HOLES in the HILLS

Joseph Bogo

Lulu Press, Morrisville, NC

This is a work of fiction. While it is based on an actual event that occurred in July of 1922, all names, characters, places and incidents either are the product of the author's imagination or are used fictitiously. Any resemblance to actual living persons is entirely coincidental. The only person accurately depicted by name is the author's father as a 12-year old boy named Albert.

ISBN: 1-4116-4711-4

ISBN-13: 978-1-4116-4711-4

Cover design (and manuscript formatting) by:
Gregory Banks (BDDesign) - Lulu.com Service Provider

Printing/Distribution provided through:
Lulu Enterprises, Inc.
3131 RDU Center Dr., Ste. 210
Morrisville, NC 27560

With love and thanks to Carolyn, my wife,
my partner in life and my encourager.
In honor of Albert and Olga Bogo
and Robert and Eleanor Jacob

Special thanks to the staff of the Avella Area
Public Library For their help and encouragement.
Special appreciation to Anne Kress for sharing
her vast knowledge of the local community in days
of yore and of ethnic and antiquated customs

To the memory of all the men who dug coal in the early
twentieth century, and for those who dig it today.
And to the men and women who fought for, struck for,
and died to lay the groundwork for today's safer and
more secure working conditions.

"Some look at things that are, and ask why. I dream of things that never were and ask why not?"

– George Bernard Shaw

Holes in the Hills

PROLOGUE

July, 1920 Western Pennsylvania

The heat of the July sun pervaded the general store in downtown Avella, a small coalmining town in Western Pennsylvania. It had been a long, hard day for Carrie. The cardboard fan with which she struggled against the heavy, humid air made very little headway in increasing her comfort.. But Carrie had no complaint. At least she had a steady, paying job, unlike the coal miners. Mining was the fuel for the local economy – that and the railroad. Though farming was important too, the town's economy flowed mainly from the faltering fountain of coal, and the railroad that hauled it away.

"Thank you, Mrs. Martin," she said as she handed the new knitting needles and yarn to her customer, accepting money in return. As Mrs. Martin walked out the door, Carrie again thought how few paying customers there were these days. The mines were only working part-time now. The miners who got a day or two of work a week were always short of cash money. They were usually paid in company "scrip," a kind of check that could only be spent at the company store or for other services offered by their coal company.

Carrie's girlfriends, who were the daughters of miners, sometimes talked about how the coal company deducted the rent for the houses they lived in from the first pay of each month. Deductions also mounted each month for food, blacksmith services, fuses, black powder and other supplies. They said there was never any money left from the first pay of the month, even when the mines were working full time. After two weeks of work the mine families just owed more money to the company.

The tingling of the bell at the front door interrupted her thoughts as it opened. A large man filled the doorway as he entered. "Good morning, sir," Carrie said politely. The man looked at her with weary eyes and mumbled a word or two of greeting. He wore rough clothing coated with a thick layer of black dust and carried a battered lunch bucket. He had apparently just come in from a long day at the mine. His bearing testified to how hard a day it had been. She looked at his face, not recognizing him. But the turnover in miners was hard to keep up with. It seemed men died or suffered injury nearly every day in one area coalmine or another. When needed, the company just ordered more replacements. But now, with little work available, they didn't need replacements so often.

"Can I help you find something?" She asked. He looked at her quizzically. Carrie realized that he probably knew very little English, if any at all. He pointed to a tiny doll, obviously for his daughter, and showed her a few coins from his pocket. Counting the money, she realized it wasn't enough. She shook her head.

The big man choked back a barely audible sound and gamely tried to stem the flow of tears that began to carve their way in ashen rivulets down his coal dust-blackened cheeks. He seemed to shrivel a little; his shoulders visibly sagging. He turned dejectedly and walked back through the front door, the bell tingling merrily as he departed.

"I am so grateful for this job, Lord," Carrie said in a simple prayer. "But sometimes it can be an awful job, too."

CHAPTER ONE

July 17, 1922
Southwestern Pennsylvania

"Unnngggghhhh….." he again cried out as a searing shaft of fire tore through the waves of pain wracking his body. He had passed beyond care, finally beginning to accept that there could be no escape from this torment – not in a doctor's office, not in his own bed, not in this life. Escape would only come when his mama opened her arms for him once more. And he wished it to be soon.

"My friend, do not give up hope. We will get you home…" his companion pledged to him. "Please do not give up." The big man glanced despairingly over at the others who had been gamely helping in his losing cause. He shifted his share of the deadening weight higher onto his shoulder as another man took his turn on the other side. They were strong, and loyal, too, but the way home was long. And their comrade was failing fast. Too much blood had spilled from his wound. Even as the big man fought to block it out, the certain outcome seeped into and pervaded his consciousness. But he could never accept it, not as long as his friend had even one breath remaining. "We will get you home…"

"Unghh…." His friend moaned.

***

The day before
Southwestern Pennsylvania

Nick was only twenty-two years old, but strong. Strong hands. Strong back. But a man had to be strong to do pick-and-shovel work bent over in a coal mine, digging under a ceiling of four feet. Yes, Nick was young and strong and brave, too. How could a coward work far underground where the only light shone dimly from his helmet lamp and the only way out was the way he came in?

Still unsure what it was all about, Nick just walked along with the others. More than two dozen of them now strode down the dusty red-dog road from P&W Patch – the mining camp where he lived – to the union hall in Avella. As they passed the small rough-built company-owned shanties and a few company houses, the others talked all excited, getting their courage up and their anger. Of course, Angelo's Dago Red wine helped. But that glow had mostly worn off, and they'd only drunk a couple glasses anyhow. As they walked along they picked up a few more men. Their numbers had since grown to over 35 men, perhaps 40. He saw more small groups joining in from other streets in the patch and the Avella camp on the way.

When they finally got to the meeting hall he could see over a hundred anxious men waiting in the hot July sun, and more coming down from the camps up around Cedar Grove, from Duquesne to the west and Donahoo to the east. The word had certainly gotten around. Somebody opened the doors of the hall and men surged in. The rush brought on by Angelo's wine was all gone now, Nick realized, but it was never about bravery brought on by wine. Their growing courage and their fury came from something stronger – desperation. The flow of men coming in slowed to a trickle now and sweaty bodies crowded the meeting room. More miners stayed outside, standing under the open windows to listen.

The union man climbed up on a rickety bench over by a window so that men outside could hear. He wavered briefly until somebody grabbed hold of the bench and held it still. "Boys," he began. "They could break our strike. The miners and the union will have no say." That commanded their attention. If they couldn't stop the coal coming out of scab mines, the strike could be broken and then there would be no union. Their payless weeks on strike would have come to nothing.

Most of the coal mines in the country were on strike, but the men all knew about the mines still working over the line in West Virginia. The union guy went on, raising his voice now: "The new owners of the Clifton Mine threw the miners out of the company houses. Now they live in tents on the other side of Cross Creek. They don't have a roof over their heads." Low murmuring began to escalate to shouts. The union man, a small but tough and wiry Italian named Mario, had to raise his hand. The noise died down. "All they did was vote for the union!"

Mario stood on his bench, steady now with an unlit stogie cigar clenched in his teeth and sweat glistening on the dark skin of his craggy and lined face. Nick knew he was about thirty-five years old, but the years had worn on him hard. It seemed that Mario always sported an unlit stogie. He supposed that Mario must have smoked sometimes, but he couldn't remember ever seeing that cigar lit – only chewed. Of course, miners rarely smoked in the mines because of the danger of explosion from "firedamp" gases or coal dust.

Mario went on: "Now they bring in scab workers to mine coal. They bring them in boxcars just like cattle! They ship them from Alabama, from the prisons!" A shocked silence filled the room, and then somebody cursed in Hungarian. Another swore in Italian. Angry shouts and waving fists filled the room. Nick looked around. Many were men he worked with, men he respected. But they all deserved respect for the hard and dangerous work that they did uncomplainingly. They wore old and patched clothing and repaired work boots – sometimes repaired many times over. Many spoke no English or at most broken English and had a hard time understanding, but even those men had a good idea what Mario was talking about. Nick noticed that a few miners were translating excitedly into Italian, Polish, Slavic, or some other language.

Mario's voice grew louder: "If that mine stays open it could be the end for all of us. We better get going. We do no good here. Next we stop at Penowa. After that we go shut down the mine!" The room erupted in a cheer. The men fought their way through the doors in their excitement, elbowing their way and pouring out of the building before heading down to the railroad tracks. Nick noticed that some men were carrying guns – hunting rifles, shotguns and a few pistols. He saw a couple more miners head home for their guns. Like most of them Nick didn't have a weapon. Yet nothing could have kept him at home. He would throw rocks if he had to. But like the others he hoped they could convince the replacement miners to refuse to work. The last thing they wanted was gunfire and death.

Soon there were nearly 200 men walking down the tracks under the bright and hot July sun, heading toward the West Virginia state line. They crossed the trestle bridge over the creek and continued on. More men from Duquesne and Burgettstown Coal joined in. They walked and stumbled along the uneven railroad ties, walking the nearby roads and paths when they could, kicking up a choking trail of dust as they went. They followed the tracks through the darkness of the first two railroad tunnels, tripping and stumbling from time to time on the uneven surface. They muttered to themselves or cursed loudly, or just dwelled within their own thoughts.

Lost in his own thoughts, and in his fears, Nick worried that this could become a bad day. Maybe a very bad day. But if a man did nothing when women and children went hungry, how could he be called a man? He could see the concerned and fearful faces on bystanders as they passed. More men came out of the company shanties and boarding houses, resolutely joining in. Some marchers went inside to bring out miners too reluctant to get involved. They joined the march, too, but they weren't happy about it.

"If we don't have everybody, we have nobody," Angelo remarked.

Walking by Jefferson Coal they picked up more marchers. By now there were closer to 300. They talked angrily as they walked, building up their courage with loud boasts like soldiers getting ready for a battle against an unknown and intimidating enemy. Some of the women looked proud as they saw their men walking by so purposefully, marching to provide a better life for them and their children. But most were crying. They worried that some might not come back. Young girls wailed, tears streaming down their cheeks. Many of the boys were cheering, and some tried to join in. While the younger ones were refused they let some of the older boys march with them, at least to Penowa. They said it would help to build their manhood. Nick knew that the boys would then be sent home.

The first of the marchers got to Penowa, the last mining town before the State Line Tunnel, in late afternoon. They began to turn out the camp's miners. More men came down from the Waverly and Seldom Seen mines – the last mines in their westward march – further filling their ragged ranks. Hot, with throats choking from the dust they had kicked up, they all headed over to the ball field where they drank thirstily from a spring and the creek. They then gathered in noisy groups, talking in their native languages from Southern and Eastern Europe and from Austria and Wales. But one thing they knew with certainly; on the other end of the last railroad tunnel men were digging coal, and they weren't union miners.

Nick sat with his group and watched the unruly scene. He saw a few more guns, but not very many. Some of the men carried mining tools like shovels, or pieces of lumber or scrap iron. The rest were barehanded. He also thought he saw a stick that looked like dynamite.

The group became attentive when they saw that a man, carrying an American flag and a pistol and wearing an old army uniform, had joined Mario. Nick had never seen him before, but he looked important. A few of the union organizers had also joined the leaders group. They talked seriously, sometimes arguing heatedly. Finally Mario wiped his brow with a big cloth and climbed up on a bench. After the marchers gathered around in a close, tight-knit knot he again began to speak.

He started out low so that the ones in the back had to shut up to hear. "They bring us to this country and make us big promises. If we work hard we will get good pay and we can bring our families to live here, too. But the big promises were all lies." Mutterings of agreement were accompanied by shaking fists. The voices grew louder. Mario held up his hand for attention. "They think we are women, too scared to complain." A huge and derisive cheer went up, ringing throughout the Cross Creek valley. Nick could hear men translating for the miners who understood very little English, but Nick understood well enough. Even with his broken English, he knew what this man was saying. He was saying that we have to stand up for ourselves and our brother miners and our families.

Mario went on: "They send us to these coal mines and put us in company shanties and charge us big rent. They tell us to dig coal, but they don't pay us for digging and cleaning slate out of the coal. And they cheat us when they count our coal cars and weigh our coal!" Shouting and jeering rang louder, with angry looks and shaking fists. "They make us buy from their store and charge us what they want. If we complain there is no work for us, and no place to live. They call us troublemakers and throw us out, us and our kids and our furniture. So we strike. We know we can only get good pay if everybody strikes. But they have those scabs mining coal over there in Cliftonville." He gestured scornfully to the hill to the west. "...and then they will bring more scabs here. Now good miners are living across the creek, with no houses and no pay!" The ball field erupted into shouts of agreement. More fists were shaken while curses were uttered in a dozen languages or more.

Somebody in back abruptly yelled: "But what do we do?"

After a moment of silence the man in the uniform with the flag walked forward and climbed onto the bench. He held up his hand and the field grew quiet again. "On my mother's name," he began, to the astonishment of his comrades. "We go through that tunnel and through the woods. We march on that mine and we shut it down. If they don't come out we drag them out and no more shifts go in!"

Above the yells of the angry and desperate men, somebody else yelled: "But when?"

Mario shouted: "We walk through the tunnel and the woods tonight. But we go into the mine at dawn. The signal will be the morning train. It comes about five o'clock. When it leaves the station blowing its whistle, we go! We do not let the day shift enter the mine, even if we have to blow that mine up. They mine no more coal while those people have to camp on the other side of the creek. We fight for their jobs, and we fight for ours!" A maddened roar went up, with everybody shouting, waving their fists and shovels and guns. One gun discharged into the air, and everybody suddenly got quiet. The shot seemed to cut through their bravado to the heart of their fears – into their very souls. They knew that there would be no turning back, not now.

Nick looked at the tunnel anew. The railroad tracks went straight into and through that dark, forbidding hole without turning away, and he knew that he must do the same.

The leaders went off to the side and started to confer while the others gathered in small groups to talk and argue, or try to rest. But they knew that few would sleep. Nobody who was there, including the ones who were forced to join the march, would go home this night. And they realized that some of them might never come home. They remembered the mine guards and their guns, and wondered if the company had called in the sheriff or even the hated Coal and Iron Police.

Nick's mind wandered to his Carmella. He worried that he might never see her again. He longed to return to her, to look into her dark eyes and hear her soft voice, feel her gentle touch and make plans with her for a life together. But he still had to do what a man had to do, so he lay down and tried to get some rest. Nick slept fitfully, but when he woke up about midnight gladness filled his heart because Carmella had a place in his dream.

Meanwhile on the other side of the tunnel the county sheriff considered what the new day might bring. "Why am I in this position?" He thought ruefully. "The mine owners need somebody to protect their property – but from what? From people who only want to work? Men I brought here might die tomorrow. And for what?" He shrugged and gave the order for his deputies, the mine guards and the specially deputized citizens to move into position behind cover near the mine. They tried to settle down for the night. But first they checked and re-checked their guns and counted their bullets. Meanwhile, across the tracks three more guards worked on a pipe cannon to be powered by black powder.

Everybody on both sides of that dark hole in the ground prepared for a long night and possibly a very long tomorrow.

CHAPTER TWO

Pittsburgh, The present

"I don't know, Sam," Joe Bailey continued. "This would be a major move for me. I don't want to sell my house in Collier Township and move to Avella. That's way out in the sticks, isn't it? I mean, how could I continue working for you if I live 25 miles away?" Joe had been a real estate agent for Sam Braden at Viewpointe Real Estate in Pittsburgh for nearly seven years.

"Joe, you need to shake up your life a bit now that Kathy's gone," Sam said. "You're beginning to act like an old man but you're only 37. When are you going to stop mooning over her? Come on, Joe. Snap out of it!"

Sam paused briefly, considering the man sitting across from him. Joe had become a very good friend as well as one of his top agents. A former policeman who kept himself in pretty decent shape, Joe still had a lot going for him, even though his close-cropped dark-brown hair displayed more gray than it had when he arrived in Pittsburgh those few short years ago. At six foot one and about two hundred pounds he kept himself in considerably better shape than most real estate agents, who tended to be sedentary. Joe's running apparently does him some good, Sam thought, because he rarely spends any time in the gym. The women around the office still considered him somewhat of a catch and occasionally tried to fix him up with a friend. But Kathy's effect just seemed to be hanging on. Sam detected a quizzical change in Joe's medium-blue eyes and realized that his mind had wandered. He gave an inaudible sigh of frustration. When would that man ever get over her?

Joe distractedly turned the letter from the lawyer over again, and opened it for the umpteenth time. It always read the same way:

... saddened to inform you of the death of your great-uncle Albert Albertini. Mr. Albertini provided in his will, a copy of which is enclosed, that if any of his line could be found all of his property and

possessions should transfer to said person or persons. As you and your parents are his sole heirs and they have deferred to you...

He still couldn't believe it. He was now the recipient of a house and two acres near a small town in the boondocks of Washington County named Avella. He had also inherited old Albert's tidy savings account. The only condition of his inheritance – contained in a codicil to the will – was that the heir had to take possession by living in the house for at least a year. Apparently old Albert really loved his house and didn't want to have somebody just throw it on the market and sell it.

Joe rattled the house's key ring nervously. He had merely to go and take possession. "Sam, I like living close to Pittsburgh."

"Just go on down there and get things under control. Fix it up a bit and after a year sell it. Then move back," Sam told him. "You can leave your Collier place vacant for a while. Your police buddies will gladly keep an eye on it for you. Meanwhile, maybe you can list and sell some of that rural Washington County real estate for me, maybe even a farm or two. I've wanted to crack that market for quite a while."

"I guess you're right. I might as well give it a try," Joe sighed. "Business is a little slow now. Besides, I've been meaning to take some time off to get back to hiking and spend some time in the woods." Joe's mind drifted for a moment, remembering how he used to love the feel of his muscles working and the smell of the earth – especially the dewy underbrush and damp soil – as he walked through endless miles of wooded trails. He would readily detect the bouquet of the rich humus and feel the undulating slopes of the trail as he trudged onward, sometimes to a destination but often to wherever the trail led him. He smiled involuntarily, remembering that more than once his trails had taken him so far that he returned to his car in total darkness, aided only by the weakening beam of his pocket flashlight. Why hadn't he been hiking all along? Even as a great way to put on some miles in a hurry, his running could never be the same as his beloved hiking. Maybe it was time for him to step back from his busy career... to bring his life back into balance again.

His mind snapped back to the office in Pittsburgh. Seeing the comprehending smile on Sam's face, his own began to flush. "Maybe I should just get on with it." He stood and shook Sam's hand. "Thanks for your advice and support, Sam." After making a few explanatory calls to clients and filling Sam and his partner in on his unfinished business, he headed his old but beautifully maintained Cadillac out the Parkway West to Collier. No new SUVs for Joe; he had always preferred a roomy but classic car to a modern status-symbol, even when chauffeuring appreciative clients around.

As he drove, Joe reflected on how his life had changed since he had come to Pittsburgh. He made some great friends, especially in the city and county police departments, and settled in with Sam's real estate firm. He also bought and applied himself to restoring an old schoolhouse in Collier Township. His sweat and imagination was turning it into a showplace. Joe had also met and fallen in love with a wonderful woman, but afterward lost her. Maybe it *was* time for a change and a new challenge.

He packed some clothes and tools, loaded cans of food into a box, and set the security system. He then called Collier's Police Chief Frank Adamson and told him his plans. Frank agreed to have a patrolman swing by the house periodically to make sure things were okay, to augment Joe's security system. Finally he filled his bird feeders for what would be the last time in a long time and threw cracked corn out for the wild turkeys. With a last glance at the entrance to his familiar running trail, he finally departed. As a man who clung to routine, Joe was never comfortable having it disrupted. Even as he drove down Route 50 to Washington County and Avella, Joe still felt conflicted with mixed emotions.

After about 35 minutes or so of scenery changing from suburban to distinctly rural, Joe arrived at the small town that had seemed so remote on paper. How did he get here so fast? The first thing that caught his attention was the old brick bank building: The Lincoln Savings Bank. Obviously it had once been imposing and impressive. It was probably the cornerstone building of the entire town. Now it stood locked up, with boarded-over windows – obviously vacant for many years – probably decades. He wondered what had happened to it. Did it fail during the great depression, or was it just the victim of a small-town business district on the decline? But he was surprised to notice that it had not been adorned by graffiti, unlike vacant buildings in some larger towns. Across from the bank stood an efficient-looking volunteer fire department with the doors open and trucks at the ready. A couple large and charming homes sat opposite each other on the corner.

Joe suddenly began to feel a rumbling through the frame of his beloved Caddy. He realized with a shock that he was driving down a brick-paved street; the first one he had seen outside of Pittsburgh. Many of that city's brick and Belgian stone streets had been paved over or ripped up and replaced with smooth pavement, along with Pittsburgh's nearly forgotten streetcar tracks. Encountering the paving was like meeting an old friend in an unexpected place. *What other surprises might this town hold in store for me?* Joe wondered.

A small family practice medical office, a funeral home and a post office were arrayed a bit further down the street – and then a hometown flower shop that exuded a simple beauty and charm. Next to it was an equestrian tack shop. He wondered at the NASCAR items in the display windows. What a combination, he contemplated: horses and stock car racing.

After passing by a steepled Presbyterian church, he made a left turn into a convenience store and gas station for a cold drink and to get directions to the old Albertini house. In the car once again, he found his way up Campbell Drive and out of town a half-mile or so.

There it awaited him: Albert's old homestead, a small brick ranch home on a large but lately unkempt lot. The house hadn't been boarded up but neither had it been broken into. It exuded a comfortable but decrepit, even despondent appearance. "Okay," Joe said out loud. "I'm here. So what do I do now?"

He parked, walked to the front door, unlocked it and went inside. His eyes adjusted to the darkened interior as he fumbled for and found the light switch hidden behind the frayed edge of a dusty curtain. The room that came into view under the dim bulb of the ceiling light betrayed its own vintage through the dated and heavily patterned wallpaper, plush carpeting and dingy draperies. But any thoughts on updating Albert's place would have to wait for the morning.

Joe busied himself with making the place livable and then prepared himself for bed.

CHAPTER THREE

Joe awoke at five-thirty a.m. to a bright May morning, with the temperatures already in the sixties. He started the coffeepot, according to his usual routine. If nothing else, he was a man of routine. But now for the first time in a long time he would be jogging somewhere other than in Collier Township. He pulled on his dingy sweats, laced up his scuffed running shoes, stepped outside, stretched, and began running at a comfortable pace.

He headed out the dusty country road past a few scattered houses. Running had always given Joe time to ponder, to work things out. Back when he wore a badge, his time spent running sometimes helped him to think through difficult cases. But he mentally cringed as the painful irony struck him again that he hadn't figured out what was happening behind his back, in his own home.

Fortunately, this time the most difficult problem was what to do about that god-awful wallpaper in the living room. But Albert must have liked that wallpaper to leave it up so long, or at least his wife did. Joe continued running as he always did; "picking them up and putting them down," while noticing the lush trees and underbrush foliage that were now in full leaf.

Joe came to a complete stop several miles later, when he saw a sign: *Shades of Death Road.* "What's the story behind that?" he wondered aloud. He shrugged and set off on his return run, his mind already dwelling on his other love from long ago: hiking. As he had promised himself, he would resume hiking and this could be a prime place. This could be a fine place indeed, with the hills, valleys, creek bottoms and deer paths. He decided to start hiking as soon as he found a likely stretch of trail.

As he neared Albert's house, an old man beckoned to him from his front yard. He veered and approached the old man's neatly kept cottage. "Hi, old-timer," he said in greeting.

"Old-timer is it? Well you're right. I am an old-timer and proud of it! I grew up when a man had to work for a living, not like now." He grinned. "The name's Andy. Andy Polack." He offered his hand, a bit feebly but with a fire in his left eye. He had only his left eye.

Joe stared at the obviously glass one on the right. The effect was hypnotic. Finally he broke his gaze away only to look at a branch behind Andy's head. Very smooth, Joe, he thought. His gaze returned to Andy's face, and to his good eye instead. He held it there; mortified that not only had he stared at the bad eye, he then looked away from Andy entirely. This time, his gaze held steady on Andy's bright and friendly face.

Andy seemed bemused. "What's the matter, young fella? Never saw a glass eye before?"

"Sorry, Mr. Polack. Yes I have. I apologize, but I was caught off-guard. My name is Joe. Joe Bailey."

"Call me Andy. Mr. Polack was my dad," he said. Joe thought he detected a flash of emotion that flickered through Andy's expression. But then the old guy winked. "You related to Albert, then? He was my buddy. He was a couple years younger than me. We worked together in the mines a lot and we retired up here about the same time. By the way, the mine is where I lost my eye. Not to mention a few other injuries. Albert, too. He got banged up some, but he came through it okay."

"You lost the eye in the mine?" Joe asked. "Did it happen around here?"

"Of course I lost it around here. How far do you think I'd have walked for a job? We walked everywhere back then. It must have been about 1931 or 1932 when I lost the eye. My memory isn't what it used to be. Anyway we walked everywhere, unless we jumped onto a railroad car. Them were welcome rides.

"Poor ol' Skinny, he hopped a railroad car for a ride to work and slipped under a wheel. He left his leg between the tracks, above the knee. Never made it to the doctor's office alive. He was a good worker, too, ol' Skinny. Just not very lucky." Andy spat some tobacco juice at the base of a tree. "Them bugs just don't like tobacco juice!" He laughed. "Want to hear about my eye?"

Joe could see that this would take a while, so he followed Andy and settled into a straight-backed chair on the shaded front porch. "So, what happened?"

Andy had a momentary faraway look, as though he could see a sight that nobody else could see. "It happened in the Penobscot mine. I was working day shift. We were trying to brace the roof in a new-cut area. The ceiling was slate and stone, which is pretty shaky. But one thing we knew. No braces, no work. So we hauled some timbers in and set to work. We were about half-finished when the back section began to fall. It cracked a couple timbers and before we could turn and run, a wood splinter about eight inches long came flying right at my face. Took me straight in the right eye, it did. It hurt like the blazes. The roof fall didn't get us, but that splinter sure did me in.

"The foreman took me out and got me to the mine doctor. The doc said he had to take the eye, or I could have lost the other one. After a while I made a wooden one. I sanded it down real smooth and painted it up nice and pretty, but people still knew what it was. Wood is wood, after all. I went nine years before I could buy a proper glass eye. This one I have now is what they call a prosthesis." He reflected for a minute or two. "How about that? I got me a prosthesis!" He laughed aloud.

Joe liked Andy's laugh. He could see that he could enjoy chatting with this crotchety but interesting old man, so old and bent but still not giving up on life.

"Want to know how old I am, Joe? Bet you can't guess."

Joe reflected. This is where you should always guess under the true age by half-dozen or so years to make the senior citizen feel better, right? "I would say about seventy-five, Andy."

Andy cackled. "Nope. Not half right. Try ninety-six!" He spat some more juice at the tree. "Bet no tent worms are gonna climb that tree, Joe." He laughed again.

"Andy, you don't look like you're a day over eighty years old." Joe had to admit that he was dumbfounded. "By the way," he continued. "What's up with that 'Shades of Death Road'? How'd it get its name?"

Andy shrugged and scratched his head. "Dunno. Nobody ever gave me a good reason for it being named that. Sorry I can't help you there."

Disappointed, Joe started to turn toward Albert's house. "Well, I should be pushing on to the house, and getting on with my day. I hope to see you again." He reached out and shook Andy's hand, amazed at the power lurking within the frail-looking skin of that hand.

Andy said with a mischievous glint in his eye. "You will, Joe. You sure will." He gave a little cackle, got up and walked inside, shooing a white cat out of the way.

Joe said to nobody in particular: "I guess the interview really is over." He finished the last two hundred feet of his tour by walking slowly, in deep thought. "What a strange man. Maybe I should start to keep a journal. This place could have something to teach me."

He opened the door and went inside. He was ready for some of that coffee that he had started just before he left. He always preferred it "just past prime," but this was way beyond the mildly bitter nuance that he favored. It now had a distinct acidic taste. He drank it anyway, thinking about old Andy and his generation. They must have been something, he decided. Really something.

He worked around the place throughout the day – dusting, vacuuming, and cleaning out the cellar. During a break he sat outside, enjoying a cool glass of water. "Bird feeders!" He exclaimed in surprise. Old Albert had bird feeders. He must have some seed stored around here, too, and of course Joe would get more. He welcomed this little something that might bring back a piece of his old routine – something to help offset the unfamiliar surroundings. He embraced the thought gratefully, and then he went back to work.

Joe slowly realized that this house offered some real potential. He had seen many of these post-World War Two generation three-bedroom ranches with one bath, a small kitchen, average dining room, and a comfortable living room. Albert had obviously maintained his home pretty well. But it had no air-conditioning. He might have to do something about that if for no other reason than salability when he finally put it on the market.

As he worked, Joe thought about Andy saying that they walked everywhere in his day. At about four o'clock he made up his mind. He left the car parked and began the walk toward downtown Avella. He knew he would be ready for a cold drink when he got there. A few people offered him rides, but he politely declined all offers. He wanted to see what it might be like to walk when he would ordinarily ride. He realized that, while he wanted to get back to hiking, a mile along hot pavement was definitely not what he had planned.

Joe had to admit that the cold Sprite, when he finally got it, tasted very, very good.

CHAPTER FOUR

July 17, 1922

The State Line Tunnel was the very bowel of the hill – almost oppressively dark and dank. Nick heard the water dripping ahead as he stumbled down the tunnel. The flickering light from the few helmet lamps barely revealed any features of the track bed just ahead before being swallowed by the impenetrable darkness. He could now feel large droplets of water smacking his head and neck as they fell from the leaking ceiling. There was no place to go to escape the falling water, so he didn't even try. He heard men stumble and curse as they tried to navigate the railroad track with its bed of stones and unevenly spaced railroad timbers. Headlong tumbles into the blackness punctuated the night as they trudged onward.

"Sonna ma beetch!" cried an Italian miner in front of Nick as he fell forward onto his hands and knees. Cursing, he exclaimed: "Railroad spikes are sticking up." Another man stumbled over him as the others backed up or wedged their ways around. He mumbled something as he picked himself up and stopped temporarily to examine the torn material in the knees of both pant legs, and the cuts on both hands, before heeding the gentle shoves from behind and resuming his trek.

"Railroad tracks were meant for trains, not men on foot," grumbled Angelo. The stone roadbed sloped off gradually within two feet of either end of the crossties, and then dropped down dramatically to where they stopped near the concrete tunnel walls. In fact, there was no easy path to walk in the tunnel, even with daylight streaming in both ends of this infernal hole. But in the empty darkness of midnight, comfortable walking became a hopeless chore. This simple fact was made painfully clear by unfortunate miners who stumbled off-balance, setting off a string of curses and domino tumbles of several men onto the rough stones of the track bed.

Hole in the Hills

In the inconsistent light of oil lamps as the men's heads bobbed along, Nick could occasionally make out the sloping walls as they arched up to a dripping, vaulted crown. The shiny surface of the finished concrete occasionally reflected a little of the light back. "They say this tunnel runs 1500 feet," grunted one man. It certainly seemed longer tonight as they picked their way along.

Nick and the others wondered whatever had possessed them to try to transit this tunnel in almost total darkness. He thought of the others outside. There were more than 200 more men making their way along the stream bed toward the ridge under a nearly full moon. They were following the creek bottom on the south side of the tracks. After receiving final instructions, those marchers had set off under a clear sky, with the moon shining in all its glory. Yes the men outside had it easy, all right. They could make their way through the brush and across wooded game trails with nary a stumble.

As they finally approached the western portal Nick noticed men beginning to congregate on the left side of the tunnel. Somebody passed the word back that there was water coming from the tunnel's side. It was a natural spring that gushed through a hole in the tunnel's wall like water pouring continuously from a well pump. Nick could see the men just ahead of him drinking greedily before reluctantly moving on. Nick also stopped and slaked his thirst gratefully, yet quickly, and then hurried onward.

As the men neared the western tunnel opening the miners with helmet lights extinguished them. They didn't want the authorities to see the lights as they exited the tunnel. Besides, moonlight now filled the tunnel portal. When they approached the mouth the leader of their group reminded them of their task. They would quietly walk to the left side of the tracks, cross the stream, and prepare to go after mine buildings from the north side. Their main goal was to shut down the generator building and the tipple, the building where coal was conveyed from the mine to the railroad cars waiting beneath it on the siding.

Meanwhile the major part of the contingent was picking its way along the wooded ridge top behind the mine opening, also prepared to go after the mine's buildings, including the tipple and the explosives shed. Both groups were tasked to prevent the day shift from reporting for work. If necessary, they would enter the mine to bring out any reluctant scab miners. Mario, who had long proven himself to be a natural leader, had cautioned them to avoid bloodshed if possible, but to do whatever was necessary to stop the scab miners from reporting to work.

Nick now found himself toward the front of his group as they slid down the steep embankment to the creek. As he moved along the streamside, tripping occasionally on a willow root or slipping on a moss-covered stone, he noticed some other men beginning to join them from their right side, nodding a silent greeting. They were from the union miners' tent camp between the creek and the railroad. One of the Clifton miners showed them the shallowest place to ford the creek, advice that they gratefully accepted. The water at that place only flowed below their knees. Nick and the others dispersed into cover on the south side of the stream embankment to dump out their shoes and wait for the dawn that was less than four hours away. And afterward the whistle of the morning train would sound as it departed from the station at 5:15.

Angelo had stayed by Nick as they walked. He whispered that he heard a few of the boys on the ridge had a surprise planned for the mine's guards, who were surely waiting in the darkness. Nick had no doubt that that the guards were waiting. He could sense their ominous presence. He only hoped that the guards were so outnumbered that they would let the miners shut the mine down without a fight.

They began to talk quietly about small things that seemed so large and important now. Angelo hailed from a small stone-cutting town in the mountains of the Italian Tyrol. He loved to talk about his village, but he mostly talked about his young wife of only three years who was waiting for him to send her money to join him. "I saved up almost enough money, Nick!" he bragged. "I know she must travel in a low class, but she is a hardy mountain girl, my Maria. Those bunks piled on each other won't bother her. And they separate the single men from the families and women traveling alone in the ships." Angelo sat there as he always did, with a look of satisfaction. "Besides she will have some food brought from home to help her to survive the trip. The ship food is not good." Nick remembered it well. "In a few months we will have enough money," Angelo continued. "I will work on the farms or wherever I have to so I can get the money."

As Angelo went on, Nick wondered why he felt so close to this man, who wasn't even Slavic. Even though Angelo was older than him, they enjoyed a bond closer than most brothers. And like an older brother, Angelo kept him out of trouble. When he had first come to Avella, Nick was ready to fight anybody. "Angelo, do you remember when I first came to this place, this Avella?" he asked.

"Nick, you were just a little boy in a man's body who wanted to fight. But you fought others because you were scared. Not scared of work, or even of other strong men. Instead you were scared of not succeeding in America- of going back home with your tail between your legs. So you fought. But do you remember what happened, my little brother?" Nick remembered only too well and reflexively massaged the place on his jaw where Angelo had hit him and knocked him down.

"Yes. You knocked me onto my pants. I have never felt such a blow. And then you picked me up and gave me a glass of wine. We got drunk that night!" laughed Nick. "And you have been better than my brother ever since. But remember, if I was as big as you maybe I knock you down!" Angelo laughed in return.

Their conversation turned to something that Angelo never tired of talking about, the rituals of his mountain birthplace. He especially loved the religious festivals in honor of their patron saint. He again began to tell of the festivals, something that Nick's people didn't do in the same way. The festivals fascinated Nick, who often asked Angelo to tell all about them. And as usual, he was more than happy to oblige.

Angelo went on: "… and six strong men would carry the statue of Saint Theresa down the streets on a chair like a throne, on two large poles across our shoulders. People would put money on the statue in offering, and…"

And then, it happened! From just below the ridge top the flash of a large explosion lit the valley briefly, exposing the features of the mine and the striking miners' tent camp. A booming sound quickly followed, louder than a clap of thunder. Another brighter flash lit up the valley, followed by yet another shock wave! Totally stunned, the men who had first looked up in surprise buried their faces in the soil and heard debris flying though the trees and landing throughout the encampment. The explosions were followed by temporary darkness born of night blindness. The sound of dirt and debris falling from the sky, and rocks sliding down the hillside, interrupted the resulting stillness.

But the explosion hadn't come from the mineshaft. It originated in the woods more than a hundred feet above. Then, all was still again. Dynamite! It had to be dynamite! Now several skyrockets were set off, arcing through the darkness before extinguishing themselves in the waning night. A few men got up to march on the mine, but others reminded them, "No, not yet. It's not the time." They lay back down amid the uneasy silence. They could hear other men talking excitedly off in the distance near the mine buildings. Angelo muttered to those nearest himself: "I know they wanted to scare the guards, but I think they did worse to me. I better check my pants!" Nick and the others chuckled. Angelo's joke was a great stress-reliever.

Nick and Angelo waited with the others for the first signs of dawn to invade the darkness from the east, coming over the hills that separated them from their honest work in Avella. An uneasy but clearly temporary peace had returned to the valley.

The stillness also weighed heavily on the sheriff and his twenty-odd deputies and mine guards, who knew they would be badly outnumbered. Their only advantage was that they were able to set up defensive positions in advance behind well-chosen cover and that, unlike the miners; they all had guns and plenty of ammunition. They waited in the moonlit darkness of pre-dawn, just beginning to suspect the full scope of what the day would bring. Across the railroad tracks, near Virginville, the other three defenders readied their pipe cannon, including the black powder charges and the pieces of scrap iron and stone that would serve as their ammunition.

Meanwhile, exhaustion finally overcame Nick and like many of the others waiting by the streamside, he laid his head on his forearms and slipped into a welcome sleep.

CHAPTER FIVE

Nick's arm slipped comfortably behind Carmella's back, his hand gently resting on her slim waist. It was as though it had found a comfortable and welcome home there. He heard her make a barely audible sigh and felt her body move slightly to press against his side as they walked along in the pleasant coolness of the spring afternoon. They now trailed the others in their group by a few feet as they walked to the wedding celebration.

Nick looked over at Carmella, walking close enough to his right side that he could smell her hair. He brushed it with his strong Slavic nose. It lingered there, breathing in the amazing scent of her just-washed tresses. She again sighed, audibly, and her gentle smile widened slightly. "She is the most beautiful and precious thing in the world," he thought. He loved how her black hair fell in small curls just over her soft shoulders, framing her delicate facial features. Carmella's nose was perfect in Nick's eyes, even the noticeable bump on the bridge. Her dark eyes seemed so deep that if he touched them they might draw his entire hand and arm inside. He smiled at the thought. "Yes," Nick contemplated, "I am the world's luckiest man to have such a woman."

Thinking back, he could still hear Camillo's words ringing in his ear after Nick asked permission to escort her to the wedding celebration. "Who else is going? And when will you bring her back home?"

"There will be seven boys and five girls," Nick responded as Carmella stood nearby, twisting her scarf nervously. "We will walk together like always," he assured her father. "We are going as a group.

. "You will not be alone with her?" the impatient and very suspicious parent asked for the third time. You will have her home when?" he repeated.

"We will walk back together, the same boys and girls. And I will have her back in your house by nine o'clock." Camillo finally relented. After all, Nick seemed to be a nice boy and a hard worker, even though he wasn't Italian. He didn't drink very much, either. Nick was Slavic, but Camillo knew some good Slavs. They were Catholic, too, at least. "Okay. She can go with you. But nine o'clock! I will be on the porch at five minutes after nine!"

"Thank you, papa," Carmella smiled gratefully as she hugged her old man. Nick admired the way she respected her father. When they were married she would respect him, too. And he would protect her with his love. They never mentioned marriage to her father, but Nick thought Camillo knew about what they wanted. The good fathers always seemed to know. After all, at almost seventeen, Carmella was maturing nicely into a young woman. She would soon be ready to marry, something the young bachelors had already noticed. *But why not an Italian boy? Why a Slavic?* Camillo threw his hands up in frustration as the two happily walked down the street to join their waiting group of young friends.

It was always like that when Nick and Carmella wanted to go somewhere. "Who else is going? What are their names? When will she be back home?" Her father wanted to protect her, his oldest daughter but still his little girl. It was she who most reminded him of his wife; let her soul rest in peace. Camillo crossed himself quickly and went into his house, glancing one more time at the little group of laughing young people.

This is one of the best times, Nick thought, as he and Carmella trailed the chattering group of young people. The others had learned to allow them some space, which is why they walked a few feet ahead. Not far enough that an onlooker would say something to her father, but just far enough. Nick whispered: "When will we tell your father? I want to marry you when we can afford it and then come home to you each night. I love you, Carmella."

Carmella smiled her little smile like she was hearing the best thing in the world, but had to keep the best thing a secret for a while. "I love you, too, Nick," she breathed. "Maybe when I am seventeen or eighteen. Can we wait until I am seventeen? My mother is dead now and I take care of my father's house for him. In a year my sister Olga will be old enough to take over. Then we can marry." Nick's spirit jumped at the thought of them finally becoming husband and wife, but his body wanted their marriage to be sooner.

"I know, I know. But I love you so much," he whispered,

knowing that their friends in front could hear a few of their words. But their friends could keep a secret. Nick's hand stayed looped around her back, not too tight, and not straying from her waist. If people saw his hand moving they would surely tell her father. It had only been a few weeks since he stopped holding her hand all the time and took a chance holding her around her thin waist. Nobody objected so he kept doing it, even though he was sure that her father had been told. Camillo could tell that they were in love and would someday marry, but they had to stay at a respectable distance for now.

The group walked around a bend in the road, out of sight of all the houses. Nick leaned over and kissed her head. He felt her sharp intake of breath. He kissed her again, this time on her cheek. She blushed, but let his lips linger there before turning her face the other way.

"Did you hear about Mrs. Ferraro?" She asked her friends out loud, signaling them to slow down so that Nick and Carmella would catch up to them. "She lost her husband in the mine only ten weeks ago, and now she is marrying another man. The other families have been helping her out a little, but it was time that she married again, especially because she has three small children. This will be her third husband and she is only thirty years old!" They all knew that Mr. Ferraro and her first husband were both killed in the mines. "She had nowhere else to go, so she is marrying a bachelor named Antonetti."

"I know him. He's a good man," Nick responded. "He drinks sometimes but he's a hard worker." As they walked they thought about it… how many women had to marry a second time or sometimes a third, just because of mine explosions and cave-ins. Too many to count, they realized. "Listen, one girl interrupted. "Do you hear it?" They stopped and strained their ears, now able to make out the faint and distant sounds. "The polka band!" exclaimed Carmella. Yes, it was the polka band, but even more so, it foretold an evening of dancing and happiness.

As they approached the wedding celebration, one girl exclaimed: "Kathryn told me that the *Starosta* had 'the talk' with her and her mother and father." The others nodded. The Starosta, an older Rusyn man named John, took his duties seriously whenever any couple of the Byzantine Rite church planned to get married. The others stopped and listened expectantly.

"He told her life to her. He said that her mother raised her right and sacrificed for her children, and her father worked in the mines all day for them. He said that her father worked on his knees every day, shoveling coal from out of the water into the mine car. He told her that she must honor what they did by being a good wife and mother and raising her children right. He gave her the whole talk."

"What did she say to him?" Carmella asked.

"She said that she took the whole thing very seriously and she would honor her parents and her husband and raise her family right."

Nick nodded his head. "She is a good girl and will make a good wife and a good mother." He smiled at Carmella. "A very good wife. The best."

They resumed walking as the draw of the music and happiness pulled them onward. Presently they arrived at the wedding celebration.

After they ate, the music started up and the young people went onto the dance floor of the social hall. The little girls practically ran onto it and began to dance clumsily with each other. Meanwhile the boys snickered nervously and punched each other's arms. Some began to wrestle near the wall, about as far from the dance floor as they could go. Several started to run and slide on their knees on the sawdust that covered the floor for dancing. A father went over and broke up their distracting play.

Nick and Carmella started to dance together, but other men and boys wanted their turns so he had to let them dance with her, too. He did his duty and danced with a few of the other girls and women. But every now and then he danced with his Carmella again. He loved the feel of her small bosom occasionally pressing against him through her simple cotton dress as they danced a waltz or a polka.

After a while the band stopped playing and the crowd grew quiet. "It's the Starosta!" A woman standing nearby exclaimed as an older man stepped forward with an air of importance. "And the bride." The crowd waited expectantly, understanding that, as in parts of Eastern Europe, this man also took charge of the reception and thus would start the bridal dance.

"Let's get in line," Carmella whispered, as she pulled a coin out of her purse.

"You do it," Nick demurred. "I will wait for you." Her eyes

shining expectantly, she joined the line of people waiting to dance with the bride. Everybody who had a coin to give could dance with the bride, who received lots of happy tears and advice as she danced, especially from the old women. The Starosta kept cutting in so that all dancers could have their turn, because the line had grown very long.

As dancers reluctantly, but good-humoredly, gave up their place to the next in line, they were offered a shot of whiskey and a morsel of cake. Meanwhile the bride gamely danced on. She knew that the coins she earned and the well wishes she received would make a difference to her marriage. Even the groom, who stood impatiently nearby, understood this.

After the bride again danced with her happy but tearful mother, she and her husband departed for their wedding night.

"Let's go outside," Nick suggested. Carmella, tired but happy, agreed. They stepped outside for some cool air.

Noticing that they were temporarily alone in the dim light of the evening, Nick impulsively kissed Carmella on her lips. "Nick!" she protested, but then she kissed him back. Made bolder, he kissed her again, this time pulling her closer to him, closer than they had been while dancing. He knew that he might have to answer for this, but he didn't care anymore. Then he heard somebody snicker softly. He pulled away, with a big but embarrassed smile on his face. Carmella turned in embarrassment. Nick then saw that it his good friend, Mike Zaretsky, who grinned at him as he stood there lighting a pipe. Mike was a true friend, the best friend that a man could have.

Realizing it was only Mike; Carmella turned and gave him a shy smile, her cheeks still red from the blush. Nick grinned at Mike as though he had just loaded one more coal car than Mike did. Nick pecked Carmella on the lips one last time before they re-entered the social hall. This is a wonderful time, he thought. May it never end.

Nick was still smiling broadly when Angelo woke him up. The joy on his face took a few seconds to disappear as his mind shifted back to the present and to where he lay, in the grass and dirt in front of a mine. He remembered what had to be done here today. Even so, he would enjoy the memory of Carmella – her soft voice, her maturing figure, her lovely eyes and wonderful lips, for as long as he could. He hoped that his brief moment with her in his dreams might give him the courage to face whatever the day would bring.

CHAPTER SIX

July 18, 1922

They could now see the first rays of sunlight brightening the eastern horizon and casting long, vague shadows over the scene. It was as though toy soldiers had been placed in position by giant unseen generals, each overlooking the montage and pondering their first move. Both sides were ready, but not exactly sure for what.

Soon the rays of dawn shone brighter as the sun crept above the hills to the east of Cliftonville, over the hill that contained that dark rectum of a tunnel. The long, diffused shadows of the early light began to take on distinct form as the sun slowly cleared the ridge. But the sun was just as much an enemy as a friend of the waiting miners. It exposed the hiding places of the men to anybody who had the right vantage point. The men in the streamside column flattened themselves fearfully into the creek side embankment. Nick looked around at all the faces that had shown such bravado yesterday. To a man they were trying to hide, some clawing at the grass and mud to dig themselves a little deeper.

Glancing up, he saw flurrying on the hillside above the mine. "It is our other people," Angelo whispered. "They will come from all directions above the mine." Nick and Angelo's group would come on from the eastern flank and below.

Angelo took a chance and raised his head slightly, staring at the mine complex. Ahead he could see the main camp, with a few large, weathered clapboard houses and the omnipresent company store on the left side. Well beyond the main camp the slope mine's opening gaped, a yawning hole in the hillside overlooking the tidy-looking rows of cottages in Cliftonville's New Camp. He chafed at the idea that faithful union miners were not the ones who rode the empty coal cars down the grade within the hillside and then sent full cars back to the surface. Instead replacement miners were digging coal and earning their pay.

Returning to his inspection, Angelo saw the blacksmith shop near the mineshaft as well as the mine's equipment shed and a generator building. Finally he noticed the large coal conveyor that led from the tipple building. Everything appeared quiet, as though nobody knew of their presence and their intent. But Angelo knew better. His instincts told him that a reception party awaited their appearance.

Following Angelo's lead, Nick saw movement in New Camp as the replacement miners – or scabs – began to prepare for the day shift by filling their water buckets at the pump and stuffing food into their lunch pails.

"See that?" Angelo whispered, pointing off to the side. Shifting his gaze, Nick only saw the tipple and the coal conveyor. Nick shrugged tiredly. "See what?" His brief slumber had given him just enough rest to want more. Angelo nudged him again, and also remarked in a louder whisper to address the men to either side of them. "Who aren't you seeing?" Nick shrugged again, too tired to comprehend details.

"The mine guards. They aren't there. Mine guards always stand outside or sit on chairs!" exclaimed another man.

Angelo nodded. "So if they aren't there, then where are they? " The nearby men passed the word down the line. "Remember, in West Virginia, mine guards have the powers of police on mine property. As if they could arrest anybody today."

"I just saw a movement behind a stone wall in front of the explosives shed," somebody whispered. Closer scrutiny revealed that the low wall was new, hastily created from rough-cut stones apparently intended for a foundation. More alert now, Nick made out what appeared to be the tops of two hats behind the wall. Somebody spotted a human figure behind a broken window in the mine tipple building. They also saw that another window in the tipple had been broken out. "There is probably a man behind that window, too," whispered the man on Nick's right.

Nick realized that he had to pee. He scooted back down the embankment a few feet and opened his fly. He let loose right there, to the amusement of Angelo and a few others. "Better than in my pants," Nick commented after he had crabbed his way back up the embankment. "I would hate to have people say that Nick Shebellko pissed his pants after he was shot. What kind of a man does that?

"A brave man who knows what it is to live and to fear death," came the reply from one of the men.

After a moment of silence several others slid back down the embankment and did the same. Angelo reluctantly followed. "You have wisdom beyond your years my young friend," he confided upon his return. "So how many guns do we have?" Angelo asked the men on both sides. The question was whispered all the way down the line. The man to the right finally reported: "Three pistols and two rifles." From the left came the answer: four rifles, a shotgun and two pistols. Angelo shook his head sadly. Not enough for a hundred men or more. Not nearly enough. They would have to depend on sheer numbers to win today. Nick hefted his heavy branch, thick as a man's forearm. It would be his only weapon.

Angelo nudged Nick. "Hear it?" He glanced up the tracks toward the tunnel.

After a few seconds, another man echoed, "I hear it," with a note of anxiety in his voice. Now, Nick could hear it, too. The morning train was arriving right on schedule at five o'clock. After a few more minutes the train's engine slowly emerged from the tunnel, as though the hillside was forcing a huge bowel movement. After the engine's emergence, billowing clouds of thick black smoke and white steam followed, enveloping the rest of the train. The steam whistle warned of its massive size and weight as the train approached the grade crossing above where Nick and his friends were waiting.

Once it reached the tiny railroad station with the signboard that proclaimed Cliftonville, it stopped just long enough to pick up one outgoing sack of mail. Two new sacks were dropped onto the platform and two arriving passengers stepped down from the Pullman car. Nick surmised that those two passengers would soon have much to remember about the tiny hole-in-the-wall called Cliftonville, West Virginia.

The anticipation was palpable. He could feel it in the air, mixed with the fear and anguish of the miners near him. They were not soldiers. Only a few had fought in the Great War, and even those men with battle experience were afraid today. He could hear many of them praying quietly. Angelo said aloud, "Any minute now. Remember, we walk to take over the mine tipple and generator building and help our brothers keep the daylight shift out of the mine. We walk. We do not run. And we do not shoot first."

After a few more minutes the engine's steam whistle shrilled and the train began to take up the slack between its cars, each knuckle connection clanking loudly as the train slowly pulled away from the station. With a chorus of low groans, Nick and the others arose on their shaky legs and began to walk toward the mine buildings as a ragged rank of Civil War soldiers might have crossed a battlefield in launching an attack. Those with guns didn't shoulder them but instead kept them ready near their hips.

Looking up, they could see the column starting from the woods heading toward the tipple, mineshaft and explosives shed. Nick saw the daylight crew of replacement miners walking toward the mine opening from the right, the morning sun shining brightly off their dangling metal lunch pails. Finally noticing the approaching horde, the replacement miners hesitated and began to mill about confusedly. Thinking the better of reporting to work, they changed direction without argument and headed back to New Camp where they remained outside of their houses, watching the scenario being played out at the mine.

Near the company store, Nick saw women from the main camp at the water pump, staring at his advancing rank of miners. They began to shout and scream, but nobody paid any attention. Nick and his men were within two hundred yards of the tipple when a shot rang out from somewhere on the hillside. He and his friends quickly fell to the ground, as though a single man, in self-preservation. It had begun. Somebody had fired a gunshot. Did somebody suffer a nervous trigger finger or had a defender of the mine decided to fire upon them?

CHAPTER SEVEN

Raggedly they rose again and began to advance at a faster rate across the field, with a few men firing as they walked. More shots rang out, this time clearly from the area of the tipple building and the explosives shed. A man to Nick's left screamed hoarsely and went down. Another further down the line to his right pitched forward into the grass. Several men reflexively fell to the ground without being wounded but got up again and rejoined the others in their advance.

The women fled inside their houses, while the scab miners did the same in New Camp. With bullets beginning to fly in all directions, this was no time to stupidly stand and watch what would surely be a battle. The bystanders comprehended it only too well.

Suddenly Nick could hear gunfire erupting from the hillside above the mine buildings, from the miners' hillside comrades. It seemed that all hell was breaking loose. Concentrated fire came from the area of the mine and its buildings, mainly aimed at Nick's line, but it seemed to be mostly inaccurate at this distance. Still, another man fell to Nick's right, calling out in pain: "Madre Mio!" He was calling on his mother, Nick knew. The man began to pray fervently in Italian.

To their surprise the miners heard a booming sound coming from the tracks near Virginville, behind them. Nick looked back as a cloud of projectiles flew through their rank, tearing though the brush with a ripping sound. They dropped down and tried to become part of the earth itself. "A pipe cannon!" somebody exclaimed. Fortunately pipe cannon aren't very accurate and the ammunition was mainly wasted on vacant ground. Still, a piece of roadbed stone struck the man lying right next to Nick in the back of the neck. He screamed out from the pain, but the energy of the missile had been mostly depleted before it hit him. They rose and began to move forward once again.

Now they could hear gunshots coming from the displaced miners' tent camp on their right. Somebody there had begun firing on the mine guards' and deputies' defensive positions. That was welcome, because Nick's group would need every advantage they could muster when they got near the mine buildings and the defenders waiting there. If shooting from the tent camp could keep some of the guards' heads down, it would make their fire less accurate.

Nick could now see that the men on the ridge top were advancing quickly down the slope with the man in the old army uniform leading them. He screamed instructions and encouragement as he ran. Either a demented radical or a born leader, or maybe both, the man was incredibly brave. He carried the American flag as his banner of battle as he passed from speckled shadows of the woods into the bright, open sunlight. The defenders couldn't concentrate their fire on Nick's group as much now, so Nick's comrades gained more courage as they kept on moving. But yet another man fell on the right flank, moaning. Nick glanced over and saw a colored miner get back up and keep going, holding his left arm with his right, a grimace of pain contorting his features.

For the first time, Nick saw a few men from the ridge top column begin to fall. Some falls were spectacular as they tumbled forward down the hillside after being shot. Meanwhile the pipe cannon blasts could still be heard behind them, but as they advanced, adding to the distance from the cannon, the blasts were becoming less of a concern. But still, a short, heavy piece of scrap iron hit a man on Nick's immediate left on the thigh. He yelled out in pain as his leg buckled under him. He stopped and picked it up to throw at the defenders when he got close enough, and staggered onward. At a closer range, Nick knew, the scrap metal weighing nearly a pound would have been a devastating missile. But the gunfire from the front had become much more deadly, especially to the men with no weapons other than what they had fashioned from nature or from their own working tools.

The group coming down the hill met some stiff resistance and even fell back twice before continuing onward, shooting as they came. Finally, the first of them forced their way into the mine's tipple building, led by the man with the flag. He kicked in the door and led them into the main floor while firing his revolver. Nick could hear gunfire from inside as they barged into the building. After a few minutes he saw several defenders slipping out a side door into the brush nearby. The shooting only slowed, however, so other defenders must have fallen back within the tipple to keep on firing from new positions. Nick knew that the attackers must have paid a heavy price for taking the entrance room of the tipple building.

Soon the tipple began to emit a dense black cloud that poured out of the windows, partially obscuring the surrounding scenery so that the escaping defenders could find new positions of concealment. Nick surmised that the invading miners must have doused the interior of the tipple with fuel oil. The uniformed man stuck his head out a broken window and reached his hand outside, waving the flag. A rousing cheer went up from Nick's group before the man disappeared back inside.

Pandemonium! Attackers were pouring out of the front of the burning tipple building while the last of the defenders ran out of the back. Nick's group had now approached within thirty yards of the front of the mineshaft, a generating plant and the explosives shed, so the pistol and especially the rifle fire from the defenders became much more telling. More men fell and one young, fallen miner began to cry. He seemed like a baby at that moment, even though he was a hard-muscled miner of eighteen years. Another prayed aloud in Nick's own language.

Suddenly a bright flash of light overwhelmed the entire scene. A deafening explosion stopped all movement and a few standing men were blown off their feet. Some were hit by flying projectiles, but most of the debris had been blown into the air and then rained down on the area without much effect. Part of the tipple's conveyor had been blown apart. Stunned attackers and defenders temporarily stopped fighting, and some began to confusedly mill about. Nick and the others wondered who had dynamited the conveyor. Was it attackers to destroy it, or defenders who wanted to stop the tipple fire from reaching the mine?

As he tentatively started forward again, Nick saw that a small group of defenders were climbing the hillside to the east, apparently trying to outflank the ridge top group. But Nick had his own worries. The gunfire had become very concentrated now and the defenders kept changing their positions. The few guns that the miners carried did help to reduce the accuracy of the deputies' gunfire because they had to spend more time behind cover.

Finally Nick and a group of men got to the generating plant and broke in the door. There, a withering fire from two deputies met them. One deputy had two revolvers blazing. A man fell silently in front of Nick, dead before he hit the floor. And then another fell, screaming out in pain. Nick was swept into the building with the small mass of invaders, who had no hope of survival other than to strike down anybody with a gun trying to kill them. Nick raised his own club over his head and rushed forward with his comrades. His fear had been transformed into a blind, hostile fury. Nick just wanted to strike out at any defender who held a weapon. Too many of his friends had been falling around him.

The man on Nick's left was cut down, tumbling forward. Then to his surprise Nick was hit, too. A heavy-caliber bullet struck him below the left shoulder and spun his body around. The pain raced through him like a blacksmith's hot iron poker jabbed into and clear through him. He screamed as he fell, hearing others near him crying out, some in pain, others in blind rage. He reached his hand over to his wound and found a hot, wet stickiness flowing through his fingers. He mechanically pulled his large handkerchief from his pocket and held it over the bullet's entry hole. As Nick's body slipped into a welcome but temporary respite from the pain it occurred to him that at least he hadn't pissed himself.

As another man fell, a miner got off a shot that hit the deputy in the face. As he collapsed onto the floor, somebody stepped forward and took his guns. Meanwhile another man pulled Nick to his feet, helping him to regain consciousness. He was somehow certain that it was Angelo. Nick mumbled that now he had a hole, too, like the hillside. "What, Nick?" Angelo said, but Nick didn't try to repeat it.

The survivors staggered outside, Angelo supporting most of Nick's weight. Glancing up, Nick could see through teary eyes that other miners were beginning to help the wounded to leave the area, fleeing back toward Pennsylvania. He could tell that the scene of the battle had been transformed in the space of an hour from a fierce conflict into a pastiche of total confusion. Miners were beginning to escape; many helping and some carrying wounded comrades. The attempt to shut down the mine had become a confused retreat by the now totally disorganized attackers.

*****

Meanwhile on the slope above, the sheriff had become separated from his group while pursuing a small group of miners. He clambered out of a thicket of saplings and berry bushes onto a large limestone outcropping. "Over there!" somebody shouted. Looking up, he saw a man with a rifle. The sheriff fired off a quick shot, but a bullet immediately slammed into his chest. He fell to his knees and looked upward. What he saw was not comforting. He looked into the faces of men who knew they had lost many comrades. In order to reach him, they had to step around and over the body of a fallen miner. They weren't in a merciful mood. Vengefully, they began to beat him as they took his guns. They shot him again – more than once – from close range. The sheriff lay there, all alone, victorious in death.

Below in the mine complex the defending deputies and mine guards were so grateful to be alive that they didn't even fire on the retreating miners. Perhaps they took pity on these men who were no longer a threat to them, and who only wanted to mine coal for a living wage. The attackers had been bloodied and were now in full retreat.

Overlooking the chaos flared the fiercely burning mine tipple and the demolished conveyor, still billowing plumes of smoke. Those unseen generals watching over the sorry tableau might have recognized the billowing smoke as a battle flag, flying victoriously over the field of a Pyrrhic victory, and the place of a tragic defeat.

CHAPTER EIGHT

Angelo staggered under the weight of his semi-conscious friend, as they struggled into the underbrush on the hillside. Nick was clearly becoming less and less able to contribute to his own escape. Another miner stepped forward and took his other side.

Angelo kept offering comforting words to Nick about getting to a doctor. "...And you will be back, ready for work in no time. It's only a flesh wound," he continued encouragingly as he struggled for breath.

While Nick was solid, he was not a heavy man. However the way home stretched long before them. He could tell that he had lost a lot of blood and that his strength, too, was bleeding away with it. The searing pain had been reduced to a dull throb in his shoulder and upper chest. Together the men trudged onward, passing the bodies of several miners. Bloodstains marked much of the underbrush, and the grass lay flattened by obvious drag marks.

Some miners passed them quickly as they hurried home. They knew they had to pretend that they had not been involved. Some began to make up stories of where they had been: hunting, visiting a friend, anywhere but at the Clifton mine. Mercifully, other miners eased Angelo's burden as they took turns helping him. Many of the fleeing miners would stop and help the able-bodied to assist, drag or carry the wounded before continuing onward with their own escape.

Nick moved into and out of consciousness as his rescuers stumbled onward in the oppressive heat of that July morning. He felt an abiding love for Angelo and his other comrades, more love than he had felt for anybody but his mother and father… and his dear Carmella. He could tell that they were risking much by helping him. Streaked with his blood they would easily be marked as men who had attacked the mine.

Nick passed again into a wonderful place of oblivion. He could now see his Carmella. It was a village corn roast, on a sweet and cool

August evening. They walked arm-in-arm at the Polar Star field as the crowds of happy revelers swirled about them. They stopped by a large pot of boiling water where Nick bought two ears of corn, his calloused hands peeling the husks back until they formed handles. Then Nick rolled each ear in butter and sprinkled salt over it. He handed one to Carmella after it had cooled enough for her to manage. They walked on, greeting friends and acquaintances as they enjoyed the succulent and juicy ears of fresh corn on the cob. "You always eat exactly three rows of corn and from the big end to the small!" he laughed.

"I know, but that is how I always did it and how I will always do it. If you marry me, this is what you will get. A woman who eats three rows at a time, not wasting any."

This is a good time, Nick realized. A very good time.

Over beyond the edge of the crowd, they noticed a group of young boys playing with a large tin paint can. Nick knew instantly what they were up to. They must have stolen a little of their father's carbide for his miner's lamp. Nick and Carmella stopped to watch. Two little boys teamed up. One put a little water in the bottom of the can and then dropped two or three nuggets of carbide into it. The other put the lid on and stamped it in place with his shoe. Then they both jumped back. After a few seconds the lid blew off from the expanding gases within and arched high into the air.

"Fire!" suggested another. With dancing eyes, the tow-headed redhead produced a nail and determinedly poked a hole in the bottom of the can, using a rock for a hammer. They repeated the process with the water, but one boy had a match this time. A dark-skinned boy stomped the lid into place, and the little instigator applied the match to the gases coming from the small hole, causing all the gases in the can to light. This time a thin column of fire spectacularly erupted from the small hole, as the gases inside the can exploded. The lid went flying toward a group of men playing "morra." One man, the father of the boy with the match, came over and said, "break it up or I break your heads." The boys scattered, giggling. He grinned at Nick. "Boys," he said, but with obvious affection.

They walked over to the small crowd surrounding the morra game. Nick, even though not Italian, had picked this game up quickly. One had merely to know the numbers in Italian from zero to ten.

Playing against your opponent, you try to predict the total number of fingers thrown by both your hand and your opponent's hand. It could be a long game with equally matched opponents cagily parrying, or a quick win by an excellent player who quickly recognizes patterns in his opponent's play.

Angelo walked up to them, giving Carmella a fond squeeze and Nick a hearty back slap. They watched the game for a few minutes, before Angelo said, "Watch Julio. When he gets excited, he always follows two fingers with three fingers. His man will trap him." After the next time Julio threw two, he again threw three. His opponent shouted "cinque!" (five) and threw two. The opponent won the point, to the disgust of Julio's teammates. "Julio is too easy," Angelo said. "Especially when he has a glass of wine." Julio lost the point, so the next man on his team stepped forward to play.

Angelo joined the next team waiting to play, while Nick and Carmella moved on. Nick tossed their spent ears of corn into an emptied oil drum and gave his kerchief to Carmella to wipe her hands and lips. "This is a wonderful time," Nick whispered to her, as the small band began to play. There were an accordion, a clarinet, a violin and a drum. Nick and Carmella moved in the direction of the music…

***

"Unngghhhh!" Nick cried out as a renewed shaft of pain coursed through his throbbing chest and shoulder. Angelo shifted Nick's torso, to center more of his weight across his own shoulder. He also tried to relieve the pressure on Nick's upper body by pulling upward on his belt. The man on Nick's other side matched Angelo's efforts.

Looking around through his pain-filled, haze-covered vision, Nick knew that they had traveled at least two miles and were well into Pennsylvania. Angelo kept giving his friend words of comfort as he himself struggled for breath. Shortly, two other miners took Nick by the shoulders and Angelo trod along behind them, re-gathering his strength. They took turns more often now as they tired more easily.

"Look!" someone cried out. "The spring!" They stopped by the long-anticipated spring in a hillside, where Angelo drank lustily. So did the others. Somebody held a metal folding cup of water up to

Nick's mouth. He tried to drink, but most of it spilled from his lips.

After a short rest, they continued onward, a small group of five men who seemed determined to assure that Nick got to a doctor, or at least as close to home as possible. During a moment of near-lucidity, Nick thought he could see buildings off to the right. "Penowa, Nick." Angelo said. "See? We are on our way home." Nick weakly nodded. Mercifully, the intense pain had again subsided, but the omnipresent, underlying throbbing ache remained, growing and receding in waves of discomfort.

Now Nick's feverish mind began to concentrate on his Carmella. How he loved that girl. How much he wanted to become her husband and provide a good living for her and their babies. He tugged weakly at Angelo's sleeve and moved his mouth next to Angelo. They stopped and Angelo held his ear close to Nick's mouth. He knew that the most important words in the world were those of a dying man. They must never be denied or ignored. Nick croaked hoarsely and just barely audibly: "Talk to my Carmella. Tell her I..." He suddenly sank to the ground, a dead weight. The realization hit his comrades that Nick had passed away.

Angelo looked at the others sadly. They silently agreed that Nick must be buried. His body must be protected from the buzzards and crows and the forest animals. They carried his body for nearly another half-mile, staggering in their dedication to this comrade, this brother. One man finally exclaimed and pointed up ahead. On a slope they could see a rock outcropping with what appeared to be a depression beneath it.

Angelo and the others carried Nick's body to the hole in the hill and found that it was the mouth of a shallow cave. They pulled and pushed his body inside and carried it about sixty feet to the back. They gently laid him on his back, and they closed his eyes. Angelo placed his own handkerchief over Nick's face, because he knew what they must do. They each said a short prayer over him, asking the Savior and the holy mother to watch over their comrade and Angelo's dear friend.

The others backed respectfully from the cave, and then one passed a stout tree branch in to Angelo. He again blessed Nick's body, and moved toward the cave mouth. He turned and pushed the branch above some limestone and shale that comprised the unreliable ceiling of the cave, before jumping backward. A portion of the roof fell in, concealing Nick's body behind the rubble. As the dust settled, Angelo and the others picked up many of the loose rocks and placed them on top of and in front of the rubble. No animal would defile the body of his friend.

Angelo said a few more words of prayer and made a promise to Nick. "Yes, my friend, I will tell your Carmella. I will tell her that her man fought bravely and died well. I will also tell her that his last thoughts and the last words from his lips were of his Carmella." He turned and despondently left, finally beginning to think of his own safety and his own future. Both were highly in doubt.

CHAPTER NINE

The tipple continued to pump out smoke, even as the flames were diminishing. As the replacement miners and the defending force of regular deputies, deputized citizens and mine guards approached the smoldering scene; the awful extent of what had transpired finally began to hit them.

During the battle, the defenders had to worry more about self-preservation than mine equipment. The scab miners and uninvolved mine employees had also felt the same need. They and the women of the mining camp had mainly tried to stay indoors and close to the floors, with the exception of the occasional perilous peek through a window at the fearsome conflict. As the mine's firefighters poured water into the tipple's main floor so that they might enter, the others had a chance to talk and to think.

"Do we have any casualties?" asked the mine superintendent. "We better call the sheriff and state police, and then the company to get them after those scoundrels."

"Boss," a foreman reminded him: "The sheriff fought right here with us, but I don't see him now. Should we get a search party out to look for the dead and wounded?" The superintendent agreed and gave the order. As the searchers fanned out in small groups to check the buildings and grounds, the super started toward the mine office to make his phone calls to the authorities.

"Hey!" somebody shouted. "Here comes a deputy, and he don't look too good." The super stopped in his tracks. A deputy staggered up to the group and gasped: "Deputy Mokinson was shot. He might not make it!" He started back toward the generator building followed by the foreman. Upon entering, they found a scene of awful carnage. Mokinson lay there all right, looking up at them weakly but with triumphant pride in his eyes. A few feet away they saw the prone and still body of a miner who had been shot in the chest. Even though the victim lay face down, they could tell the site of the wound because of the gaping exit hole in his back. It had no doubt been made by a slug from one of Mokinson's .45 caliber revolvers. Mokinson remained conscious, but barely so. He had taken a bullet in the mouth that exited through the right side of his oral cavity.

The foreman turned and gave the order to call for the mine's doc and for an ambulance. "On second thought," he amended, "Better make that lots of ambulances. Better call the Weirton and Steubenville hospitals, too. Mokinson will be coming in and we don't know how many others."

After completing his first calls, the super hurried back to the scene, where a small crowd of onlookers jostled each other to peer into the building. He brushed them aside and forced his way in, where he saw first aid being performed on Mokinson's wounds from a box of bandages. "It's the chief deputy," somebody offered. The super nodded. He glanced around, looking for damage to the building's equipment, his gaze passing over the dead miner. Vast amounts of blood had been splashed on the floor and splattered on the wall near the doorway. "More men than just that one died here today," he remarked to nobody in particular.

Unable to accomplish anything more in the building, the super stepped outside to collect his thoughts. The defenders were straggling in now, small groups beginning to collect around him. "I saw a dead miner on the hillside," one exclaimed. "There's one over by the supply shed," another said excitedly. The group buzzed with excited side chatter. Another offered that he had peeked into the mine tipple after the intense heat in the main floor had died down. "I saw at least two badly burned bodies in there. One man still held a burned-out torch!" he exclaimed. The super cleared his throat loudly, interrupting the chatter. Everybody fell silent and looked at him.

"Okay, boys. I want an accurate count of the dead and wounded. Help any injured guards back here if they can walk. Let the miners lay wherever you find them. But if they're not dead, put a guard over them." About then he heard sirens off in the distance, coming closer on the road over by Virginville. "Somebody get out there to show them the way back here. Now, where's the sheriff?" A guard explained that he had last seen the sheriff, his son and a few other deputies heading up the slope during the battle but they hadn't come back since. The super directed that a party be sent out to find them, led by the guard who last saw them disappear up the slope.

"Now, who blew up my mine conveyor?" he demanded. A

guard stepped forward, hat in hand, and stood with head bowed before the super. "We did, sir. We had to. The tipple was burning so hot that we thought the fire would heat the mine and set it on fire, too. That conveyor acts like a chimney and it could have turned the mine into a blast furnace. Besides, there were men hiding in that mine," he concluded nervously. The guard knew that he and his friend had put themselves on dangerous ground here. If the super or the owners didn't like their decision, it would mean permanent unemployment in the coalfields. He and the other guard who planted the dynamite would be blacklisted at the very least. Not to mention jail time for willfully destroying undamaged mine property. He waited for the super's judgment.

"Boys, you did what you had to do," the super said after a moment. "We can always rebuild it before the mine reopens. We have to rebuild the tipple as it is. You did just fine," he assured the two guards. "You might have saved the mine, not to mention a few lives. But I have to tell you, your dynamite job sure got everybody's attention!"

The first of the police cars had just pulled into the mine property and were driving through the creek bottom, followed by a fire truck. The super walked over to meet the small group of state and local police who were now proceeding toward him. The fire truck drove bumpily toward the tipple to add its pumps to the firefighting effort as two firemen began to lay hose from the stream bed. Several more cars and trucks arrived, followed by an ambulance and a horse-drawn hearse. Somebody up at the generator building waved wildly for the ambulance and the doctor.

By now, most of the searchers had returned. There were no living miners found on the property, but several dead ones had been located, including the two who could be seen in the now-cooling tipple. "Where's that sheriff?" the super wondered aloud.

***

Up on the hillside, the sheriff's son and three other deputies searched desperately for his father. They split up and struggled onward up and around the steep slope, slipping and clutching at saplings as they went. The son rounded a bend and saw a large boulder jutting from the hillside. A body lay prone on the outcropping. He approached the figure, which he quickly recognized as that of his father. The sheriff lay still. The blood drying on the stone, still warming in the heat of mid-morning, attested to his death. He shouted: "Over here!" The others made their way to the boulder and gathered around, standing silently over the prone sheriff and his kneeling son. After a few minutes they gathered him up and carried him from the scene.

Below, the dead had since been rounded up from the grounds of the mine, the generator building, and the still-smoldering tipple. The count totaled five miners killed and found on mine property that day. They suspected that more bodies were yet to be found.

The injured deputy waved weakly at the concerned onlookers, as the rescuers gently carried him to an ambulance. "What a hero," one guard commented, and the others nodded agreement. "What a hero." Meanwhile the dead miners were being loaded into the bed of a truck to be hauled away, like so much garbage.

A guard suddenly exclaimed and pointed. He had noticed the small group of deputies struggling with their burden as they approached the camp. The super looked up, followed by the police and the other bystanders. First one man and then the others recognized the sheriff's son and the other deputies carrying their precious burden. They quickly realized whose body was being carried back into the camp. The heroic lawman had fallen in the line of duty .

"Let's get those bastards." A policeman muttered angrily. "They have to pay for this."

CHAPTER TEN

The Present

After a threatening overnight sky, the day dawned breezy and overcast, but the sun was already forcing its brilliant light through the quickly dissipating cloud cover. Now, in mid-morning, the day promised perfect weather for hiking. Joe had long looked forward to testing his legs and cardio system on a rugged trail. He parked along Meadowcroft Road and studied the trailhead he had noticed. It didn't look like much of a trailhead really, just a place where deer crossed the road from the lower meadow and creek to their cover and browse on the wooded hillside. He locked the Caddy, checked his few hiking supplies, and tied his favorite kerchief on his head.

After a brief hesitation he forced his way through the thick, damp brush that, competing for the available sunlight, crowded into the trail's opening next to the road. Nature was always like that, Joe thought, especially in the spring when foliage grew at its most aggressive pace. Survival of the fittest, or at least the fastest, he mused. "In the old days, Joe," Andy had said just that morning. "Things were different. We lived in boarding houses and we men ate supper together. If you were slow to a piece of meat on the tray, you probably lost it to somebody with a faster fork."

Once inside, he found an open trail that he could hike without much difficulty. He set off at a fast pace on a gentle upward slope, following the contour of the hillside. Those deer could always pick the best way to negotiate a terrain, he thought. The deer taught the Indians, and often the Indians taught the white men. Something like that. He sighed contentedly, trying to slow his constantly wandering mind, and pressed onward

He maintained his swift pace for a few minutes, to bring his heart rate up, before settling into a comfortable but brisk stride. In the shade provided by the forest canopy, the dirt of the worn trail hadn't yet dried out from the rain of a couple days ago. He found that it was muddy in a few places; the mud sometimes mixed with a slippery seam of clay. But grass dominated most of the trail, and that offered its own kind of slickness to a hiking boot. As he rounded a bend into deep shade, Joe abruptly slipped on exposed damp clay and nearly fell, catching himself on both hands and one knee. Selecting a stout walking stick from a piece of broken tree branch, he walked on; this time striding more securely by using his handy new third leg.

As usual, Joe's mind fell back to its wanderings, to the important issues and the mundane. It didn't take him long to think of old Andy. He had to admit that the old guy was quite a character. Fast approaching the century mark but only slightly wizened and bent, the man still seemed indefatigable. Joe could tell from the lines of Andy's face and his large, gnarled hands that his life hadn't been an easy one. He could still remember the old man's words from one of their conversations: "Joe, nobody made us any promises when we were brought into this world. There were no deals struck. But when we got here we each had a chance. The most important thing is what you did with whatever hand you were dealt." He could still see the distant look on Andy's face. "I worked hard and played fair, Joe. Nobody can take that away from me."

Worked hard and played fair, Joe pondered as he trudged onward, following the gradually increasing slope of the trail. Had Joe done that, too? He hoped so. Sudden movement in the tree ahead attracted his attention. Two huge blue jays were flitting around in a courtship dance. They noticed him and began to noisily chastise him for disturbing their play. "Okay, okay. I'll be out of your territory before you know it," he said as he passed. "Sheesh!" Glancing back, he saw them resume their game. Obviously he offered only a temporary – and at the most a minor – irritation in their avian world.

He stopped, wiped his brow and drank thirstily from his water bottle. That water sure did taste good. He felt no concern about drinking most of the contents to replenish the lost sweat. As an outdoorsman, he understood that the woods held more sources of water than he would ever need. Joe swatted a mosquito on his forehead. Well, they had found him. He applied a little repellant and moved on.

Joe's mind restlessly moved back to his old neighbor. The other morning, Andy told him that he had worked in the mines during the late twenties and thirties, before hooking up with a strip-mining outfit. How had he said it? "Mining? Hard work, Joe. About as hard as you could imagine. But a man got used to it and worked without complaint. Those days you were lucky to have a job, even one deep under a hill. A man would chance having that hill serve as his tombstone if there was a paycheck in it. Not to mention a true miner learned to love the work and wouldn't want to take an outside job if he could help it. The earth called to him. And by the time I started they were beginning to pay a fairer union wage."

Joe wondered about that: a fairer union wage. What exactly did he mean? He would have to ask Andy to explain it to him. He also wanted to know how a man could love such a dangerous occupation. He paused and scribbled in his little note pad, and then replaced it and the pencil stub in his breast pocket. He ate half of his granola bar and trudged on.

How he had missed this pleasure, Joe mused. It had been so long. Even when running for miles along a country road or his usual trails, his body never really had to deal much with continuous undulations of the earth's surface. But now his legs were constantly adjusting to the changing terrain and surface texture of the ground. He would slip on greasy wet clay and catch himself. He would trip over a tree root or falter on an unevenly jutting rock. But he also knew that all of this effort forced a strengthening of his legs and building up of the reflex speed that could make the difference between a minor ankle turn and a serious knee and ankle sprain someday. What did they call it? Muscle memory? Proprioceptive feedback? Now, how did that term work its way from somewhere within the deep recesses of his mind? An instructor had used it at the police academy; it was what your body told you about itself. If the signal regarding a sudden problem with your footing or body position could shoot from your legs to your spinal cord fast enough, your reflexes could adjust quickly and avoid a sprain or worse.

All that aside, he just liked the feeling of his legs doing his bidding as he tuned them up, along with his heart and lungs. Hiking, he realized, constantly involved your upper body as well. You adjusted your weight, used the walking stick, or grabbed for saplings or rock outcroppings to help you along a steep stretch or to keep from slipping over an embankment. Balance. As much as anything else, it was about balance.

The sudden flash of a white tail deer explosively bursting though the underbrush nearby broke that wandering line of thought. Two yearlings quickly followed the big doe, also racing away with tails vertical as warning flags. He stopped again and sat on a rock to take a break. He also took the opportunity to filter some spring-fed water from a small ravine into his water bottle as he studied a clearing just coming into view up ahead.

What did Andy say about this part of the township? There were small outcroppings of coal, and some men would dig into them for fuel to heat their houses. In fact, a small, clandestine wildcat mine started on such an outcropping could provide coal for sale to help support a family. Andy said that the free coal could make the difference between a painfully cold house in the winter and a tolerable one. Most men and boys didn't mind the work of digging and hauling, not when it made their family's life a little more bearable.

Joe decided that while the meadow would be a welcome respite from the hard slogging of the slippery trail, he would hold off on taking a break for lunch. As he passed through the open area he quickly appreciated the drying sunshine, but then the bites of waiting sweat bees confirmed his decision to keep on moving. Given a choice, he would take the occasional mosquito in the woods anytime over the persistent little biters. Joe followed the contour of the hill, re-entered the woods, and finally began to enjoy a gentle downward grade.

The sun overhead told him, without need to check his watch, that lunchtime had finally arrived. He started looking for a welcoming place to eat. Farther on down the trail he saw another small meadow with a wooded area and rock outcropping just beyond. Joe welcomed the relief that the shade would offer from the hot sunshine. He quickened his pace and speedily arrived at the outcropping, dropping gratefully onto a flat stone underneath. Pulling out his lunch, he attacked his first sandwich; he had always looked forward to and appreciated this hiking moment. Joe settled in to the cooling shade of the protective rock ledge and tried to absorb the beauty of the sylvan setting.

Thoughts of the indomitable old coal miner flooded his mind again. The man had a stronger spirit than most people he knew, and frankly he couldn't think of anybody under thirty who could begin to compare in Joe's regard. How could a man work, bent over the way Andy tells it, unable to stand upright for hours on end while digging and loading coal? Or work from one knee, using mainly his upper body's strength to shovel coal out of a foot of water into a waiting coal car? The very place where miners worked, beneath thousands of tons of dirt and rock, had to be the most threatening in the world.

He scooted back and, glancing under the outcropping, saw that a small cave reached thirty or more feet back. He dug out his flashlight and peered inside as his eyes began to adjust from the bright sun to the dim interior. Nope, no bears in there, he wordlessly chuckled. He crawled inside and began inspecting the interior. It had been carved from the soft earth between layers of limestone and shale. It contained a minimal amount of litter, mainly candy wrappers and a couple empty water bottles, apparently left by other hikers, hunters or children out on a wooded foray. The cave's ceiling didn't exceed five feet in any place. Tiredly, he laid his daypack down and stretched out with his head on it for a brief but welcome nap in the cool comfort of the darkened hole in the ground. As he drifted into slumber his thoughts turned again to Andy's coal mining stories. What kind of men were these? And would he ever see their like again?

Suddenly vivid dreams hit him! They inundated him; overwhelmed his consciousness! But there was no Andy. Instead, scenes of coal mining tragedy spilled all over each other; shocking in their invasiveness. A black miner cried out his final breath along with his life's essence as the crushing weight of coal and rock expelled the air from his chest. A young miner's last mental image was of his bride and baby, just before exploding fire damp gases flashed through the main tunnel and into his workspace. Faces frozen with fear watched the billowing cave-in as it rushed toward the doomed men. They turned to run but had nowhere to go. They resignedly faced the certainty of their doom.

Scenes of mining camp life, polka music and carefree dancing irrationally worked their way into these visions of tragedy. But then an image of scores of men running across a field, cursing, falling and dying bruised its way past the other scenes; one miner dying instantly as his heart was blown away. A young miner cried out for his mother after his leg was shot out from under him. The apparition of another pain-wracked miner fervently sobbing and praying in a foreign language banished the other images from Joe's consciousness.

Then the mining tragedy vignettes fought their way back and tussled with the others for his dreamspace. All the images merged, overlaid, and shoved each other out of the way, like surreal vaudeville players bizarrely and continuously attempting to upstage each other. But Joe was far from an appreciative audience. Shocked and beleaguered by the sensory overload, he struggled to push these intrusive visions from his mind. But he couldn't wake up and they just wouldn't leave. After more minutes of desperate struggle, he finally forced himself awake.

Joe found himself sitting rigidly upright with an unaccustomed look of abject horror on his face and sweat streaming from his forehead. It took all of his self-control to refrain from leaping upright and crashing his head into the rock ceiling in an attempt to run from the cave. After a confused moment, he finally focused on his escape route and reached for his daypack.

Joe shivered uncontrollably. The cave no longer served as a cool retreat from the heat of the mid-day sun; it now infused him with an enveloping, oppressive coldness that seemed to cling to and permeate deep within his flesh. His body shuddering, he grabbed up his pack and scrambled through the entrance, relieved to escape that hole. Stumbling to his feet upon exiting the cave, he rushed a short distance away. He sank gratefully onto a stone outcropping super-heated in the early-afternoon sun. All too slowly the heat permeated his body, finally drying out his sweat-drenched shirt and purging the coldness from his very bones. After awhile the shivering ebbed and he crawled back to the cave mouth and shined his light within. He saw nothing in there, absolutely nothing. But no hot rock could purge the horrors he had witnessed. Joe turned and rushed down the trail.

The way back to his car took less than a half hour of hurried walking and occasional frantic running. Arriving at the roadside, he ran to the car. He fumbled with the keys, flung the door back on its hinge, tossed in his gear and shoved the key into the ignition to start the engine. Peeling the tires and scattering gravel, he wasted no time at all in escaping that dreadful place.

CHAPTER ELEVEN

Joe awoke with a start. For the fifth time tonight he sat bolt upright, driven relentlessly and mercilessly from his slumber. As he stared into the enveloping darkness, it finally became clear to him that somebody was determined to tell him – or show him – something. He turned on the bedside lamp and lay there, staring at the plaster designs on the ceiling. What was it? Who was it? And why wouldn't they just leave him alone?

Joe tried to re-capture that last dream, but found it slipping rapidly away. He could never seem to remember his dreams more than a minute or two after he awoke each day, each one no more than an elusive apparition that winked at him, gave a flippant wave and then dissolved. This usually disappointed him, especially when his dream involved a beautiful woman or a pleasurable event. However this time his desperation to find out the source of the terrors that vengefully appeared each night overwhelmed him. Why did that dream beleaguer him so? He concentrated, closing his eyes and trying to return to the dream state – trying to get past the feeling that he could never return to a specific dream. The hopelessness of trying seemed to overwhelm his efforts, even before he started.

Wait a minute! The cave, that damn cave again! What was it about that cave? Suddenly he could see himself coming into view at the cave mouth under an overcast sky. Strangely, he began to hear a new and unexpected sound. He detected a rumble of coal cars on a narrow-gage track, shuttling tons of coal back and forth. What the hell were coal cars doing in a shallow cave?

Joe thought he could hear the faint "tink, tink, tink" of pickaxes far within. He listened closer, finally getting into his dream, or if not his dream, his vision. He could hear a song being sung by men in a foreign language. It had a rhythm that matched the sounds of pickaxes and shovelfuls of coal being flung into an iron and hardwood mine car. The chanting reminded him above all else of old movies of chain gang prisoners, turning big rocks into little ones with sledgehammers along the roadside. The sounds from the cave swirled around him, enveloping him. Chanting, chanting, tink, tink, tink; chanting, chanting, thunk, thunk, thunk. Pickaxes? Shovels? And what about that language? So indistinct, so elusive. Was it eastern European? Was it Polish? Slavic? Russian?

Now the sounds became clearer to him. No longer a foreign language, he heard instead a lone voice, chanting as though in time with the work: "Tink, tink, tink, who, are, you; thunk, thunk, thunk, who, are, you…" The sounds drove shivers and a feeling of dread throughout Joe. Suddenly the sounds of work stopped and he heard heavy tools being tossed against a wall. He thought the chanting had ended, too.

But no, it resumed, simple and plaintive: "Who are you. Who are you…" But then it became more intense – more strident. Joe forced himself to lie in bed and face his demon.

As he watched, his dream self backed away from the cave entrance but waited and watched also; apparently too terrified to stay but too engrossed to leave. Joe stayed in bed with his eyes clamped shut, tensely watching the scene being played out against the interior of his eyelids. He now realized with undeniable certainty that somebody was in there, approaching the inside of the cave mouth.

Joe merely had to open his eyes and the petrifying vignette would disappear. Or at least it would go away until he fell asleep again. He tried to detach himself as a mere observer, but his connection to Joe at the cave entrance was much too strong to allow that. He felt a sudden pall fall over the cave mouth. The chanting stopped. He forced himself to continue focusing on the scene unfolding on that lonely hillside.

The dream Joe felt a sudden chill as an even darker cloud passed in front of the sun. The darkness intensified his feeling of anxiety and dread as he waited, emphasizing his helplessness to affect the cards that were about to be dealt to him.

He watched the entrance, having backed away about six feet, and then ten. He felt rather than heard somebody stop inside the cave entry, still hidden in the darkness within. Joe nervously shouted out in an unexpectedly weak and squeaky voice born of tension and anxiety: "Who are you and what do you want?" Silence answered him, as though somebody or something inside had to ponder the meaning of his words before speaking; somebody who seemed unsettled that Joe stood outside of his cave mouth asking questions.

Silence. Embarrassed by the unmanly squeak that had issued from his lips already, Joe said, more quietly this time and with all the self-control and authority he could muster, "Is somebody in that cave?" This time his voice took on more of a manly tone. But still, the response remained silence.

After what seemed like an eternity, he heard somebody say – or did he feel him say it? "Who are you and why are you here?"

After another moment Joe answered: "My name is Joe. This isn't a coal mine. Who are you?"

The scene being played out at the cave fascinated the recumbent Joe, who had lost some of his fear. He continued to watch; his eyelids no longer scrunched tightly shut. But he wondered if he could have opened his eyes even if he wanted to.

At the cave, Joe awaited the answer. "Who are you? And why won't you come in?" the voice demanded

Joe thought about that for a minute. As the clouds overhead dissipated and his world lightened, he edged closer to the cave. Or was it a mine? No, it couldn't be, but for the hollow sounds of mining he had heard. Were they real or the product of his feverish imagination? He edged closer still until he stopped by the entrance. "Why should I come in?"

The voice seemed surprised at the unexpected question. "Because I can't come out."

Joe decided to look inside. He edged closer to the opening, keeping his body well aside, and peered into the darkness. His eyes, accustomed to the daylight, took a few moments to adjust to the semi-darkness within the cave. There he saw a shape taking form. He soon realized that it had taken on the shape of a man, but yet it also appeared indistinct, ethereal. The face slowly swam into view.

Startled, Joe in bed was poised to fling his eyes open and stop the whole business at once. Yet, he maintained control and lay still, watching. A curious but not detached audience of one to the one-act drama being acted out.

To see better, Joe edged his head farther into the cave. Yes, one man sat there now, wearing rough clothing. The man's face was finally discernible. Even though smudged with grime, it was one he instinctively felt that he could trust. Joe surprised himself by crawling quickly into the cave's entrance, kneeling there with the sun on his back and his face in darkness.

Strangely unafraid, it was as though in the light of day his fears had plagued him, but in the darkened recess of the earth his doubts illogically dissolved. He sat down and waited. The stranger sat quietly as they each had a chance to gather their thoughts and size each other up. After a few moments, Joe nervously asked, "Who are you and why did I hear the sounds of a mine working? How long have you been here?"

"I can't say how long," the man replied. 'I know my name is Nick and that I shouldn't be here. How long have I been here?" He pondered his own odd question and Joe's. "All I know is that after all this time I'm not even hungry." Studying the man, Joe noticed something odd. His lips moved but Joe couldn't hear any words. He just felt them and understood them. The man went on. "You can understand me?"

"Yes, very well," Joe answered. "I can't hear you, but I can understand you."

"Strange," Nick replied. "I speak very broken American. I mostly speak Slavic, but I understand some Italian and a little German. You can understand my American?"

"Yes, very well," repeated Joe.

In bed Joe opened his eyes with a start and sat abruptly upright. He had begun to fall asleep and didn't quite know how to handle that loss of control. The scene at the cave dissipated suddenly and both actors disappeared.

CHAPTER TWELVE

Joe spent the next few days dreaming at night, hiking in the woods near Shades of Death Road and working on projects around old Albert's house. He found that he detested removing old wallpaper. It was sweaty and unrewarding work in the non-air-conditioned house. "How could they have ever expected this stuff to peel back off?" He exclaimed. "What did Albert use for glue? Mortar mix? I bet if I took away the wood framing, the paper and glue walls would stand up on their own!" He liberally wetted the wallpaper a few more times and actually removed a few strips. "Just what I need: older wallpaper under the top layer." He gave the entire room a final wetting and left, covering his containers of water and chemicals. But as he exited the house one glance in the living room mirror revealed a man who – troublingly – talks to himself.

The sun had already risen very high in the sky, he noticed. Catching Andy's eye, he sauntered over to the old man's garden. "Looks like the lettuce and onions are coming along nice, Andy." He looked closer at the recently transplanted seedlings. "Are those pepper plants? Hot or sweet?"

"Some of each, Joe. Some of each," Andy replied with satisfaction. "This is an old-fashioned garden. I'll eat all I can during the season, parboil and freeze some, and give the rest away. Some of the ladies around here still preserve food, and they seem to appreciate the gift. Especially the widows.

"I remember the old days, Joe, when each house had a small yard and it was like every inch of space was planted, except for the clothesline and maybe a place to sit out on the back stoop. Kids didn't play in the yard like now; they played out in the street and in the woods, or they played ball in a vacant lot. We would share food from house to house and everybody would can what they could for the winter. When money became scarce, which was most of the time, those jars of food would keep a family going." Joe could see it in his mind's eye. Yes, rows of jars filled with food in the fruit cellar would be a mighty welcome sight when funds got low.

"Well," Joe said. "I think I'll take a little walk down to Avella, and maybe get a little something to eat myself. And who knows? I might bump into somebody I know and catch up on what's happening around town. I could use some trail mix for my next hike, too. I'll bring back something for you, too, okay?"

"Sounds good," replied Andy. "Hey, Joe, before you go, do you mind telling me about your hikes? I notice that you hike more than you run these days." Andy looked at Joe pensively. "Anything interesting happen on those hikes? I don't mean to pry, but lately you seem a bit... distracted, I'd say. Yep, distracted. Anything you want to talk about?"

"You are one perceptive old coot," said Joe in response. "To tell you the truth, I found kind of a little cave under an outcropping down toward Penowa. I stopped there to eat on one of my hikes." Andy noticed the distant look on Joe's face. In fact it was more than distant. It seemed that something was very troubling to his young friend. Joe finally looked at Andy with a start. "How long was I like that?"

"A minute or two. Yep, a good two minutes." Andy responded. "Want to talk about it? I can keep a confidence, Joe. Would you like to go inside for few minutes and maybe have a cold one before you start that walk?"

"Yeah, I would like to talk." Joe made up his mind to finally share some of what has been troubling him. "And I can't think of a person I'd rather talk with. Let's go inside. Do you really have beer chilling? I think I could use one."

Inside, Andy opened two cans and extended one to his new friend. "Okay, shoot!" He plunked down into a kitchen chair with a laugh. "Remember, in my ninety-six years I likely heard it all. You ain't gonna surprise me."

Joe looked him squarely in the eye. "Maybe you haven't heard it all, Andy. And maybe I will surprise you." He took had a good, long swallow, consuming about a third of the contents of the 16-ounce can. Oh, did that ever taste good, he thought. "Okay, get ready for a story. But first, do you remember any miners from your boyhood days named Nick?"

If the sudden question surprised Andy he didn't let it show. "I knew several miners named Nick, but I don't recall any in particular.

Why that strange question? Do you know a miner named Nick?"

"I doubt it. Heck, I didn't even know about my great-uncle Albert. Our family tree got pretty mixed up during the Depression and after World War Two, when they traveled out west for jobs. Anyway, as you well know I've been doing some hiking for relaxation. But lately, I haven't been very relaxed. Something happened to me, Andy. Maybe you can make sense of it," he said hopefully. "I know I'm stumped." He related the story of his first hike, the small outcropping and the cave within. He described the sudden coldness that had enveloped him.

"Caves can be cold, Joe," Andy offered, but without conviction.

"I know that, Andy. But this was different. It didn't feel natural, and the cave is shallow. It didn't connect to a larger cavern where a sudden blast of cold air could have come from. Anyway I've never felt coldness like that.

"And lately," he continued uneasily, "I've been having these bad dreams of me in the cave. Another person is in there too, but this isn't a flesh-and-blood person. Remember these are only dreams, but there are lots of them, sometimes four or five a night." He laughed nervously, studying the old man's face for any hint of mockery.

Andy looked thoughtful. "Tell me about the man. Can I assume that was Nick?" Joe nodded gratefully. That Andy's mind might be open was his first hurdle to overcome.

"Well, in my dreams he tells me in life he was a miner named Nick. But I don't think the dreams are what I can hang my hat on right now. In fact, I could probably blame Nick on my vivid imagination. But I think I have to go back to that cave just to be sure. Either Nick is there, or he isn't. I've been hoping that he would be waiting for me, but on the other hand I'm afraid that he'd be waiting, too. I mean, what do you do with a ghost when you have one?"

"It seems to me that you have a darn good imagination," Andy reflected with a bit of a twinkle in his eye. "Just going on what you told me, a lot of people would consider calling for the nut wagon and the guys in white coats. 'You could probably do with a nice long rest,' the doctors might say. But you'll never prove anything in bed. Only the cave will tell. Know what else I think?"

"What's that, Andy?"

"I think even if it's all real and you do meet an old miner named Nick, you could still find yourself in a big tub of real hot water. And people could be piling logs on the fire underneath. I mean, who besides me would believe you? In fact, I'm not all that sure about me. I think you should go to your cave and set your mind at ease. But even if you do find a dead coal miner wanting to have a little chat, I'd keep it to myself if I were you. Except for telling me all the details, of course." Andy's expression was loaded with conspiratorial amusement.

Joe started on his walk to Avella, mulling over his friend's opinion and taking his warning seriously. If word got around about Joe chatting with a ghost, people just might get the wrong idea about his sanity. Or even worse, they might get the right idea.

He made it to the convenience store and bought a cold Coke that he downed on the spot. He bought another for himself and one for Andy, plus enough trail mix and dried fruit for his next two hikes. He spent a few minutes chatting with Les, the amiable chief of the local volunteer fire department, who also enjoyed an occasional walk in the woods.

Joe always looked forward to seeing Les Wilson, one of the first people Joe met after arriving in Avella. A fit-looking man of about 35, his dedication to the fire department was apparent in the amount of time he spent there. Fortunately he had an understanding wife and two little tow-headed boys at home who aspired to be firemen, just like their daddy, and who wanted to be with him at the fire station whenever possible. They preferred clambering on the big fire trucks to pushing toy trucks around with their tinny sirens.

As Joe turned to leave, he bumped into a young woman who had distractedly hurried through the door of the store. Bending over to retrieve his purchases he knocked her off-balance, just managing to catch her as she stumbled backward. "I'm so sorry!" she mumbled as he helped her to her feet. "I'm so clumsy, and I was hurrying too fast. I always hurry too fast. And I can be so clumsy."

"My fault," he objected as he helped her pick up her car keys, wallet and purse, before attending to his own now-split open bag of treats. "I wasn't paying enough attention." The woman bent down again to help him, and as they stood up in unison he finally stared into her eyes. What a lovely shade of green. Her face blushed a deep pink to complement the green of her eyes. It was a very fascinating effect.

Joe could feel his own cheeks flushing. "My name is Joe," he said to break the uncomfortable silence. "Joe Bailey."

"I'm Jessie," she answered. "Are you new here, Joe? I don't think I've ever bumped… I mean seen you before," she said, again blushing. He noticed more about her now. Tall – about five feet nine, slender, straw-colored hair falling just past her shoulders. Probably in her late twenties, very nice full face, leaning toward round but with a fetching set of dimples. A shy smile that tugged at him immediately. She paid for her gas and began to leave. Or to escape? He hoped that wasn't it, and followed her out the door.

As they approached her car Joe volunteered some information to extend the encounter: "I'm new here, Jessie. I've only been here a few weeks, fixing up a house. I usually sell real estate in Pittsburgh. Living here is like a vacation to me." He struggled for something to keep her attention. "In fact, I developed a fondness for hiking in the woods around Avella. In desperation, he ventured, "Are you from here, Jessie?" He liked the sound of her name. He also realized that he had verged on babbling.

"No," she responded shyly. Joe noticed Les watching with amusement from over near the bag ice dispenser. "I teach elementary science at Avella. Well, Joe, it was nice meeting you. Maybe we'll... bump into each other again?" She had obviously recovered from the awkwardness of the moment faster than he had. As she turned away, Joe wanted to reach out and take hold of her as a drowning man might grab onto a floating dock. Why did she have this sudden impact on him?

"I see you two already met," Les remarked as he walked over, to Joe's relief. "Now, how about a formal introduction? Jessie, this is Joe Bailey, a pretty good guy and a good friend, too. Joe, may I introduce Miss Jessie Randall, science teacher extraordinaire." Les grinned, having a little fun with the both of them but also serving a critical function for his floundering friend.

"M'lady," Joe gravely took her hand and bowed, to Les's amusement and Jessie's increasing interest.

"You may rise, kind sir." Jessie glanced toward Les, who found himself enjoying the show as well as facilitating it. "A pleasure to make your acquaintance, Joe. Any friend of Les's must be alright."

"Well, I better be toddling on my way," Les concluded. "We have a work party going on at the fire hall in five minutes." He shook their hands and began to cross the street.

"Joe?" She said as she turned back to him. "You say you hike? Do you know much about nature?"

"I'm actually a pretty experienced hiker, and I know most of the mammals, birds and reptiles, as well as some of the edible plants. Why do you ask?"

"I have a unit coming up in environmental science, and I was planning to take the kids on a nature walk. Would you like to help? You would have to formally apply through the administrative office to be a volunteer and submit to a background check, but it could be a rewarding experience for you as well as the students."

"I served as a policeman before getting into real estate, so I shouldn't have any trouble passing the background check. I'm willing if you are. These days, walking in the woods is my favorite pastime."

Jessie looked thoughtful. Joe liked the way she looked thoughtful. She pursed her lips slightly and her eyebrows made a tiny frown. "Okay, just go to the elementary principal's office and fill out a form. They will be expecting you. After the office receives your clearance, we can schedule the walk. Just ask the secretary to call for Miss Randall." She opened the car door. "You did say Joseph Bailey?" He nodded.

Jessie slid behind the steering wheel and started the ignition. She waved gaily as she started to drive away. Joe's eyes finally focused on her left hand. No ring! He gave a short wave after her, conscious of Les still watching him from across the street. Glancing sheepishly at Les, who finally turned toward the fire department, he began his trek up Campbell Drive. Damn, he thought. He had met a girl and made sort of a date. Back at home, Andy was already sitting on Joe's front porch to make sure that he didn't miss out on his soft drink and on any news from downtown. Finally, Joe had something special to share.

CHAPTER THIRTEEN

Joe knew that this had to be the day. After yet another night of recurrent and very troubling dreams, he just knew that he had to get closure about this Nick thing. He had been lying starkly awake for well over an hour now, staring straight at the ceiling light fixture, and it was still only five-thirty a.m. Sighing tiredly, he sat upright and swung his legs out of bed. It was time. He resignedly accepted the fact that he could have no peace until he found closure to this Nick thing. Joe started the coffeemaker and poured a glass of juice, to drink as he dressed. He then filled his backpack with snacks and other supplies and drank two cups of strong coffee. Satisfied that his water bottle was full, he packed a spare and then tottered out to his old caddy and drove toward – what?

"What would I say to him?" Joe asked himself aloud, pondering what would take place if he were actually to meet a dead miner named Nick. It seemed that he talked to himself the entire way there, sometimes holding two-sided conversations. He planned what he would say, and how he would console himself if he found nobody at all. What would he ask Nick? "How did you die? Did it hurt? How old were you? Have you ever been to heaven? Did you meet Elvis?" Now that *really* qualified as a stupid question. "What *does* one say to a dead person?" he wondered out loud. "Sorry you're dead?"

He could well be on the way to losing it, he thought, as he parked the Caddy. This Nick thing and his lack of sleep had to be affecting his mental stability. His and Jessie's first date could very well be holding hands in his mental ward's visiting room.

It was nearly eight o'clock on a cool and overcast morning when he finally grabbed his daypack and headed for the trail. He wouldn't waste any time this morning. The dew still adhered to the grass and underbrush, but it willingly gave itself up to wet his hiking shoes and saturate his pant legs as he passed through the overgrown entrance to the trail. The trail inside still had that slippery clayey, muddy quality that made hiking so difficult. He found his walking stick propped against a tree, noting again – with satisfaction – that it equaled his six feet two inches. It felt good and substantial, having a nice heft. Taking a deep breath, he strode briskly up the winding trail.

Joe pressed his gait to what would have been an uncomfortable, nearly impossible speed before he began hiking these hills. But today he had the advantage of stronger legs and more endurance. He also felt the urgency of an appointment today, one that could be more important than any he had ever had with his police chief, his clients, or doctors. While unknown and unscheduled, this appointment was more compelling than he could have imagined a few short weeks ago.

Strangely, he very seldom entertained any doubts about Nick's actual existence. It had been confirmed through his visions and by a growing conviction carried deep within his soul. Right now, denying Nick's existence would have been like denying the existence of his image in the mirror. But the cop in him laughed at the thought. Had he taken evidence this flimsy to his chief or the prosecutor, they would have recommended a long and restful leave followed by retraining in Evidence 101.

Who was this Nick? Joe wondered. Again, a doubt flared in the analytical segment of his mind. Was this Nick real or only the figment of his overactive imagination, as it bubbled in this new and strange environment? Could somebody actually assault the dreams of a man in bed miles away? And if so, to what end? What purpose could it serve? The image of Nick's face forced its way into his thoughts. There was a lot of detail in that image. How would his mind have generated that? But then, could Nick be merely a composite of others he had met during his abbreviated law enforcement career or his current real estate profession? After all, he had met numerous people, often under very trying, and occasionally life-threatening, circumstances. In his past, vivid images of criminals – and even more so victims of violent crime – would plague his sleep. Such intrusions haunted the dreams of cops who lived their professions more than they worked them. But this was different, he argued to himself. These dreams were extended and chronic. In them, he and this Nick regularly interacted.

Joe tripped over a tree root on the muddy trail and slid down a small but steep slope. "Well, that's nice!" Joe exclaimed after he bounced into a tree, forcing him back to the here-and-now. He opened his daypack and began to inspect the contents. His spare water bottle had sprung a leak. He quickly drained it, taking advantage of the remaining contents. Emptied, the bottle went back into his backpack to be discarded later. Luckily he always carried his snacks, matches and other supplies in plastic sandwich bags. Even in his partially sodden pack they all remained completely dry. "So Boy Scouts did teach me something useful," he remarked under his breath. Still sitting next to the tree, he eyed the ten feet or so of steep slope back up to the trail. He leaned his weight on his walking stick to get up, feeling a lot older than usual. Nope, no injuries beyond a deep bruise in his left thigh, a minor scrape on his left wrist and a blow to his manly pride. He clambered back up to where his slide had started and continued on his way.

The clearing came into view. This would be a good time to stop in the meadow, he decided. "The sweat bees won't be out in force until the sun heats up," he remarked, realizing that he was talking to himself again. He stopped and sat on a downed lightning-split tree trunk to chew a granola bar and a little trail mix, washing it all down with a few more sips of water. "What time is it, anyway? About ten o'clock," he said, answering himself. He then turned sheepishly to see if anybody else was approaching. He didn't want to get the reputation of a man who talked to nobody at all. But he *was* talking to himself a lot lately. Unable to wait any longer, he arose, wiped his brow and headed toward the edge of the clearing – and toward, again – what?

Joe pushed onward, knowing that the walk to the cave would take at most ten minutes unless he slowed down. He slowed down. It wasn't really that he was all that tired. Suddenly he didn't look forward to the possible rendezvous quite as much, now that the distance separating him from it could be measured in feet instead of miles. Relentlessly the interval narrowed until he knew that the outcropping awaited him just around that next bend.

He stopped and took another sip of water, asking himself again: "Do I really want to do this?" He wondered what harm there would be in his just taking a different route back to his car. It suddenly became a very appealing prospect. For a coward. No, he had to see for himself. He had to confront and overcome the growing apprehension that welled up within his soul. Was this his personal demon? Would it become his personal hell? If so, he had to face up to it. The place was here and the time was most certainly now.

Joe squared his shoulders and pressed on. Around the bend, the outcropping came into view. As he approached it, he realized that his inner turmoil had subsided and finally he looked forward to confronting his anxieties. He stopped outside the cave. After a minute or two, he asked out loud: “Is anybody in there?” There was no answer. “Is anybody there?” Still, no answer. He walked to the cave entrance and peeked inside. After his vision adjusted to the dimness, he inspected the small confines of the cavity in the earth. His pocket flashlight further revealed nothing but an empty, shallow cave.

Relieved but also disappointed, Joe bent down and duck-walked inside. Yes, he was alone, with no sign or feel of a spiritual presence. He sat on his piece of stone to consider things. It had been so real, he thought – so damn real. How could his mind have tricked him so? He had so many dreams about this one hole in the earth and one fictitious man. Did they have a purpose? Could there even *be* a purpose to this?

The thought that had been lurking in the recesses of his mind suddenly thrust itself to the forefront, confronting him with its unwelcome possibility. Could it be that he was actually slipping over the edge of reality and might soon need professional help? He shoved that thought back into its hiding place, to be dealt with later or, he hoped, never.

So, he pondered. This didn’t pan out. He still liked this little place and would visit it when in the area, but now he could continue to hike in other places. The field trip with Jessie and her students would be in an entirely new place, after all. Maybe Jessie would like to try hiking with him sometime. That thought was much more welcome to dwell on than his possible burgeoning madness. Bone-weary, he leaned back against the wall of the cave and soon dozed off.

CHAPTER FOURTEEN

After an undisturbed nap Joe woke and checked his glow-in-the-dark watch face. He had slept for nearly an hour. Thankfully he didn't dream, and definitely not about a miner named Nick. Now he could get serious about his remodeling and... And his mind returned to spending time with Jessie, too. What a nice thought. Jessie. How he liked that name. "I hope she isn't attached." He said aloud. Stretching, Joe looked around. He really did like this cave.

Then, suddenly a figure caught his eye. Nick sat casually with an amused look on his face. Joe looked at him with amazement. "Nick! Is that you? I mean, are you Nick?"

"I'm not John L. Lewis," Nick replied. "And do you always talk to yourself like that?"

"More often than usual lately," Joe retorted, "and I think I can blame it on you." It seemed remarkable to Joe that he could talk so casually with this stranger, this apparent ghost.

"I don't understand it, Nick. I don't exactly hear you but I can understand what you say just fine. Like in my dreams. How *did* you get into my dreams?"

Nick considered the question for a moment. "A while ago I was traveling around to the places where I usually go; mainly some of the old coal mines. When I returned to my cave I felt a strange sensation, like my spirit had been warmed a little. Actually it felt pretty nice. I think I might have touched you, or passed through you. Maybe something happened then. All I know is that you were here, in my space. But you didn't see me."

Joe remembered vividly the inexplicable, sudden blast of terrifying coldness, and the visions that had flooded through him on his first visit. It might have been Nick. "Are you saying that because we might have touched, that could have caused us to be linked somehow? How do I know that feeling of coldness *was* you?"

Nick said: "I can only think of one way to prove it. Touch my hand."

"Touch your hand?" Joe asked dubiously. "I don't think I can do that. No. No, I can't." Without warning, Nick reached out and touched Joe with his forefinger. The finger penetrated Joe's skin.

"Hey!" exclaimed Joe. It had cut like an icy dagger sliding through his skin, but with no actual pain. In fact, other than the unexpected, intense coldness, Joe felt no unpleasant sensation at all. He pulled his hand away and began rubbing it to restore the warmth where Nick had touched him. Joe thought ruefully about what had just happened. "Well, we won't be arm-wrestling any day soon. By the way, my name's Joe. Joe Bailey."

They both sat there, each lost in his own thoughts: the miner who had had no human contact on a personal level for over eighty years and the real estate agent who had discovered a very unusual property indeed.

After a while Nick posed a question: "I still wonder why you can see me. Others have stopped in here and none of them ever saw me. Only you. Do you suppose that's also because I passed through you that one time?" They both fell silent again. Clearly, they were now connected by something, some kind of bond. Was it just a random event or could there be a purpose to it?

Feeling a bit strange and a little ill at ease with each other, they continued to sit in silence. After a while Joe made up his mind to ask the one question that he most wanted to have answered. "Nick, what happened? How did you die? I mean, how did you happen to be here? I mean..." His voice trailed off.

"That's kind of a personal question, isn't it, Joe? Do you often ask men how they died?" Nick laughed. "But considering the circumstances it's a fair question, too." He finally decided how best to answer. "Back in 1922, times were very tough. The mines were on strike. Over the line in West Virginia, some miners who wanted to join the Mine Workers were thrown off company property at the Clifton Mine. That's just on the other end of the railroad tunnel by the state line. It happened suddenly, and they showed no mercy for their women or kids, either. The coal and iron police tossed furniture, clothing, everything they had onto the side of the road. With no place else to go, they set up a little tent camp nearby. Meanwhile, the owners brought in a couple boxcars of replacements from down south. We called them scabs, because they took food from our mouths.

The local miners asked for our help, so a bunch of miners from around Avella decided to go to Cliftonville and shut the mine down. I walked with that bunch. Anyway, our try at shutting the mine down turned into a fight. During the battle I was shot and hurt bad. My friend Angelo and some other men helped me back toward home. I don't remember what happened then very well. The next thing I knew I woke up in here. I don't know how much time went by before I woke up, or how long it's been since. Know something, Joe? I don't know what's going on out there. I have no idea. Would you tell me about it sometime?"

"That's a pretty big order – a lot has changed. But sure, Nick. I'll tell you what I can." Noticing the dimming light outside, Joe realized that dusk had begun to fall. He had been sitting with Nick longer than he thought. Stretching his limbs, he remarked: "I better be getting on home. But I'll be back. You can depend on it."

"Thanks, Joe."

He eased his way out of the cave entrance. After a final look back, he started down the trail toward his car, and toward home. A sudden realization hit him. He had begun to think of old Albert's place as home. He smiled to himself. "I guess a man can have two homes," he remarked. "My old schoolhouse in Colliers and this one in Avella. They both sure feel like it."

CHAPTER FIFTEEN

Joe's eyes sprang open, but he saw nothing but near-total darkness. Where was he? Back in the cave? In his grave? No. Not in his grave, he realized immediately. Nor was it the cave, he concluded, as reality finally began to set in. He lay disoriented in the darkness of a shade-drawn bedroom, cloaked in the isolation of a late, moonless night. His confusion receding, he reached over, touching the bedside lamp. Light immediately flooded his bedroom. A quick look outside verified that the first rays of dawn would tarry for at least another hour. It had been another night of dreams, but not as intense as some others. But he had slept nearly five hours this time. Fatigue from remodeling the house had helped him to get a few hours sleep. But Joe realized, with a sickening certainty, that more sleepless nights were undoubtedly ahead. Unless he could soon find a way to bring peace to Nick, that is. Only then could he also know his own peace.

Joe swung his legs over the bedside, squirming his feet into his slippers. "What's my purpose in all this?" he asked the empty room. "Nick – are you why I'm here, now?" Nick provided no answer, but he didn't really expect one. Scratching his side, he stood up and headed for the bathroom. While brushing his teeth, Joe considered the man in the mirror. He had never seen him so haggard looking, except possibly the first time Kathy left him… and then the second. Tall, with slightly graying black hair, he still looked fit; actually more fit than in a long time. He liked most of what he saw. Except, of course, for the unwelcome gauntness that entrenched itself over his facial features.

After starting the coffee, he pulled down his journal and removed the note pad from his shirt pocket. He began to write in the journal, slowly at first, referring often to his scribbled notes. But soon the words began to spill faster into his consciousness than he could put them on paper:

I met Nick. How abrupt that statement seems, but I can write with some satisfaction that I finally met Nick. That is his name – or was his name. No, it is his name. He seems like a nice enough fellow, somebody I might have shared a beer with. Except that he has an underlying anger to his personality. He didn't really turn the bitterness on me, but I could sense its presence. I will have to ask him more about that sometime. Is it a part of his nature, or a product of his decades-long solitary confinement – neither a part of this life or the next?

Nick had a hard life and a harder death, in a mine riot that occurred in 1922. I have to find out about what happened. I wonder if Andy knows anything about it. Does anybody else? It's been over eighty years now. Few people who were old enough to remember anything about it would still be alive and they would have been little children then.

And finally, do I have a purpose here? What could it be? I am Nick's only link with the living, and I feel uncomfortable that he seems to be stuck wherever he is. I didn't think that spirits could remain trapped in the ground, but he surely is. Is he unique in that way? Is there a reason that he remains, while others may have moved on? Are there more like him out there? One per cave? Is he like a spirit trapped for decades – or for eternity – in a haunted house?

If I have a responsibility here, those dreams imply that I couldn't duck that responsibility if I wanted to. I don't see how I could just walk away. It's a prison for Nick down there, and I'm his only visitor. He has certainly seen others, but if they don't see him, they hardly count as visitors – more like someone walking down a cellblock past rows of cells, ignoring every prisoner. Does he have buddies there, too? I wonder.

Closing the book, he replaced it on its shelf.

Joe walked through the still, early morning to the kitchen for his coffee, his mind still turning over his apparent duty to Nick. The thought nearly overwhelmed him, especially with his physical and emotional reserves at an all-time low. Shuddering, he poured a cup, noticing with no small measure of satisfaction that his coffee was now "just past prime."

Joe waved at his neighbor as he walked to his car with his daypack. Andy shouted from his garden: "Gonna see Nick, Joe?"

"I just might, Andy. In fact I do believe I will." The sun was on the rise now, well over the eastern hilltops. This would be a nice day to tramp through the woods, with a cold front just coming in and the possibility of light showers during mid-afternoon. With renewed purpose, Joe climbed behind the wheel and drove down toward Meadowcroft. "Yes," he said aloud, resolve growing within him, "I think I do have a purpose. I just need to figure out how I can help him – if I can help him. I must be able to. Otherwise, why am I here?" He stopped at his by now well-worn parking space across from the trailhead. Slipping out of his loafers, he laced up his hiking shoes.

He started up the trail. Even in his bone-weary tiredness he stepped out with a fast gait, thinking of his new and quite unusual acquaintance. He arrived at the cave before nine o'clock, having stopped only once for a sip of water. Despite the cool weather, his shirt was sweat-soaked. Joe shouted out: "Anybody home?"

"What took you so long?" The response sounded within his head.

"Oh, come on, Nick!" Joe retorted: "Your concept of the passage of time is pretty limited!"

"Well, it seemed like the thing to say," the spirit responded. "So, what's taking you so long now? Come on in!" Joe lowered his head, took a minute for his eyes to adjust, and crawled inside. "Good to see you again," Nick continued. "So what's happening out there?"

"I've been wondering about that. You're seriously telling me that you don't keep track of what's going on in the world?"

"Nope. I don't, because I can't. That world is closed to us, or at least to me. I can see that all the old mines around here are closed, though. Mining is honest work. Don't they need coal anymore?"

Joe mulled over about Nick's question. "Yes, they still mine coal, but not around Avella. I'll make you a deal, Nick. I'll tell you about today if you tell me about your time first." With that, they sat down to talk. "So, what was it like in your day?

Nick paused and began his story. "It wasn't easy for us. But nobody said it would be. It was the spring of 1921. I was born in a little village in eastern Slovakia. We did some mining there. But then stories started coming in about America. Some people said that America had so much money that the city streets were paved with gold. Nobody believed that, of course. But we also heard that a miner could make a decent wage and his children could grow up to be anything else they wanted, like a policeman or a shopkeeper or even the mayor. There wasn't much to keep me in my village, because my mother died in childbirth and my father was killed in the mine. So I saved my money, bought a ticket and set off for America.

"We walked up a long ramp onto a big steamship. While we were boarding, we in fourth class were the only ones we saw. We knew there were rich people traveling, too. I heard all about them, but we never saw them. We carried all our stuff below to the big area where we were going to sleep. We hadn't even left the dock before the place began to smell. You could smell salami and sausage and unwashed bodies. Some passengers had walked or ridden oxcarts for many days just to get to the ship.

"It didn't take long before the place began to stink. Men lit up cigars, too, but at least it didn't bother the women and families because single men were separated from them. I didn't act very fast, so I got a top bunk that I had to throw my bag of clothes up on and then climb to reach. But it turned out to be a blessing when seasickness hit later – if you know what I mean." Joe thought he understood. How many people vomit upward?

"Anyway," Nick continued. "The trip wasn't as bad as I heard it could be. The ship went through one storm but it wasn't a big one, only three or four hours. I stood the confinement okay because the mine I worked in made living quarters seem big. The food was filling, but my brother could have cooked it better than they did. We got mainly vegetable soup with some kind of meat in it and hard bread. We got water with our meals, too. With my smoked sausage from home I got along okay.

"Finally, we felt the ship slowing down and could see buildings off in the distance. We crowded the rail and saw a big statue on an island outside New York City. We all gawked like schoolchildren as we passed it and saw the wonderful city off in the distance. They loaded us onto smaller boats or barges that took us to an island with big buildings. They lined us up like cattle, with doctors poking us and officials stamping our papers. I saw some people herded into another room. I think they had a lung disease or an eye disease.

"A man from a coal company was there who spoke my

language. He told the authorities that he would give me and some other men from Italy and Slovakia a job in the mines, so they let us pass.

"We took a boat to New York. But we didn't find any gold in the streets. I didn't really expect to see any because people would always be digging it up, but I was hoping for at least shiny streets. Instead, the streets were real dirty. Well, we didn't stay in the city at all that day. They took us to the train station, bought us all tickets and put us on a train for here."

Nick paused. "Do you want to hear something?" He asked, realizing as he said it that Joe couldn't 'hear' a word he said. Even if Joe could hear him, he probably wouldn't have understood very much because of Nick's badly broken English. Joe just understood Nick's tale without hearing anything at all.

"I bought my own ticket to America, but some others had their way paid by the coal companies. The company didn't give out gifts, so they had to pay the company back, just as we had to repay the company for the train trip. That was a large hole for men to start out in. Also, some of the others had wives and children back home. They had to try and save up the money to bring their families over. Worst of all, some of the married men were killed in the mines, so they never saw their families again."

Nick fell silent while both men thought about what he had related. Joe realized that while the concepts were understandable, he could never have imagined the reality of life in those days. Nick went on. "Well we finally got to this area and the men were dropped off at different towns where the boss told them they would be working. Four other men and I got off at Avella. No, the streets weren't paved with gold here, either. Most had no paving at all. They were mostly dirt, and some were red-dog or cinders. Do you know what red-dog is?" Nick answered before Joe could shake his head no. "It's made when bad coal is heaped high and the pile starts burning inside. After a long while the only thing left is something like soft red stones. They spread it on the roads. Anyway, some of the roads were red-dog.

"We were taken to a boarding house, where we shared rooms and got to eat every night. We also got a lunch packed each morning. They took the money from our pay. I met another Slavic miner who had worked here for two years. He said they hired us because they didn't want English-speakers. Miners who spoke the same language as each other could cause trouble, like trying to organize a union. They liked it that most men knew very little English and spoke so many different languages like Italian, Slavic, Polish, and Russian. We would be less trouble to them that way. Keeping us apart kept us weak, or so the companies thought. But they sure liked our strong bodies!

"So I went to work in the mine and, later, I got shot. Maybe I'll tell you more about that sometime." He looked at Joe expectantly.

Joe realized it was now his turn. As he began to collect his thoughts, he pulled out his little-used pipe and filled it with tobacco. Seeing the wistful expression on Nick's face he commented, "The funny thing now, Nick, is that a man can't smoke in very many places. They have 'no-smoking policies' – and plenty of no-smoking laws – mainly for eating places and where people gather to watch a show. In hotels you can't smoke in most rooms, either. There are fewer and fewer places where a man can have a smoke these days, even sweet-smelling pipe tobacco. You don't have a no-smoking policy in here, do you?" He asked with a laugh.

"Nope, smoke doesn't bother me none," Nick responded with a smile, but also with a hint of seriousness. "I really did like a stogie after a hard day in the mine. And sometimes a bowl of tobacco. Go ahead and light it up. Maybe I can pretend to enjoy the smoke. I know that I'll enjoy the feeling you get when you're smoking. I feel like I'm inside your feelings sometimes as it is."

"I know you get into my dreams. Or at least it seems like you do." He paused. "Is that really you, or am I just imagining that you're there?"

"It's both. I was in your dreams before you knew I existed, because I found myself there. But most of the time now it's just you dreaming – most of the time," Nick said a bit apologetically.

Joe wondered where to start. "Coal mining has changed a lot, Nick. Would you like me to tell you how?" Nick seemed surprised, but nodded for Joe to go on. "These days there's very little pick-and-shovel work. You probably won't believe this, but they have huge machines that grind their way through a coal seam, with the coal spilling onto a big conveyor. The miners mainly tend the machines these days, or take care of the coal after it comes off the seam.

"You men dug coal by the room-and-pillar, right? More

specifically, you opened up a new room in the coal seam, shored it up when you had to, and left coal pillars in place to help hold up the roof. You would have to mine like that to have a chance at survival, right?" Nick nodded again, with a hint of uneasiness betrayed in his expression.

"Anyway I don't know how they do it, but this huge machine just grinds its way through the seam, tearing out coal as wide as dozens of your rooms put together." Nick's jaw dropped. Joe wondered briefly how he did that. Just like he's actually alive, Joe thought. "Somehow the machine and its operators don't get crushed, doing what they call 'long wall mining'. I think they use temporary roof supports as they keep moving forward.

"Most people don't like this system, even though it's efficient. Because there's no shoring or pillars left, the ground up above sinks right away, maybe three or four feet. Houses collapse sometimes, roads can cave in, creeks and ponds dry up, wells and springs go dry, and who knows what else happens? Not me."

Clearly having difficulty coping with Joe's description, an incredulous Nick burst out, "do you mean men don't walk into the mine in shifts and dig coal anymore?'

"Not in most mines around here anyway. I'm telling you the truth, though I don't know much more than what I read in the newspapers. My job is selling houses and land for people, so I can see the mine subsidence first-hand sometimes. When long-wall mining is coming, houses and land aren't worth as much, and after it goes by people have to pick up the pieces. Don't get me wrong. The coal companies have some responsibility. They try to stabilize a house before mining under it, and they have to pay for damages or buy the house if it can't be fixed. But really, who wants to live in or buy a fixed-up house?

"The companies have to replace the lost water, too. Some families have to work from a big water container – called a water buffalo – in their back yard. Sometimes the wells and springs never come back and the creeks and ponds remain dry."

Nick looked pensive. "Things sure have changed a lot. Do men still get killed in the mines? And how are they paid?"

"Men still get killed, but not as often. Mainly in the mines where they still do room-and-pillar work. But it isn't very often anymore. And I understand they get an hourly pay, and they make some pretty good money. But there aren't very many jobs."

"Well, at least there's that," Nick said after a moment's pause. "At least there's that."

Joe glanced at his watch. "It's getting pretty late. I better get going. But I'll be back to fill you in on some more things happening in the world, okay? Nick nodded vigorously.

"Just one more thing, Joe?" "I know this will sound silly, but if they still have stogies, would you bring one in here and smoke it for me? If you enjoy it, I think I'll enjoy it, too. And who knows?" he laughed. "Maybe I can even catch a whiff of it now and then."

"I'll be happy to. What do you like?"

"Marsh Wheeling made some nice stogies, and there were some little Italian cigars named Parodi and De Nobili that I liked now and then. They looked something like pieces of tarred rope, but I liked the flavor. I also liked a tobacco called Cutty Pipe. Just bring anything in, okay?"

Joe jotted the strange-sounding names down in his little notepad. "Will do." Slipping the pencil stub and pad back into his breast pocket, he gave a final wave and headed to the cave entrance. He blinked his eyes into adjustment with the outside light, scrambled outside and then went on his way.

"See you," he heard – or felt – from behind him. He looked back at the outcropping but saw only the same gaping hole in the hill.

CHAPTER SIXTEEN

"Funny thing," Joe pondered, finally accepting the nagging fact that he hadn't done a lick of real estate work since coming to Avella. He now spend most of his time hiking, talking with Nick and Andy, talking to himself, working on the house and walking to Avella. Why did he walk down there so often? His question was partly rhetorical, because deep down, he knew the overriding reason for so many of his trips. He hoped to see Jessie again. There was just something about her, a simple kind of openness, not to mention her obvious nice looks... Joe waved off an offered ride, smiling his gratitude. "I just feel like walking, but thanks a lot!"

On the way, he waved at some of his newfound neighbors. Many sat on their front porches while a few busily worked in their flowers or landscaping shrubs. "Front porches." Joe turned the words over under his breath. Just like in Pittsburgh, this place has lots of front porches. Just when had back patios and decks made porches obsolete? There's something nice and homey about a front porch, he thought; actually a row of them up and down the street. People would sit out just to talk, to catch a cool breeze, and to keep an eye on their kids playing. Is that why crime is up so much now? No front porches? Backyard patios and decks seemed to symbolize a retreat – from the society of the street into more cocooned lives. And society is probably the worse off for it.

Joe remembered his most recent sales of more expensive homes; in the $200,000-$400,000 range. At the most, they had a covered front stoop, not a porch; just enough room for an arriving visitor to barely stand out of the rain. They spent more on their master bathtub than on their front stoop, and far more on their back deck.

Walking is another way of being social, Joe realized as he strode along. You see people and they see you. You make eye contact. In a car you rarely get to make real eye contact before the fleeting opportunity for recognition dissolves. In fact, you usually have no idea who's in the other car as they zip by, unless you recognize the car. Funny, you can know a person's car more than you know them. He considered that for a moment, happy that he could reflect all he wanted as he walked. While Joe's mind wandered, it did so at a safe walking rate of four miles per hour. It could be dangerous to get too involved in problem-solving while driving on the highway, or even worse on a stop-and-go street. Not to mention the escalating use of cell phones in cars. How many times had his own attention been distracted from the road while using his cell phone and trying to scribble down a hasty note?

Joe contemplated finally unpacking his cell phone. *But why?* After all, Sam and the other agents seemed to be handling his open business well while he was on sabbatical. Sam hadn't bothered him on his house phone yet, because his notes and files were well organized. In Pittsburgh, Joe never had his cell phone beyond arm's reach, and it was his 24-7 companion. What became of the cell phone withdrawal others talked of? He was enjoying the break, but just in case, he decided, he would carry it for a while. Who knows? He could fall and be injured or be bitten by a copperhead snake on one of his hikes. A copperhead strike, while usually not fatal, is very life threatening and he'd much rather have help on the way.

Joe waved at Mrs. Johnson over in her garden. She must be eighty years old, but still stooped over pulling weeds or watering the plants for at least an hour each day. He hoped he could be that active at her age. "Hey, Mrs. J! I see your grandkids are helping you! Are you well today?"

"Yes, young man. Thank you. When they come over they are quite a help." Her young grandson looked up from the foliage and waved, while her teenage granddaughter, reading a fashion magazine on the front porch steps, glanced up and smiled a greeting. Joe strode on, nearing downtown Avella.

Here I am, walking, he thought. Me, walking everywhere. Heck, nobody walks anywhere anymore, except to get exercise. They even drive to a gym and then try to find the closest parking space before climbing on a treadmill. Heck. As a cop in Arizona I never walked, but I ran for exercise. And then after moving to Pittsburgh, and even changing my line of work, I did the same. Talk about a creature of habit.

He waved at Charlie the mechanic, and at Charlie's young

daughter working on her car's brakes. A teacher, maintaining her own car! "My Caddy needs inspected, Charlie," he called out. "Is Saturday morning okay?"

"Bring it down anytime," Charlie responded. "I'll work it in."

Nearing the convenience store, his spirit darkened as he saw that Jessie's Camaro wasn't parked at the pumps. Sighing audibly, he walked in. Jessie wasn't there but Les was, waiting with a grin on his face. "Hey, Joe, let me buy you a cold Coke." Les selected a can and paid the cashier. They walked outside to sit on the curb.

"I thought we should talk about Jessie," Les began, none too subtly. "She's a damn nice girl. I've known her for several years now, since we served on a school committee together. I like you, and frankly we've become friends. Just be careful with her, okay?" Joe gave Les a questioning look. "She saw me in here a couple days ago and asked about you. I gave her the low-down on you, but only the good stuff!" Les laughed. Joe chuckled, but wondered where this was all going.

"Jessie is a great gal and a better human being. A couple years ago she was hurt badly in a relationship. He was a young doctor from Washington. They were in love, or at least she was. After a while, she learned that he was seeing somebody else. When she asked him about it he dumped her. But he dumped her with no compassion at all. I know how much it hurt her. It took her a while to get past the pain. She really did love the guy. And she hasn't dated seriously since."

"I understand, Les," Joe assured him after studying the label on his Coke can for a moment. "I never told you about this; in fact very few people around Pittsburgh even know about it. In the Phoenix suburb where I worked as a cop, I was married to a woman named Helen. We loved each other, but she was exceptionally beautiful and very obsessed with preserving her looks. I think that's probably why we never had a child. She avoided getting pregnant just to protect her body. Anyway I was gone on duty a lot, and I guess plenty of men desired her. So, what happened next was inevitable I suppose.

"I came home early one night, and saw my partner's car parked a couple blocks away. I entered the house quietly – at the time I didn't even know why – and turned on the bedroom light. There they were, in my bed. My own damn bed! I'm surprised I didn't pull out my piece and blast the two of them, or at least him. I know at that moment I wanted to. But instead I just walked away. I walked away from them and I walked away from Arizona and I walked away from police work. Funny thing, though; I still like being around cops. Most of my buddies are cops. We just have a kind of bond.

"And then, in Pittsburgh, I had another relationship that went sour, but that's a story for some other time. Anyway, you can see that I know what it is to be vulnerable, too." Shocked, Joe realized how much had spilled from his own private reserves of pain. Why would he do that, even talking to a friend?

Les nodded sympathetically. "Joe, you're a good guy. I hope you and Jessie each find the love you deserve. Les stared into his sports drink, as though he had just realized that an empty bottle filled his hand. Struggling to his feet, he stretched out his cramped legs and said: "I better get on home. By the way, you don't stop by the firehouse often enough, Joe. The guys really like and respcct you. You should stop down more often."

"I'll do that. You know, I still can't resist being around uniforms. And there's nothing quite like polishing a big fire truck to work out your upper body. The last time I helped wash the trucks was really satisfying!"

"Yeah, we liked the extra help, too," Les grinned, "You aren't all that bad for unskilled labor, and your rates are reasonable. By the way," he offered as he turned to walk away. "Have you noticed who just turned into the lot?"

CHAPTER SEVENTEEN

The sleek, red Camaro pulled up to the gas pumps and eased to a stop. A pair of long, slender legs slid through the car's doorway. Jessie smiled as she saw Joe approaching her.

"We provide full service at no extra cost here, ma'am," he deadpanned. Would you like your tires and oil checked along with your gas purchase? I'm also a whiz at washing a windshield."

"Just fill 'er up," Jessie retorted, laughing. "And don't be too slow about it, or the tip could be drastically affected!" He started filling the tank with regular gas and lifted the hood.

"Oh, this is too bad," Joe said after a moment's inspection. Startled, Jessie ducked her head under the hood, too. He liked her proximity. Even with a full foot of airspace separating them, he could feel the warmth emanating from her body and invading his own, or at least he imagined that he could. He liked the feeling.

"What's wrong?" Jessie demanded.

"I'm afraid your framatizing spark converter appears to be loose. It's a good thing I saw it in time. It so happens that I'm the east coast expert on framatizing spark converters." A shy smile crept slowly over Jessie's face.

"A framatizing spark converter, you say? Are they expensive to repair? I'd hate to neglect it until it failed on a backcountry road. Then I'd have to call somebody to rescue me."

Joe pretended to push the coil wire tighter into the distributor cap and gave a gentle push on the distributor cap itself. "It should be okay now, ma'am. I think you're good to go for another 20,000 miles or so." After a quick check of the engine's fluids, Joe closed the hood with a satisfying click of the latch.

The gasoline had already stopped flowing, so he shut off the pump and twisted the gas cap securely. Joe then made a show of carefully washing all the windows, lingering over the driver's side as he pretended to look for the missing driver within. Jessie laughed appreciatively.

"How about a soft drink, Jessie? And have you heard yet if my background check was approved?" They walked inside so that she could pay for the gas while he picked out two Cokes.

"Your background check came back just fine. If you're ready, we can plan the field trip. It should be quite an outing," she said with enthusiasm as they walked back outside. "We already have permission slips for forty of my students, and I have seven parent volunteers who agreed to help. Why don't you come by the school Monday morning and meet some of the students? Is ten o'clock okay?" Jessie asked as she slipped gracefully behind the wheel. Gallantly and with an exaggerated, sweeping gesture, Joe closed the door for her.

"You bet it is. See you then!" He watched as she waved gaily and drove away. Still no ring! He thought about that. She still displayed no ring.

***

On Monday Joe didn't bother to hike, knowing that Nick would be waiting for him whatever day he showed up, because he doubted that Nick had any real concept of the passage of time. A day could seem like a year – and a year as a day. Or more likely, any time interval would feel the same as no interval at all to Nick. Not to mention the miner seemed to know where he could find Joe whenever he wanted. It was only necessary that Joe be asleep.

Joe walked over to see Andy, working in his garden. "The pole beans are coming along nicely. They already climbed two feet up the little trellises."

"Yep, they're doing just fine. That's my magic touch! Where are you off to today, Joe?"

"The school. I met a teacher and told her I like to hike, so she asked me to help out on a biology field trip. I have to go and meet the class this morning. It should be fun. I have some things to show the kids that they probably don't know, but I'm sure they'll try to teach me a thing or two, too."

"A teacher you say? Something tells me she isn't a 55-year-old spinster." Andy paused. "Did you tell her *everything* about your hikes, Joe?" A more serious look hid just beneath Andy's smile.

"No, I haven't mentioned even the hint of that to anybody but you. Speaking of which, we have some catching up to do. I learned from Nick what it was like to come from the old country to America and go off to a coal mining town in some god-forsaken place and then start trying to make a living. Did you know that some family men got killed before they could even begin to save up the money to bring their wives and kids over? They never saw their families again."

"I know. I knew some of those men, but a few years after Nick did." Andy's face took on a very serious look. "Could you do me a favor? Ask him if he knew my dad, okay? His name was Andy Polack, too. He would have been older. About 35 years old then."

"I'll be sure to do that, Andy. You can count on it. Oh by the way," Joe remembered. Do you know where I can buy some… let me see…" He pulled out his notepad. "Parodi's? De Nobili's? Cutty Pipe? Marsh Wheeling stogies?

Andy scratched his head. "He doesn't plan to smoke, does he?" Andy joked. "I suppose some of those brands are still around. I know Marsh Wheelings are. But one thing; the little Italian cigars could be rough on a man who never tried one before. I recommend you stick with the stogies. They ain't too bad."

"Sounds like tried-and-true advice. Thanks, Andy. But I better get going. Don't want to keep the kids waiting!" Or their teacher, he secretly thought.

***

As he drove up Route 50 to the school campus, his mind flitted all over the constellation: the field trip, Nick, Andy, the beautiful weather, the foliage now in all its green finery, and even old Albert's house and selling real estate. But only one person was securely rooted in his mind and made every scene nicer.

He pulled into the parking area between the two buildings and parked in a visitors spot for the second time. He sat back and smiled at the day spreading before him.

Joe went to the principal's office where he was to pick up a visitor badge. The secretary directed him to Miss Randall's classroom. He paused outside her door, knocked, and waited expectantly. "Come in" he heard a recognizable feminine voice say. "Come in!" a chorus of pre-teen voices repeated, accompanied by a wave of muffled laughter. He tentatively opened the door and entered, not knowing quite what to expect. Jessie's smile warmly greeted him, along with the furtive giggles of twenty boys and girls.

Mr. Bailey, this is one of the classes that will be going on the field trip. Class, this is Mr. Bailey. He loves to hike and he knows lots of things about the outdoors. And Mr. Bailey was once a policeman."

"Oooooohhhhh!" The boys who had been withholding their admiration were immediately impressed. Most of the girls had seemed sold on him the moment he entered the room. "I must have cleaned up pretty well today," Joe thought.

"Does anybody have any questions about the field trip for Mr. Bailey?" asked Jessie.

A small girl tentatively raised her hand. "Will there be any snakes, Mr. Bailey?"

"That's a very good question. We may see some, but I doubt it. Snakes are afraid of us, and when they know we are approaching they usually get out of our way," Joe responded. "Who else has a question?"

Another little girl's hand went up. "Mr. Bailey, how do you keep from getting lost in the woods? Getting lost scares me."

"That's also a very good question. An important thing is to know where you are going and pay attention to where you have been, including landmarks like a big, dead tree or a boulder. The most important thing is to stay on the path, and to have a map and a compass with you. Do you know what a compass is and how it works?" Joe held up the compass he had brought with him.

A skinny tow-headed boy with a band-aid on his chin piped up. "We learned all about maps and compasses in Boy Scout orienteering. The compass shows us where magnetic north is, and the map helps us to know the way. It has north marked on it, too. I'm the assistant patrol leader in the black panther patrol," he concluded proudly.

"Very good," Joe responded. "Maybe we can break up into patrols, with a Boy or Girl Scout as patrol leader and a parent helping each patrol. If that's okay with our senior troop leader, that is." He indicated toward Miss Randall. The children broke into laughter.

"That sounds like a very good idea, Mr. Bailey," Jessie said. "Are there any more questions?"

"Did you ever shoot anybody when you were a cop?" a freckle-covered boy asked mischievously.

"Well only once, but he tried to shoot me first," answered Joe truthfully. "Are there any more questions?

A pudgy boy with an impish grin raised his hand. "Are you and Miss Randall gonna get married?" The room exploded into laughter.

"I don't think we will have any more questions!" said a visibly blushing Jessie. "Thank you for coming, Mr. Bailey. We will see you at nine o'clock on Thursday." Joe excused himself and left the room. He leaned against the wall in the hallway and enjoyed a hearty laugh. But the mental picture the question left him with also made him tingle.

CHAPTER EIGHTEEN

Two nights later Joe again slept fitfully. Vivid dreams repeatedly invaded his rare moments of slumber. They all seemed to take place in that same dark hole in the ground. Nick was there each time, his body and facial details clearly visible. In the dreams his spirit seemed to have more substance. In spite of Joe's lantern there was a surprising absence of illumination around them. It seemed that all the light in the dream emanated from their very essences. Nick challenged Joe to arm-wrestle with a flat stone as the field of friendly battle. Their hands joined and the light spread along both arms until the only light in the cave emanated from them. Nick easily won every time, except for once when it was painfully apparent that Nick had been taking it easy on him. Joe took no pleasure in pinning Nick's hand to the stone's hard surface that one time. He could not relish such a hollow victory.

Even in his dream state, Nick had that same friendly look, the very image of a fellow conspirator or perhaps a boyhood chum out behind the shed sneaking a cigarette from a pack stolen from Joe's old man. Joe enjoyed the thought of having Nick for a friend, despite the fact that in life he would be more than a dozen years older than Nick's twenty-two, and in death he would be Nick's junior by more than seventy.

Joe awoke abruptly, as usual, with the despairing thought that he would sleep no more this night. After several fruitless attempts at returning to slumber, he finally got up. It was only 4:15 am. He went to the kitchen, poured a glass of orange juice, and began to write in his journal.

Yesterday, I again met Nick in his small cave. While my visits are interfering with the work on Albert's house, I just don't care anymore. I'm pleased to write that he and I are becoming friends. I really look forward to my hikes these days. No matter where I may intend to go, I find my way to 'Nick's Place' as he and I have come to call it. He finds it funny that it might even be his tomb as well as our place of meeting. It's not all that funny to me, but some people say I just don't get a joke.

As I think of my friend, I wonder how hard life must have been for him and how terrifying his death. I wonder at the tales he tells me of mining coal in his day. They only had a large hand auger, some black powder to blast the coal loose, and a pick and shovel to tear that black gold from the bowels of the earth. They had only one objective in mind: to make a living. They never shrank from their labor, because they knew that they had to work, no matter how hard on their body and how demanding on their spirit. They just had no other choice. They were like indentured servants in a strange land who had to work constantly to live.

Theirs was honest work but dangerous. But unlike mining precious metals, it provided no prospect of fortune for them or their families. At most they could look forward to saving a few dollars to buy a house of their own, or a few acres to farm. They prayed for their children to live better lives than theirs. But one painful fact never strayed far from their minds. The company held all the cards, and only the owners would ever get rich.

But I still have this unsettling feeling, and I will follow up on it if I dare. Nick tries mightily to protect me from whatever troubles him at his core and he seems to value me as a friend. But I have to try to find out the force within him that is so troubling. Is it anger over his virtual imprisonment? Fear? Misery? Bitterness? What does he want? I have to learn all I can about him now, because someday he will surely be gone; or I will.

Joe sighed and closed his book. There would be more entries the next day or the day after that. Joe couldn't hold his journal to a schedule. It was at best a book of inspiration, not routine.

When he finished his coffee, Joe decided to go for a quiet walk instead of a hike or run. Joe slipped on his jeans and sneakers and went out into the cool morning air. The light from Andy's kitchen spilled welcomingly through his curtains, so Joe decided to give him a little company. He headed over to the house where he knew, with a feeling of comfortable warmth, that he would always be welcome.

Andy had seen him coming and now stood in the open door with his usual mischievous expression plastered on his face. He also held forth a cup of coffee. “Wanna cuppa Joe, Joe?” he asked with a laugh. “I saw your lights on when I got up and I had a feeling you would make your way over here. Frankly, I was getting a little tired of waiting.” Joe chuckled and walked right in. “So, what’s on your mind?”

Joe sat down at the kitchen table. After a minute he seemed to arrive at a decision.

“Andy? Do you remember anything about the Cliftonville Mine Riot? It happened in 1922. I know you were a youngster then…”

“What’re you talking about? I’m just a youngster now,” Andy laughed. After a minute of rubbing his chin, he also sat down. He stared at the table with a faraway gaze and then looked up contemplatively. “I don’t often talk about that. But for you I can make an exception.

“Them were troublesome times, Joe,” he said seriously. “It seemed like the whole country was on strike, or at least the mines were. Not all of them, but most of them.” He paused and went on: “The miners around here were fighting to unionize then, and most families had very little food and less money. The Communists were beginning to have some success in organizing the miners, mainly because they were able to provide some food like coffee and bread for breakfast. For the kids at least. And sometimes they set up a soup kitchen. People didn’t care about Communism, but they did care about getting some food in their bellies. The food made a difference, Joe. But on the other hand, the Communists asked us to go to the farms and beg for spare food. They also took kids to beg on Pittsburgh streets for money. Most people had too much pride to let their kids do that, not to mention they never trusted them Bolsheviks.

“The United Mine Workers under John L. Lewis were also trying to unionize the miners and they were doing a better job of organizing. They didn’t preach no philosophy except union brothers banding together for a contract and better wages and working conditions. Meanwhile the companies were beginning to hurt, too. Less demand for the coal meant lower prices. The companies were cutting back on workdays and pay per ton. Anyway, most of the mines around here were voting UMWA, and the companies didn’t like it. For a while whenever the union organized a mine, the company would fire the lot of them and bring in replacement miners. My dad called them scabs so I did, too. Anyway, around Avella the mines weren't working and no coal was being dug.

"I was just a youngster back then, so when I wasn't in school I usually hung out with my good buddy, Albert. Not your great uncle Albert, mind you. Your uncle and I got to be friends in the mines. My boyhood chum Albert was an Italian kid. People started calling him Brink when he was little and it stuck. His family started a small pop bottling company here in Avella. He and his dad would deliver soda pop to the local bars and clubs. Sometimes I would ride with them and help with the deliveries.

"I mainly remember two things about the riot. They've been stuck in my brain for all this time. The day before, all the miners were fired up about the scabs and we watched them walk down the tracks. It looked like a big adventure, so I wanted to go too but my dad wouldn't let me. He made me stay home. But my dad walked with them." Joe listened as intently as he ever had, waiting for each sentence, each word, as though it were a drop of water for a thirsty man.

"There was a lot of anxiety around town. My mother and the other ladies visited each other, crying. It seemed like my mom washed the kitchen floor about ten times that night. She always washed the floor when she was worried, and that night she was beyond worry. She was distressed. Do you believe me, Joe?"

"I believe you, Andy."

"The next morning the town was even more on edge. We boys felt it, too. We didn't go fishing or to the ball field or nuthin'. We just hung around and waited like everybody else. I was glad they wouldn't let me go.

Andy got up and poured a cup of coffee, creating a little time to get himself together. Joe could see that talking about it cost his old friend dearly. "Brink and his dad and I went out delivering pop down to Browntown and Penowa. We started passing groups of men who looked all tired. Some of them looked to be hurt, too. They called up to his dad and asked us if they could ride under our tarp on the truck. Of course Brink's dad let them. They weren't just riding, Joe. Brink and I could tell that they were hiding. His dad gave them a ride back to town or wherever they were going, and then he went back again. He took three or more loads of men back to town that day. The sound I'll never forget is while those strong men were under that tarp hiding, I could hear some crying and others trying to shush them up. I knew that the bumpy ride aggravated some injuries. I didn't see no bullet wounds, but there might have been some. Mainly bad bruises and maybe broken bones. Every man was tired, discouraged and thirsty. Brink's dad gave them a bottle opener and said they could help themselves to the pop in the cases. Anyway, his dad helped a pretty good bunch of them get back to town.

"I told Brink's dad maybe I should go home. He drove me home and I went inside to sit with my mother and sisters. We waited and waited. But you know what?"

"No, tell me," Joe said, a darkening cloud beginning to loom over his soul. He couldn't fend off the ending he couldn't forestall.

"My father never came home, Joe. He never came home. I heard later that some men had to bury him on the way. They put him in a shallow ditch and then covered him with dirt and rocks. They told my mother about it and she thanked them for that kindness." Andy sat there, thoughtfully staring into his coffee cup, as though it held a secret that he could never figure out. "My father never came home. And I don't know where he is."

"I'm sorry, Andy, truly sorry," Joe said after a moment. He reached across and touched the old man's hand. Andy didn't draw it away. This tough little man who had seen so much in his long, hard life still felt the need to have somebody say: "I understand and I'm sorry." And Joe thought he truly did understand. Until he had met Nick he never could have really understood, of course, but today he thought he finally could. They sat together in silence at the worn kitchen table.

After a while Andy said, "nobody knows how many men didn't come home that day because they were from all the mining camps around here, not just the ones in Avella. Most of them were bachelors or still had families in the old country, so they weren't missed as much here as the family men like my father. And a few more just pulled up stakes and left; I guess they ran away to avoid the law. So that made it even harder to figger out who lived and who died.

"But it still wasn't right. They only wanted a decent wage but nobody was willing to give it to them. Even though they earned every penny of whatever wages they could get." Andy reflected for another minute or so.

"Funny thing. After a while, the United Mine Workers put up a monument to four or five miners who died at Cliftonville. Heck, I'm not even sure that was all of them whose bodies were found there, let alone the ones buried in the woods. And I don't know if any of them are even buried in that cemetery, anyway. I don't know where they can be found. My dad and so many other miners got no recognition or remembrance, even in death. Except for their widows and kids and a few buddies, they were just forgotten." Andy looked up sadly, suddenly looking very old.

They sat in silence at the old kitchen table a while longer, and then Andy stood up abruptly. "I better get to my garden." He walked quickly outside, and after a moment Joe got up, too. He waved goodbye to Andy and went to his own home. How sad, he thought. And after all these years. How very sad.

He went into his house and poured a cup of his own coffee, then got his journal down from the shelf and pulled out a pen. He stared thoughtfully at the next blank page, but instead he closed the book and put it back in its place. This was no time to write; it was a time to think. He sat at the table and stared into his coffee, occasionally taking a sip as it got colder and colder. Somehow, the temperature of his morning coffee just didn't seem very important.

CHAPTER NINETEEN

Joe awoke with a start after yet another night of intrusive dreams. He had the persistent impression that Nick wanted to see him and wasn't in the mood to wait for him to take his own good time about it. He groaned, climbed tiredly out of bed, and tottered off to the bathroom for his morning ritual. Then, he went about supplying his daypack. "I wonder what Jessie's doing?" he wondered aloud as he examined a pair of worn white socks. Funny thing, he muttered. "Even with all the wondering I've been doing about Andy, I think I actually dwell more on her now. But if Andy knew Jess, even at 96, he'd be thinking about her, too." Joe grinned at the prospect.

He tossed a final spare pair of white socks, an extra granola bar and a pack of waterproof matches in his pack. The matches were for the stogies that he had sealed within a sandwich bag. Satisfied that he'd remembered everything, he finished dressing, turned out the lights and walked out the door.

"Hey, Joe!" Turning from locking his door, he saw Andy standing in his own front doorway with his hand outstretched, offering a cup of steaming coffee. Now, how could Joe turn that down? He sauntered over to Andy's and, dropping his pack on the front porch, he took the mug and headed straight inside. He knew the routine well: Go to Andy's kitchen table, pull up a white-painted but well-worn chair, drink coffee, and talk about whatever was on Andy's mind. Clearly there was something on his mind. Joe sat on the sturdy old straight-backed kitchen chair and waited.

"Heading off to see Nick this morning, looks like," Andy started. "I mean, if you were planning to take your Jessie on a date dressed like that and at this hour, I'd think you a bit strange." Joe pondered his escalating strangeness, but didn't mention *that*. "Seriously, you heading off on another one of them Nick hikes this morning?"

"Well, it being a bit too early for an actual date and me with nothing else to do except chat with old coot neighbors, I thought I might take a little walk in the woods." Joe became suddenly aware that he was starting to talk a little like his old friend. "Anyway, I thought I'd go and see Nick for a while. It's been a couple days now."

"You got those cigars with you, then? Any of the little Italian ones could kill you if you aren't used to that kind of smoking, especially in a cave!" (Now, how on earth did the old guy guess that's what he wanted them for?)

"Yep, Marsh Wheelings," Joe said, recovering from his surprise. They were all I could find in town. And I don't know if I could have found the others anywhere. I know the locals don't know about them these days. It's strange, Andy. Nick seems to think he could get some enjoyment from me smoking in the cave. And you know what? I think he could, too. Somehow, he seems to be wired into my body." And even into my soul, he thought.

Andy nodded knowingly. "The only thing more strange is that I believed you almost from the first minute about Nick. No hesitation. I think something in your eyes and in your voice convinced me." Joe's eyes thanked him now. He gulped the last few drops of coffee and started to get up. "Joe?" The old man reached out and touched his sleeve. Joe sat back down at once.

"Could you do me a favor, Joe? I told you I don't know anything about my dad, except that he's buried out there somewhere. Ask Nick if he knows anything at all?" Andy's one good eye got watery beneath his wrinkled old brow. "I never realized until after I grew up just how big a hole my dad left in my heart. I mean, we never went fishing again, and he didn't get to teach me when I started out in the mine. He liked to talk about how one day he'd show me the ropes. Will you ask him, Joe?"

Joe took out his pad to make sure he didn't forget this assignment, although their first conversation about Andy, Sr. had burned so deep into his heart that he could never forget. "I'll be sure to do that, Andy." He put the pad back in his breast pocket.

"I know I already asked you to find out if he knew my dad. Now I want something more. You understand?" Joe nodded, comprehending what was coming. "I just want to know if he has any current information on him. Know what I mean?"

Joe wasn't going to screw up this assignment. "I'll learn all that he can tell me, Andy. You can count on it." Andy reached out and took Joe's hand sincerely, shook it and then just held it for another moment, looking into Joe's eyes with his own good one.

"Thanks," he said simply, releasing the hand. "Well, I know I kept you long enough."

"The company and the coffee were both well worth it," Joe responded sincerely. He got up and left hurriedly, not wanting to see his strong friend unravel. "Seeya, Andy," he said lightly as he pushed open the door.

Each day that Joe made the drive to the trailhead, the trip seemed shorter and shorter. He hardly had a chance to dwell on the things that worried him anymore, or even on more pleasant topics like Jessie. As he pulled into his regular space, he realized from the well-worn grass just how often he parked his old Caddy there. He laughed aloud, wondering if one day he would find a valet standing next to a "private parking" sign reserved to his name. Still amused at the vision, he laced up his hiking shoes, stepped out into the warm morning air, and purposefully strode off on his latest trek

As he trudged onward and upward it occurred to him that very few people could remember the early days of Avella and its surrounding coal camps - the social life and the hard work. While interviewing a ghost was not exactly standard research protocol, he realized that a unique opportunity had been offered to him. He would like to chat for years to come with his new buddy, but it was painfully clear that he could lose Nick at any time. Heck, he should lose Nick, if only to find his place of peace, whatever that is. Heaven? The enormity of his next thought stopped Joe in his tracks. It slammed Joe between the eyes. He could also lose Andy! Yes, he had to take full advantage of the hours – minutes – he could harvest with both men. Joe fought back a tear at the prospect of losing his near-centenarian neighbor.

Joe turned the bend before the outcropping way earlier than usual. At only eight-thirty he would have all the time he wanted. He stopped outside the cave, saying nothing. He waited.

After a few minutes, he felt the message: "Well? Why not step inside out of the sun? Do you expect me to sit here all day waiting for your highness to stroll in? I could be off inspecting abandoned coal mines, you know." Joe laughed.

"I hate to keep you waiting, your majesty. Besides, I can't stroll through a hole that's not even four feet high. Joe crab-walked in. When are you going to enlarge your opening? I'm not getting any younger, you know. The "rheumatiz" is settling into these old bones as we speak."

Nick grinned at him. "Hi, good buddy." Boy, did Joe wish that he could shake Nick's hand, but there was a rather obvious problem there. Nick had no hand, only some very cold vapors. "Well, I know you're here to talk and get some things straight in your mind. I saw that in your dreams and I can see it now in your expression. So, shoot!"

Joe tried to collect his thoughts… where to begin?

CHAPTER TWENTY

"Nick, I might as well jump right in. I know times were tough back then, but you folks had some fun, too, I'm sure. Frankly, there aren't very many people alive who can talk about times before the 1930s and 40s. What was it like?" How *can* he remember, Joe wondered as he awaited Nick's response. Is memory found in the spirit as much as in the brain cells? He waited patiently.

"I told you some things already. What do you want to know?"

Tell me about mining. Tell me about pick-and-shovel work underground and stuff like that?"

"Mining, huh? Why not let me show you instead?"

Joe gasped at the unexpected possibility. "Show me? You can really do that? Do you have some kind of time machine or something? I'd really like to see it first-hand, but I just can't see how it's possible." He leaned forward now, all his senses on full alert. Nick laughed.

"Nope, I don't have a time machine. I don't even know what one is. Do they have such things now? Anyway, we don't need one of them time machines. I just happen to know where there's a small mine that they never properly closed up. I think it might be safe enough for you to go in, but I wouldn't lean on any timbers or make loud noises if I were you. Then there might be two of us in this fix!" Nick laughed wryly. "You better bring a light with you if you want to give it a try. One of them lights with no fire like you use in here would be okay."

"I'll do it!" Joe exclaimed excitedly. "When and where?"

"Whenever you want. I have don't have much of a schedule. About a mile from here, following the creek toward Avella, there's a hillside with the opening about halfway up the slope. You'll have to look hard to see it now. I'm sure it must be all grown over and hidden. You'll have to come here first, though, and let me know before you go, so I'll know to meet you there." Amazed at the prospect, but also disconcerted by the potential dangers, Joe nodded his agreement

"You asked about how things were, Joe. We had it tough because even when all the mines were working full time we couldn't make enough money to get ahead. Do you know what a miner's check was? No, of course you don't. It was like a numbered tag. Each man had his own number, stamped on circles made of brass or some other metal. When we had a coal car loaded – about two-and-a-half tons usually – we would fix our own check onto it before it left our mining room. That was supposed to give us credit for a full load of coal, one for each car we sent out. On a good day we could do eight or ten cars by working real hard. Like I told you, the coal seams weren't very high here, so we worked in four or five feet high rooms, all stooped over or kneeling down. A foot of water on the floor made shoveling harder yet.

"The coal cars were usually pulled out by mules, but sometimes they had a big machine up above. We hooked a car onto a heavy bull rope or cable and it pulled the cars out. After they got up top, the cars were counted and weighed. We were supposed to get full credit but it usually didn't happen. Sometimes another miner tried to switch tags. If we caught a guy doing that he had to leave town after he healed up. But usually it was the company that flat-out cheated us by not giving us credit for the tons or the number of cars we sent up. We worked all day and never knew how much of the work we got credit for."

Nick looked thoughtful and a smile brightened his face. "Know what we did to relieve the stress? Sometimes we left the mine and went to play baseball. They still do that, don't they? Some days we would work a full ten-hour shift and then go out and play until dark. On days off we played a double-header. Every camp had its own team. Those were good times." He paused, reflecting. "We were really tired, but it was a good kind of tired. We played soccer, too. We had some real good players around here. They were about the best you could find. We whipped the teams from a lot of other towns." Nick smiled wistfully, remembering.

"And oh, how we liked to dance! You could dance with anybody's wife or girlfriend and nobody got mad. That helped the bachelors stay happy. Did I tell you that I had a girlfriend, Joe?" A new light stole over his expression as he paused, remembering something wonderful. "Her name was Carmella. She was the best thing in the world for me. She understood me and made me laugh when I got discouraged. I really wanted to marry that girl and make her happy. She was almost seventeen when I … you know. I wonder what ever happened to her. Think you could find out for me?" His tone turned a bit more serious. "Her name was Carmella Antonini. Her father was Camillo Antonini. She was born in 1905 if I remember right. Her Mother was Olga. Her sister was a year or two younger. She was Olga, too. I hope Carmella had a good life." Nick looked wistful. "Think you could find out for me?"

"I will sure try," Joe said in all earnestness.

"I wonder about my good friend, Angelo Ballino, too. He practically carried me away from the battle. He and some other men got me to this spot. That's three miles or more! Angelo was my best friend in this country. He was six years older than me, but sometimes he was more like my father or brother than my best friend. I knew I could always count on Angelo, and he proved it again that day. But he could count on me, too.

"I worried about him, Joe. He had to have my blood all over him. How could he say he wasn't at the mine? I hope they didn't catch up with him. They'd have killed him or put him away for sure. He was a good man, Angelo was. The best. Would you do me another favor?"

"Sure, Nick. I'll try to find out about Angelo, too."

"Thanks, Joe. Thanks a lot. You're a true friend. I feel like I've known you all my life. Now, what are you here for? Not just to entertain a dead miner, I'm sure." He laughed again, breaking the somber mood.

"Well, I have a similar favor to ask. My neighbor is now a very old man and a former miner. He tells me that his father went on the Cliftonville march and never came back. He said other men told his mother that he died and they buried him in the woods in a small ravine or ditch. His name was Andy, Andy Polack. His boy was twelve years old at the time and he misses his dad something awful. He's named Andy, too. Me showing up and asking about the riot opened some old wounds. Any chance you can find out about him? How's he's doing? Is he still around?"

Nick looked at Joe with a mixture of sincerity, amusement, and solemnity. "What do you think? That we have reunions down here?" He chuckled mirthlessly. "I'll see what I can do. Now, did you bring me a little something?"

Joe reached into his pack for the cigars. Just then his cell phone went off and he reflexively answered it. He moved toward the cave mouth to improve reception, holding it against his ear. "Sam? Yes, it's me. How are things? Okay, huh? Sounds like you're not missing me at all. Is there a problem? No, not here either. I haven't even spent much time thinking about real estate lately, Sam. It's been better than a vacation. Usually I take the cell phone and do business while I'm away, but not this time. Okay… Okay…. Okay… Thanks Sam. If things are still going well, I'd like a little more time away before I get back into the grind. Yes, I know that I can work from the house in Avella most of the time. Yes, I know… Okay. I'll call you next week. Take care, Sam." Joe pocketed the phone.

Nick looked curiously at Joe's pocket. "What was that? What was that thing? Did you really talk to somebody just now?"

Joe retrieved the phone. "Do you remember what a telephone is, Nick? Did you ever see one?" Nick tried to rub his chin, without success.

"I heard the mine super could talk to people in other places, but he had to do it in his office. Did he have one of those things?"

"Sort of. His would have been much bigger and connected by a wire to a big switchboard somewhere else where a woman, called a telephone operator, would fix it so he could talk to people. As you can see, there are no wires now, at least for these little phones you can take anywhere."

Nick shook his head in amazement. "I missed a lot, being dead and all. And I really missed that stogie." Joe glanced down at the one in his hand that he'd forgotten. "Are you going to light it or plant it outside to see if it'll grow?" Laughing, Joe struck a match and lit the cigar.

"At least I know what that thing is. It's what they called a Lucifer match. But I remember them being a whole lot bigger, and they were made of wood." Joe puffed through the cigar to keep it burning, without actually taking much smoke into his lungs. After a minute or so the tip burned with a red-hot intensity and he took a little more smoke into his lungs, for Nick's sake more than his own, hoping that the nicotine effect would somehow be transmitted to his friend. Nick smiled in satisfaction, watching the familiar show. "I like watching you do that. And it's like I can feel and taste the smoke."

Joe puffed away for a while, with his back propped against the wall, just sharing this companionable moment with Nick. After a while his eyelids became heavy and his hand dropped away from his side. He saw Nick get up and move toward him. Through half-closed eyes and a haze of cigar smoke building up in the cave, he saw Nick reach down for the cigar.

After fifteen or twenty minutes Joe began to come to. He glanced at his right hand and saw where the now-burnt down cigar had rolled away from his fingertips. He looked suspiciously at Nick; surely he had been dreaming. Oxygen deprivation – carbon monoxide – something like that. "Nick, did something just happen here?"

"You fell asleep."

CHAPTER TWENTY-ONE

Thursday! Joe woke early, but not because of restless sleep and intrusive dreams. He had actually slept pretty well. Did Nick decide to go easy on him because he could tell, somehow, that Joe had a big day planned? While he couldn't explain his restful night of sleep, he gratefully embraced it. Even though he had awakened very early again – this time before six o'clock – he felt ready to conquer the world.

Joe lay for a few minutes in the slowly lightening room as he played out in his mind how the day would go. He would arrive at school and meet all the children and adults who would be going on the field trip to Cross Creek Park and Lake. They'd be very interested in him because of his rugged manly looks and his outdoor awareness. He'd sit with Miss Randall on the school bus, the focus of admiring glances. After arriving at the park, they would venture into the wild areas so that he could share his awe-inspiring knowledge with them. He'd also steal a few moments with Jessie. Later they would all climb back on the bus, tired but happy. It would be a great day.

He practically leapt out of bed, poured a glass of juice and started the coffee. Having already filled his daypack, it was all ready to go. He unpacked it again, compulsively working to make it just perfect. Compass. Topographic map. Granola bars. Water bottle. Spare. Water filter. Trail mix. Extra white socks. All this other stuff. He re-filled the pack. (Probably overkill for a nature outing.) Oh, well. With a sigh, he finished getting dressed, downed his juice, and barely noticed the cup of coffee. All ready now, he took his journal down from the shelf and began to write.

To date I have written mostly about what I learned from Andy and Nick. Now I can't help but focus on Jessie. There's just something about her. Or is it something within her? Whatever it is, I just can't help thinking about it. Perhaps it's the inner strength that I admire. Today I will venture out with her and seven or eight other adults, plus about forty or so rambunctious children. And I illogically hope to spend some time alone with her! When did

I become so irrational?

I know why I'm going, but I'm still not sure why she asked me. Jessie is an experienced teacher and has been on nature field trips before; she probably doesn't need me to be there at all. Is she just being nice to me, or does she really hope that I can contribute? Or is she beginning to see me as I have come to see her?

Joe closed the book and placed it back on the shelf. Might as well see how Andy's getting along, he thought. It would look strange if I showed up at school two hours before the bus arrives. He took up his daypack and closed the door behind him as he left. Sure enough, Andy's kitchen light made it clear where Joe's first stop would be.

"Joe! Didn't expect to see you this morning. Aren't you going with thc kids today? Well, come on in, I can put some fresh coffee on." Joe walked past Andy to the kitchen and sat at the table, as though he had lived there his whole life. Andy chortled. "You've been headed to some strange destinations lately, but you sure know where to come for some coffee and company!"

Joe sat quietly for a few minutes while Andy pottered about. "Why the glum face this morning, Joe? I thought things were going okay for you lately. Anything I can do to help?"

Joe sighed heavily. "I have to admit that I really like Jessie and I hope to make a good impression today. I mean I really do like her." His expression deteriorated from glum to despairing. "I've been giving myself this rah-rah pep talk, but underneath it all I'm afraid of screwing it up with her. If not today, maybe tomorrow." He looked up with a pleading expression. Andy put his hand on his shoulder.

"Like is the wrong word, Joe. You are smitten," Andy laughed. "Seriously, you're a very good man, and you know the outdoors better than most people. Just do what you know how to do and be what you are. Answer their questions if they have any, and try to keep the kids safe and out of trouble." He removed his hand from Joe's shoulder and went back to the stove. "You'll do just fine," he said reassuringly. "Now let's have coffee and I'll fix you some eggs and ham. You never have enough to eat in the morning. That granola just won't cut it. I'm thinking of starting up a Bailey feeding line."

Joe laughed. "Okay, you win. Now update me on that garden."

They talked and ate and talked some more. Finally he checked his watch. "Half-past eight already! I better get going. Thanks for the food and for keeping me occupied, Andy. I don't know how I could have stood the wait without you."

"Anytime, young friend, anytime," Andy said as he gathered up the dishes.

Joe arrived at the school just before nine o'clock and immediately spotted Jessie and her crowd of kids at the front entrance, awaiting the bus. He detected a kind of controlled orderliness that verged on mayhem. He parked nearby and waved as he approached. As Jessie introduced him to the group of kids and parents, the bus arrived.

The trip to the park was a short one, less than fifteen minutes, but sitting next to Miss Randall it seemed to fly by a whole lot faster than that; far too fast. Craning his neck around, Joe noticed something strange. The noisy, ebullient busload of children had become oddly quiet. Forty-eight sets of eyes were watching him and Miss Randall. Glancing over, he could see this wasn't lost on Jessie either. She wore a contemplative look, and her lips were pursed in a very fetching way.

They arrived next to a pristine lake, the lush foliage from the opposite hillside reflected on its placid blue waters. Re-animated, the children practically tumbled from the bus. Jessie clapped her hands and gathered everybody together.

"The other day one of our boy scouts inspired Mr. Bailey to conclude that a patrol leader system could be useful for us today, so we will try it like this. I have already chosen and talked with boy and girl scouts, who will be our patrol leaders. They each have a cardboard badge. Each adult will be an adviser for a patrol, including Mr. Bailey, who will advise the 'Jungle Rats'." Giggles. "Johnny Black will be their patrol leader. I will be senior patrol leader and will accompany the Jungle Rats, too. More giggles. I'll read through the list that says to what patrol you are assigned. I also have a checklist for each patrol so that you can record the animals, plants and trees that I want you to find. If you have any questions, check with Mr. Bailey or me."

"Yes, Miss Randall," came from a chorus of voices. Joe thought he heard a little boy's voice add: "Mrs. Bailey." A few giggles erupted from the rear of the group. Several parents tried to hide their smiles. Jessie blushed slightly and pretended not to notice.

Though she decidedly did not look his way, Joe thought he could see her eyes flicker in his direction. After a few minutes of getting organized, they trooped off after Miss Randall.

The trail followed the shoreline of the lake, where they would occasionally stop and look for creatures in the water or under rocks. One girl shouted: "There's a great blue heron!" Following the outstretched, pointing arm and hand, they could clearly see the bird standing on a partially submerged log further up the shoreline.

"Very good, Virginia," Jessie said. "Look at the long legs and neck and the mainly blue-gray coloration," she explained. As the children stood in silent admiration, the ungainly-looking bird lazily flapped its wings and then flew across the lake. What a great start to the outing, Joe thought. The first part of the hike went remarkably well, except for some muddy shoes and pants when children slipped while looking for hellgrammites and tadpoles.

About halfway through the hike they stopped for a snack and relaxed. Joe and Jessie walked a short distance away, but still within everybody's view. They sat on a log. Jessie seemed happy.

"So, how have your hikes been going, Joe? Anything interesting? You seem a bit pre-occupied."

"Actually Jessie, there is. But it's way beyond interesting, verging on bizarre. Maybe I can tell you about it someday," he said, off-handedly, hoping to move on to a lighter topic.

"Joe…" she admonished. "We are here now, so if something is troubling you, I'm listening."

He made his decision. "Well, I can give you the short version, if you like." Jessie nodded, with an intrigued look on her face. Joe briefly told her, to her growing astonishment, about meeting and talking with Nick.

"You are sure about this, Joe? This seems beyond belief. I never heard of this riot and certainly nothing about any ghosts. I can't say that I believe this story." She hesitated, and then went on, "but strange things have been known to happen."

"It's all true, Jessie. Every word. He even offered to show me an abandoned coal mine." They sat and pondered what he had just related; he, reassured that she hadn't rejected his tale out of hand, and she, not sure of what to believe. Shortly before they got up to call the group together, the two fifth-graders who had been spying nearby, hoping to see a stolen kiss or overhear some words of romance, slipped away and returned to their own patrol. They didn't notice Jessie giving Joe's hand a brief and impulsive squeeze. Joe noticed, and his heart leapt.

"I think we should talk about this some more, another time," Jessie whispered as they got up to join the re-congregating group. She gave a Joe a smile that seemed to him to be both conspiratorial and cautionary, indicating the children with a slight nod of her head.

Shortly after the break they heard a loud scream from the trail near the lakefront, followed by childish laughter. Rushing in that direction, Joe and Jessie found a small garter snake in the hands of a young girl. "What happened here!" demanded Miss Randall. The girl, Bonny, said that Bucky had used the snake to scare her friends, so she took it from him. Bucky now looked much less happy than he probably was when wielding the snake. "Thank you, Bonny," Jessie said as she gently took the obviously frightened little creature and placed it in the high grass near the lake, surrounded by the excited and curious students. "And, Bucky? We may have to talk about this later."

"Yes, Miss Randall," the guilty one said contritely. Joe smiled inwardly, secretly sympathetic towards Bucky's cause.

The rest of the hike went very well. Jessie occasionally called all the patrols together so that Joe could explain some basic orienteering pointers and how to not get lost in the woods. He also showed them some edible plants, like cattails, and sources of water if they were ever lost. He cautioned that they should study the subject further, because some plants and water sources can sicken a person. Johnny Black, the Jungle Rats patrol leader, nodded his head knowingly.

A happy but tired group climbed back onto the bus. Even in the fifteen minutes it took to return to the school, several children fell asleep. At the school there the kids gave a rousing: "Thank you, Mr. Bailey and Miss Randall," accompanied by a lot of nudging of small elbows.

Just before he left, Miss Randall whispered to Mr. Bailey that she would need gasoline at about five o'clock p.m.

CHAPTER TWENTY-TWO

At four-thirty, Joe started his walk downtown. After chatting briefly with Mrs. J. and a few others along the way, he arrived at the convenience store at five minutes to the hour. He bought two soft drinks and took up his station near the gas pumps. After another minute or so, he saw it. The Camaro! Jessie pulled her car to the pumps.

"Sir," she inquired. "Is this station still full service?"

"Until they fire me, it is," he retorted as he handed her the spare soft drink, which she sipped while he began servicing her car. He started her gasoline flowing and opened up her hood. She moved next to him and looked under the hood, too, perhaps an inch or so closer to him than the last time.

"I hope the framatizing whatzit is okay," she said with concern. Joe glanced at her abruptly, and then saw her wide grin. "Gotcha!" she laughed. As they walked toward the door to the store, she said in a low voice, "I wonder if we could go up to your house, Joe? I would like to meet Andy and talk over all this stuff in greater detail." Slightly unnerved, he nodded his acquiescence.

After she paid for the gasoline, he gallantly opened her door so that he could admire the way she slid into her driver's seat. Then without anybody to open his door for him, he opened the passenger side door and got in. "Where to?" Jessie asked. He directed her up Campbell Drive, and in a few minutes they pulled to a stop in front of old Albert's house.

"So this is the house you are fixing up?" she questioned. "And is that where your friend Andy lives?"

"Right, and right again," said Joe as he walked her toward the door.

"Wait," she stopped him. "Could we sit out here? I'd like to chat about these ghosts you were telling me about." Joe sighed and directed her to two porch chairs.

"Where do you want me to begin?" he asked resignedly.

"At the beginning," she said. "Just at the beginning." For the next full hour he patiently worked through how it had all come about, including the first hike when the sudden chill hit him in the cave and the dream-filled nights that followed. He explained the bizarre dream where he first met Nick, too. He then took her through the first actual meeting on the hike when it occurred to both him and Nick that Nick's spirit must have inadvertently passed through Joe's body, bringing them together. He told of the cave meetings that they had enjoyed since then, and of all the colorful information he had learned from Nick and Andy about the Cliftonville Mine riot of July 17, 1922, and of mining town life in the early 1920's. "I have some of this recorded in my journal. I started the journal only because I met Andy and found him to be quite a character; I had no idea that I would be using it to document the paranormal."

"That is an amazing story, Joe," she quietly remarked. "Do you suppose Andy is home? He sounds like quite a guy."

"Andy? I really admire that old-timer. He's 96 now and still going strong. There's lots of spirit in that old man. Let's walk on over there." Joe got up and gave Jessie his hand to help her from the porch chair. She took it, rose, and they turned to go to Andy's.

As usual, Andy stood at his open door, this time holding a pitcher of iced tea. "Hey, Joe. Usually it's coffee in the morning that you bum from me," Andy said amusedly. "So is this your Jessie? She's everything you said she was, and more. No wonder you're smitten." Joe had no response to that, other than an embarrassed shrug. Jessie said nothing, but a slight smile peeked through. "Let's sit out in the garden, okay?" Andy offered.

They all took seats at a patio table. Joe gratefully noticed that Jessie took the glass eye in stride. "I am very pleased to meet you, Mr. Polack. Joe has told me a lot about you. I understand you were a coal miner?"

"Please call me Andy. I'm not old enough for you to call me Mr. Polack," Andy cracked. "Me and my dad… my dad before me," Andy replied. "We were both coal miners. We worked hard and we paid our bills. What more can I say?

Jessie wouldn't be deterred. "Joe tells me that you lost your father, Andy. I was sorry to hear about that. He took part in the riot that Joe told me about, is that right? I never heard about that riot."

Andy's expression changed, and he slipped into his faraway gaze for a brief moment. "He was killed alright. We don't know how many men were killed. But we do know about my dad."

"What do you know about Nick?" Jessie pressed on. "I understand he was a miner, too?"

"Aaah, I see you broke down and told her," Andy glanced at Joe. Turning back to Jessie, he looked contemplative. "If you are asking if I believe what Joe tells me, I do believe it. For an outsider, Joe learned an awful lot about old time stuff during a very few hikes. He told me things that he had no right to know. Is Nick for real? You betcha he is!" Andy spoke the last few words with an unusual fire in his voice.

"I think I believe what he tells me, too. It's far too bizarre a story to be made up. But I also think we have to go a bit further. After a few moments of silent concentration, she summarized. "We could go to the library to see what resourccs arc available there, and we can also search the Internet. Perhaps we could also see if any other older peop… I mean youngsters like you, are still around that we can talk to." Jessie smiled fetchingly, but then her tone changed dramatically. "And one more thing…"

Her demeanor changed to a very serious one. Andy and Joe both leaned forward expectantly. "I want to go to that cave and meet Nick," she concluded firmly.

Andy nodded. "I want like the devil to go to that cave, but I don't think I could make it. I'm not as young as I would have you believe." They all burst out laughing.

Joe had been sitting quietly while his bizarre recent history was laid bare for both to see. He finally spoke up. "You really want to go to the cave? It could be a bit strange, and I don't know how Nick would like it. But he does seem a reasonable sort. He's certainly likable enough, except for that underlying mood I told you about. You probably won't see or hear him, anyway. But he should at least see you. He's seen other people who stopped by his cave."

Jessie looked at him with a firm set to her jaw. "I still have to go. And don't forget this, Mr. Joseph Bailey. Andy hit the nail on the head when he said that if this gets around – and I have the feeling that it will – your credibility could stand or fall on what we are able to do to support what you say. That includes field research as well as what we can find within the bookshelves."

Joe stroked his chin thoughtfully. "I was planning to meet Nick at an old, abandoned coal mine on Saturday, but I'd have to go to his cave first. Maybe you could accompany me there. I'm not sure if I want you to go to the old mine with me, though. It could be unstable, and I can't see us both putting our lives in jeopardy. But I've been brewing another idea. On the other side of the State Line Tunnel is the site of the Clifton Mine. I was thinking of taking a day trip down there."

Jessie clapped her hands excitedly. "I want to go, too, Joe." She reached over and squeezed his hand. Joe blushed visibly in front of Andy, who displayed a toothy grin.

"But you don't understand. While you can drive to the area of Virginville and Cliftonville from the West Virginia side, I want to walk the whole distance… all of it. The walk would be from Avella through the two railroad tunnels before Penowa, and then through the State Line Tunnel. It will be a lot of hard walking along uneven railroad tracks and over some trestles. And, when I get there, I want to poke around the site of the mine. I have a topographic map plus some data on where things were probably situated… although I understand it's pretty much gone back to nature now"

"I'm going," she said firmly. "And you can't stop me." Joe looked at Andy and shook his head. "Women," he said with feigned dejectedness. But secretly he knew that any moments he could enjoy in the company of Miss Randall would be welcome indeed, no matter how peculiar the circumstances.

Jessie looked at him with an excitement growing in her eyes. "This is very weird. There's nothing logical about it. But do you know something, Joe? I really do believe you now. And I want to be part of whatever comes next. I want to be there with you. And I want to help you research the riot and the men who died. Perhaps we can use genealogy to help us."

With that, she got up and said, "It's beginning to get dark. What time will we meet for that hike on Saturday, and where?" She said it with a 'no-nonsense and don't even try to stop me' tone. Joe sighed with a less-than-heartfelt look of exasperation.

"Eight o'clock Saturday morning, Jessie, right here. And bring sturdy hiking shoes. By the way, I know where we can mooch a free cup of coffee before we leave."

"Aye, aye, captain!" She smiled, gave Andy's hand a gentle squeeze, and gave Joe a brief hug. As she walked to her car, she stopped and looked back. "Nice Caddy. Will we be riding in it on Saturday?" Joe nodded dumbly.

She hugged me, Joe thought. She hugged me.

CHAPTER TWENTY-THREE

Friday morning! Only one more day and he would not only see Jessie again, but spend most of a day in her presence. Joe sighed heartily. Just one more day. And if he worked it right, she might spend Sunday with him, too.

"Well," he said to himself. "I don't think I can take that walk down the tracks today. She made it clear that whenever I go, I won't be going alone. No point in hiking to 'Nick's Place', because I'm going there tomorrow. I guess it's time to check out the library, like Jessie said. Then maybe time schedule a CAT scan. I'm spending way too much time talking to myself."

This time Joe drove instead of walking. He found the public library on top of the hill in Avella. He parked in front of the red brick community center that appeared to have once been a school and glanced around.

"A coal mine coal car!" he exclaimed. On display under a pavilion roof a mine car with steel wheels rested on two rails. He also noted some sort of large bell on display. "I wonder how long it would take me to fill a car like that," he said, whistling in wonder. "Nick said each car usually held about two-and-a-half tons. That's a lot of coal!"

Making a mental note to stop talking to himself, Joe entered the building's main hallway and made a right-turn into the library. Without comment, he started studying the bookshelves. "Just like a man" the older, redheaded library staffer remarked jokingly, after he had wandered aimlessly for over five minutes. "You obviously want something specific, but just won't ask for help."

"You have my number," he answered sheepishly. "I want some information on local history, especially early coal mining days and a coal mine riot that happened in the 1920's."

"I can help you there. By the way, my name is Nan Cross, but you can call me Nan. We don't have very much information about the Cliftonville Riot, but I can show you what we do have. We learned much of it through Internet research, and we have a file of printouts, magazine and newspaper articles and an old research paper. What would you like to start with?"

"Whatever you can show me. By the way, I'm Joe. Joe Bailey.

"You're new in town, aren't you, Joe Bailey? While some local people are interested in our history, people new to the area are often more curious. Wait a minute. Are you the young man who is living in old Albert's house?"

"Guilty as charged, ma'am. I inherited it and now I'm fixing it up a little, while I take a welcome break from selling real estate. What do you have here for me?"

Nan nodded approvingly. "We have the articles I told you about regarding the Cliftonville Riot, and there is a local historical section next to the checkout desk. You also might find the historical displays in the main hall interesting. There are excellent sketches showing how many of the local mines were laid out in their heyday."

"The Clifton Mine?" he asked hopefully.

"I'm afraid not," Nan replied consolingly. However its layout had to be similar to the other slope mines in the area. Most of them were cut into a hillside, and they used the same tipple method of filling railroad cars with coal. But if you don't mind my asking, why all the interest in the Clifton mine and the riot?"

"I just heard about it from some locals is all," he lied. "One man is my neighbor, Andy Polack."

"Old Andy? What a character!" Nan laughed. But he's really sharp in his old age, isn't he?" Joe vigorously nodded his agreement. "Here, Joe. Let me get our file of Cliftonville material out for you to look over. I can make you a copy of whatever you want. Just don't take any originals, okay?" Nan's voice remained gentle, but she said that with a dangerous look in her eye.

Joe decided it would not be a good idea to trifle with Nan. He sat at a table and began to review the materials, mainly reprints of old articles and printouts from web sites. The recollections of witnesses were rather sketchy, in part because many eyewitness accounts were given decades after the event. Also, some accounts were by people who were away from the scene of the action and who spent a good deal of their time with their heads down. Newspaper articles related the meeting in Avella and the trip to Penowa plus a basic recounting of what happened, more so than how it happened. The articles attempted to describe the gunfire, the tipple fire and explosion, and the beginning of the retreat back to Pennsylvania. Joe noticed some discrepancies that he would have to scrutinize later. Unfortunately, there were no graphic accounts by actual participants except for quotes by law enforcement people. Not one miner's story was told.

The accounts were consistent in saying that at least some of the miners were armed and that a gun battle ensued, with the defenders getting the better of the fight. The mine's tipple burned and the conveyor was blown up with dynamite. The attackers were then beaten into a retreat. Only the victorious defenders and some carnage were left.

As the smoke cleared, several miners were found dead on mine property, including two whose remains were found in the burned-out tipple. After several days, the count of miner bodies totaled eight. Of the survivors, more than two hundred were arrested. Some arrests were by West Virginia authorities, but most were by Pennsylvania law enforcement officers who then turned them over to West Virginia for prosecution. A series of trials in Wellsburg, West Virginia, resulted in nearly four dozen men convicted plus 126 miners eventually set free. Strangely, nobody was convicted of killing the sheriff, even though that was the most serious charge. Prison terms were handed out for conspiracy and the convicted men were sent to the state prison in Moundsville, West Virginia.

Joe paid for copies, to be scrutinized later at home. While the copies were being run off, he walked out into the main display area and looked over the old photos and drawings, and the mining artifacts. Yes, he thought, these drawings give a pretty good idea of how slope mines were laid out. He made a few quick sketches and headed back into the library. He thanked Nan for the copies and left.

After a tiring week of sporadic sleep and the expenditure of lots of physical and mental energy, he retired to what he hoped would be a second restful night. It was not to be. The dreams came back with a vengeance, and they induced images of scenes from the fighting, and men dying terrible deaths. Whenever he awoke from a dream and forced himself to relax and go to sleep again, more dreams of mine tragedies forced their way in. One frightening vision was that of a blindingly realistic explosion of mine gases followed by a cave-in, and another of men being crushed under a roof fall. The visions invaded his slumber and blew it apart, as though somebody had drilled and tamped black powder into his very sleep.

After begging for at least a little rest, he managed to fall into a deep slumber.

CHAPTER TWENTY-FOUR

He awakened to a loud pounding on his door. *Oh, no!* He thought, struggling to his feet. He threw on a light robe and staggered to the door. There she stood, all ready and right on time. "Come in, Jessie," he pleaded. "I'm so sorry. I had the dreams all night and they wore me out. I know I only got two, maybe three hours. And here you are, right on time. Will you give me ten minutes?"

Jessie looked at him with a compassion that gratified Joe. "I'll scrape you up something to eat. And where do you keep your pack? I'll fill your water bottles while you dress." While she busied herself over his pack, Joe washed up and dressed in his bathroom.

He came out, feeling somewhat refreshed. "You look almost human, Joe," she said as she glanced up. He smiled and thought: "This is a remarkable woman. Nothing fazes her." He took the offered glass of juice and the slice of peanut butter toast that she had prepared, and downed both thankfully.

"Thanks loads for being so understanding. Those darn dreams kept me up most of the night. Now, what say we wander over to Andy's Diner for some fresh brewed coffee?"

Andy waited in his doorway again. "Joe! What was wrong with you? You never turned your lights on. I was getting ready to head on over when I saw Jessie show up and practically beat your door down. Here, have some coffee. You look like you could use it."

"I sure can, Andy. I think Nick must have decided he was too easy on me this week. He came after me with a vengeance last night. I got very little sleep until about five o'clock." Andy frowned sympathetically.

"But here's something you two might be interested in. I went to the library yesterday just to check out local history, like Jessie suggested. I got a few article reprints on the Cliftonville Riot." Jessie's eyebrows rose slightly, but she said nothing. "Just about everything Nick said checks out, but I learned even more than that. There were arrests and trials and convictions. Many men were sent to prison. There's still a lot more to learn about the riot, I'm sure."

Joe checked his watch and pushed his chair back. "Thanks for the coffee and the company, Andy. Sorry that my sleeplessness cost us some visiting time this morning, but we have to be on our way." Joe got up and Jessie started to follow him to the door.

"Wait," said Andy with a new, more sober tone. "Please wait a minute. I have something for you." He reached onto a shelf and handed a small photo to Joe. "Would you mind showing this to Nick for me? Maybe he saw this feller during the march. He's my dad. It's one of only two photos I have of him." Andy showed them a close-up photo of a young man, carrying his helmet and lunch pail.

"I sure will." Joe put it in a sandwich bag to keep it dry and then placed it in his breast pocket. "See you later, Andy." He shook the old man's trembling hand and they started across the grass to his Caddie. Jessie paused, then went back and gave Andy a little hug and a kiss on his cheek. Andy's face crumpled, and he sniffed loudly to divert attention from his tears.

They silently got into the Caddy and started down the road toward Meadowcroft. At the trailhead, they stepped off at a pretty good pace up the slope. Jessie kept up easily, only beginning to gasp for breath after a half-hour or so of steady uphill walking. Even with all his recent hiking, Joe faltered, too. After stopping for water and a snack, they were at the clearing in just under an hour. "Just ahead, into the woods again and around a bend. We'll be there in about fifteen minutes."

Jessie nodded excitedly, her face jubilant. "Well, what are we waiting for?"

After they rounded the bend, the outcropping came into sight. A dark area indicated the cave mouth. Joe pursed his lips in a silent "Shhhhh." They stopped outside the cave mouth and said nothing.

After a few minutes, Joe felt Nick say, "Well, what's taking you so long?"

"Did you hear that?" She shook her head no. Joe sighed. "I'm here, Nick. And I brought somebody. I hope you don't mind. She really wanted to come and meet you." Silence.

Finally, "You brought somebody? Well, might as well bring her in." Joe ducked and crabbed his way inside. After a moment's hesitation, Jessie did the same. Joe spotted Nick sitting in his usual place. After his eyes acclimated to the darkness he could see a sullen look on Nick's face.

"Well? Why did you bring her here? Although I do have to admit that she's a whole lot prettier than you. Maybe you didn't have such a bad idea after all."

"Nick is sitting there with a sourpuss look on his face but he had to confess that you are pretty." Jessie beamed into the vacant darkness.

"She looks familiar. I've been competing with her for your attention in your dreams." Blushing, Joe refused to pass on that message.

"But how can I be sure that there is a Nick here?" Jessie wanted to know. I mean, I think I believe it, but how can I be sure?" Joe and Nick both thought about that.

"I have an idea," said Joe. "You extend a certain number of fingers behind your back and I will guess them, okay? Nick will look for me. Go." After a moment's hesitation she did as asked. Nick passed on the message. "Nine," said Joe. She did it again. "Seven." Again. "None."

Unnerved, she claimed that it could be a trick. Joe thought for a moment. "Okay, Nick. How about that fingertip? Show her." Nick touched her bicep with his fingertip.

"Ouch! Hey!" Jessie yelped, and began to rub her arm. "That was cold! It felt like it pierced me. Did Nick do that?" Joe nodded. Nick laughed.

"It seems he has a problem stopping at the surface of the skin, not having a sense of touch and all. Can you imagine how it felt for me when Nick inadvertently passed through my entire body with no warning?" He glowered at Nick, who now sat there with an innocent grin. He seemed to be enjoying the show immensely.

Jessie nodded ruefully as she rubbed her arm. "Joe? Would you please translate so that Nick can tell me some things? I want to know how it has been for him, living here in the cave for over eighty years." Joe told Nick, who nodded his acquiescence.

"He says, shoot. But remember. He has no true concept of the passage of time. I have to stop by here before I meet him at the mine, because we can't make an appointment to meet somewhere else. By the way, I think he likes you."

"Tell him thanks, but I might already be taken," she said,

knocking Joe totally off his pins for once. Nick smirked.

For the next several hours Jessie asked questions, many of which Joe had never considered. Nick answered them all, adding layers to his life, the riot, and his death. She considered all the answers solemnly, while Joe occasionally jotted down some facts in his notepad.

"Nick? There are just two more things if you don't mind. Number one is that you are going to show a mine to Joe, right? I want to go, too. I hope that's okay."

"Tell her it's fine with me if you don't mind. But just remember that she has to be real careful to not lean on any timbers. It'll be slippery down there, too, with some areas ankle deep or worse in sulfur water. And the roof could be shaky in places. What else?"

"Joe has a picture in his pocket. We would like to see if you recognize the man in the picture." Joe pulled out the photo and shined his flashlight on it. Nick looked it over thoroughly.

"Yep, I remember him. He was in our group. I think maybe he went into the same building where I was shot, but I'm not sure. That was a confusing morning. But like I told you before, we don't hold any family reunions down here. But I can check around if you want," he concluded.

"That's Andy Polack," Joe explained. "He's the one I already asked you about, the dad of my neighbor, Andy." He then passed on the information to Jessie, whose face brightened with mounting anticipation.

"I just thought of another thing," Jessie offered suddenly. "Would you pass through me, too, sometime?" Shocked by her nerve, Joe was at a loss for words.

Nick thought for a moment. "I'm not sure you really want that, or that it would be a good thing." Relieved, Joe told Jessie, who acknowledged the answer with obvious disappointment, coupled with what appeared to be a tiny measure of relief.

Stretching their legs, they prepared to leave. "Okay if we do the mine tomorrow, Nick? I keep a couple hard hats for construction sites in my car's trunk that we can use. Of course we'll come here first… to wake you up." Joe laughed at his own ludicrous statement.

"We can do that. But, Joe? Don't run any tours down here,

please? 'Nick's Place' could get pretty crowded."

Joe and Jessie left, feeling like conspirators in a secret that the rest of the world might never know. But about that, they were entirely wrong.

CHAPTER TWENTY-FIVE

"Thanks, Nick." Joe muttered it to himself, but also to Nick, in case he was lurking around Joe's subconscious someplace. "I really did need that sleep. I'll see you in a couple hours, okay?" He felt foolish even saying it because logic told him that his acquaintance could not hear it. Or could he? Joe just didn't know, and didn't have the psychic energy to spend deliberating it.

He would be seeing three of his favorite people in the world today: Nick, Andy, and Jessie. Especially Jessie. Joe couldn't prevent a broad grin at the prospect.

"Did she really say yesterday that she might be taken? Could she have actually meant me?" The thought set him about his work with renewed energy. He showered quickly and shaved slowly, and then put on clean hiking garb. He even brushed off the dried mud sticking to his hiking shoes. Juice and toast set him up for the day, except of course for the obligatory cup of coffee at Andy's. At 7:45, he turned off his lights, plunging the house into darkness. Daypack filled and at hand, he sat near the front door and waited for his lovely hiking companion.

Ten minutes later he heard the Camaro pull up in front of his house. Hurried footsteps approached the door and practically before she slid to a stop, she started banging on it. He opened the door, pack in hand, and said: "May I help you, miss?" He turned and locked the door as she stood there, shaking the confusion from her face.

"I've been had! She exclaimed, and then laughed merrily as they headed over to Andy's. She collapsed against him on the way. "You got me good there, Bailey. But you know what they say about payback." Joe thought to himself that whatever punishment she decided to mete out, he doubtless wouldn't complain.

Andy was waiting in the doorway again, with two full mugs in his hand. "I started the eggs and bacon when I saw you starting over, so there's no excuse you not eating." Dutifully they took their places at the table and watched him continue his cooking, which he did with no small measure of verve. He knew that he had an appreciative audience. Soon he set plates in front of them, laden with food. Joe dug in lustily, while Jessie ate a bit more ladylike.

"So you're heading out to an abandoned mine, are you? It mighta been a wildcat mine. It probably won't go too deep, but I have to warn you. Wear those hardhats all the time, and don't burn any flame. Keep away from all roof supports and any other old timbers. And don't go too deep, because there could be mine damp gases collected. They can suffocate you. And don't separate, except that one should always stay behind the other. In fact you should be tied together on a fifty-foot line, which I have ready for you right here. It's nylon and not very heavy. In case one feels faint, the other might be able to pull them out. And remember it'll be slippery in there! It'll stink, but that'll probably be sulfur. But be careful of another smell, a sour one. It could be methane. If you think you smell it, don't waste any time getting out.

And whatever you do, be careful not to go too deep into a dead end area. That's where the heavy air could be collected. Boy, I wish I could go with you to protect you. Just be careful and listen to anything that Nick tells you. Promise?" They nodded, serious expressions on their faces.

"We'll be careful," they said in unison, before glancing at each other in surprise.

"See? You made an impression on us." Joe finished his last bite, slurped the last of his coffee, and wordlessly agreed with Jessie's expression that it was time to leave. "Well, thanks again, Andy. I'll tell Nick you said hello. And we will be careful. We both have cell phones in case there's a problem.

"OH! We nearly forgot the most important news!" Jessie interjected. We showed Nick your dad's photo, and he remembers your dad being there, and thinks he was part of the group that went into the building with him, when Nick… you know. But he definitely recognized your dad's picture. He couldn't make any promises, but he told us that he would 'check around,' whatever that means." Andy smiled sadly but with a grateful expression on his old visage.

Jessie hugged Andy and they left. As they crossed the lawn to his Caddy, Joe muttered: "Old coot gets more hugs than I do!" Jessie stopped, turned to him, and gave him something more than a gentle hug, flinging her arms around his neck and leaning her body into him, as she gazed coquettishly up into his face. Joe didn't remember his shoes touching the ground during the last thirty feet to his car.

They drove to the trailhead and hurried up the now well-worn path to the cave. Nick wasn't there, so they sat and waited in the darkness, illuminated only by the reflection of a flashlight beam shining against the wall. Joe finally remarked "You hugged me."

"I know," she said. They sat in silence.

"Are your intentions toward me honorable?"

"Purely honorable, sir," she responded. More silence.

"Why only honorable?" They both laughed. "I guess you know that I've grown to like you, Jessie. A lot."

"I know, Joe. And I like you, too." Joe's heart turned itself upside down with a happy flip.

"Now ain't that sweet," came from the corner. Nick had materialized there and sat studying the two of them with an amused look on his face.

"Nick is here, Jessie, and he heard you profess your undying love for me, the kind that endures to the end of time."

She laughed. "I didn't intend to lead you on, sir," she said merrily. But I might give you a few months. Is he really here?"

"Right over there," he said, motioning to where Nick sat grinning. "I do believe we provided the entertainment to complete Nick's morning."

Jessie looked miffed. "So, why didn't he just pass through my body, like he did yours, on his way back?"

"He says he just came back from checking out the mine again, but these days he's more careful when he enters this cave. He wouldn't want to get familiar with the wrong people. Although I doubt that he'd consider you to be the wrong people. He just says he's more careful these days, is all." Jessie glowered in Nick's direction. "He saw that," Joe reported.

"This chit-chat is all well and good. But do you plan to see a mine today?" Nick asked grumpily.

"Okay, I guess it's time we left. It's about ten o'clock. We'll see you there." In a feigned whisper he said to Jessie: "It's best you can't hear or see him. He's all grumpy today." Nick chuckled. Grumpily.

They hiked back down the trail and then drove to the area that Nick had described. They could just make out the likely location of the mine mouth, but the slope would make it hard going and the loose stone and overgrown brambles in front of the opening made the prospect a daunting one. They started through the brush to the hillside and climbed to where they could see some boards behind the foliage. Joe shoved the foliage aside, breaking the shrubbery that didn't stay put.

At the mine entrance they saw some rotting boards with painted letters scrawled across them. Though now illegible, it didn't take a genius to tell that they were intended to warn people to stay out. They took firm grips with gloved hands on the ends of the boards and pulled. The boards split and fell apart, their wood sliding off the rusted nails. Inside, the light from the entrance dwindled into near blackness. Joe turned on one flashlight. Nick was just inside the portal, waiting. "Welcome to our home," he said. They both adjusted their helmets and Jessie turned on her flashlight. Without further ado, they carefully stepped over the rubble at the entrance and walked inside, finding that that they could stand comfortably.

"This is the main entry," said Nick. Joe passed on that obvious bit of information to Jessie, who began to get a frustrated look on her face.

"Where is Nick right now?" she asked. Joe answered that Nick was standing about three feet directly in front of him, pointing down the passageway. Without hesitation, she launched herself in that direction.

CHAPTER TWENTY-SIX

Jessie sailed through the space that Joe had described and fell to her hands and knees, avoiding a more severe tumble. As the two men stood temporarily frozen in shock, she lay there for several seconds, unassisted. She was shivering violently and holding her hands across her chest, rubbing her shoulders and upper arms. Joe glanced at Nick in wonder and lurched forward to help her to her feet.

"Hey!" Nick exclaimed. "She jumped right through me!" He stared at her, his ghost eyes wide, while Joe pulled her to himself to try and share some body warmth. "You better take her outside for a few minutes," he advised Joe, who was already turning her toward the portal. Still holding her close and feeling an occasional shuddering convulsion interrupt the continuous shivering, Joe walked her slowly outside, guiding her over to a nearby stone outcropping. Two copperhead snakes that had been taking advantage of the warming rays of the sun on the flat granite sensed their approaching footsteps. They slid off the rock, slithering away through the brush to an underground den.

Now on the rapidly heating stone, in the full sun of late morning, Joe held the still-shivering Jessie close for a while longer. Finally, her shivering slowed and then stopped and she pushed herself away from him. "I think I can take it from here," she said with a smile on her face. "I mean the extended hug was very nice, but I think the sun and the hot rock can handle the job now."

"What were you *thinking*?" Joe demanded, having already realized, of course, exactly what she had been thinking. "Why didn't you just ask him?"

"Well, Mr. Bailey. I wasn't sure that Nick would have agreed and once I put you two birds on notice what I had in mind, you and he wouldn't have been as forthcoming with information regarding his whereabouts. Am I right, or am I right? Or am I right?" Joe had to admit that she was right. "Now let's go back inside and see if my little idea worked. Okay?"

"Yes, Ma'am," Joe said as he took her forearm to assist her

back toward the cave. She was still a little unsteady, but her unwavering confidence helped her manage the walk back to the portal. As they entered, her coldness had nearly dissipated.

"That was quite unexpected but very funny in hindsight," Nick remarked. "Besides, the little warmth I got from her was a nice kind of feeling." He played as though he was suffering from an internal conflict, and finally concluded: "Know what? I liked her warmth better than I liked yours." He and Joe both laughed.

Jessie had a confused look on her face. "Why don't I see him?" she demanded. "I can tell he is there." And then it struck her. "I can tell he is there! I could never tell before," she said with a feeling of wonder.

"I couldn't see Nick right away, either. Who knows? Maybe it will just take a little time and patience. You might even have to start out seeing him in a dream." But noticing the expression on her shining face in the dim light of the portal, Joc knew that the lady was a bit short on patience.

"Well, Mr. Bailey," she laughed. "I can wait a while but if it doesn't get any better than this, I want you to tie that ghost down with ghost ropes so I can do the job right the next time." Nick and Joe both laughed in admiration, but they were still a little wary from her unexpected performance. She rubbed her shoulders again. "I just hope a next time won't be necessary! Now let's get on with it, Nick."

"Joe, if you two ever get married she's going to be a handful. I hope the kids are more like you. I can't imagine how you could manage her and more like her, both."

"Did Nick just say something?" she asked, trying to listen very intently.

"Yes, he did. But I don't think I'll chance sharing it with you," a mildly embarrassed Joe responded. "No, I better not." Jessie gave him a strange but comprehending look as though she didn't have to be told. "Well we better get on with this tour," he concluded as he turned toward Nick.

"Yes, there's no doubt you'd have your hands full with just one of them, never mind the kids," Nick cracked. "Now you both better turn your lights on." Jessie turned her flashlight on, followed by Joe. They both looked at her in amazement.

"I don't know. It just seemed to be the thing to do," she

explained, as she turned away from the entry and shined her light down the passageway. Joe followed suit, remarking aloud that he seems to have lost all control of his little historical experiment. Nick bent over, laughing.

"Okay. The passage is that way, as Jessie already figured out. You see that the ceiling isn't very high. That's because they only wanted coal and didn't see any point to digging above the top of the seam. So you tall folks will have to bend down pretty far from here on in. Myself, I don't have to bend at all. Watch this." Nick passed through the wall and came back with his head passing through the ceiling. "Nick" said Joe. I think you have to save that act for Jessie. It's pretty disconcerting but I think she'll appreciate it."

After he caught a glare from the lady, he looked over at Nick, who continued, "I already had a good look down the passage. I think I can take you about 200 feet or so without too much danger. Ready?"

Joe passed on Nick's information to Jessie, who nodded her head vigorously, a look of excitement building in her eyes. They took out Andy's rope and tied it around both their waists and to their belts, to Nick's indulgent interest. Following Nick, Joe led the way, followed by an obviously miffed Jessie. He surmised that she wasn't too happy depending on a man who was as much a rookie as her.

"Do you see where they once had railroad rails here?" she asked, staring downward.

Following her gaze, Joe had to agree. "Nick says they would have pulled the rails out from the back of the mine to the entry as they abandoned it. They'd have saved everything they could reuse or sell for scrap metal.

About fifty feet into the mine the ceiling had already decreased to less than five feet. Joe bumped his helmet on a small outcropping in the ceiling, causing his neck to jam back into his shoulders. "Hey! That really hurt" he cried out. Nick nodded knowingly, and explained that it happened all too often back when he had a body.

"I think I just heard… or felt Nick say something," Jessie exclaimed excitedly. She pushed ahead of Joe, brushing heavily against a timber column next to the sidewall. The column shifted slightly and some loose dirt sprinkled onto the floor as the timber groaned. "Oops," she said. "I guess I shouldn't have rushed past that timber like that, right?" Joe and Nick both nodded in agreement. She saw Joe's nod but not Nick's.

With both their flashlights pointing ahead now, further along the passageway, they realized they were in what would have been total darkness without the flashlight beams. The passageway proceeded downward on a slant, curving very slightly to the left. Both living beings had to crouch way over and bend their knees just to keep moving under the diminishing height of the ceiling. They ducked their heads even more whenever they came to a rotting beam supported by two pillars. Their backs, unaccustomed to the strain, began to show the early promise of future pain.

Joe gently moved ahead of Jessie again in the narrow corridor, keeping her just behind his right shoulder. "I can see Nick but you can't, so for safety's sake I think I should go ahead. This could be dangerous." She reluctantly agreed, but he could tell that she didn't like it at all. "How far have we gone, Nick?" he asked.

"Seventy steps," Jessie responded. "In this cramped area and with my mincing steps in here I would guess a little over one hundred feet." Not showing their admiration at her planning and presence of mind, the two men walked carefully onward. "I would like to try something here, if you don't mind."

"Do we really have a choice?" Nick asked his friend, who shook his head.

"Let's sit and turn off our lights." She sat and turned off her light, followed by Joe. He had to admit that she had a good idea. They sat there in the darkness, Joe reaching out to hold her hand.

"I'm scared," he said jokingly. She squeezed his hand. Joe admitted to himself that the total darkness was very unsettling, with his only points of reference the wall behind his back and the floor under his seat. Had he been standing upright he would have probably wavered and toppled from disorientation. But her hand grounded him. He passed his left hand within an inch of his nose and saw nothing.

They sat for nearly five minutes, just pondering what it would have been like to be a miner whose light had failed. They were both grateful that they each had two flashlights plus Joe's pocket flash and the one from Jessie's purse.

Joe then suggested one more exercise. "Let's stand up, very carefully." They struggled to their feet, again bent forward to avoid hitting the ceiling. "Sure enough," Joe reported. "I could easily lose my balance. My only points of reference right now are my feet and Jessie's hand."

"Okay, playtime's over," Muttered Nick. "Let's get going."

"I agree," said Jessie to everybody's sudden astonishment, including her own. "Nick? I agree!" she repeated triumphantly. She flashed on her light and saw two people with her, Joe and a man-sized vapor just swimming into shape. "Nick! Nick! I see you!" she exclaimed joyfully. "I mean I can't see you clearly but I can see where you are! I feel like hugging you but I don't want that coldness again. So I think I'll hug Joe instead." She hugged Joe ecstatically. Joe hugged her back eagerly. "Now," she continued. "Let's see what this mine is all about." She carefully stood with knees bent and back hunched, watching Nick's form and substance become much clearer to her senses. "By the way, Nick, can already see you are a handsome man. I like that strong nose."

Joe was also ready to move on, grateful for the respite the sitting had provided for his back, despite the damp chill that had soaked from the wall through his back muscles. They turned down the passage, with Nick leading the way. "Remember, don't touch or lean on anything in here!" They glanced at each other, in caution and in agreement. After another sixty feet or so, they could feel water washing under their shoes as they walked. This is about the farthest we can go in this mine," Nick stated. "You can see the rubble ahead and to both sides."

"Did a cave-in happen here?" Joe asked.

"Partly, but mostly it was the result of them taking out pillars as they mined backward. When they figured the mine was about done they worked from the back to the front, removing coal from the pillars as they went. Then the only things holding up the roof were smaller pillars and the timbers, and they weren't up to the job. About all they did was slow down the collapse of the ceiling.

"After the coal cars were loaded in a mined-out area they took up the rails from the track bed and hauled them out. They basically left an empty hole for the earth to reclaim in its own good time. Now don't get me wrong, some of the roof collapsed right away, so it was a real risky business, taking the coal pillars. In fact in many mines they were left in place. But not in this one."

They stood there, gazing at the destruction of decades past. Jessie moved forward, followed by Joe, sloshing through water well over their ankles to examine the rubble close up and to shine their light over the fallen stones and earth. They could see more cavities in the distance, some wide open and some partially filled with rubble. "Those are more rooms," Nick explained, needlessly.

After toying with the idea of climbing over the rubble and exploring further, they thought the better of it. Neither Nick nor Andy would have forgiven them had they gone further. Plus it would have been a stupid thing to do. They mutely turned and began to retrace their steps back up the passageway. "I noticed something," Joe soon commented. "As we proceeded I never felt any kind of a change in my breathing and I only picked up a mild sulfurous smell."

"I was careful about my breathing, too," Jessie replied. "And I was trying to make sure that I didn't feel faint. In fact, I found the air to be refreshing and clean. Not what I expected at all. Is that because we were in a pretty shallow mine?"

"It is shallow," Nick responded. "Plus I think fresh air is coming in from another hole somewhere. Maybe a natural cut in the hillside or a vent opening. Another thing is that all the coal dust has settled. You wouldn't believe how hard it could be trying to breathe with all the coal dust floating in the air, especially after we blasted a section loose. Men had their lungs ruined by it."

They proceeded slowly back up the passageway, walking a little easier this time with the rising roof and upward slope. As they neared the entry portal Joe began to obsess that a few minutes – or hours – lying in the hot sunshine would do his aching back some good. "My back hurts," Jessie said, as if reading his thoughts.

Finally they got to the entry where they could actually stand upright, stretching out their aching backs. "You worked down there for full shifts?" Joe asked. Nick nodded modestly.

"Once you got used to it you could put up with it," he said. "But coming topside and walking outside was always a treat. Except maybe in the winter when the outside air was really cold and the weather miserable. Sometimes you wished that you could have a bed down there!" Then he corrected himself. "No, I wouldn't want that. Not as long as I had Carmella in my life. She made any place warm for me."

Jessie looked at the now clearly formed Nick and nodded compassionately. Joe felt a brotherly understanding for his friend. "Well, we better go on our way. I think my back needs about an hour or so lying on a hot rock and another hour in the soft grass before I can ever be productive again. We'll see you back at 'Nick's Place' soon, okay?"

"You sure will, Joe. And I'll be waiting. I don't have much of a social life as you well know." As they turned to leave, he said, "Oh, by the way…" They turned back. "Tell your friend that Andy Polack is doing okay. He's like me, but he's doing okay. He just kind of wishes that he could get on with his… his life. If you know what I mean."

They could only nod, wrapped in their own private thoughts about this new development. With a simultaneous final glance back into the cave's opening, they saw Nick looking after them. "I wonder what he's thinking right now," Joe posed. Jessie could only shake her head in wonder.

"Race you to the rock!" she squealed as she hurried away. Following right on her heels, Joe reached the flat outcropping and carefully eased himself down beside her in the bright sunshine. Gratefully they lay there, letting the heat that had soaked the stone find its way into their aching backs.

After a few minutes, they took off their shoes and dumped the remaining water out, letting the sun and air begin to work on drying them out, too. Wiggling his toes in his wet socks, Joe remarked: "You didn't notice any copperheads, did you?"

"I didn't look," Jessie answered tiredly. "But if they were here, I hope they left."

CHAPTER TWENTY-SEVEN

"Joe?" Jessie's voice coming through his cell phone sounded tight and strained.

"What's wrong?" he answered, immediately concerned. Why would Jessie be calling him during a school day? It was Monday; she should be in class. There had to be something wrong.

"Joe, I'm in Principal Landers' office. They wanted to talk to me and I think they would like to talk to you, too. Could you please come to school now? It's about Nick." Dazed, Joe agreed.

Joe had not yet started working on the house, so he only needed a quick change into more presentable clothing. Then he found himself following Route 50 to the school campus. The journey did not include the happy anticipation he enjoyed during his other two trips. Joe parked his car and entered the school, where he signed in and went directly to the elementary principal's office.

An unsmiling secretary welcomed and ushered him into the principal's private office, where he found a worried-looking Jessie, Principal Landers and two women he'd never seen before awaiting him. "Mr. Bailey, may I present Mrs. Jones and Mrs. Granger."

Mrs. Granger – a severe looking and slightly overweight brunette with short-cropped hair – interrupted the principal. "Do you talk to ghosts, Mr. Bailey?" she asked him with a piercing look. The sudden and accusatory question took Joe aback, but his cop sense quickly kicked in. Rule number one: Try to answer a question with a question.

"Would that be important, Mrs. Granger?" he asked. She appeared to be taken even more aback than he was. Joe thought he detected a slight smile pushing through Landers' frown.

Mrs. Jones – a taller and thinner woman with gray-streaked black hair and with what seemed to be a perpetual scowl – jumped into the gap. "Well? Do you, Mr. Bailey? My daughter Lisa told me that you were discussing talking to ghosts last Thursday. She said she… overheard you. Do you really talk to ghosts?"

Joe surmised that Landers was either a trained negotiator or had been principal long enough that he recognized the game being played out. He apparently didn't see a reason to intervene… yet.

"How did she happen to overhear me say anything, Mrs. Jones? You say it happened on Thursday. Was that at Cross Creek Park? If I recall correctly I was there to assist in a nature walk and talk about compasses, maps, wildlife, and edible plants. Miss Randall thoughtfully invited me because I have some outdoor experience. I understand that my background check went well." Jessie seemed to relax her bearing a little as Joe appeared to take some measure of control of the situation. Of course, it was her place of employment and her job that could possibly be in jeopardy, not his. "So how did little Lisa happen to overhear me?"

"She… well, she happened to be nearby while you and Miss Randall were talking." Mrs. Jones blushed noticeably.

"I see, Mrs. Jones. Your daughter apparently wandered nearby while Miss Randall and I chatted during the break. I don't recall seeing anybody, but perhaps I wasn't looking. Maybe that's because I have nothing to hide. Now what did Lisa say she heard?"

"Lisa and my daughter, Jenny," interrupted Mrs. Granger, who had by now regained her composure. "They said that you told Miss Randall that you talk to ghosts. We just want to know what this is about and whether you are a fit person to accompany our children on a field trip. We want to know why Miss Randall asked you to participate," she said with a righteous finality.

"So, what did Miss Randall tell you?" he asked.

Jessie leaned forward and said: "I told them the truth, Mr. Bailey. Because of your outdoors experience and because you passed the required background check, I found you to be a suitable addition to the other volunteers on our nature walk. Your talk confirmed that you have a wealth of outdoor knowledge, which you shared with our students. Frankly I was glad to have you along."

"And why is that, Miss Randall?" asked Principal Landers encouragingly.

"For several reasons, Principal Landers. First, a mutual friend whose judgment I respect recommended Mr. Bailey to me. Second, Joe – Mr. Bailey is a former police officer. Also he is an experienced outdoorsman who has much knowledge to share. And finally, as may be seen by the fact that all other adults on the nature hike were women, we could certainly use a man to serve as a model for our young boys, and our young girls, too. And again, he did pass the background check. So with your permission I asked him to participate, Mr. Landers."

"Tell us about these ghosts, Mr. Bailey," the principal asked Joe.

"I don't 'talk to ghosts' I assure you all," he began. "I happened to stop in at a small cave under an outcropping during a hike. In that cave I encountered a spirit. The spirit told me that he died during a mine riot in 1922."

"Cliftonville?" the principal asked with surprise, now leaning forward more intently.

"Cliftonville," Joe replied. "The Cliftonville Mine Riot of July 17, 1922 to be exact. Until I met Nick I had never heard of that mine riot. But since he first told me about it I learned even more from an old ex-miner who lives near me, as well as through research at the local public library." The two women seemed bewildered.

"What some people called the Clifton Mine was located at Cliftonville in Brooke County, West Virginia," explained Principal Landers. "Apparently a large group of miners from the Avella area walked down the railroad tracks in July of 1922 to the Clifton Mine and tried to shut it down. There was a considerable amount of gunfire and some damage to mine equipment. A number of miners were killed as well as the Brooke County sheriff. A large number of miners from here were arrested and tried in Wellsburg, and dozens of them were sent to the state prison in Moundsville. It is a quaint but troubling piece of local history, ladies."

Turning to Joe, he continued: "Are you saying that you have been conversing with a miner who died in 1922, Mr. Bailey?"

"Yes, I have," Joe admitted. The room fell quiet, with the two ladies apparently unable to find a reason for further complaint. Mr. Landers finally broke the silence.

"The way I see it, Miss Randall acted appropriately in inviting you on the nature walk, Mr. Bailey." Turning to Jessie, he continued. "You identified ways that Mr. Bailey could enrich your class's outdoor experience and your lesson plan. He submitted to the required background check and passed with flying colors. According to policy, my office officially invited him to accompany you. Mr. Bailey refrained from being alone with any child or children, and there were an adequate number of registered parent volunteers accompanying the group. I find no fault with you, Miss Randall, nor with Mr. Bailey. But, Mr. Bailey, I recommend that in the future you limit your conversation to the lesson plan when within earshot of the children. Thank you all for coming," he concluded, standing up. Joe shook his hand.

Jessie seemed to be relieved at the show of support she had received from administration. She rewarded Joe for his part with a little smile. Joe excused himself and started to leave the principal's office. Mr. Landers said, "I'll see you out Mr. Bailey." They walked out into the main hallway. "Mr. Bailey, I've been aware of the Cliftonville riot for several years now, and I'd like to learn what you found out. In your library research, of course." They shook hands again.

"Certainly, Mr. Landers. But I'm concerned. Could what just happened be a problem for Jessie? I mean Miss Randall?"

"I hope not." Landers responded. "And I hope this does not interfere with her becoming a principal. She worked hard at studying for her principal papers, and I think she will make a strong administrator someday."

Joe had a lot to think about during his drive back to town...

For the rest of the day he worked around old Albert's house. He finished some tasks in the living room and began to work in the kitchen. For the next week or two he would be eating mostly microwave fare, until he had completed the cabinetry makeover and installed the new appliances. But try as he might, he couldn't quite give full attention to his project. Thoughts of Nick and Jessie kept intruding.

It being a very warm day in June, Joe was ready for another shower after he quit work at about four o'clock. The hot needles of spray beating down upon his still-sore lower back provided welcome respite, from not only the physical discomfort but also the unanticipated confusion earlier in the day. After pulling on clean clothing he began his trek downtown. Arriving at his intended destination at nearly ten minutes to the hour, he knew that Jessie would make a point of being there, too.

Instead he found Les there, apparently waiting, with two soft drinks in his hand. He passed one to Joe. "I saw you coming. What's this I hear? The word around school is that you've been talking to ghosts and Jessie could be in trouble for asking you to go on a nature trip," he admonished. "My son told me about it."

"Les," Joe protested. "I don't really talk to ghosts. I mean I never have before…" he stopped fumbling for words when he saw the Camaro pull up to the pumps. They both headed over to help Jessie with her gas purchase. As Les filled the tank and Joe washed the windshield, Les casually asked Jessie how things were going at school.

"You heard?" she asked, with a small frown breaking through what had been a pleased smile.

"I heard," Les replied, still not looking at Jessie so that people wouldn't think a serious discussion was going on. In fact, a serious discussion had started. "The story my son brought home was that two mothers complained because you invited Joe to go on the nature walk and he says he talks to ghosts. They claim he isn't fit to be with young children."

Clearly troubled by what Les had said, she suggested that Joe and Les meet her at Joe's house after she paid for her gas. Once back behind her steering wheel, she pulled away from the pumps and headed up Campbell Drive. The two men followed in Les's fire-engine red four-by-four pickup truck. When they arrived at Joe's house she had already parked and awaited them on Joe's front porch.

"A take-charge woman," Les commented admiringly.

"I think we owe you an explanation," Jessie began when they stepped up onto the porch. "Go ahead and start the story, Joe." Joe filled an incredulous Les in on how he had met Nick and what he had learned about the Cliftonville Mine riot of 1922. Jessie brought some of the more recent developments into focus, including their trip to the abandoned mine.

Tipping back in her chair, she exclaimed, "Look! There's Andy now. Let's go and chat with him." She stood and walked quickly to Andy's house, with the men dutifully following in her wake. Andy looked up in feigned surprise.

"I saw you having a pow-wow over there and thought mebbe you had forgotten about old Andy Polack. Thanks for honoring me with your presence." He gave them an exaggerated bow, and then exclaimed, "Oh, my rheumatiz!" as he reached for his back. Joe knew better but Jessie and Les fell for the act, until Andy cackled and directed them to the patio table. On it Andy had prepared a pitcher of iced tea and four glasses, as though their arrival had been anticipated, which of course it had been.

After they sat and Andy had poured iced tea for each, Jessie began. "Andy, you know Les, don't you?"

"Know Les? Sure I know Les, I know his father, and I knew his granddad. Yep, I know him all right. How are you doing, young fella?"

"Just fine Mr. Polack. But I hear you people up here are chasing ghosts now? Is it something in the air up here, or what?" While Les laughed, Andy had been put on guard. He did not plan to look like a senile old fool.

"What's he talking about?" Andy asked the others. Joe explained what had happened at the school.

"Didn't I warn you about that, Joe? I warned you, didn't I? I warned you both."

"Yes, you did. I guess it was bound to come out, but I didn't think it would be this soon. But we can talk about damage control later. For now, we want to fill you in on the old mine. Okay?"

The old man nodded seriously. "I hoped you'd get around to that. So, how did it go?"

"Pretty much what we expected, but your gal here did something we never anticipated. I'll tell you about it in due course." Joe continued, with Jessie's considerable involvement, to describe the visit to the mine. Les let his jaw drop open in utter amazement after they described how Jessie had leaped through Nick's spirit and afterward was able to see and hear him, too. He shook his head in amazement so often that it began to look like a bobble-head doll.

They concluded the tale with what Andy had most wanted to hear: that his dad had been accounted for. Andy's eye misted over, but he fought back the tears. "Thanks," was all he could muster. They sat in silence for a few minutes, Joe and Jessie recovering from the telling and Andy from the listening. For his part, Les still had not fully recovered when Andy brought out four cold beers to top off the evening. Les turned his beer in his hand, appearing to read the front label and then the back and then the front and the back again, while he struggled to comprehend how a simple gossip story brought home from school had turned into such an overwhelming tale.

"You say there may be a dozen or more buried in the woods?"

"Possibly," Joe responded. "Nobody really knows how many men were buried along the way. Not to mention the midnight burials that were said to have taken place later. There are also reports of miners who later died and were buried under assumed names in regular cemeteries. What we do know is that many men died, unheralded and unrecorded. We know two by name. They didn't get a decent burial with the mourners who should have been there, although I'm sure the men who piled dirt and rocks on them must have showed respect at the time. They probably stood or knelt in silence and possibly said a quick Lord's Prayer, muttered a "Hail Mary" or at least whispered a few simple words of goodbye."

"So what's your plan?" Les wanted to know. "I hope you have a plan."

CHAPTER TWENTY-EIGHT

"Plan?" Joe shrugged wearily. "Frankly, I haven't had much of a clue up to this point, let alone a plan. Mainly I've been reacting to whatever happens. But I do want to visit Nick again and learn whatever I can, and also walk the tracks to Cliftonville. Other than that I have no plan. Maybe it's time we worked one out, huh?" Joe looked at the three others expectantly. Jessie reacted first.

"I think a plan to protect my job would be a good thing," Jessie responded. "I doubt we have heard the last of those two women… or their friends. Mrs. Jones, especially, has a reputation for starting up bandwagons and convincing people to pile on. If she dislikes somebody she can make his or her professional life very difficult. In fact, I overheard Mrs. Jones say something about the school board to Mr. Landers."

"That could be a problem," Les remarked. "The board just spent weeks working through the annual budget and they're negotiating the teachers' contract now. Their sessions have been pretty intense and I doubt they'll be in a mood to deal with controversial chaperones. Even though you have a very good reputation and have done absolutely nothing wrong, the pressure on the school board and on you could get pretty harsh. I've heard those women become very shrill once they are in front of an audience at a board meeting. And their friends in the audience can treat anybody rudely who speaks against them. Not to mention that they can take the smallest incident and make it into a crisis."

"I think you hit the nail on the head," Joe added. "We should assume that Jessie and I will become a focal point of the next school board meeting. When is it scheduled and what can we do to pull their teeth before they bite us?"

"I think the board meets on the second and third Wednesdays of each month, so the next meetings will be in June," Jessie offered. "But frankly we have to do more research on Nick's story, too. Let's look at what you were able to compile from the public library and then check out the Brooke County Library in Wellsburg. They should have relevant materials in their local history section. Also, the State Archives in Charleston might be able to provide more information. That could be a long shot, though. Brooke County seems to be our best chance."

"If you don't mind me saying so, I think we have to work on Joe's image," remarked Andy. "Who is he now? A nice kinda feller who walks to town when everybody else drives. That right there could be seen as strange. Not to mention selling real estate, which a few people liken to selling used cars. Not me, of course, but some other folks. They think you want too much of their money to do what they could do better for free." Joe winced, knowing that in the eyes of some that was exactly true.

"But we work hard for our money, Andy. We're not employees, and we get no salary and no benefits. We just pay our expenses every day and get the occasional commission check when something sells. We take on the marketing costs and risks. Wc hclp our clients to do better financially than they could have done without us. We earn what we are paid," he said glumly.

"You know some people might question why you're an 'ex-policeman'," Les added to Joe's increasing chagrin. "They might wonder if you were kicked off the force or were forced out under a dark cloud. I know your police friends in Pittsburgh would support you, but it should never come to that. We have to do something to prevent the situation from becoming a full-blown crisis for you, not to mention Jessie, who would get splattered by the mud."

"You really know how to cheer a guy up, old buddy," Joe commented weakly.

"Do we have any natural allies?" Jessie asked. "My teacher friends would support me. But then again, negotiations are going on right now and they wouldn't want to jeopardize the new contract. Administration would have to be neutral at best. They can't incur the wrath of the school board, nor risk getting that small group's guns trained on them. Most of the public is pretty great, but it only takes a few vengeful people to stir things up and put them in the worst possible light."

"Joe made a number of friends at the fire station," Les said thoughtfully. "When he shows up, he works side by side with them washing the trucks and maintaining the hall and the landscaping. They also like his company. Firefighters have a kind of affinity for the police because we work together at accident scenes and fires. Not to mention that when we get Joe going, he can tell a good story or two about his days as a cop." He nudged Joe and gave him a conspiratorial look that everybody else saw, but nobody but Joe and Les understood. Jessie decided to ask Joe about these stories some other time. "We should be able to drum up some moral support from the guys in the department. And the women firefighters, too," he added.

"The Memorial Day parade and ceremony is Les continued. "Joe, if you have a little spare time on Friday evening we have a work party scheduled for about six o'clock. Come on down. We could use the extra hands, and maybe we can do a little early damage control. The firefighters we don't see then, I can talk with on Monday while we're shining up the trucks and getting ready for formation. I'm sure that Joe will have their support around town and at the school board meeting. If work doesn't keep most of them away, that is." Work schedules these days are so unpredictable, he knew. Joe caught the momentary flicker of doubt in his friend's eyes.

"Les, I know you'll do your best to help me out, but even more important is protecting Jessie. Her job and professional reputation should get first priority."

"That's all fine and good and noble too, sir," Jessie interjected, with a mini-curtsy in his direction. But we have to deal with the whole situation, not just my precious job and reputation. You live here now. Remember that your reputation is worth something – even though you sell real estate." Joe laughed uncomfortably. She was entirely correct. "Furthermore, we have the small matter of at least two dead miners to consider, and whatever it will take to bring closure for them.

"By the way," she continued. "The science teacher in me has a problem believing that Nick accidentally slipped through your body. There's something more to it than that." The others sat silently, considering what she had just said. "Cause and effect," she added.

"Of course in my case," she went on. "Nick had no choice because I… Wait! I intentionally jumped through Nick. I knew where he stood and I made that decision. Now I am even more certain that Nick was drawn unerringly to Joe, even though he didn't realize it at the time. But again, why?" Nobody even hazarded a guess.

"So let me get this straight. You will work on building a base of support for Joe, especially if it is needed at school board meetings, and Joe and I will do further research in Wellsburg. Also, we will work on the best way to present the facts on this ghost to the townspeople, should that become necessary." She paused. "Why don't we all go over to Joe's house to look over the printouts and newspaper articles from the public library, for whatever hidden facts may be there? His journal could even reveal a forgotten clue. I thinks that's about the most we can do for now."

"I'm getting tired in my old age, so I have to pass." This from Andy.

"I'm late for supper already, so I have to pass, too. I wish you both luck, though – in your research." Les slyly winked at Andy and got up to leave. Les headed for his truck, but then turned and approached Joe. "One more thing. I know that Jessie over there has first call on your time. No doubt followed by your buddies Nick and Andy. But do you mind me tagging along when you walk down to Cliftonville? You sure stirred up my interest!"

"Of course," Joe responded. "The more the merrier." He and Jessie then headed over to his house to begin their review of the literature. As they entered, Jessie glanced back at old Andy. That sly dog was grinning smugly.

CHAPTER TWENTY-NINE

Joe awoke the next morning after sleeping for a whole five hours. He was in that somewhat rested but still tired state that was about the most he could hope for these days. Jessie had lightly kissed him goodnight at nearly midnight, seemingly satisfied with what they had accomplished.

"Oh, no!" he gasped in recollection, clamping his hands over his ears. It all flooded back to him again. While he reviewed old clippings, she had been browsing his journal for anything important that he might have overlooked. It was just after he heard a catch in her breath that he realized what he had written about *her*. She didn't say anything and quickly moved on, but he knew that she had seen it. That little part was more like his diary than a journal. "Oh, no," he repeated, before wrenching his attention from the incident of the night before. He forced his thoughts to move onward.

Because this was a regular school day, it he knew he would visit Nick alone. Stretching his tired bones before climbing out of bed, he dwelled on how Jessie's welcome presence had added so much to his bachelor existence. While Joe's mind and body were beginning to yearn for her, his spirit was entirely happy with her more and more frequent visits.

"Six o'clock already!" he said aloud. He rolled out of bed and hastily loaded his daypack, skipping the usual juice and coffee. He knew Andy's Diner would be ready for his early-morning patronage. In well under an hour he had dressed and walked out the door. "Yep, he's open. I hope the coffee's good and strong this morning. I sure need it." He turned, locked up and started over to Andy's, where he could see his host standing in the front door.

"Morning, Joe. Sleep well?" The sly grin had reappeared on his lined face. "Breakfast is almost ready." Joe nodded wearily, walked directly to the place prepared for him at the table, and plunked down heavily into the chair.

"I owe you some food, Andy," I have to do some shopping, so when we're in Wellsburg researching the riot I'll swing by the supermarket."

"Suit yerself," Andy responded. "But I keep plenty of peanut butter and jelly on hand here, in case we run out of the good stuff." He placed a dish of hot food in front of Joe and filled both their coffee cups. "I really wish I could go with you, but I just know it's not possible. I wouldn't be up to it."

"I know," Joe said consolingly. "I wish you could go, too." As he ate his friend chattered on about what they had discussed last night. Andy had slept on the matter and said that he had a few ideas to try out.

"Rain showers today," Andy commented. "It could be heavy at times. I hope you don't get trapped in the cave. Or go sliding off into a ravine."

"I should be fine. I have a poncho in my pack and my walking stick awaits me. Besides, I don't plan to stay long. I'd just like to find out some more about the old days. One thing I want to ask him about is the Coal and Iron Police."

"The 'yellow dogs?' Andy interjected. "I remember them well. Want me to tell you a thing or two about 'em?"

Joe put down his fork and the last slice of toast, and leaned forward attentively. "Shoot."

"They had all the power, Joe," he began. "And they knew how to use it. Back in them days they had a barracks down by where the fire hall is now. I have to admit those guys were impressive to look at." Andy sat back and disappeared into his thoughts. Joe could plainly see the range of negative emotions on the old man's face, capped by an angry frown. After a minute Andy seemed to remember that Joe was patiently sitting in front of him and he returned to his story.

"They were mostly big men, some were six-footers or better, all dressed up in fancy police uniforms and riding on big horses. The uniforms brought them more fear than respect. They preferred black horses, too. They had everything they needed, including their barracks building, a stable and even a blacksmith shop. Believe me, they weren't the most popular people in town. Do you know what they were all about?" While Joe had a notion, he shook his head 'no.'

"Well, the iron and mining companies decided they needed more protection than the sheriffs and state police could give them, so they got a law passed letting them hire their own police. And they did. The yellow dogs acted like spies against union organizing and they'd protect strikebreakers on their way to work. If we tried to have a meeting they could break it up and even arrest people and punish them. And meetings weren't the only things they broke up. They broke more than a few heads."

It didn't take Joe long to clearly visualize Andy's tale. He could imagine those big men on their prancing mounts – their horses probably fifteen or sixteen hands tall at the withers – the policemen in the middle of a picket line, smacking the head of anybody they could reach with their clubs. The miners wouldn't have had a chance. He pulled out his pencil stub and pocket note pad and jotted down a few lines as Andy chattered on.

"But the miners were pretty smart, too. They'd meet in real small groups; just chatting on a front porch like the discussion was about baseball or something. But underneath it all they were plotting how to organize next or even planning a picket. Oh, the yellow dogs could break up any gathering they wanted to, but real small groups didn't attract their attention much. The miners also fooled them with bigger meetings from time to time, like when they met in the store down in Penowa or in somebody's shed with darkened windows and only a small light lit. They just had to watch out for stool pigeons, but it didn't take long to tell who they were.

"I remember one feller who turned some men in and testified against them. From then on, whenever he walked downtown men would cross the street to avoid him. I don't know if he ever had a friend after that. I don't think so. Anyway, the company's police were so powerful that sometimes fear of them could turn neighbor against neighbor.

"I could tell you stories about how they'd come into a sick man's shack and drag him out of bed just so he would get in a day at the mine. They were even harder on a man who was hung over. The company didn't want production to slip. The yellow dogs were also the company's agents for any dirty work that needed done. I wouldn't have wanted their job, even with the regular pay that came with it. I think mebbe the job turned a regular man heartless. I wouldn't want that to happen to me. That's why I couldn't have been one, even if they offered me the job. The yellow dogs were done away with not long after I grew up and started mining.

"Well, the sun's getting way up there and I bent your ear long enough. Now you know if you want to get out of here at a reasonable time, don't get me started talking about the yellow dogs." Andy laughed mirthlessly. "You better be on your way. I see it's clouding up out there."

Joe nodded. "Thanks for the info on the Coal and Iron Police, Andy. I'll try to remember it all for my journal." Replacing the pad in his pocket, he arose and headed for the door. "Give me a shopping list next time, okay? I'll replenish your supplies when I get to the store."

On the way to the trailhead Joe pondered the yellow dogs. What kind of men joined that force? Were they sociopaths who loved the power and fear that came with it, or were they regular men who just wanted a job? Did the companies try to hire mean men or did they turn mean because of the power they were given? Were some of them sympathetic under their brutal exteriors? Most surely must have had mixed feelings as they went about their business of enforcement and intimidation. He hoped Nick would be able to fill in the gaps.

Before he even realized it, he pulled into his parking spot and headed up the trail. Two weeks without rain had left the ground nice and dry, so he enjoyed a fast and uneventful hike that allowed him time to think about his favorite subjects. By nine o'clock he found himself standing outside the cave entrance, under a darkening sky. "Nick?" he inquired.

"Come on in," Nick replied. Joe squatted down and crawled inside on his hands and knees. Nick sat there in obvious anticipation. "I can tell you have something on your mind. So, what is it?"

Joe sat back in his accustomed place. "What can you tell me about the Coal and Iron Police?"

Nick sat as still as stone, as though he had not expected this question. "You heard about them, did you?" he finally responded. "Well, I can tell you about them. Better yet… Would you mind closing your eyes?"

"If I close them I could go to sleep," Joe replied. "I'm really tired today. Dog-tired."

"I doubt that you will, Joe. Just close them. I want to try something." Joe did as directed. He sat there for perhaps five minutes with his eyes closed and his breathing becoming more regular, slower, deeper – a pre-slumber. And then, in his mind's eye, he saw Nick coming into focus.

***

It was an overcast day. Nick stood beside a dusty street in front of a general store, bemusedly looking at him before he turned and began to walk. Joe found himself following. They passed several businesses and a doctor's office with a coal company truck parked outside. A horse-drawn wagon was tied-up outside a general store. Other people were walking along, too, but not with Nick. Most seemed to be going in roughly the same direction, but purposefully not as a group.

"We're going to look at the barracks," Joe could feel Nick tell him. They continued down the road, seeing swirls of reddog dust and coal powder kicked up by people trudging along, and by a passing horse cart and an old jalopy car. Near a newer mansion house they turned left at a corner and started down a small grade toward a large whitewashed building with a stable attached. They stopped about seventy or eighty feet away, across the dirt access lane. "This is the barracks," Nick told him. It was the most impressive building he had seen so far. Behind the building there was a paddock, where three black horses grazed on the little grass remaining within the dirt enclosure. Just then he saw men in black uniforms walk their mounts outside the stable, swing up onto their saddles, and begin to ride at a trot past Joe and Nick. One man gave Nick a strange look but didn't react to Joe at all. The other nodded slightly to Nick.

"This is where the yellow dogs are housed for the mines in the Avella area," Nick explained. "Their blacksmith shop is right over there." Joe noticed a low building near the creek bank, with a large open doorway. He could see smoke and steam coming out of the open doorway as the smithy worked at his forge, clanking a piece of hot iron with his hammer as he turned it over and over. Several men lounged by the smithy's shop. Suddenly a large man in a police uniform walking directly toward them caught his attention. Nick nodded at the man and said, "Just looking."

"Well, don't look here," the man growled threateningly. Nick turned and began to walk hastily up the hill, with Joe in tow.

Then Joe could feel something change. Nick and he had walked out the main road toward a small mining patch to the east. They now stood expectantly across from a miner's shack, one of a long row of drab and dreary-looking shanties. With peeling paint, it had one door and a window and appeared to have only one room, or at the most two. The bare boards that formed its shell didn't completely meet, leaving substantial cracks between them. Joe doubted that the shacks had been provided with interior walls, because he could see some sort of material stuffed in the cracks in an obvious attempt to keep the chilling winds and rain from blowing through. Nick told him, as though he read Joe's thoughts, that some of the larger houses actually had plastered walls within.

Nick appeared to be waiting patiently, so Joe waited, too, while still looking up and down the monotonous row. He turned as two yellow dogs rode up on their horses and dismounted in front of the shanty. They walked directly into the house without knocking. Immediately the two observers heard a commotion and shouting going on inside.

"But I'm sick!" He heard a man protesting. "I can't work today!" The man's wife was screaming and pleading as they all came outside, but the police ignored her as though she were a part of the furniture or a yapping family dog

"Here! Put your clothes on! Woman, make him a lunch and fill that water bucket." The man, wheezing, sat on the front stoop and pulled his work pants on over his long john underwear. He then laced up his work boots. As he finished getting dressed, his sobbing wife handed him his lunch bucket and water pail. He staggered to his feet and, with a halting gait, turned onto the road and trudged off toward the mine. The men mounted their horses and followed him. His sobbing wife watched them go, still wringing her hands.

The sky darkening even more, he followed Nick a few hundred feet down the road. After a few more minutes, Joe heard the sound of hoof beats. He looked up and saw two more police pull up to a stop in front of another company shanty. With only a passing glance at Nick, whom they obviously didn't consider a threat, they dismounted.

"Damn union sympathizers," one said angrily to the other. They both walked inside, with the angry officer leading. A few people, including two women and three small barefoot children, came out of nearby houses to watch. Joe realized that what they were about to witness was not unusual to the bystanders. The women stood in front of their own front doors, far enough away to stay out of trouble. They wore blank expressions on their haggard-looking faces. The small children took shelter behind their mothers' skirts.

Presently, one officer came to the front door and threw a chair into the front yard, near the road. Mumbling, he walked back inside. The other officer came to the door and tossed a few articles of clothing into a pile near the chair. Within minutes, all the meager possessions from the shanty were scattered next to the street. "That'll teach him to be a union man!" said one officer scornfully.

The other laughed as he firmly closed the door to the small shack and heard it latch. "He better not try to go back into this house. He don't live here anymore." The first officer placed his boot into his stirrup and swung athletically up into the saddle. The other did likewise, and with a loud guffaw they both rode away, not bothering to acknowledge the onlookers. It was all in a day's work, Joe realized.

"Just wait," said Nick. They stood there a while longer until they saw a group of miners coming down the street, covered in black dust and talking in low tones. The men stopped when they saw the mess outside the shanty. Finally, one man stepped forward and began to gather his possessions. "We are sorry, Ernie," another miner said in consolation. Three men helped him to recover his things from the dirt. As a light rain began to spatter up the dust, they walked down the street carrying everything the man owned.

"He may stay with another man for a few days, but too long could be dangerous for both. He's a marked man now. He will no longer work in the Donahoo mine, but he could try to find work in one of the Avella mines. Or he will probably just move on to another place."

"Follow me," Nick said. They walked the railroad tracks through a drizzling rain, back to Avella where they regained the road and crossed the wooden bridge that spanned the rail line. As they continued up the road Nick told him: "I knew a man named Attengo, a family man and a good, hard worker. A union organizer. There he is now." Joe could see Attengo wearily plodding home from his shift in the P and W Mine. Even caked with the ubiquitous black dust, his lined face still displayed the smile of a man with a clear conscience, looking forward to supper with his wife and kids. Joe wondered if Attengo and Nick were friends. The man's steps, while obviously spent of much of the energy that his legs had held only that morning, were still firm and purposeful. He stopped with his lunch bucket dangling from one hand as he attempted to light a stogie with the other. Joe liked what he saw in Mr. Attengo.

"You say you knew him?" Joe asked.

"Yes, I knew him. I worked in the P and W mine, too." Suddenly a car careened around a curve several hundred feet behind the walking figure, throwing a choking cloud of dust up to mix with the drizzling rain. It sped down the road, seemingly out of control, passing several other miners who scrambled for their lives. Mr. Attengo heard it coming far too late to escape his fate. As he tried to jump out of the way, the car hit him directly in his back, knocking his crooked body like a rag doll over the roadside embankment. The driver screeched to a stop a hundred feet or more down the road. After sitting there for a minute or two, he approached the body. Inebriated, he made a clumsy show of remorse at what he had done, as other miners gathered around. Somebody picked up a work boot from the dirt and placed it next to Mr. Attengo. His lunch bucket was nowhere to be seen. While he still lived, it was pretty clear to all that he could not recover.

"The driver was a mine guard. He was never punished," Nick reported to Joe as they turned and walked away. "People who saw it happen said it was no accident."

"I've seen enough," Joe responded. Far too much, he thought.

In the cave, Joe woke up and lay still for several minutes, staring transfixed into the darkness. He didn't bother to ask Nick the obvious question about this unique experience. But yet he wondered: What *had* he just experienced? Had he really seen the actual death of a man as it happened, for example, or was it instead the shadow of what had taken place? Lately very little surprised him, so he knew instinctively the truth of what he had just seen. What he had just witnessed was no auto accident.

He finally noticed the steady drumming of a heavy rain on the rocks of the outcropping. A quick look through the opening told him that the entire sky had opened up. What would ordinarily be a beautiful walk back to his car now held the promise of a nasty hiking experience. Joe pulled on his rain gear and bade Nick farewell.

Joe realized morosely that the downhill trek to the car was as muddy and slippery as he had feared. But the steady downpour fit his mood. As he trudged along he sullenly reflected that that the poncho might as well be dry in its plastic pouch for all the good it did him this day.

CHAPTER THIRTY

The next morning the radio confirmed the forecast for frequent showers and a few thunderstorms, good for the gardens but not very promising for a pleasant stroll in the woods. Joe had laundered his garb from the day before and hung it on a clothesline in his basement. "Well, time for Plan B," he said to his loyal audience of one, Joe Bailey.

After a short visit to Andy's Diner to chat with his astonished friend about his adventures with Nick in the 1920's, he arose from his chair. "Funny thing, Andy. Nick asked me once before if we had time machines, after I said something about them. Apparently, he doesn't need one to show a friend around. I doubt that I will ever know how he created that vision, or if it was more than a vision."

After venturing out into a light rain, Joe glanced back. Andy, standing in his backlit doorway, was still shaking his head in amazement.

The trip to the library was much more pleasant by car than it would have been were he to "walk everywhere" on this chilly and wet June day. He soon pulled into the community center parking lot and parked in front of the building, again glancing admiringly at the coal car. Inside he found Nan, who introduced him to the library director, Carol.

"I wonder… could you could help me? I guess I'm stumped." That piqued their interest: a man who asked for information right away for once. It was like a man voluntarily asking for directions during a car trip. He could see it in their eyes. "I'm trying to track down whatever became of two people from the early 1900's. Their names were," he pulled out his notepad and scrutinized the fading pencil markings on the still-moist paper, "Carmella Antonini and Angelo Ballino."

"Wait!" interrupted Nan. "Does this have anything to do with the ghosts you've been talking to?" She explained the rumors to Carol, who had been away visiting her mother for several days and thus was out of the usual gossip grapevine. Joe sighed and heavily dropped into a chair.

"First, I don't talk to ghosts, Nan. At least I never have before. And now there's only the one, the spirit of a long-dead coal miner. It's the reason I asked you all that stuff about the Cliftonville Mine riot. If I tell you the story would you give me the benefit of the doubt, at least until you've heard it all?" They both nodded, intrigued.

"Eighty-year old gossip is the best, Joe," Carol laughed. "I hope it's good and juicy!" They settled in to listen.

Joe began: "While hiking a wooded trail down toward Penowa I stopped in a shallow cave for a break and to eat my lunch..." Joe continued, relating his barely plausible tale. But he had no intention of telling of Jessie's involvement.

"When I began inquiring up here about the mine riot, I did it because he'd told me all about it. Since then he shared many things with me about what life was like during that period. Now I think I can put his mind at ease if I can learn whatever became of his intended bride, Carmella, and his good friend, Angelo. He really hopes that they both went on to have good lives." Nan and Carol nodded sympathetically, but still with a healthy helping of skepticism.

"What can you tell us about them?" Nan asked. "We have a person on staff, Ben Jenkins, who specializes in genealogy. In fact he should be here any time now."

"Well, I know that Carmella was born in 1905 to Camillo and Olga Antonini, right here in Avella. Apparently Camillo came over as one of the early Italian immigrants who worked on a gang building the railroad and its tunnels. He brought his wife over after a couple years, and then Carmella was born. He later worked as a miner. Nick says Carmella was 16 when he died in 1922. They also had a younger daughter, named Olga like her mother. She would have been about 14. Camillo was widowed sometime before 1922, so the entire family consisted of him, Carmella, and her sister Olga.

"As for Angelo, he was Nick's best friend in America, practically a big brother. He says that he and this Italian man enjoyed a special closeness. Since Angelo was twenty-eight in 1922, he would have been born about 1894, in a small village in the Tyrol. He took part in the riot, too. He and some other miners practically carried Nick into Pennsylvania before he died from his gunshot wound. Then they buried him, which is why he's in – as he describes it – the 'fix' he's in right now, unable to move on to his reward. What he wants most is to be assured that his special friends went on to have good lives."

The two women glanced at each other as he continued. "Nick also told me that Angelo had a young wife in his home village, named Maria. He hopes Angelo was able to bring her over. He tells me that many men died in mining accidents here without ever seeing their wives again.

"He's especially concerned because his smeared blood probably marked Angelo for arrest. Angelo could have suffered imprisonment or worse. The other miners who helped carry him would have been marked, too, but he didn't know who they were. They'd just pitched in to help when they saw Angelo struggling."

"Wow," said Nan. "Let's get this information written down for Ben. He has some census records that can help determine who lived here in 1920, 1930, 1940, and so forth. He also recorded the information from most of the tombstones, headstones and burial records in the nearby cemeteries. While it's remotely possible that Carmella could be alive now – if so, probably in a nursing home – there is no realistic chance that Angelo is alive, nor his wife because they were older. So we would be looking for death records, probably for all three. Also, we can look up surnames and descendants. And, I will make a poster for the bulletin board asking for information on possible ancestors with their names."

"If either one moved away it would make the job harder," said Carol. "One thing we can also do is check the listing of miners sentenced to prison at Moundsville, in case he was sent there." She added, "I can't say I believe your story, Joe. But we will follow up on the genealogical, historical and public records for you. Ben is a whiz at that research. In fact, here he is now."

A lean, graying man had just walked in, carrying a heavily loaded satchel. He hauled it up onto the desk.

"Ben" said Carol. "Perfect timing. This is Joe Bailey. He needs to have some research done on people who were alive in the early 1900's in the Avella area."

The two men shook hands. "I'll be happy to do whatever I can to help, Mr. Bailey. Do we have any starting information?"

"Please call me Joe. The ladies and I are already on a first-name basis," Joe responded. "And all the information I know is now written down on this legal pad." Ben glanced at the information scrawled on the lined yellow paper and frowned.

"It's a bit sketchy but I've worked with less. I'll try to not let you down. By the way, does this have anything to do with you talking to ghosts?" Joe moaned in frustration.

"I'll let the ladies fill you in, Ben. They've already gotten an earful. I better head over to Wellsburg to do some grocery shopping, and get to the Brooke County Library before it closes. They might have some historical data on the riot and the trials."

On his way to West Virginia, Joe spent the next twenty minutes pondering what had just happened back there. The library staff members were very helpful and sympathetic, although unconvinced regarding his story. But what really troubled him was that two of them had already heard about him and his ghost. The word apparently spreads very quickly, like verbal wildfire. That could be a very bad thing for him – and especially for Jessie.

At Wellsburg he stopped at the library, an attractive white-trimmed brick Colonial building next to the wide Ohio River, still flowing high and fast from the heavy runoff of the recent rains. He inquired about Cliftonville, especially any newspaper clippings from the time of the riot and the trials that followed. The immediately available information pretty much mirrored what he learned at Avella, so they offered to search deeper within their local history collection and to call the State Archives in Charleston. The helpful staff members said that they could have more data for him before the end of the week.

Finally, Joe found the supermarket and filled his own shopping list and Andy's list as well. "Funny," he remarked under his breath. "They sell beer and wine here, right in the supermarket." As an afterthought, he bought two six-packs to replace Andy's beer.

Joe drove home in a drizzling rain under an ominous sky. He pondered that his own sky did indeed look dark, with storm clouds hanging low and heavy on the horizon. Unless he was mistaken his storm clouds were advancing far too quickly.

CHAPTER THIRTY-ONE

Saturday dawned bright and cloudless. The warmth of the post-rain morning held the promise of a hot and humid day ahead. Joe awakened with the birds, unable to sleep any longer. But with both Les and Jessie scheduled to meet him at seven o'clock he had little time to dawdle. He rolled out of bed and began to pack his gear. "Now I have three people buying into my fantasy," he muttered. "And two of them are walking down railroad tracks with me today. Am I that persuasive or are they just trying to keep me out of trouble?"

The signs were that this would be a strange hiking day indeed. The railroad walk of perhaps six miles would encompass three long tunnels and several trestles over the winding Cross Creek. Then they would walk through the now-wilderness site of the old Clifton Mine. Finally, of course, the walk back would be just as daunting, six miles again of rough walking on unevenly spaced railroad ties and oversized roadbed stones. All three hikers would probably be exhausted at the end of a long day.

Joe could hear a car pulling into his parking space, and then Jessie's familiar knock on his front door. "Morning, sunshine!" she brightly exclaimed, grinning at his tired appearance. "I hope you're ready to go on our little stroll down the tracks." At that moment Joe's energy resources were at their lowest ebb, and frankly he had little inclination to face the day's hike. If he had planned to go it alone, he would probably have fallen back into bed.

"Of course," he lied. "I hope it won't be too much for your tired, educator's legs."

"I think your old, sedentary real estate legs will give out first," she parried. Then she finished with her thrust. "And I do mean old!"

"Now wait a minute!" He protested. "I'm only seven or eight years older than you, depending on birthdays, and I'm in pretty good shape, too." Then he caught her teasing expression. "But seriously, Jessie, I haven't walked railroad tracks more than a few hundred yards in years. I hope nobody turns an ankle."

Just then Les's truck pulled into Joe's yard. They could hear too many footsteps crunching in the gravel for it to be only him. Jessie threw the door open for Les and for Leo, a tall, rangy fire lieutenant. "I hope you don't mind," Les offered. I mentioned our plans to Leo, who of course wanted in on the hike. He's in better shape than any of us, being an iron worker and an avid hunter." Joe remembered Leo from work parties at the fire hall. He had to admit that Leo was not only fit, but he might even be strong enough to carry Joe home if necessary. Well, maybe not.

"We'll see about that," said Jessie. "This won't be your usual walk in the woods." Leo shrugged. One thing Joe knew well was that Leo didn't waste words.

"My boys wanted to come, too," Les continued. "But I told them that it would probably be too hot and grueling today. We can let them come on another hike sometime. If that's okay with you, of course." Feeling things spiraling further out of control, Joe could only nod his acquiescence.

"Thanks, Joe. They're becoming big pests about it. In fact, they're talking about their scout troop taking a hike someday, hoping to see your ghosts." He paused. "Isn't it getting a little late? I'd hate to have to pass on Andy's coffee."

Joe and Jessie picked up their packs and hats and they all headed out the door and over to Andy's lighted kitchen. "I put on more coffee when I saw our morning breakfast club had got bigger," Andy said as he swung open the door. He poured the coffee into huge mugs and handed them to the grateful hikers. "Eggs are ready, too. And don't worry, Leo. We have plenty."

"Thanks, Andy," Joe said, between mouthfuls. "I know our group is growing…"

"Don't you worry none. I'm just happy I can help. You know how much I'd like to go with you, but you stopping by here is the next best thing. You're keeping me involved, and at my age that's about the best thing that could happen. This is a lot better than hanging out at the senior citizens center." Andy picked up their wiped-clean plates. "If I were two years younger you couldn't stop me!" They left him, still laughing.

The area around the old Avella railroad station provided plenty of parking, so they could head out immediately without any extra walking to get to the tracks. "Hey, Les," Joe observed. "The town looks pretty festive this morning. Is it for Memorial Day?"

"We decorate the main street and the war memorial with flags the entire week before Memorial Day. You just haven't been down here. You should take the day off and check it out. We have a small parade, a ceremony with the high school band and choir and the American Legion and then lunch for everybody at the fire hall."

Joe pondered the possibilities. "Maybe the bystanders will be more interested in the guy who thinks he talks to ghosts than in the speakers, Les. Maybe I better stay away."

"Maybe," Les responded. "Maybe." Without another word they set off walking westward toward the first trestle, the first railroad crossing and the first tunnel.

"This isn't so bad," offered Jessie. "Just try to walk on the railroad crossties. They are pretty evenly spaced.

"Yeah, right. They might be spaced okay for you, but not for me," muttered Les. They're too close for me. It's terrible."

"Yeah, I agree," Joe chimed in. "You can walk on each crosstie, but then your steps are too close together. It's kinda like the 'baby steps' when we played 'Simon Says' as kids. You want to take 'giant steps' but skipping every other tie makes your steps too long. Not to mention the ties are too narrow for a man's shoes. There's no comfortable walking pace, not to mention the roadbed stones that roll under your feet." They walked in silence.

"I have to agree," Jessie finally admitted. "The crossties aren't spaced very well, and now they are varying in their spacing." She trudged on.

"Nick said they took nearby roads whenever they could, or they walked along paths. But when they came to a tunnel they had to walk through it, with the exception of the ones who walked the creek bottom during the night. Hey, let's try the path that follows the roadbed. It's full of stones, but it has to be better than up here on the ties."

They tried the walkway and, while it made walking better, it could hardly be described as comfortable because it was made from stones, too. "There's a trestle coming up," Joe informed them. "We'll have to walk the railroad tracks and hope a train doesn't come while we're on it. There's nothing underneath but wide open air and a creek fifty feet below." With those foreboding words they began to walk across the trestle, listening carefully for any approaching train. Finally, they were across.

"How's your balance, guys?" Jessie asked the men. "The rail is smooth enough to walk on and it isn't even hot, yet." She stepped up onto the rail and began a balancing act, compensating for her unsteadiness by extending her arms. Joe, Les and Leo looked at each other, shrugged and did the same. Joe immediately slipped and fell off, scraping his anklebone on the rail as his foot fell hard to the railroad tie. "Ouch!" he complained. "That hurt."

"Here. Give me your hand and don't be a baby. Didn't you do this when you were a kid?" She reached her hand over to him and he grudgingly took it. After a few missteps on his part, her natural sense of balance seemed to infuse him, too. They walked along more or less steadily, holding hands across the space between the rails. Joe smiled to himself.

"I refuse to hold your hand, Les," Leo stated firmly. "I'll take my chances on my own."

"No offense, but I don't need you anyway. We used to walk the railroad all the time when we went fishing as kids. I'm an old hand at this. Hey, that's the Craighead Tunnel coming up. We must have walked close to two miles." They dismounted the rails as they approached the tunnel, and then walked the ties into its depths. "This isn't so bad," Leo decided. While the roadbed was easier on their feet in the tunnel than outside, Joe had to wonder if it was as smooth during the 1922 march. Or, being maintained mainly by manual labor instead of machines, was it instead a mish-mash of various sized rocks strewn all along the crossties with iron spikes sticking out all around?

"It might be a bit dark in here, but at least it's cooler than outside, and less humid" Joe remarked. "This might be a good time to rest and have some water. We can refill our bottles later with water run through my filter." They all sat down in unison on the rails. "You say you walked the railroads to go fishing, Les?"

"It seemed we went fishing about every Saturday," he responded. "And most days during the summer. Some fishing holes were best reached along Route 50, and some by railroad. But it had to be one or the other. Walking cross-country, slipping and falling and being scratched by thorns took some of the magic out of fishing.'

"So, boys, why don't we push on?" Jessie suggested.

Begrudgingly they agreed and joined her in standing up. Soon they exited the western portal into sunlight so bright it hurt their eyes. Joe squinted his eyelids hard and pulled his ball cap down over his face. After a while their eyes adjusted and the brightness became tolerable. "I think it will be a hot one this afternoon," she concluded. They continued walking westward toward the Buxton Tunnel, the second of three.

While their legs and feet silently protested the rough walking surface, they realized that the walking had actually gotten a bit easier as they got used to the adjustment. Soon they came to the Buxton Tunnel and took another break inside, consuming more water and some fruit and grain trail mix.

"I think we better let our eyes adjust near the tunnel exit this time," Leo offered. "It won't be as brutal when we hit the sunshine." Near the western portal, they paused to discuss what the miners must have been thinking as they traversed each tunnel. Did they wonder if each successive one took them a little closer to a better future, or towards death at the hands of gun-wielding deputies? Or to imprisonment and never seeing their loved ones in the old country again? Were they merely marching along with their comrades on a great adventure, or did they instead suffer grave internal conflicts over the possible consequences of their actions?

"I think most of them must have been terribly conflicted," Jessie concluded. "But I can also see you three taking part in such a march if the situation were desperate enough." Internally, each man had to agree with her. Given the right motivation they would surely do the same. "Well, back to reality. Ready to walk?"

Exiting the second tunnel they marched onward with a renewed purpose, and with the satisfaction that came from conquering a walk that very few people even attempted anymore.

Checking his topographic maps, Joe explained, "That place off to the right is Jefferson and the one way to its left is Penowa. According to Nick and the records, the marchers all stopped at Penowa and gathered more miners from the Seldom Seen, Waverly and Penobscot mines. They held a final rally at the old Penowa ball field before they made the trek through and around the State Line Tunnel. He told me that the mood of the Penowa rally grew much angrier than the meeting in Avella. When they finally left Penowa, they were bound and determined to close down the Clifton Mine, 'by hook or by crook' as he put it."

"I'd say by at least one of those, but I'm not sure which," observed Les. "But I believe that if I were alive then, I'd have gone with them."

"I've been thinking," Joe declared, quietly interrupting. "I'd like to do a day-night walk; a kind of lone pilgrimage. You know, to connect with Nick's walk on a solo basis. I thought I'd stop at the Penowa ball field like they did, rest, and then go through the tunnel…" He paused, eyeing the two men who were edging away as the lady advanced on him.

She moved forward, all right, right to his chest, and glared into his eyes.

"What do you mean by solo, Mr. Bailey? A lone pilgrimage, you say?" She asked piercingly. You were perhaps going to leave me – I mean us – out of your little adventure?" She challenged him with her most outraged look.

"Well, I thought it was a kinda crazy idea, and you wouldn't want… Well, maybe you could tag along…" he back-pedaled, stammering. Satisfied, she stepped back and rewarded him with a winning smile.

"Do you mean return after midnight?" Les asked, after a pause to make sure the sparks had all died down. "Well, it's a nutty idea if you think about it. I mean, who would actually do something like that? Not many people I know. Except maybe for us, I mean."

"If we go through the tunnel around midnight, we'd be starting back in the middle of the night," Leo offered. "But we could have somebody waiting to pick us up so we can ride back."

Joe added: "We could try to match their schedule as exactly as we can, including traversing the tunnel around midnight. It would be a way of honoring them and really getting a feel for what they went through. I mean, they sure went out of their way to help the local miners, so why can't we recall what they did by doing the same thing?"

"I hope without the battle in the morning," Leo remarked dryly.

"We can leave that part out," Joe agreed. The others laughed.

They doggedly walked onward until they came to a grade crossing. Beyond it they could see the ominous opening of the trip's last "hole in the hill." They paused there for nearly ten minutes, lost in their own thoughts. Finally they set out again and approached the tunnel, seeing the legend on the concrete outer wall: "1904". They entered its gaping maw and began the trek of about 1500 feet toward the western end. "According to Nick, the night sky was clear and a nearly full moon shone outside. But you can imagine how little that moonlight benefited the miners traversing the tunnel. Once inside they must have walked in total darkness."

Joe paused, listening. "There's the water that he talked about, dripping from the ceiling!" The water began to drip down on their heads and shoulders. "Nick told me that you couldn't escape the water drops, so you might as well walk right through them. He also mentioned a spring up ahead…"

"There it is," exclaimed Les, shining his flashlight ahead. "It's on the left side of the tunnel." As they approached the steady stream of water gushing from a hole, Joe suggested that they drink their fill and use his filter to top up their water bottles. They gladly complied. "There will likely be a spring on the mine property, but we can't be too careful."

As they exited the western tunnel mouth a thin blanket of clouds shielded their eyes from the harshest rays of the sun. There it awaited them just ahead – West Virginia. They walked onward to a railroad grade crossing where Joe checked his topo maps. "That should be the remains of Cliftonville to the left and that's Virginville to the right. That would jibe with what Nick said. I can see where Nick's group would have infiltrated near the stream down there to the left and then crossed it in a shallows like that one. That area between the creek and the railroad would be where the displaced mine families set up their tent camp."

Jessie interjected: "I saw in the library materials that the law went through the tent camp after the battle, ripping everything down and driving the occupants out. We talk about homeless people today. Those people were not only homeless but most were homeless immigrants in a strange land." Jessie's eyes misted over at the thought.

Joe checked his watch. "It's getting late. How about a short walk through New Camp to get the lay of the land? But be sure to watch out for copperheads!" He picked up a stout stick to help him walk but also to fend off snakes. They continued down the tracks and crossed one more trestle. To the left they found a path leading into the woods, following the contour of the hillside. Sure enough they found a spring by the side of the path. "The catch basin looks as clean as it must have looked eighty and more years ago," Joe said in wonder. "Look at the clarity of the water." In celebration they each consumed most of the contents of their water bottles, knowing they could filter more for the trip home.

Following the path, they noticed that the lower side had apparently been provided with supports to keep it from sliding over the hillside. Somebody had long ago installed timbers and logs that were held in place by pieces of iron. Farther along they found the first group of foundation stones that roughly outlined what would have been cottage-size buildings. More stone outlines then followed in even rows. Jessie photographed first one arrangement, and then another and another. Passing more rows, they came upon a single cottage-style house in the middle of a clearing, obviously still habitable but not occupied on this day. It appeared to be a vacation home, preserved just to keep the memory of New Camp alive. Gesturing to the right, Joe remarked, "the mine portal should have been up there." He began to start clambering uphill but Jessie grabbed him by the shirt and yanked him backward in a startling display of strength. All three of the men gasped.

"Don't piss her off, Joe. I think she could take you," Leo exclaimed..

"It's getting late," she said, ignoring the remark. "I think even if we hurry, the last part of our return trip could be in darkness." The men reluctantly agreed to leave further exploration for another day. After filling their bottles from the spring, they began their homeward trek. Sure enough they didn't reach Avella until nearly nine o'clock p.m., needing flashlights for the last half-mile. "My feet and legs hurt," Joe admitted. "And my knees, too."

"Mine, too," the others chimed in.

"Tomorrow will truly be a day of rest," Jessie opined. Nobody disagreed.

CHAPTER THIRTY-TWO

"Julie? This is Brenda," Mrs. Jones said breathlessly into the phone, to her friend and frequent ally Julie Granger. "I know it's early, but this is important. We just can't let this ghost-talking business drop. Even after we complained to the principal he didn't do a thing about it. Doesn't the opinion of the parents matter anymore?"

"I agree completely. But what can we do? Go to the superintendent? She'll only support her staff like she always does."

"I thought of that, too. What we need is a nice, public stink, so the school board is where we have to go next. But first we have to win some people over to show support. And then we have to register on the agenda so we can be heard. If we each take our five minutes to talk, we can definitely raise some eyebrows. And maybe even push Principal Landers closer to resigning. And that little witch, Jessie Randall, has to go! How dare she invite somebody like that Bailey person to walk with our young children? She didn't even apologize for it."

"I know what you mean," Mrs. Granger affirmed. "You remember when she chastised my Lisa for talking back to her? Lisa was only exercising her right to free speech. When she didn't apologize for that, either, I told her I would have her job. Now looks like the perfect opportunity. How do we go about it?"

"Well, we can complain that Joseph Bailey isn't a fit person to be with our children because he's mentally unstable," responded Mrs. Jones. "And Jessica Randall should have known about it before she invited him on the outing. I think we have her there."

"That's perfect!" Mrs. Granger agreed. "This is the crack in their armor. The principal is in charge, so we can finally force him out. And maybe that little witch, too. And who knows? We might even come closer to getting the superintendent. Not to mention if we can have a few friends elected in November, the school board majority will swing our way. We can eventually get rid of all the so-called 'educators' who don't toe the line."

"The first thing tomorrow morning I'll register to speak at the next board meeting," offered Mrs. Jones. "I'll talk on… let me see.

'Why are unstable persons allowed on field trips with our young children?' I'll then ask why teachers continue to be employed here when they make such bad decisions."

"Good! I'll follow up with an angry outburst because of their incompetence and demand their resignations. Our supporters will shout their agreement."

"We'll show them we're a force to be reckoned with. Now let's make some phone calls. We need lots of loud and angry support. And, we can talk to even more people on Memorial Day."

***

Back at old Albert's house, Joe massaged his calves thoroughly with liniment. He had not had such a wearying hike in a long time, except for some very steep slopes. His feet and calves had borne the brunt of the unyielding and uneven walking surface.

Suddenly, the crunch of gravel heralded somebody pulling up in front of the house. It had to be Jessie, he realized, even before confirming it with a peek out the window. He put down the liniment and pulled his pants on.

Just as she reached out to knock on his front door, he opened it and quickly pulled her in, giving her a big hug. "I'm so glad you came!" he exclaimed, looking fondly into her eyes.

"I'm glad, too," she replied, brushing her lips across his cheek. "I've rested long enough. While a hot shower did my legs a world of good, I'm in no shape to walk anywhere today. So, I think a nice Sunday drive would be welcome. Are you up to it, old guy?"

The shower image lingered in his mind a moment longer, but he finally answered. "Well, it so happens, young lady that I already planned to check on my regular home in Collier today. Would you like to join me in a jaunt in my old Caddy? We should be back in about four hours or so."

Before Joe knew it, she had planted herself in the driver's side of the Cadillac, holding her hand out for the keys. He dutifully handed them to her and slid onto the passenger seat. "You look nice in those slacks and top," he offered lamely.

"Where to?" she asked as she started the car and shifted it into gear, pulling out onto Campbell Drive. "Route 50?"

"Yes. Up Route 50." Joe sat back to enjoy the ride – and the view.

After a half-hour, Joe directed Jessie onto I-79 North, then finally onto an exit into Collier Township. As they headed up the dirt road to Joe's house, she exclaimed, "It *is* a schoolhouse, Joe Bailey. You weren't kidding!" He could see the delight dancing in her eyes. Until just that moment he hadn't seen the irony in taking a female teacher to his home in a converted schoolhouse. The irony was rather delicious, he realized.

Alighting from the car, they approached the house and Joe slipped temporarily into his former cop mode, checking the entire exterior carefully for any sign of intrusion. There were none, so they went inside where he disabled the security system. Jessie inhaled audibly at the renovations he had made.

"I always enter my house using a trick I learned on the job," Joe explained as he surveyed the panorama. "Both jobs, actually. I walk in as though I have never seen the place before and try to see it with a fresh eye. Kind of how a cop surveys a crime scene or as a real estate agent would see the house when previewing it. Every time, something different strikes me about my little home. The great room has the original hardwood floors, only recently sanded and refinished. The ceilings were removed to expose the second-floor storage area rafters, giving me those cathedral ceilings you see. It cost me some attic space, but I decided I could live with that. I live alone and don't need much storage.

"The school was originally a large two-room type from the 1890s that had been chopped into five rooms by previous owners," he went on. He followed Jessie as she walked around, absorbing the effect. "The wood-sided frame structure had been improved by the school board over the years, and by the couple that owned it before me. Now, the exterior is bricked, as you saw, with old bricks from a demolished brewery. The fireplace is Belgian stone that had been pulled up and hauled away from some of Pittsburgh's streets when they re-paved."

"That's huge!" said Jessie, admiring the six-by-ten foot fireplace set into a wall of stone, with a firebox measuring an awesome three by four feet. The solid chestnut mantel would have been too much for most fireplaces, but it seemed to fit this fireplace just fine.

"The mantel was cut from a downed tree on my own lot," explained Joe. The hearth is of rough-cut fieldstone. It bears the sooty carbon smears I like so much. When I clean the stones I always leave some soot." They moved into the kitchen, which had only recently been finished.

"I can't take all the credit for the kitchen," he professed modestly. "The good folks who owned the house before me did a lot of the work in here. Of course, I couldn't leave well enough alone and had to change a few minor items like the counter tops. I also added the rack for hanging pots and pans around the light fixture."

Jessie stared upward at the vaulted ceiling with two skylights tucked away between the rafters. Lowering her gaze she looked around in a slow circle at the immense working area, with thirty feet of counter space and cabinetry. In the middle of the kitchen there stood an island with an uncluttered countertop.

"I make pizza there and – please don't laugh – chocolate chip cookies," he admitted, blushing. "Did you notice the cherry cabinets?" he asked, trying to take the focus off his fondness for baking. "If you want to go into the great room and get comfy on the couch, I can bring something to snack on." Still speechless, she just nodded and ambled into the great room.

When he joined her, carrying a tray with two glasses of beer and a bowl of mixed nuts and some chips, Jessie gazed up at him with wide eyes. "I just never expected anything like this, Joe. This is beyond belief."

"I just made it the way I like it is all," he replied, setting down the tray. "Would you excuse me for a minute? I have to call the local police. They keep an eye on the place for me while I'm gone." Joe called Collier Police Chief Adamson and informed him that he would be home for a few hours, but should be gone before nightfall.

"No, sorry, Frank. I just don't have time tonight to visit. I'm kind of busy." He looked over at Jessie. "Next time I come out we might get a poker game going, okay? Thanks, Frank."

He walked over to the massive sofa and settled in next to Jessie. "Cheers!" he said, as he held his beer glass out to clink it with hers.

"Cheers," she replied, as she clinked his glass with hers. "Can we make some cookies later?"

CHAPTER THIRTY-THREE

Joe slowly came awake into a bright, bird song-filled Memorial Day morning. As he lay in bed basking in the light spilling through his bedroom window he began to pick out the various calls. It occurred to him that this just might be the best part of his day – and the most neglected. The songs of his feathered friends penetrated his sleepiness and his heart as easily as the songs infiltrated the screens in the open windows. He never could sort them all out, and he frankly hoped he never would. His relationship with the frequent drop-ins to his feeders, and the visitors to the neighboring trees and berry bushes, had always been a refuge from his cares. Were the songs and calls to ever be fully predictable, they would lose some of their value as a diversion in his very strange world.

This morning one of his two favorite woodpeckers had returned, the big pileated woodpecker with its strangely high-pitched cheeping and the following "tokk-tokk-tokk-tokk" against the insect-inhabited dead tree. Joe lay there, enjoying the natural concert, although he missed the red-bellied woodpecker with its faster "thumming" sound.

The mournful, owl-like sounds of the doves from their pine tree perches were a comfort to him right now, although the way they seemed to be in bereavement over something – or somebody – usually brought back old anxieties.

He easily recognized the chattering of the robins, happy after the overnight rain shower, gorging on worms flushed to the surface of the ground. They seemed to be congregating in greater numbers today for their breakfast buffet. Baby robins in their nearby nests clamored for their breakfast, too, with their harried parents apparently only too happy to oblige.

A pair of blue jays noisily bossed other birds around the feeder, while feasting on his sunflower seeds. But the indiscernible songs of the array of finches at his thistle seed feeder didn't betray any alarm at the jays. What colors were there today? There would be goldfinches for sure, he knew. There were always goldfinches,

He realized with some perverse delight that he had lain in bed until nearly eight o'clock. He had promised to swing by Andy's before heading down to the war memorial, so he struggled out of bed. He showered, shaved, and dressed in non-hiking garb for once. A polo shirt and slacks comprised his uniform of the day. How long has it been, Joe wondered, since he wore 'real estate clothes' like a suit or sport jacket with tie? It seemed like forever, although only a few weeks had slid by. He stepped outside into the clean, sweet air ready for a new day.

"Joe!" he heard Andy call out, predictably. Unpredictably, he saw Andy dressed in his American Legion garb, with his hat tilted at a rakish angle. Old Andy seemed to be standing taller today, even as he retained his slightly bent posture.

"You aren't marching today, are you?" Joe asked, trying to conceal his concern.

"Nope, my marching days have been over for a few years. I'd like to do it, but instead I will be one of the old farts sitting by the memorial waiting for the parade to come to me. By the way, I have some coffee staying hot in the thermos on the patio table. Want some?" Joe nodded, amazed at this new side of at his old compatriot. While Andy poured, Joe admired his uniform. "I remember you said you joined up for World War Two, the second 'war to end all wars', as they called it. You fought in Italy, right?"

"Yep, I sure did, and they had us ready to ship out for the Pacific when old Harry dropped the big one on Japan, taking away the necessity. Believe you me, I didn't look forward to invading Japan. Chances were that I would not have made it back alive, along with a good number of my buddies." That bomb did us a favor, although it killed lots of innocent civilians.

As they drove downtown Joe and Andy saw the parade beginning to form at the base of Campbell Drive. The marchers parted willingly when they saw the grizzled old legionnaire being chauffeured to the memorial. Joe parked his car after letting Andy out near the chairs set up for him and his fellow "old farts".

Noticing Jessie standing near the old bank building with Les's wife, Nancy, and their two sons, Joe went over to greet them. "Mr. Bailey, will you let us meet your ghost someday?" Timmy asked, before his mother could shush him up.

"I don't mind, Nancy," he explained. "No, I doubt that you can meet him, Timmy, but who knows for sure?" He caught a cautioning look on Jessie's face. Glancing around, he saw some knowing looks on the faces of bystanders who had obviously been alerted by the high-pitched question and Joe's low answer. "Well," he thought to himself. "I guess it's begun." He returned Jessie's silent communication with an "I'll try to keep my head down so it won't get it shot off" look.

A high-pitched firehouse siren abruptly broke up the quiet that had fallen over their small group. "That signals the beginning of the parade," Jessie explained. While craning to see the first marchers appear at the other end of the main street, Joe happened to see somebody standing nearby.

Oh, no. A sense of foreboding settled over him like a black cloud. Mrs. Granger had button-holed some bystanders only thirty feet away, talking earnestly with a man and two women. They looked over at him and then averted their gazes. She moved away and started talking with another woman and a man. "Why do I feel like I'm in a fishbowl?" he whispered to Jessie.

"Me, too," she quietly told him. "Me, too. But at least we're in this together. Sharing any kind of bowl with you is okay with me, even your transparent fishbowl."

Nancy caught the meaning of their exchange. "I understand how you feel, or at least I think I do. Les told me all about it, and I've heard what those trouble-makers have been up to… are obviously still up to. But I think you'll come out of this okay. There are some people who support you, and most are neutral. Some people even say that whatever you do is none of their friggin' business. But the school board meeting will likely be the real test."

Nancy stopped talking as the parade came into view, with the American Legion and a boy scouts color guard carrying Old Glory and leading the way. The rest of the parade consisted of 'Sons of the American Legion', boy and girl scouts, firemen, and the high school marching band belting out a Sousa march. It was not a large parade at all, Joe realized, but the earnestness of it touched him. A low flyover by two C-130 transport airplanes interrupted Joe's brief patriotic trance, but also amplified the feeling as well. The people lining the main street fell in behind the parade and followed it to the little town square where the ceremonies would be held.

The Legionnaires and the other groups went to their places. The band sat in seats arranged concert-style, where they soon took up playing a patriotic medley. Joe noted with some relief, albeit temporary at best, that he was no longer the center of attention by bystanders. Everybody focused on the memorial, where the Legion's commander started the program. The boy scouts quickly raised the American flag and the 'POW/MIA' flag to the top of the mast, before slowly lowering them back down to half-staff. Everybody stood at attention and those in uniform saluted.

The program went on with the Pledge of Allegiance, prayers, citizenship awards, recitations by school students, and a speech by a guest speaker. Joe looked around periodically. Every now and then he caught somebody looking at him contemplatively and then averting their gaze. The saluting of the dead with the firing of seven rifles three times indicated that the service had wound to an end.

Finally a trumpeter from the high school band stepped proudly forward, brought his horn to his lips and played 'taps', with the very poignant catch in the melody. Joe's heart lurched, as it always did, to that sound, causing his hand to seek out and squeeze Jessie's. Hers understandingly squeezed his in return and she moved slightly closer to him. Off in the distance, the music notes were echoed hauntingly by another musician, causing chills to pervade Joe's very being and – he suspected – those of all present. The ceremony concluded, the commander invited everybody to the fire hall where a meal had been prepared.

"I don't think I'll go to eat," Joe said. "I'm becoming too much a focus of attention." Jessie, Nancy, and Les – who had just rejoined them from where he had stood with his fellow volunteer firefighters – all looked at him in surprise.

"Sure, you will, Joe. Most of the people there don't even know about you, and those who have heard probably couldn't pick you out of a crowd," Les asserted. "Anyway I see Andy walking over here now and he has never missed this meal!" They walked to the fire hall together. After a few minutes wait in the buffet line, they repaired to a table with chicken, rigatoni, bread, salad and dessert.

"Well, what did you think?" Nancy asked.

"It made me feel good. Really good," Joe answered honestly. "I think this kind of thing is America at its best. It gave me gooseflesh several times during the ceremony. It wasn't a huge parade with floats and majorettes and officials and princesses riding in convertibles. It was just a simple parade and ceremony that I think really tells a lot about the roots of America. It can be found right here, in towns like this one." Joe hadn't realized that his voice was rising a little and that some others nearby had heard what he said.

"That's right, young man," a woman of about sixty said, while others nodded their agreement.

"I don't care if you do talk to ghosts, your heart's in the right place," a man remarked. Blushing, Joe nodded his thanks.

"You bet!" responded Andy. "And he's a good feller, too."

While Joe's group and some others nearby continued their animated conversations, Andy and Les's sons went back for second helpings. Finally, as the crowd thinned out, they got up to leave. Les poked Joe's arm unobtrusively and quietly remarked, "don't look now, but your two dedicated admirers are working the crowd over there." The others looked to where he had indicated. Jones and Granger were still at it.

CHAPTER THIRTY-FOUR

Joe awoke well rested again, savoring the day that lay in wait. He had already decided that he would ask Nick for a special favor, in Nick's own heyday as it were. Even better, because Jessie still had two days of school left, he could spend some quality time with Nick without her also tagging along. While Joe loved Jessie's company and missed her terribly when she was away, he also appreciated his man-to-man (or spirit-to-man?) time with Nick. Men sometimes need masculine time with their buddies – tangible or not – and Nick was fast becoming his buddy.

He dressed quickly, determined to visit Nick as soon as possible and spend a full day with him. After throwing a few items into his daypack, he set off to visit 'Nick's Place."

But first he had to spend a little time next door. Over the usual eggs and coffee, Joe briefed Andy on his plans. "I want to see what village life was like in Nick's time. Did they have any recreation? What were their customs? How did the men and their families cope with the stress of such dangerous work? I hope he can somehow guide me like when he showed me the yellow dogs," he concluded."

"I expect he can," said his old, trusted friend. "Somehow I think that very little is impossible for him and for you. You make quite a team. Now, have another cup of coffee and then get outta here. But I still wish I was going with you. Now remember, only a full report will do!"

Joe grinned his agreement. "You're becoming a pretty demanding old codger, Andy Polack. If you didn't run such a fine breakfast and coffee diner, I doubt I'd even come over here." He smiled fondly at Andy. "Full report it is, sir!"

As Joe approached the cave, he lingered, pondering how to explain to Nick what he wanted. "Well?" It came from the cave. "Are you going to stay out there debating, or just come in and ask me straight out?"

Joe stooped and crawled inside, letting his eyes adjust to the limited lighting. "Ask you what, you ghost?"

"You know what, Joe. But you have to ask me or I won't do it."

"Okay, okay. Would you please, kind sir, accompany me in a little visit to a time or place when I can learn first-hand about local coal camp life in your time? I want to experience, if I can, what it was like to live back then."

"I'm not exactly sure how it happened the last time we did that, Joe. I didn't know what to expect myself, even though I kind of thought it could be done. In fact, I'm not even sure that we went back to my time."

"I know." I've thought a lot about that, too. Maybe we just went to a reality that duplicated what happened then. Did you notice how some people saw and reacted to you, but it was like I wasn't even there? I mean, I wore strange clothes and all, and they didn't even blink an eye. It was bizarre. I was there, but maybe not there. Like I existed but wasn't a factor in their world. But you were real to them, I think." He stopped and looked thoughtful for a long minute. "I'm ready to try it again if you are."

"Sit back and close your eyes," Nick directed. Joe sat with his back to the wall as comfortably as he could, flipping off his flashlight and letting the semi-darkness seep in. After a few minutes his breathing became slow and steady, deep and regular. Joe felt as though he were dropping off to sleep.

***

Joe found himself with his friend walking in the warmth of the dawn, sky streaked red in the east. His eyes began to stream from the sulfurous odors emanating from the smoking, mountainous slag heaps. The late-spring foliage pushed forth lush and vibrant, even with the fine coating of road and coal dust and soot blessing each leaf. As they walked a well-worn path, they came to a small grouping of company houses. "This is good, Joe. Sometimes even when I wasn't working I would get up just to see this." They approached the rough fence that surrounded the vegetable garden of one house, joined to the fences of yards to either side.

A woman had just rushed outside with her family's soiled

clothing and dumped it into a steaming laundry tub. An acrid smell gave away the presence of lye soap in the hot water bubbling within. She looked around in satisfaction and cackled, her voice barely audible. "Ha! This morning I beat them!" She took a large crooked stick and used it to stir the clothes; raising them out of the water for examination before dumping them back in, satisfied. She leaned a corrugated metal washboard against the side of the tub and tottered off to the pump for a bucket of rinse water. She soon returned, staggering under her load, but looking pleased indeed.

Her neighbor to the left came rushing outside and took on a crestfallen look. "This morning you beat me, Maria!" she exclaimed as the other woman hung the first of her clean clothes on the clothesline strung across two wooden clothes poles used to keep the line from sagging. "But at least you beat Nicola, too. I heard she put wet clothes on the line the other day just to make us think she was first and then finished washing them after!" Maria covered her mouth in shock. Moving on, Nick pointed out fellow miners who were aggressively pulling weeds from their vegetable gardens as their wives prepared the lunch buckets for that workday. The nearest man's wife filled the bottom compartment of his lunch bucket with water before snapping the top section into place and filling it with fruit and other food. She then pressed the cover onto the lunch pail and admired her work with satisfaction.

One man groaned as he rose. He approached the fence. "My tomatoes are ripe before yours, Frank," he bragged. I will be having juicy tomatoes in my salad tonight!"

"Yours might be ripe first, but mine are already bigger. I will have thick slices on my sandwich this week, as big as the bread." He surveyed both gardens. "I see that your banana peppers are ready," he conceded. "But here! Try this one. Mine have more red in their skin and will be hotter."

Stan tentatively bit into the pepper, wincing as the fiery juices and seeds mixed with his saliva. Containing his pain as best he could, he breathed out hoarsely. "See you later, Frank. The wife is calling me." He practically staggered toward his back door as Frank looked on in smug satisfaction. He would have a story to tell at lunch today. He bit into the rest of the pepper and then ran for the water bucket.

Nick grinned at Joe and they moved on. "I had some of those

banana peppers. Sometimes they were as hot as a good cherry pepper." Joe winced at the thought, and swallowed the saliva that began to flood his own mouth as he remembered a few hot peppers in his past.

"Do you see Frank's water barrel over there?" Nick asked with a sly grin on his face. "One thing that helps their vegetables to grow big and fast is that they sink a gunny sack of old mule manure in that barrel filled with rain water. The water takes on lots of fertilizer for when they pour it around their plants." They resumed walking as Joe tried to absorb the unfamiliar sights and sounds of early morning in a simple village.

Down the street they saw a small group of miners approaching them. The men nodded in greeting at Nick. "The day shift starts about seven o'clock and ends at about five in the afternoon. The mine they are going to has been dug far into the coal seam. They will really appreciate the coal car ride into the mine this morning. It's called a 'man-trip.' Riding to their coal digging rooms will leave them more strength to mine. They will appreciate it even more when they come back out."

Trailing the group were two more miners, talking earnestly. "That is a man I know named Bernie. With him is his son, about sixteen years old now. A miner and his son work in a room together where the man teaches his boy all about mining. They work together until his next boy is ready, then the first one gets his own room and the man trains the next boy. There is no better teacher for a boy than his own father… if his father still lives."

They walked onward.

Shortly they saw a group of children walking toward a vacant field, carrying a battered bat and a baseball wrapped in tape. Nick and Joe tagged along.

After they arrived at the field, they arranged four pieces of wood in a diamond pattern and chose up sides. There were boys and girls, ranging from about eight years old up to about fourteen. One boy pitched a ball and a girl swung. "Crack!" the ball flew to a larger boy who caught it with ease. Again, the pitch. "Crack!" The grounder rolled to a little girl who seemed confused with what to do.

"Run with it to first, Anna!"

"Throw it to first!" She finally tossed it to the boy waiting impatiently at first while the batter stormed down on him.

"Safe!" shouted the member of the batting team who served as umpire during this half of the inning.

"What do you mean safe!" yelled the first baseman. "I tagged him out!"

"No, Lenny" the pitcher intervened. "I think he was safe." A girl of about ten years walked tentatively to the plate for her "tips" or her time at bat. Nick turned to go and Joe, who clearly wanted to watch this pick-up game a little longer, grudgingly followed.

They walked over to a muddy stream that flowed through town. There they sat and watched two small boys and an old man lacing worms on hooks and casting the fishing line into the water. After a few attempts, the old man caught a nice sucker about a foot long. "Supper!" he cried out. They tried a few more times without any success, so the old man decided, "Now we try some doughball." He pulled out an old tobacco pouch with a sticky mixture of cornmeal in it. He applied small balls of it to all three hooks and helped the boys throw their baited hooks into the stream near the opposite bank, aided by heavy lead sinkers. Shortly one excited, tow-headed boy screamed excitedly and pulled in a small catfish. "Stop yelling, Nicky!" The old man good-naturedly chastised him. "You will scare away all the fish!"

Joe realized that they must have sat there watching under a pussywillow tree for perhaps two hours because the sun had climbed high in the sky. With a sigh, Nick got up followed by Joe and started away from the streamside.

As they walked back into town, a sudden piercing steam whistle tore through the stillness. "P and W mine!" Nick exclaimed and then hurried away. Joe tried his best to keep up with him in the crowd of people, mainly women and children, who came streaming out of houses. The crowd thronged to the mine, where guards kept the people away from the mine entrance.

"A roof fall," explained an exhausted, blackened miner, who had just emerged, to some people nearby. Shortly a group of miners went back in with timbers, jacks and shovels to help in the rescue effort. "There are two men still missing," a miner said. Women searched for their husbands as more survivors streamed from the mine.

"Frank! Where is my Frank?" one woman screamed.

"Julio!" Did anybody see Julio?" another cried out.

After a long wait a man-trip car exited the mine with one man sitting slouched in it and another lying under a tarpaulin. The mine doctor knelt in the car, too. He was treating the sitting man but ignoring the one lying in the car.

"Julio!" The second woman screamed in relief and rushed toward the man-trip, only to be restrained by a foreman.

"Frank, Frank, Frank…" sobbed the other woman, who by now had a little girl clinging to her leg and was surrounded by friends trying to comfort her.

"Was that Frank from the garden?" Joe asked. Nick shrugged, not knowing for sure.

With the afternoon sun well past its mid-point in the sky the men dumped out their water buckets, a common signal that they would mine no more this day. Nick and Joe turned and walked away. "It happens," Nick said simply. Joe felt a deep sense of compassionate loss, even though these people were strangers to him.

When they returned to town, Nick said, "we stop here for a while." They looked over a backyard fence, where an oval washtub filled with hot water had been prepared. The man of the house came home from his shift, covered with coal dust. He could have been of any race or nationality, because his features were so well concealed by the fine, shiny black powder caking his face. He began to cough up a thick, black phlegmy mixture that he spat into the edge of the garden, before repeating the process. "Take off your clothes, Mario," his wife directed. Mario complied, until he stood there only in long john underwear bottoms. He sat in the tub and leaned forward with his forearms in the water, as his wife washed his back with a soapy rag and a brush. The blackness flowed like thick cola from his body into the water. Nick turned and began to walk away, followed by a very quiet Joe.

"Nick?" Joe asked. "How often did men die in the mines?"

"It seemed like every day somebody died or was badly hurt in some mine around Avella," Nick replied simply. "Maybe not that often, but that's the way it seemed." Joe was troubled by that thought. These were *people* after all. Not mine mules. Heck, if mine mules existed in the twenty-first century and died at that rate, numerous animal rights organizations would have banded together and the government would have shut the operation down right away.

"The men and their families will be eating now," Nick estimated. "The women pride themselves on having dinner ready for their husbands. The boarding house ladies also have dinner ready for the men baching it." Joe glanced questioningly at Nick. "Living like bachelors, even though some were married and had wives still in the old country," Nick explained.

They walked onward. "Look!" Nick exclaimed. "Mrs. Ferrari is first!" He pointed to a lady who had just come out to sit on her front porch in a clean apron. She had the look of a person who had just won a race. In fact, she had. "This is important to them. Her kitchen is clean and things have been put away. She can now relax on the front porch and as the other women come outside, they will see that she was first." Mrs. Ferrari sat there with a look of obvious satisfaction, as she basked in the glances of each woman who came out after her. "The sun is going down now, Joe. But we have a little more to see."

As darkness fell they strolled on in solitude, enjoying the warm but humid air. Nick took obvious delight in occasionally kicking a stone off the dirt road, trying to hit a fence post. Joe realized that Nick still had some boy in him.

Suddenly Joe stopped, straining to hear somebody singing off in the distance. Nick walked toward it. The remarkably beautiful tenor voice rang clear, singing indistinguishable but very melodic Italian lyrics, perhaps a folk song or an aria from some opera. "This has to be the most romantic song I ever heard, and I don't even understand the words," Joe quietly remarked. The neighbors who had been talking on their front porches stopped to listen. Shortly after the song ended, somebody began to play a concertina – a small accordion squeezebox – in an inexpert but melodic rendition of a hauntingly familiar melody. The people started talking again.

Suddenly Joe heard shouting and occasional laughter off in the distance. As they got nearer, he began to make out the now-familiar numbers: "quattro" "cinque!" and "sette!" he recognized the game of morra. The growing enthusiasm as the game progressed, and the loud bragging after each point, made it clear that some homemade wine likely aided their play. "It's not my language," Nick remarked. "But how I loved that game"

After a while two men could be seen coming down the dusty

road, apparently inebriated either on somebody's wine or from a local bar. They walked homeward in a semi-controlled kind of stagger, aiming their lurching bodies in the direction they intended to go, like sailboats tacking into the wind. One broke into song, joined by the other. "I wouldn't pay to hear them sing," Nick observed dryly. Joe just had to laugh.

And then, he found himself back in the cave.

"You'd better be on your way, Joe. I think it's getting dark outside."

Joe turned on his flashlight, climbed through the opening and started on his way down the dusky but familiar path. Before he found his car, the moonless night had already become pitch dark

Joe realized that there would probably be hell to pay whenever Jessie found out what he had done – alone – this day. What did that they said about a woman scorned? A woman left out of an adventure would be at least as hostile.

CHAPTER THIRTY-FIVE

"School's out!" Jessie proclaimed to Joe and Andy. "I thought this day would never come. Another cup of your finest brew, please." She had arrived bright and perky that Tuesday morning in mid-June, anxious to hike to Nick's, do more research into genealogy, and help plan another trek to Cliftonville. Not to mention trying to forget, at least for a little while, the small matter of the upcoming school board meeting. She had heard it could well turn into a circus.

Joe pondered his situation aloud. "Here I am with two of the best friends I have ever known, and I have even more friends in town. No matter what those two and their allies may do to me, they can't change that. I've made some irreplaceable friends here. Jessie, my main hope is that they don't take you, or even Principal Landers, down with me."

Andy's weathered face took on a pensive look. "I don't think they will get you, Jessie. Or even you, Joe. There's something coming together here. While I don't know what it is, I doubt it can be stopped. Not by any human force. Not even by vengeful meddling women or their cohorts. All we have to do is to let it happen."

"What are you saying?" asked Jessie, intrigued.

"I've been wondering about that," said Joe. Maybe I'm here for a reason, as though I was chosen or selected or something. There have been times recently when I thought things were way beyond my control. I mean, why did I get old Albert's house, and why now? Why me at the cave and not somebody else? After all, I show up in this little hole-in-the-wall town some eighty-odd years after the riot and all this stuff suddenly happens."

Jessie pondered this new line of reasoning. "Maybe you two are right. Perhaps something is going on here. But if it is, we won't find out about it in Andy's Diner. Library time!" She drained her cup and placed it in the sink. Reluctantly, Joe did the same. He had come to notice that he could practically hang out with Andy all day and be happy doing it. The old codger was just that interesting. But Jessie now prodded him into action and this time Andy insisted on going with them.

When they pulled into the library parking lot, Andy's eye was immediately drawn to the exhibit with the mine car. "See that? We used to ride in them, way down into the mine. The cars took us deep into the coal seam, and they took out the coal that we dug." His eye misted over. "They would tip them at the tipple and then send the cars back down empty."

Nan's expression brightened when the three walked into the library. "Joe! I guess this must be Jessica Randall, and I recognize Andy Polack, you old coot. How is everybody?" She introduced herself to Jessie, and introduced all three to Ellen, the pleasant and cheerful English woman, another library staff member. "By the way we have some information for you, but we should wait for Ben before we tell you what he discovered. I admit it's not very conclusive yet, but once Ben has something in his sights, he can be unstoppable in his search for the facts.

"In the meantime, I've been searching for more information about the riot's aftermath. I see that many of the articles listed in the West Virginia Archives are from the Wheeling newspapers. The Ohio County Public Library in Wheeling has decades of the Wheeling newspapers on microfilm. I called them and you can look them over any time their library is open. Even better, you can print the articles to take home."

"Are they open today? If so, we could drive down there. After you share what you've learned, of course," Joe looked at Nan expectantly. She smiled and nodded to Ellen.

"Well," Ellen began. "An article from the Wheeling newspaper that we found on the Internet shows that while forty men were sentenced to prison, at least sixty-nine were set free in some kind of plea bargain. The article is rather confusing and the numbers don't really add up well; perhaps the original article on microfilm will be clearer. In any case…" she smiled at Nan.

"In any case, an Angelo Ballino had been indicted and jailed, but he was one of the men set free in February of 1923." Joe and Jessie hugged each other, and Andy turned away, wiping his eye. Joe grasped Nan's and Ellen's hands in appreciation. Meanwhile Ben walked through the doorway and hoisted his satchel onto the desk.

"Ben! I understand you might have something for me?" Joe exclaimed without any preamble or niceties. Ben smiled knowingly.

"I'm at least on the trail, Joe. I found out that the 1930 census had an Angelo Ballino, age thirty-six; wife Maria, age thirty-three; and twin sons Angelo and Nicholas, age four living in Independence Township, Avella."

"She made it!" Joe burst out. "Maria made it over from Italy! What else?" He searched Ben's eyes pleadingly.

"I know they weren't recorded as living here during the 1940 census, and I could find no record of them in any local cemetery. They must have moved away during the 1930's, perhaps because of the Depression. I'm still working on that." Joe momentarily looked crestfallen, but then brightened when Jessie pointed out that wherever he went, he went with his wife and children.

"And one of the kids was named after Nick! Joe added. That will make him very happy." After a thoughtful pause, he asked, "What about Carmella?"

"I found that a Mr. Camillo Antonini was buried next to his wife, who had preceded him in death, in 1938. They rest in the cemetery at Patterson Mill. His daughter, Olga Antonini of whom you inquired, does not appear on the 1930 census, but there were several young wives named Olga. I will see what I can find.

"I haven't yet found a Carmella Antonini in the 1930 census, nor any married woman named Carmella," Ben went on, referring to his notes and some photocopied pages. But on the other hand the records of that day were very sketchy, especially in regard to foreign-born people, who were sometimes missed in the count. But I'm not giving up yet."

Andy had been sitting in a chair, thoughtfully taking in what he heard. "I just remembered something…" he began. The others turned to him. "I remember a woman named Carmelita or Carla something like that. It might have been Carmella. She was married to a man named Mike who kept the best garden I ever saw. He could grow anything. They lived on Italy Hill, or at least they lived there for a while; I'm talking about 1927 or 1928 or thereabouts. They were nice people and I… I remember a little girl running around. They had a daughter. I don't know what happened to them, he said apologetically.

"That would be Cross Creek Township," Ben said. "I'll have another look at their census from 1930. And Nan, didn't you say that the posters you put up in here and at the senior center were getting some attention?"

She nodded. "Yes. I had several older people comment on the posters and the names of Angelo, Carmella, and Mike. Unfortunately Angelo and Mike were relatively common names, but we still might get a clue from the posters, because the senior citizens are talking about it.

"Thanks, Nan, Ellen, Ben," said Joe. "You're providing a great service here, even though we might not realize the scope of its impact yet," Joe offered.

"Oh, Joe?" Nan tried to look casual. "Are you going to the school board meeting tomorrow night? I understand it's been moved to the high school cafetorium." Catching Joe's momentary look of confusion, she explained, "it's a large cafeteria with a stage at one end. They're expecting a crowd because of the teachers' contract. And also because they may be discussing you and Miss Randall." His stomach fell, as it had been doing regularly of late.

"Just to put the icing on the cake," Jessie added. "I understand that I will attend that meeting too. It's possible that I may be called into executive session to discuss our nature walk and… and you, Joe." The room suddenly grew quiet. Andy patted Joe's arm, and Jessie squeezed the other one.

"For whatever it's worth we will all be there," Nan added, her jaw set firmly. "We don't want to give those people a reason to turn their guns on the library so we probably can't speak up, but we'll still be there for moral support. And we've each talked with trusted friends who said they'd be there, too."

"Thanks." All Joe could manage was, "thanks."

CHAPTER THIRTY-SIX

Interesting. The first two times Joe had arrived at the school campus, his mood had been so much better. His arrival each time had included the expectation of some quality time with Miss Randall. The third time he had no idea what to think, because of Jessie's unexpected phone call. But this Wednesday evening as he parked next to the high school building, his anticipation was tinged with dread. Not so much for himself or his reputation, because he was basically a transitory Avella resident. He could tough it out if he had to. Jessica Randall was most at risk here.

"She's parked over there," said Andy. Following Andy's pointing finger, he noticed the Camaro already parked, with Jessie still sitting behind the wheel. How long had she been sitting like that? He saw a pronounced slump, as though she were deep in thought or marshaling her reserves of strength.

"Hi, Jessie," he said brightly, concealing his underlying worry, as he tapped on her driver's side window. "Ready to join me in bearding the lion?" She laughed and immediately brightened.

"Hi, Joe. Hi, Andy," she said as she opened the door and gave them both quick hugs. "I'm a little surprised you knew that quote from Sir Walter Scott."

"Sir Walter Scott? I thought it was just a saying."

"Basically, it means to go into somebody else's place – the lion's den – and confront them," she explained. "I think there are more layers of meaning, but that should sum it up. On that note, are you ready to beard the lion? If so, we might as well go in".

There's no longer any slump in this girl, Joe thought as they walked through the double doors. Bring on those women.

"My union steward is waiting for me," she commented, indicating the worried-looking local education association official, a fellow teacher. She walked directly to the steward, who pointed toward the closed cafetorium door, where the executive session was likely in progress. Joe and Andy watched them both disappear behind closed doors. Principal Landers and the superintendent are probably already in there, Joe reflected.

After Joe confiscated one of the few available chairs for Andy, they waited outside in the hallway with the slowly growing crowd of citizens. As Andy chattered on about today's generation being more troublesome, Joe noticed an occasional furtive glance cast his way. With the public meeting scheduled for an hour later, the crowd numbered fewer than thirty people. But at least some of the attendees apparently knew of him.

Les arrived with Leo and a few of the men and women firefighters Joe had met while washing and shining trucks. "Ready for another stroll, Joe?" Les asked. Leo just grunted, still a man of few words.

"I'm still planning the day-night hike to Cliftonv..." then Joe realized that the question was merely rhetorical. He grinned ruefully at Les and his group. "Anyway, I'll let you know when."

Les laughed and put his arm around Joe's shoulder in a show of encouragement. "Is she in there now?" he asked. Joe nodded resignedly.

"Yes. I hope it goes well for her. I'd hate to see her get splattered with the paint meant for me." As the hour continued to erode, the crowd grew. Joe now noticed Mrs. Granger and Mrs. Jones standing outside the main entry door, collaring people as they prepared to enter the building.

Presently the door opened and Landers beckoned to Joe. He looked at his friends and sighed. He followed the principal inside.

In the cafetorium, the school board sat studying their papers on the stage with the superintendent and, Joe assumed, their legal counsel. Jessie stood on the floor below. Principal Landers began: "This is Mr. Joseph Bailey, Madame President and board members." Joe waited silently.

"Mr. Bailey. I understand that you accompanied a group of elementary children on a nature walk?" the board president began, in a neutral voice. Joe said yes and remained quiet. "What can you tell us about that experience, Mr. Bailey?"

Joe began, "I met Miss Randall through a mutual friend, the local fire chief. She learned that I'm an avid hiker who knows more than most people about the outdoors. While my regular business is real estate sales, mainly in and around Pittsburgh, I currently live in Avella in an inherited house that I'm renovating. While here I've been hiking whenever I have the chance."

One board member – a middle-aged man with thinning hair combed over his bald spot and a hawkish nose – interrupted: "Mr. Bailey, what's this about you and ghosts?"

"Why not cut straight to the heart of the matter?" Joe thought ruefully. He began to tell about his experiences with Nick in the cave. The board members sat silently, hands folded, with no small degree of skepticism on their faces. As Joe talked he glanced over at Jessie, who stood nearby, obviously in some distress. She appeared to be verging on tears but bravely held her emotions in check. Joe realized that she must have endured a stressful experience in here, and now she was forced to hear him say things that she knew many people would never believe.

Joe included the most important things in his talk, but excluded the most bizarre, such as Jessie jumping through Nick's spirit. He explained the Cliftonville Mine riot and its connection to Avella's history. He also discussed the recent research that supports what Nick had told him, including the genealogical research that identified Angelo and Carmella. When he concluded his story, he awaited their response.

After an uncomfortable silence, the board president finally spoke. "This is very difficult to believe, Mr. Bailey. But in fact we are not here to judge you in any way. The story that you just related agrees with the one Miss Randall previously gave. The significance of it lies in how it reflects on her and Principal Landers' decisions. Our concern is whether Miss Randall should have invited you on the nature walk in the first place. Do you have any comments about that?"

Joe briefly reflected. "As I said, Miss Randall and I were introduced by a trustworthy mutual friend, Les Wilson, the volunteer fire department's chief. She perceived that I could add something to a local field trip because of my knowledge about the outdoors and its flora and fauna. I underwent a background check, where I presume they confirmed my former service as a police officer, and that I served with some distinction.

"When we began the field trip, it surprised me to find that every parent volunteer was a woman. I presumed that it would be a good thing to have an occasional male role model for both boys and girls. The children seemed to enjoy having a man on the trip, to counterbalance nine women… as though any man could ever do that," he added, to a few chuckles from the board members.

"In any case, Miss Randall and the principal must have followed procedures in inviting me. They surely took advantage of the protections afforded by a background check. I should also mention that no harm resulted from my involvement in the outing, with the exception that some children apparently eavesdropped on a conversation.

"All I can say is that Miss Randall did not invite a man who says he talks to ghosts. In fact, she didn't even know about that. She invited a man whom she believed could add something to her students' educational experience." As he waited for a response – any response – he assessed that some board members appeared to verge on open hostility toward him while others were more warm and accepting of what he had said. Others still seemed contemplative over his testimony.

"Thank you, Mr. Bailey. You are excused from this executive session."

Joe left the room and was stunned to see a horde of well over a hundred people in the hallway and spilling out into the parking lot. He realized that the public meeting would soon begin. And, yes, Mrs. Jones and Mrs. Granger were nearby, glaring at him. He walked over to Les and Andy for moral support.

Over his shoulder he saw a television news truck parked just outside.

CHAPTER THIRTY-SEVEN

After a few minutes somebody opened the doors to the cafetorium. The attendees filed in, and each person signed a guest register. Joe and his friends took seats in the middle of the fourth row. Scanning the agenda for the night's meeting, he was dismayed to see that both Mrs. Jones and Mrs. Granger had signed up to speak during the public input period.

"The meeting will now come to order," the president began. "We will stand for the Pledge of Allegiance. The flag is near the door where you entered." After the assembled group recited the pledge, she began the meeting with routine teacher and principal input, where several educators reported on programs that they had implemented or were planning. The schedule called for the public input session to be next, but the president stated that it would be held at the end of the meeting after the regular agenda, which included the proposed teacher contract.

The agenda went off rather smoothly, except for a cluster of people who frequently interrupted the board to ask questions and in some cases to make accusations. Joe wondered why the president allowed the interruptions, but concluded that it the board wanted no accusations that the public was denied the right to speak.

"I think there's a small group of perhaps eight or ten people who may have an agenda of their own," he whispered.

"You picked that up that fast, did you, Joe?" responded Jessie, who had taken a seat next to him. "Yes, they appear to coordinate what they plan to do. They target certain board members, administrators, faculty and coaching staff with their criticism. If they ultimately get their way it could get pretty bad around here," she said sadly.

Finally the proposed new teachers' contract was addressed. The president explained the revised terms, including the pay increase. With very little argument from the floor, except from members of the now-obvious faction, the board approved the contract by a 6-3 vote. "People don't mind paying higher taxes, as long as they think it will result in a stronger educational program. People here take pride in the accomplishments of the students and faculty," Jessie whispered.

Joe waited through several minor items, noticing again that the nay-sayers very clearly directed their antagonism at certain board members and members of the school staff. "What's up with these people?" he whispered to Jessie. "Don't they like anybody? Maybe they need to get a life."

A woman nearby exclaimed, "Amen", while an overweight woman in what looked like a housecoat glared at him. Apparently his whispers had been gaining in volume.

"Shhh," Jessie cautioned, flickering her eyes worriedly toward people nearby who were obviously listening to him. Meanwhile Joe had noticed a young, African-American man writing carefully in his notepad, and concluded that he must be a newspaper reporter. As a former police officer Joe prided himself on being a fast study, somebody who could walk into a situation and evaluate it quickly. It didn't take him long to determine who the actors were in this scenario. He had most of the dissident group tagged now, starting, of course, with Mrs. Jones and Mrs. Granger. One person who stood out was a rotund, balding man operating a home video camera. He interrupted the speakers a number of times with challenging questions and comments. Each time, he then took on what appeared to be a self-satisfied look.

"Time for public input," Jessie quietly informed those near her. "There are only two speakers from the public tonight, two women talking about 'appropriate staffing for elementary field trips.' They must have rushed to get on the list," she concluded. Mrs. Granger approached the microphone.

"I want to know – we want to know – why the elementary school would assign a man who says he talks to ghosts to accompany our young and impressionable children on a field trip. We heard from children involved that this occurred and we also were in a meeting with Principal Landers where this man admitted that he thinks he talks to ghosts. We want to know why Jessie Randall allowed…"

The president of the board interrupted: "Any discussion regarding a specific staff member will be held during executive session, as a personnel matter. Please refrain from discussing specific staff members. You may continue." Joe noticed again, as Mrs. Granger spoke, that two members of the board were openly supportive of her, in their facial expressions and manners.

Mrs. Granger quickly veered toward outright belligerence. "Well? Why were our children subjected to this man, this stranger, named Joseph Bailey?" The mention of his name caused a commotion that the president had to eventually gavel down. The newspaper reporter wrote furiously now, and Joe could see that the light from the Channel Eight news video camera had been turned back on. The television reporter spoke quietly into her microphone.

Many in the audience turned to look at him. The reporter and the others who didn't know him by name took the cue and also looked in his direction. Mrs. Granger stoked the crowd. "We deserve our answer." The president gaveled the ensuing uproar into submission again, and then she spoke.

"We have already discussed this matter in executive session and have found nothing wrong. Policies and procedures were followed to the letter. Mr. Bailey passed all required background checks. That is all that this board will say on this subject. I see that your five minutes are up, Mrs. Granger. Thank you for speaking."

Mrs. Granger took her seat to a loud murmur, mainly from her cronies. Mrs. Jones walked to the microphone after briefly conferring with her friend. "Why don't we have Mr. Bailey stand up here and tell us about the ghosts he talks with?" she challenged, staring directly at Joe.

"If you care to relinquish your time to Mr. Bailey, who is not scheduled to speak, perhaps we will allow him to talk. Mr. Bailey?" The president gave Joe a small smile. Joe remembered that she had at least been open to his explanation earlier, so he decided to accept the offer. He arose and walked to the microphone. "I remind you, Mr. Bailey, that any matter regarding a member of the staff is reserved for executive session. However, you may discuss your own recent activities."

"Thank you, Madame President and members of the Board. I have to admit that I was not prepared to talk tonight." Jessie and Les smiled their encouragement. "But this is my story. I came to Avella because I inherited a house that I am renovating. I'm also taking a break from my real estate career in Pittsburgh.

"As a long-time hiker I took advantage of the interesting terrain around here and began to explore. I found a small cave during one hike, where I happened to come in contact with the spirit of a miner..." An explosive gasp escaped from two hundred throats, and the room erupted into chaos. Mrs. Jones took on a look of smug satisfaction at what she had accomplished. The president finally gaveled the meeting back into order with a threat to clear the room if necessary. Joe noticed that he now had everybody's rapt attention, and that the television camera was trained squarely on him. He continued.

"Please understand that I knew essentially nothing about the area, except vaguely that it had once been a coal mining center. Anyway, this spirit identified himself as Nick Shebellko, a miner who had been shot during a mine riot just over the West Virginia border at a place called Cliftonville, on July 17, 1922. Apparently this is a part of local history that few Avella people are aware of, so I'll recap it. Several hundred miners from mines in the Avella area marched down the railroad tracks to the Clifton Mine, where non-union labor had replaced the regular miners, and attempted to shut it down. A fierce battle ensued, wherein the sheriff of Brooke County was shot and killed. Many of the miners were killed or wounded as well. At least eight miners were confirmed dead at the scene, and it is believed that several more of the wounded died during their escape back to Avella." The room had become entirely quiet, as both the skeptical and the open-minded hung on his every word.

"Nick told me that he had been badly injured by a gunshot during a fight in a mine building. He said a friend named Angelo and some other miners assisted him back into Pennsylvania. But he died on the way and was buried somewhere in the woods. I also know of at least one other miner whom we know to be buried in an unmarked grave. There were likely many more, but their final resting places are unknown.

"Over two hundred of the surviving miners were arrested and put on trial in Wellsburg. After a long series of trials, about forty men were sentenced to imprisonment in Moundsville, West Virginia, but at least sixty-nine men were acquitted. However, there were no convictions for murdering the sheriff.

"Just to clarify, I don't speak to ghosts but I have communicated with this one spirit, of a miner named Nick Shebellko, who died in 1922. Exactly how and why I can do this is inexplicable to me. Anyway, Nick told me that he left a great friend behind named Angelo Ballino, and a young woman whom he had planned to marry named Carmella Antonini. We are trying to find out whatever became of Angelo and Carmella. Nick also told me a lot about the early days in the Avella area coal mines, and of village life. He also said that he's concerned that so many of his comrades have never been given decent burials."

"I heard about that riot," an older man remarked out loud.

"He's crazy!" Somebody else shouted.

Several others began to talk loudly, but Mrs. Jones' voice carried above all the others, "he's insane!" After nearly a full minute of gaveling and threats to clear the room, the voices died down to a low murmur.

Joe stood there quietly the entire time. As a policeman he had learned how to give testimony. While waiting for order, he saw that the television crew was eating it all up. They were having an unexpectedly big night. This goes well beyond a routine school board meeting, even one with a possible tax increase, he reflected. He wondered briefly which member of Mrs. Jones' group had called Channel Eight.

"Can you see this – this *ghost,* Mr. Bailey?" The man behind his home video camera shouted scornfully. Joe considered him for a moment, wondering if causing trouble at meetings was his idea of having a good time.

"Actually, I can see him. Somehow, we connected in such a way that I can see him as he was at the age of 22."

"So, Bailey, tell me about him," the man pursued. Joe regarded him for a few seconds, while the audience waited breathlessly.

"No," he said simply. "If I ever describe Nick to anybody, it certainly won't be to you." A roar of appreciative laughter went up, causing the man to lower his head slightly and adjust the controls on his camera. Joe turned away and looked questioningly at the board president.

"Thank you, Mr. Bailey" she concluded, trying to suppress a grin. "With there being no further business to discuss, I will entertain a motion to adjourn." The motion was made and seconded and passed unanimously. Joe and his friends left via a side door. As he departed, he saw members of the radical group head for the newspaper reporter and television crew. Apparently they wanted as much "face time" as they could get to air their views.

"Well, that wasn't so bad now, was it" Les observed dryly. "What do you plan to do for an encore next week?"

"I don't know," Joe responded. "I doubt that Jessie's job is on the line anymore, or at least I hope not. The focus now is squarely on me, and where it counts the most – in the court of public opinion. Anyone want to head back to my place to hash this one over?"

Jessie, Andy, Les and Leo converged on Joe's living room. They talked until about 1:00 a.m. Jessie lightly kissed him good night as the others departed for their vehicles and Andy to his home. "You are a remarkable person, Joseph Bailey." Then she, too, turned toward her car.

"Wait," he said urgently, catching her by the arm. She turned in surprise. "Sorry," he apologized. "I didn't mean to bruise your arm. But I've been wondering about your hopes to become a principal."

"I have my papers now, Joe," she said. "And I sent out feelers for open positions at a few school districts. But I just don't have much of a chance. I have no administrative experience, just my certification. Maybe in a year or two… or three…" She shrugged.

CHAPTER THIRTY-EIGHT

"Is this Mister Bailey?" the voice on the phone asked. It was a feminine voice, not at all strong, and it wavered slightly.

"I am Joseph Bailey," he responded instinctively, kicking into his real estate voice. "How may I help you?"

"My name is Carmella Cook," the woman responded. Joe's heart suddenly lurched. "My mother was also named Carmella. Have you really been trying to find out about her?" Joe heavily dropped into a chair at the kitchen table and leaned forward, his head lowering onto the table surface as he listened. Jessie came over and touched his arm with concern.

"You say that your name is Carmella?" he managed to get out, in part to verify in his own mind what he had just heard, but also to signal Jessie. He wondered how a call from a woman he had never met could cause such a physiological change within his body; an almost unbearable sadness layered over an incipient hope. Jessie sat next to him and craned her head close to the phone, which he then held slightly away from his ear. Joe realized that he had been mashing his left ear with the phone's handset. He moved it farther away. "Was your mother named Carmella Antonini?"

"Yes, she was Carmella Antonini. I understand that you have something to do with a person named Nick Shebellko?" Joe detected a cautious restraint within her carefully selected words. "Is this true?" By now, Joe managed to raise his head and his sagged shoulders back to a nearly normal sitting position. Jessie matched him, continuing to strain to hear every precious word. He finally opened his eyes and looked deeply into Jessie's, as he forced out his response.

"Yes. I know Nick," he finally stated. "I know him," he said, finally understanding the full meaning of the words. The other end of the phone connection went quiet for a few seconds, except for a little sob painfully audible to both of the listeners.

"But it would be impossible for you to know Nick Shebellko, or at least the one I know of," she tentatively offered. "It would be impossible." Joe detected the catch in her faltering voice, as though somebody had constricted her chest as she forced out the words. "Impossible..."

"I know Nick Shebellko," he repeated, more forcefully. "It may seem impossible, but I do know him."

"I think we should talk, Mr. Bailey," she finally decided. They agreed to meet at a rustic log house restaurant along Route 50 near Hickory later that day. As Joe replaced the receiver back on the phone's cradle, he found Jessie's hand placed over his own. They hung the phone up together.

He gazed into her eyes and saw her looking wonderingly back at him. Overcome with emotion, he reached out and placed his other hand behind her head, pulling her to him. They kissed, but with a kiss born from something much deeper than physical longing, or even their growing affection. The kiss was a statement that they could barely begin to understand, with its roots probing an intimacy that neither could have ever anticipated.

***

That afternoon they pulled into the restaurant's gravel parking lot and entered the building. "I believe a woman is expecting us," Jessie told the hostess, who nodded her head toward a table near the window where two women were seated. A middle-aged woman was studying something in the newspaper, while a frail-looking woman of perhaps eighty years smiled and waved them over. As they approached the table the robust-looking first woman placed the newspaper, carefully folded, on the table's surface.

"You are Mr. Bailey?" the older woman asked. "My name is Carmella Cook, Mrs. Ronald Cook. This is my daughter, Mrs. Carla Jacobs. Please join us." Joe and Jessie took seats at the table.

"May I present Miss Jessie Randall?" Joe responded. "She is my... my friend." He blushed slightly, as Jessie and the two women exchanged greetings and knowing looks.

"Did you, by any chance, happen to read today's Washington newspaper, Mr. Bailey?" Mrs. Cook asked. Carmella slid the paper over to him, and both he and Jessie began to read. He noticed a report from the school board meeting of last night, headed:

Avella Board Meeting in Uproar over Ghost

The story sketchily but factually reported on the events of the meeting, also going into considerable detail about the accusations from Mrs. Jones, Mrs. Granger, and a male member of the audience. They asserted that Joe thinks he talks to ghosts and therefore could be a danger to Avella's children. The reporter also summarized Joe's talk, including the names that he had cited: Angelo Ballino and Carmella Antonini.

"At first I assumed it would be a funny story, Mr. Bailey, until I read those names, and that you said you had been conversing with a spirit named Nick Shebellko, a miner killed in 1922 and buried in the woods. Then the article lost all its humor. Mr. Bailey, you wouldn't toy with the emotions of an old woman now, would you?" she asked him seriously, with searching looks into both his face and Jessie's. "It says here that you were hiking."

For the next twenty minutes Joe told his story. As he went on, the waitress who had been about to ask for their order stopped her chore and hovered. Soon a couple at the next table and then a party of four gathered around. None of those at the table seemed to mind their presence at all. "It may sound crazy, Mrs. Cook, but…"

"Please call me Carmella, Mr. Bailey. I feel as though I've known you for a long time. Joe," she added.

"…Carmella." He continued. "But that's what happened. I can't change it, and frankly I wouldn't change it, even if it does cause people to look at me strangely. Now, please tell me about your mother."

"First, I would like you to read something that I found among mama's papers and personal effects. She and dad often told us about her first love and his good friend, Nicholas. She also apparently kept one treasured memento, a sealed letter that she had written addressed simply to 'Nick'. It seemed too personal for me to open, so I have refrained from doing so… until I retrieved it this morning. Please read it." She shakily handed the opened letter to Joe who, along with Jessie, began to read the words blurred by the time and tears of years past:

by Joseph P. Bogo

My sweet Nicholas

It has now been more than one year since Angelo told me of your death. He said that you died bravely, and your final thoughts and words were of me. I loved you long before he told me that, and I have loved you ever since, Amore mio.

I thought my life was over that day. Oh, how we planned to spend the rest of our days together. We knew that it would be a hard life, especially when we first started out. But the hardest times would have been when we were at our best. Your love for me was strong, and mine for you even stronger. This I know in my heart.

But your love, while as strong as you, my handsome man, was also as gentle to me as a butterfly floating through my spirit on wings no more heavy than air. I could tell that you would protect me and provide for our children each day of your life and of mine.

Nicholas, we spoke many times of the children we would have. The first boy would be named in honor of you and your father.

Sometimes I think of the little violet flower that you picked for me as we walked along that path. There were many violets, but you only picked the one. The perfect flower, you called it. The violet was like our lives together, with its promise of a beautiful life, a sweet life.

You held the violet up to me and said that it was ugly when placed next to me. I protested and cried that it was beautiful and would always be beautiful. I kept that violet, Nick, pressed in a book as my treasure from our love and the promise of the life we would share.

But still, I knew that even as you held it up, it was already dying. Just as you took the flower from the earth, you are now torn from me and our life together. Now I have only the violet and the sweet remembrance of your love for me. For this year I have looked at the flower every night, but now I put it away. I will always have the violet, Nick, and I will always have you as my love, my love in my heart.

But now I must give my heart to another man. I will love him as truly as I loved you, if that is possible. He knows that I will always hold you in my heart, too, but he is happy with the love that I can give to him. Your gift to me, my Nick, was that your love caused my own to grow so that there is more than enough for him and for your memory.

In the spring, your friend Mike and I will marry. He tells me that the first boy will be named Nicholas. We will tell our son about you. I think he will be proud of your name.

Ti amo. Il mio Nicholas. Ti amo.

Your Carmella

They silently placed the paper next to the envelope and sat there, stunned by the personal nature of the letter, as though they had somehow violated a sacred relic by reading it. "Joe," Carmella went on. "I discovered something else in with the letter, sandwiched within a piece of waxed paper. Here it is." She offered the folded wax paper, which held a pressed and dried violet blossom.

Joe and Jessie pondered the strength of emotion behind the decades-old love note, as did the small crowd of bystanders, none of whom were at all embarrassed to be there. Nor were they resented. The intimate moment had become communal as well as personal.

Carmella pressed Joe's hand with her own withered one. "When you next see Nick, and I now believe that you will, please share this last message with him. After all, she intended it for him all along." She pushed the envelope containing the letter and the flower across the table to Joe, who carefully placed it in an inside pocket.

"Please tell us about your family," Jessie asked carefully. "Whatever happened to Nick's Carmella – your mother – and your father, Mike?"

"After a few years, when I was six, we just moved away to where employment possibilities were greater and sore memories were fewer. Dad – Mike Zaretsky, that is our family name – and mama had a good life. My two little brothers, Michael and Nicholas, grew to be hulking, handsome men who married and moved with their families to Arizona where they started a construction business. I lived with mama and dad until I married. First dad died, and then a year later mama followed him, not even fifteen years ago. They are buried less five miles from here. Would you like to see the grave sometime? It might interest you."

"Might we see it now, Carmella?" Jessie asked. "Do you feel up to it?"

"Not today, dear. I'm much too tired, and I have a doctor's appointment tomorrow. Why don't we meet again here the day after that, and then we can visit the cemetery together? They agreed to meet at ten o'clock on the appointed day.

"Oh, Joe?" Carmella added. "You might be interested in the Channel Eight news broadcast. You look handsome as all get out on television, but some of those people look very mean."

"I don't have a television in my house in Avella, but I saw the original version last night. I doubt that the news story is much different."

"I saw it," a woman standing next to the table added. "And I think those people were mean, too."

CHAPTER THIRTY-NINE

The next morning Joe awoke early, and after preparing for his hike he took his journal down from the shelf. He began to write:

This is happening so fast now. I have grown so close to Jessie and have also made such good friends here, only now I'm reluctant to show my face in town. What will people say? Will they crack jokes, empathize with me, or ridicule me?

And my good friend, Nick. Jessie and I will be visiting him today. We hope to show him the letter and the flower. How will he handle that? And how about the news of Carmella and Mike's marriage and their children, including his namesake? Clearly, they never forgot Nick, and in fact shared their memories of him with their children. I don't know if I could have been as accepting as Mike was of Nick's memory without also being threatened by it. Mike apparently had a greater love than most men are capable of. I respect him tremendously.

Joe placed the journal back on the shelf, just as Jessie arrived outside. He heard hasty footsteps on the gravel and a loud banging on his door. He rushed to let her in. As the door opened, he threw his arms around her and gave her a welcoming kiss.

"Joe!" she said breathlessly, pulling away. "I finally saw the television news report. I didn't like the slant that they took on it. While they didn't accuse you outright of being crazy, they implied that your story was too bizarre to believe. The footage was accurate, but they edited it in such a way that the statements of the people who had called them to the meeting offset any good points you made. I didn't like it at all."

She pulled back even more and stepped outside the threshold. "And will you look at this?" He stepped through and looked in the direction she was staring. "Ghosts!" she exclaimed angrily. "Halloween-type ghosts hanging from your tree!" He stared upward and then a grin spread over his face.

"Kids," he said. "It had to be kids playing a prank." But inside he felt a mounting, sickening sensation. As he laughingly began to tear down the offending decorations he realized that this was likely indicative of a rising tide of trouble in the near future.

They locked up and headed next door for a fast cup, anxious to get on with their day. A solemn Andy met them at the door. "I saw what they done, but I didn't see them do it. Sorry, Joe."

"If anybody could have seen them it should have been me. But it was probably just some kids' idea of fun." Joe shrugged it off. "Now, are you interested in hearing the breakthrough we learned yesterday? Or maybe we should just move on without bothering you with the details."

"If you do, your coffee and grub supply is permanently shut off, Bailey," Andy glared, then laughed and slapped his knee.

"I like it when you call me that, Andy. I know it's in good fun. But when that guy called me Bailey the other night, I felt like punching him out. I didn't hear any humor or respect in it at all." Joe and Jessie then filled Andy in on what Mrs. Carmella Cook had told them about her mother and father, including that they never let Nick's memory die.

"That's very – very touching," breathed Andy, obviously fighting to stem a groundswell of emotion.

"Show it to him," counseled Jessie. Joe handed the letter to his old friend, removing the wax paper first and placing it on the table within easy reach. "Andy, nobody ever opened this letter until yesterday morning. Carmella apparently wrote it in 1923, a year after Nick's death." As old Andy read the letter, his slumping shoulders began to shake.

Placing the letter back on the table, he looked at the wax paper. "Is that what I think it is?" Jessie handed it to him, and as he opened it the pressed, dried violet fell out. "I never knew the man…" he gasped, as the flood finally broke. "But he's like a brother to me. My own, dead brother. I'm such a sentimental fool." Joe suddenly recognized that the brotherhood of men who mined ran even deeper and thicker than the coal veins they dug.

Joe and Jessie placed the envelope and its precious contents within a larger envelope for protection and then inside a zip-lock bag.

They took their leave, Andy still sitting at the kitchen table and only glancing up once as they walked out the door. They quietly closed it behind them.

"Andy has seen many hard times in his century of living," Joe commented. "I saw him cry only once before, and those tears were for his father's memory." In silence, they drove to the trailhead and set off on their hike. Their legs carried them up the trail faster than usual this time. They had exciting news for Nick.

At the cave, a voice floated out. "Is she there, Joe?"

"I heard that, Nick!" Jessie laughed. "And just for that, I am coming in first." She ducked and shouldered her way past Joe. "Ahhh, there you are, you ghost!"

Joe grumbled as he duck-walked his way in. "Women," he said. "Can't live with 'em, can't shoot 'em." With an exaggerated sigh, he sat back against the wall next to Jessie and studied Nick's face intently. "I'm happy to see you. Each time I come here, I take away with me more than I bring to you."

Still holding Nick's gaze, he said, "but this time we have something special for you. It's about your Carmella." Nick's eyes widened in surprise and then in hope.

"You're not funning me are you, Joe? You saw Carmella?" Joe shook his head.

"No, but something almost as good. We have word of her, and even more importantly we have word from her. Jessie will explain it, and I'll chip in from time to time." He nodded at Jessie to begin.

"Yesterday we met a Carmella Cook, the married daughter of Mike and Carmella Zaretsky, and Carmella Cook's daughter, Carla Jacob." She stopped talking briefly to allow Nick to digest what she had just related.

"Carmella married Mike?" Nick gasped. "I can't think of a better man to take care of my Carmella. Tell me about them. Where did they live? How many children did they have?" He leaned forward expectantly. With a few words added by Joe, Jessie related their surprise phone call and what they had learned from the two ladies, including that both Mike and Carmella had passed away.

"Mrs. Cook – Carmella – agreed to take Joe and me to the graves of your dear love and your friend. We will go tomorrow." She looked meaningfully at Joe. "And there's something else…"

"Nick," Joe started. "I have something here that Carmella Cook gave us yesterday. She never opened it until yesterday morning, and she wants us to share it with you." He carefully withdrew the plastic bag from his inner pocket and began to remove the larger envelope with Carmella's envelope within. He next took out Carmella's envelope, and finally the letter that had been in the Zaretsky family for more than eight decades. After giving the folded wax paper to Jessie, he explained Carmella's note.

"The envelope had only one name on the outside, yours. Carmella wrote the note inside as a love letter to you, apparently. Do you want us to read it to you?" Nick nodded dumbly, his head in his hands.

"Please, Joe. Please read."

Joe began:

My sweet Nicholas

It has now been more than one year since Angelo told me of your death. He said that you died bravely, and your final thoughts and words were of me. I loved you long before he told me that, and I have loved you ever since...

Joe continued to read in the faltering light of his flashlight, not wanting to stop even to change batteries. When he finished, the silence was palpable, so thick that it took several minutes before Nick started to talk.

"She thought of me and she remembered me. And she and Mike preserved my memory."

"And they lived a good life," Joe said. "And had good children, too. They named their daughter Carmella, and their sons Mike and Nick. But there's one more thing. She mentioned a violet blossom in the note. Jessie?"

Jessie held the wax paper out toward Nick and carefully opened it, revealing the delicate, dried and pressed blossom within. "You picked that blossom, and you gave it to Carmella. She wanted you to see it but knew that you never could. I hope that somewhere she and Mike are looking on, happy that you have finally seen her precious violet and heard her words."

Choking back his emotions, Nick looked upward. "I think you're right. Somehow, I think they know." Nick smiled, weakly at first but then with a growing conviction. "They know."

"There's even more," Joe continued. "A person in the library found out some things about Angelo, the man you were especially close to."

"He was like a brother to me, closer than a brother. We could have been cast from the same mold. What did you find out?" Nick looked searchingly at Joe, with a mixture of hope and dread.

"First, Angelo was never convicted like some of the others. He spent some time in jail until the trial, but he never served prison time." Nick breathed a sigh of relief. His posture lifted as though a great weight that had been pressing down on him had just been removed.

Joe continued, "Angelo brought Maria over and they had two twin boys, named Angelo and Nicholas. That's all we know so far. But there are people trying to find out what happened to them. Apparently they moved away."

"That's good. Angelo and his Maria had a family. That's very good. Thanks, Joe. Thanks, Jessie. I just can't tell you what this means to me. I would kiss you if I could… Jessie," he said with a wink.

Breaking the mood, Joe put the letter away and then began his own story. "Do you want to hear something funny? Half the town thinks I'm crazy, because word got around that I talk to ghosts."

"Do you really do that?" Nick asked. And then, "oh, you mean me?" They nodded, laughing. "Tell me about it."

Joe and Jessie took turns, filling Nick in on the recent events including their research, the school nature walk and its aftermath, and finally the school board meeting. Joe made a few failed attempts at explaining television to a disbelieving Nick. "So you see, without realizing it you've been entertaining a crazy man in your little cave."

Jessie gave him a sharp elbow to his ribs. *"Ouch!"* He complained.

"If you're crazy, then it's catching because I must be crazy, too."

Nick grinned broadly. "I already knew that. But what are you going to do about what they say? And more important: would you read Carmella's letter to me again?"

Jessie opened and read the letter again as Nick's face took on a dreamy expression. After a few more minutes his spell of remembrance dissipated and he came back to reality.

Nick then turned directly to Joe, becoming very serious. "It seems to me that you need some proof, right? I mean Carmella's letter is all well and good, but how about some first-hand evidence?" His visitors, exchanging glances, had no idea what to expect. "Would it help if you knew where they buried me?"

After a shocked silence, Joe responded, "I don't think I'd want to see that. I like you as you are, whole in spirit, perfect in the body that I see. I just don't know that I can handle seeing your body after years of decay."

"I'm not as bad off as you think. Not like the other boys who were covered up in the dirt. Actually, you might find me in pretty good shape." Jessie grabbed her hand over her mouth and hurriedly crawled from the cave, retching when she reached daylight.

After a few minutes she crawled back in. "Sorry about that, guys. I thought I could hold up better. Just for the sake of argument, where are you… buried?"

Nick chuckled. "Just behind you, right back there. Angelo pulled down the ceiling making a false wall in front of where they put me. You take down that wall of stones and you will see me lying in an open place. All things considered I'm still in pretty good shape. He paused again. "Do you know how to use a pick and shovel?"

Joe made up his mind. "I can't come back with them tomorrow, but I can do it in the next couple days after that. We still have an appointment with Carmella and her daughter to visit the graves tomorrow, and I don't want to break that date."

"You'll need to bring somebody who knows what they're doing, just to make sure you don't get buried, too," Nick cautioned. "I like you and all, but I don't want to spend the rest of my days looking at another ghost in here."

CHAPTER FORTY

"What time is it?" Joe practically shouted as he awoke with a start. Had he overslept? The appointment with Mrs. Cook was for ten o'clock but he had been extremely sleepy last night. Nope, his bedside clock assured him it was only a few minutes after eight. But why hadn't he set the alarm? "Calm down, Joe. You have plenty of time." Gotta stop talking to myself, he thought. But then his mind moved on to happier topics, like meeting Jessie, Carmella and Carla at the restaurant.

First things first, though. He had lots of input for his journal this morning! He took it down and filled two pages with notes from yesterday, concluding with his trepidation over the task to come. *What about Nick's remains? He practically asked me to dig him out. I mean, how do I do that? Should I call 911 or some county officials? I better ask Les.* He placed the journal on the shelf again and dialed Les's number.

"Les? This is Joe. I need to talk with you about something that a fire chief might know. Could you meet me at Andy's?" Les agreed to be there in fifteen minutes, so Joe hurriedly showered and dressed, just walking out the door as Les came screeching into the yard with his truck's brakes grabbing.

His rush wasn't just because he sensed the potential seriousness of the situation. "I like to do that sometimes," he explained as he trotted over to Joe. It must be the hidden stock car driver in me." Together they walked over to the "Diner" where Andy was waiting with coffee. "So what's this all about? I hope it's good."

"Oh, it is!" said Joe. He then related the meeting with Carmella to Les as Andy prepared some toast. He then told the two of them about Nick's suggestion that they dig him out. "Are there any legal implications here, Les?" Joe asked. "I mean, if I dig him out, what then?" Les rubbed his chin.

"I'll check into it. I'm pretty sure that the county coroner will have to be involved, and as Nick suggested there should be a skilled team of diggers. Maybe I can call the United Mine Workers for some volunteer miners. He was a union miner after all… or he wanted to be.

It's been over eighty years now, so I guess he can keep for a few days longer." Les checked his watch. "Meanwhile, shouldn't we be heading over to that restaurant?"

"Yeah, we should," Andy chimed in. It's getting late."

"It's also getting out of hand," Joe remarked good-naturedly. "But you two are buying your own breakfast. Remember, I'm only a poor, currently out-of-work real estate guy." Joe suddenly slapped his own forehead in sudden realization. "Oh! That reminds me. I better call Sam and let him know that my break from real estate could last longer than I thought." He pulled the cell phone – which he never used anymore – out of his pocket and dialed Sam's office.

"Sam? It's me, Joe. Yeah, I know I used to work there in the old days... wise guy! How are things going there? Thanks... I appreciate that... Sam? I think I may have to extend my break a bit longer. I'm pretty involved in some local matters and... You heard? ...Channel Eight? ...Damn. Are many people talking about it? ...Other brokers are calling you, too? What are they saying? ...Oh... What kind of jokes?" Joe listened intently; his expression growing more worried, as the others watched. "All I can say is that I'm truly sorry, but I have to do whatever it is that I'm doing... Yeah, I know. But there aren't any ghosts, just one spirit..."

Joe's side of the discussion made it clear to the others that Sam didn't take the matter lightly.

"Anyway, Sam. I just can't help that. I hope you can understan..." Joe sighed audibly and stared off into nothingness while he listened. "Okay. I know. Anyway I think it'll blow over. Sooner or later." He seemed to stiffen and an expression of resolve overcame his face. "Sam, I'll do whatever I can to minimize any damage to Viewpointe's reputation, not to mention my own career."

Joe's resolve grew even firmer. "But I think there's something bigger going on here than any of us realize, and I just don't see how we can change that." Joe nodded with an air of finality. "Yes, I'll keep you posted. Thanks, Sam. Goodbye for now."

***

Arriving at the restaurant, Joe's heart sank when he didn't see the Camaro in the lot. Not mentioning it to the two passengers in his car, he parked and they walked inside. The hostess pointed them toward the same table near the window.

"We need a bigger table," Carmella remarked. "Our crowd is growing." The two ladies, plus two teenagers, got up and followed Joe and his friends to a much larger table. To be sure of adequate space, Joe and Les pulled another table over, too.

"Carmella and Carla," Joe began. "Please let me present Mr. Andy Polack, a neighbor and good friend of mine in Avella, and Mr. Les Wilson, another good friend and the town's volunteer fire chief. And of course you know Jessie." The late arrival had just walked in the door and was striding toward the table.

"These are my two grandchildren, Carla's daughter and son, Jenny and Joey." The teens appeared to be about 15 and 13 years old. "We would have had to beat them off with a stick to keep them away today because of all the stories they heard from Granddad's day, especially about his good friend Nick."

"Yeah!" Joey offered. "So you really talk to Nick?"

Joe nodded. "And so does Miss Randall." The two looked suitably surprised.

"Can we talk to him, too?" asked Jenny eagerly. She looked questioningly at Jessie.

"Well, I can see and talk to Nick," Jessie responded. "But I think it's something mystical that's limited to Joe and me. I doubt that anybody else could see him or hear him." Joey and Jenny looked crestfallen.

"Well, if I ever get the chance I'm gonna try!" Joey responded determinedly.

"Shall we order, ladies?" Joe asked. They all placed their order for brunch items, and spent the rest of the meal discussing what Joe and Jessie had learned, omitting for the time being that Nick had told them where his body could be found. It was hardly appropriate fodder for a mealtime chat, those in the Avella group had individually concluded.

As they were eating, Jessie broke the astonishing news that Andy had faint memories of Mike, Carmella, and their little daughter who now sat before them as the oldest woman in the place.

"I was just a young miner, but I remember. I remember your dad's garden like it was yesterday but I only vaguely remember your mom. You were mebbe four or five years old," Andy related. "Next thing I knew, your family moved away." They finished their meal in silence, thinking over the completed circle – one of many that were sure to be revealed.

"So you say, Joe, that you are worried about public opinion?" Carmella asked concernedly. "While I am a very private person, as long as I am sure that you are sincere, and I believe to this point that you are, I will be happy to help in any way that I can. That we can," she added, looking at her daughter meaningfully.

"I wouldn't want to have you held up to public scrutiny and possible ridicule," he answered after an obvious internal personal conflict. "But frankly, right now I would grab onto any help that I can get." After a final cup of tea or coffee and a bathroom break for Andy, they departed. Contrary to his earlier warning, Joe insisted on picking up the total tab. Les left a handsome tip.

In a small caravan of three vehicles, they left for the cemetery near Hickory. Joe had switched so that he rode with Jessie in her Camaro while Les drove the Caddy. Joe frequently admired the line of her legs, albeit clothed in a pair of well-fitting slacks, as they chatted.

At the cemetery they all followed the two women to the gravesite where Carmella placed a small spray of flowers, freshly cut. Jessie caught her breath when she realized that the tiny, purple flowers were in fact violets, probably picked that very morning by her grandkids. They stood there in silence, with heads bowed.

After a few moments, Carla asked: "Do you notice anything unusual about this grave, Mr. Bailey?" Joe looked at it carefully now… Zaretsky… Carmella to the right, Michael to the left… Jessie grabbed his arm and practically squeezed the life out of it. "Joe!" she exclaimed. "Look to the other side!" Then it hit him, and he could tell that Les and Andy had finally seen it, too.

Another stone stood about five feet from theirs. *Nicholas Shebellko. Born May 2, 1900; died July 17, 1922.*

The place had been prepared for a man who could never use it. The ground was perfectly flat and the soil undisturbed. No mound or slight depression attested to the presence of a corpse, as with the nearby graves. Joe turned questioningly to Carmella.

"They never even dreamed that this place could ever be used," she explained. "They put the stone there in remembrance of a man important to both of them. But the site has been available all along if Nick could ever be found."

After quickly exchanging glances with his friends, Joe finally made the decision. "Do we ever have a surprise for you! Yesterday Nick told us exactly where his body could be found, and we are considering how to best recover his remains. He told us that he's ready for a proper interment." The two ladies stood there in stunned silence, and as the senior Carmella began to falter, her grandson stepped forward manfully to support her. "I believe that a proper burial would give him the peace that has eluded him all this time."

"You are serious, Mr. Bailey? You know where Nick can be found?" Carla asked the question with hope rising in her breast. "I think that you can begin to understand the relationships within our family all this time. Grandma loved Nick, who was taken away from her, but she learned to love Grandpap with all her heart. They both treasured the memory of Nick, and talked often about him and their times together. If he could be found, it would complete a shattered circle." Her mother began to cry unabashedly, and everybody else standing in that little group at the graveside also began to weep, each lost in his or her own thoughts, and their tears.

Joe finally offered consolingly, "the best part may be that he's lying in a place where the dirt has never touched him. It's a cave with the floor and ceiling made of stone. If Angelo did his job as well as he wanted to, Nick might not be covered by soil at all, or perhaps with only a layer of dust. He could as well be lying in state." The women began to weep again. The men, including Joey, apparently decided they had cried enough and began to comfort the others.

"I'll keep you ladies informed," Joe finally said. "We won't do anything unless you know about it in advance. It's just that we have to work with the authorities in recovering his body. Trained people will have to do the work, perhaps a mine rescue team or volunteer miners."

"And we will help you do anything necessary to preserve and hopefully enhance your reputation," responded Carla. Saying their goodbyes with numerous hugs and handshakes all around, the little group disbanded.

CHAPTER FORTY-ONE

Seven a.m. Already seven a.m. Joe slowly opened his eyes into the bright daylight that forced its way through his window, despite the drawn shades. He rolled over and gratefully lay there in appreciation of his third night in a row with no disruptive interruptions of his slumber. "Nick," he said under his breath, "Thanks." After a few minutes he arose and went about his morning ablutions.

"Well," he said to himself, louder this time. "Time to get started." Les had enthusiastically taken the role of point man in finding out how to excavate Nick's body, making the first theoretical "what if?" contacts, as it were. Joe had little to do today but work around the house and maybe take a walk into town for some treats and hiking supplies. He decided to take the walk first, before the heat of day came at him full tilt. He dressed and, after waving at old Andy, started into town.

"Interesting" he remarked after waving at several neighbors. "Nobody seems to be acknowledging me today." He walked on, deciding to take the initiative.

"Hi there, Mrs. J!" he called to Mrs. Johnson. "You're having an early start on your garden this morning. Is it to beat the heat?" She looked up.

"Yes, Mr. Bailey." She abruptly looked back down, intent on pulling weeds. But he saw no weeds in her hands. Joe walked on. "Are people intentionally turning away when I approach?" he asked himself. A few more people busied themselves in their morning newspapers or stared into their teacups as though they were attempting to divine the future within. Joe walked on.

"Hey, Charlie," he yelled.

"Hey, Joe." Charlie smiled and gave him the thumbs-up sign, before returning to his duties under the hood of a Range Rover. "At least Charlie hasn't turned on me," he muttered.

Finally, Joe made it to the convenience store. As he walked in the clerk assumed a grim look. "Seen any good ghosts lately, Mr.

Bailey?" a customer standing next to the coffee machine remarked, humorlessly. Somebody else laughed. The clerk didn't crack a smile, clearly trying to remain neutral.

"Are they telling any good ghost jokes these days?" another man cracked. Joe selected a few items, paid up, and went on his way. Somebody made an unintelligible remark before the door closed and the others erupted into laughter, including the clerk.

As he continued down the street towards the dry cleaners, he saw three old men discussing whatever they did every morning. As he passed they fell silent. After he had gone by, one of them said something, eliciting a hilarious response from his cronies.

Freshly ransomed dry cleaning in hand, he wandered over to the fire hall where he saw two volunteers working on the landscaping. "Hi, Joe," one called to him, smiling. The other stopped and grinned. "Seen any good ghosts lately, Joe?" she said good-naturedly.

Joe perused the two and smiled ruefully. "Somehow when you make that joke it sounds a whole lot funnier than when some others say it." They nodded in agreement. "The difference," the woman explained, "is that we know you."

"If I can hang these things up somewhere I'll help you trim the shrubbery or pull weeds," he offered. He went inside and hung his clothes next to the firefighters' turnout gear that was always hanging ready in event of a fire.

"Where do you want me to start?" he inquired.

"You help Sheila fix up around the firefighters memorial," Jim, a lieutenant, directed. "I can keep working over here." They worked in silence for an hour more before Jim stood up, apparently satisfied with their efforts. "Now, how about a soft drink?"

They entered the welcome shade of the fire hall engine room, where Jim inserted change into the machine and handed Sheila and Joe each a cold can of ice tea. "So how are things, Joe?" he inquired seriously.

"Not bad, except for this sudden case of leprosy I must have caught," Joe chuckled grimly. "It seems that people just don't want to know me these days."

"Well you still have friends here," smiled Sheila. "And thanks loads for the help this morning. We'd still be trying to finish up out there if not for you." After a moment she continued, "You really should think of joining. You have lots of skills from your law enforcement days. You could be fire police from day one, and a hoseman just as soon as you underwent training."

"I do think about it, Sheila. But I just don't know how long I'll be living here," Joe responded. "I have a lot to think about," he said glumly.

"Look, if you're only planning to stay a year like you said, that's okay," Jim answered. "But if idiots are going to try to run you out of town, I don't think it's at all like you to let that happen. Just remember that you have friends here. Some others just don't know you."

"Thanks, guys. I know I can count on you." He drained his can, tossed the empty into the recycling bin, picked up his dry-cleaned clothes, and began to trudge back home. It was more like drudgery than in the past, as he continued to encounter occasional stares and averted eyes.

Back home he walked over to Andy's, where a pitcher of lemonade awaited him. "Lemonade never tasted so good, Andy," he said appreciatively. His old friend glanced up and observed, "That sight should pick up your spirits even more." The Camaro had just pulled into the parking space.

"Well, gents, are we ready for a library trip this morning?" Jessie burst out as she hurried over. They liked the way she hurried over. "We have to see if anybody has more information on the friend we never knew, Angelo." She poured herself a cold glass of lemonade and pressed it against her forehead. "Feels so good," she remarked. She then drained the glass. "Ready?" They nodded agreement.

***

At the library, Nan was on duty with Brenda, a library clerk. "I've wanted to meet you, Mr. Bailey, and you too, Miss Randall. The others have told me so much about you," Brenda exclaimed. "And rumor has it that Ben just might have something more for you, too."

"Oh, now don't steal my news, Brenda!" Nan said. "Joe, I heard from a senior citizen that she remembers playing with Angelo Ballino's daughter. She thinks Angelo and his family moved out west.

She recalls they went first to Michigan, and then she heard afterward, to Arizona or New Mexico. Ben took that ball and ran with it. Speak of the devil! Here he comes now." Ben walked in, placing his trusty satchel on the desk surface.

"Hi, Joe. I have something for you. My contacts reveal that an Angelo Ballino and his family moved first to the Detroit area, where he found work in an auto factory, and then afterward to Arizona to work in the housing construction boom of post-World War Two. Their line apparently included several children, including two sons who both served in the US Navy in the Atlantic. Fortunately both returned alive, although young Angelo had been seriously injured when German surface and U-Boat forces attacked his ship's convoy. It appears that he never fully recovered from his injuries and he died less than two years after the war ended.

"We're trying to find out where Angelo and Maria finally settled. But, Joe, there's something else. It appears that their son, Nicholas, later Americanized his name when he became employed in management of a communications firm. He took the name Nicholas Bailey." Joe staggered to the nearest table and clutched its edge, wavering. "Not Ballino anymore, Joe. His Americanized name was Nicholas Bailey." Joe sank into a chair as the impact of what Ben just revealed slammed him between the eyes.

After a few minutes, he shakily began his story. "I never knew much about my family's history. I was never all that concerned with it. Of course I knew my parents, but my granddad Nick and grandma Rachel died in an auto wreck in 1967, before I could know either one. I didn't really know my grandparents on my mom's side very well, either. They lived in California where mom met my dad, and we didn't see them very often."

"Are you saying, Joe, that Angelo Ballino might be your great-grandfather?" Jessie gasped.

"I can't say, because I just don't know," Joe replied unsteadily. "But I guess it's possible. I was never into family history. I sure didn't know about any Ballino in the family. I suppose that means Angelo must also be related to my great-uncle, Albert, who I was not even aware of. I just – I just don't know. This is all so sudden." He shook his head as if to clear it. "Thanks for the good work, Ben. And thanks to everybody else at the library. I have to go home now."

CHAPTER FORTY-TWO

Joe and Jessie had arranged to make the trek once more to Nick's cave, to bring him up to date on the possible Angelo-to-Joe connection. Joe fidgeted as he waited for her, pacing the floor in his living room, all dressed and packed and ready to go. The sun had already risen well over the horizon.

Finally at ten minutes to eight, he heard the familiar sound of tires slowing and coming to a stop on the gravel outside. Yes, even without looking he identified it as the Camaro. Joe counted the footsteps as they hurriedly approached the house.

"I just love the sound that those small hiking boots make!" he exclaimed. Not to mention how he felt about the feet wearing them. Opening the door, he was met by an onrush of woman. Jessie grabbed him around the neck and pressed her lips to his. "Wow!" he thought delightedly. "Wow." Jessie felt really good, and he truly savored the way she smelled in the morning before the humidity, heat and exertion brought out her womanly sweat. But he also liked the gentle but hot aroma that she emanated later in the day, after a long hike. There's just so much to like about this Jessie, he thought.

"So does this mean you're happy to see me?" he inquired as they separated.

"You betcha!" she exclaimed. "I'm really getting used to having you around, Mr. Bailey. Now, how about that hike? We have some more things to talk over with our ghost, like how his buddy Joe just might have some of Angelo's blood in him. We're stopping at Andy's first, though, aren't we?" she told him more than asked. "I really look forward to our visits with him. I wish he could go to the cave with us someday."

As they walked next door, Andy again stood in the doorway with the accustomed mugs of coffee. "Going to see Nick, Joe? Sure hope so. I hear in town you're the butt of more jokes than the lawyers." Andy welcomed them inside and placed bowls of hot oatmeal in front of each one. "I think it could all blow over in a few weeks, but we should do something to hurry up the process if we can."

"Like what?" Joe inquired.

"Dunno. But I think we oughta do something."

Joe slowly dragged his spoon through his oatmeal, staring into the bowl. "A while ago I began to wonder whether I had a purpose here," he said, looking up. "I mean, why me? And, why now? Is there a reason for me being here with all this stuff going on?" He slowly ate a few more spoonfuls and then sat back in exasperation. The others listened intently. "I had a strong feeling, maybe closer to a revelation, that I have a true purpose, one that must be fulfilled. Things seem to be coming together, like the way the planets line up from time to time or how they come together in the morning sky."

"I agree," said Jessie, never behind and often a step or two ahead of him. "If it's a kind of fate – a process that has taken nearly a hundred years, ready for culmination now – then those small-minded people will have no impact at all. Things will work out despite what they say or do."

"They might as well spit in the wind!" Andy exclaimed, grinning broadly. "And all they'll get is a face full of their own spit!" He cackled hilariously as his young friends took on more confident expressions.

"Well, we better be on our way." Joe swallowed the last few drops of his coffee. "A full report later, of course!"

"I won't take anything less. Now you two youngsters get outta here, so I can clean up this kitchen." But he accepted a hug from Jessie before they departed.

They rode in silence, anticipating how Nick would receive the news about Angelo and Joe. "It's not easy to perplex a ghost," Joe remarked out of the blue as they rode along. "But this Angelo thing just might do it." Presently, they arrived at their parking spot to find three cars and a pickup truck already parked along the roadside.

"Uh, oh,'" Jessie said quietly. "This could be bad – very bad." They saw a woman sitting in the cab of the pickup truck listening to a country music station. "Excuse me, miss," Jessie asked, dreading the answer that would surely come. "Why are all these vehicles parked here?"

"Haven't you heard? There are ghosts in a cave up there somewhere and my boyfriend and his buddy and some other people want to see them. This is where the car…" She stared at the Caddy, realization finally setting in. "Your car… is always parked." Without further hesitation Joe and Jessie turned and hurried up the trail. "Wait!" the woman called out after them. "Tell me about the ghosts!"

"Damn." Joe cursed as they hurried along. "Why did I have to use this one trail so many times and always park in the same place? Stupid! Stupid! Stupid!" He slapped his own forehead with the heel of his hand. "Stupid!"

Jessie could see clearly that he was right. The trail was actually well marked by their frequent use. It would be easy, even for a greenhorn, to find the cave. She dreaded what they would find when they got there. They hurried onward, rushing most of the way, until they were past the meadow. As they neared the outcropping, they heard resounding laughter coming from just ahead. They rounded the last bend.

"What are you doing here?" Joe demanded.

"What's your problem, man," a boy of perhaps seventeen said. "We just want to see the ghosts is all."

Joe pushed past him and muscled his way into the cave. Several more people were just inside the entrance. "What's going on here?" he demanded. Inside there were three men, in their early twenties, and two women. His flashlight's beam revealed several empty beer cans strewn around and a six-pack of unopened beers. The stagnant air hung heavy with cigarette smoke. The place grew quiet. "Well?" he demanded again. Jessie crawled inside, too, and squatted next to him, holding her stout walking stick at the ready.

"Hey, man! We just want to see the ghosts. This is where they are, right?" Glancing around, Joe and Jessie both noticed an unhappy-looking spirit sitting in the corner. In fact, Nick looked totally pissed.

"Joe, I told you we won't have any group tours down here," Nick complained.

"Get out," Joe told the others. There are no ghosts in here, so get out." One man took a step toward him, but a glare from Joe made it clear that he meant business. Jessie brandished her staff, not menacingly, but with a world full of meaning in her eyes. The disrespectful guests looked at each other sullenly and, without a word, decided to leave.

Joe tossed their empties and the full six-pack after them. "Here. Clean up after yourselves. And by the way, I jotted down your license numbers and we got a good look at your faces so you better leave my car alone."

"Well there goes the neighborhood," Jessie remarked. "And, Nick, we never brought or sent them here."

Nick broke into a large but rueful grin. "I know that. But I still didn't enjoy their company none. I mean, over all these years I hosted plenty of hikers and hunters but this lot beats them all. Most of the others just sat a while, had something to drink or a snack and maybe a smoke, and then they left. But this bunch was really wearing on my nerves. I thought of sticking a cold finger into their muscles but that would have told them I was here." Joe laughed at the thought of miscreants getting poked by invisible frigid icicles. But Nick was right; it would have just confirmed his presence.

"Anyway, Joe. Once they dig me up there will be no reason for me to hang around this cave, and after I get a proper and decent burial you might not see me at all." The truth of it hit both Joe and Jessie suddenly. Nick's spirit would surely move on to some other place.

"Nick, I'm not ready to lose you!" Joe exclaimed. "Not ready at all…" Jessie reached out and clutched his hand.

"Me, neither," she said simply.

"Look, you two. You're some of the best friends I ever had and I will remember you forever. But look at each other now. Please?" Joe and Jessie looked at each other – into each other's face, eyes, and soul. "What do you see?"

Joe answered first. "I see a woman who I care for very deeply. I can't imagine not having her in my life." It momentarily startled him that he could say that so easily.

Jessie had tears forming in her eyes. "I have the same feeling when I see Joe," she said, squeezing his hand.

"Now look around. Who do you see for me?" They didn't have to look. They knew Nick had nobody. "Do you see? All I have is a few dead miners scattered around to talk with." He paused for effect. "Believe me, that's not a very fulfilling future to look forward to," he said, with a wry smile on his face. "But when I do move on, who will be waiting for me?"

"Carmella and Mike," Jessie answered, without thinking.

"And Angelo," Joe whispered understandingly. "They'll surely be waiting for you." After another moment, Joe offered: "Let me help you pack."

Jessie laughed. "I think Nick travels pretty light. Joe, why not tell Nick what we found out yesterday? About Angelo?"

Now Nick dropped all pretense of joking and looked squarely into Joe's eyes, as though he wanted to suck the truth out about his dear friend before Joe could even form the words. Joe hesitated, and then began. "Nick, we had some people looking into where Angelo went. I already told you that he brought Maria over here, and they had twin boys named Angelo and Nick." Nick smiled at the memory. "Well, we learned something more. Angelo took his family to Michigan so he could work in a factory building new cars.

"Angelo didn't stay in mining?" Nick asked. "He quit mining? I always knew he was a smart man."

"Yes, he quit mining because there wasn't much work in the mines anymore. But people wanted to buy cars."

Jessie jumped into the conversation. "And afterward he moved farther out west with his family to work on building new houses. His sons grew up and went to war. But they both survived and came home. "Now it gets interesting. Do you want to hear the rest?"

"You're not leaving this cave until I do," Nick said, flexing an ethereal bicep.

Joe laughed in appreciation of the dark humor and continued. "His son, Nicholas, decided to Americanize his name, like many sons of immigrants did. That means to change their name to make it sound less… less foreign. Sometimes people did that to get ahead in the world of business or in society. As I said, Nick Ballino did that. He changed his name. He changed his name to Nicholas Bailey, so his descendants through his sons are also named Bailey."

"Bailey? But isn't that your name?" Nick gasped. "What are you saying, Joe?"

"We don't know for sure yet, but my grandfather's name was Nick Bailey. Granddad Nick, my father used to call him. I never knew him because he and my grandmother died when I was very young. I don't know for sure, but it could be that Granddad Nick was Angelo's son. If so, I would be directly descended from your friend, Angelo."

"You – you have Angelo's blood in your veins?"

"Maybe, Nick. Maybe. And even more so, my spirit might

have attracted your spirit when you returned to the cave. You might have passed through my body, instead of somebody else's, because of the Angelo in me."

CHAPTER FORTY-THREE

"Mr. Bailey?" The voice on the other end of the phone line sounded like that of a young man. "Mr. Joseph Bailey?" Joe decided to play along, even though he had already received over a dozen crank phone calls during the past several days. But he did have to chuckle over the variation on the old one: "Do you have Prince Albert's ghost in a can?"

"I'm Joseph Bailey. And you are...?" Joe answered as neutrally as he possibly could; ready to hang the phone up gently, or even crash it down into its cradle, depending on the caller's next few words.

"Mr. Bailey, my name is James Christopher. You might have seen me at the school board meeting. I report on local municipal affairs and meetings for the Washington Chronicle newspaper. Might I ask you some questions, just to follow up on what you said at the meeting last week?" He sounded sincere, Joe thought. But on the other hand, he could be trying to enhance his own reputation at Joe's expense.

"What do you want, Mr. Christopher? Do you plan to make a joke of me, too?" Joe asked cautiously.

After a momentary pause, the reporter continued, in the sincerest tone he could muster. "I don't plan to make a joke of anything, Mr. Bailey. I thought I picked up on a real story underlying what you said, and I was hoping you would share it with me... with our readers. How about this? If and when I write a story based on our interview, I can run it by you first, if you wish. Okay?"

Joe hesitated. Perhaps it really was time to put all his cards on the table, in full view of everyone. These half-truths, half-lies and unfunny jokes at his expense were severely damaging to his credibility, not to mention his peace of mind. When he responded his voice betrayed his tiredness. "Where would you like to meet, Mr. Christopher? At my place, or maybe the library?"

"Either one will be fine, Mr. Bailey," the reporter responded. "Whichever makes you more comfortable."

They made arrangements to meet at the public library later that afternoon. Joe called Jessie and Les and asked if they wanted to participate, or at least sit in on the interview as credible witnesses to what he said. Jessie promised to be there. Les apologized that he had to work and couldn't be available. Full of misgivings, but with hope for relief looming on the horizon, Joe organized his research documents to serve as memory aids during the interview. As an afterthought, he called the library just to confirm that the interview could be conducted there.

***

Joe and Jessie arrived early. She pulled him aside before he could enter the building.

"I just wanted to warn you," she confided seriously. "Principal Landers assured me that my job is safe, in part because of my union's backing. But even considering the patent stupidity of their charges, those two women and their group are still expected to make a scene at the board meeting tomorrow night. I don't think they can do much real damage, but the spotlight would shine on you again… and on me. Nobody is quite sure what they have planned."

"I don't worry about them anymore, Jessie. They're the least of my problems. How about this one? How do we get a buried miner exhumed without it becoming the circus act of the year? Now, *that* will be a problem. Am I worried about what will be splashed all over the newspapers and television in the next week or so? Or about my real estate reputation? No, those issues have become of little importance compared to finally putting Nick to rest and the other miners too, if they can even be found."

She nodded seriously. "Perhaps we should touch base with the library staff before Mr. Christopher gets here. They should be available just in case questions are asked of them. But otherwise, they probably should lay low." The two went inside to chat with the staff, and to wait. Precisely on time, the reporter arrived with notepad, tape-recorder and camera in hand. The locals readily recognized him as the man who had been scribbling madly in his note pad the past Wednesday night.

"Mr. Bailey?"

Joe introduced himself and Jessie. The three went to a library table to sit and size each other up. Mr. Christopher, who insisted on being called Jim, began the interview.

"At the board meeting, you described meeting the spirit of a deceased coal miner. Would you please fill me in on the circumstances?" Joe sighed loudly; so loudly that he caught the startled attention of Carol at the checkout desk, and even Jessie's eyes widened in astonishment. It appeared that Jim understood the sigh was born of well-founded frustration. He waited patiently.

"As the trite saying goes: 'where to begin?' There's just so much to say, Jim. I'll start by giving you some background stuff. You'll recall that I said I love to hike, and I'm actually very new to the area. It all began like this..."

He related his story, interrupted only by the changing of the cassette tape.

"... So, we have established the identities of two men who are buried in the woods somewhere. There are undoubtedly others buried out there, too. A battle that resulted in nine deaths at the mine, and involved so many combatants, had to have resulted in even more deaths from mortal wounds.

Jim sat, looking in some disbelief at his notes and tape recorder. "You say that there are people today who are descended from these miners and can be identified?"

"Yes, there are. I've spoken with several. I won't give you their names, but I will promise you this: I will give them your name and contact information. They may decide to contact you. That would be up to them." He shrugged. "It's the most I'll do."

"Joe, you said that one fallen man is this Nick person. The other was the father of a local man. The man must be pretty old. After all, the son of a man who died in 1922 has to be at least in his eighties or nineties..."

"He is that old, but it would be up to him to decide whether to share the story of his father's tragedy with you. But I wouldn't be surprised if he did decide to contact you. He's a real character, but perhaps the sincerest and most honest man I know. And he can really tell a story."

"You also said that you and Miss Randall used the resources of this library, Brooke County's public library, and the Ohio County

Library in Wheeling to confirm what Nick told you?" Joe nodded.

After initially hesitating to speak, Jessie jumped in. "I realized that what Joe was getting involved in – this friendship with Nick – could come to be a real problem for him. I suggested that we check historical records and perhaps genealogy, to support whatever Nick told him. The staff of this public library," she indicated the three employees standing conspicuously within earshot. "And its genealogist, were very helpful. We have some reports from newspapers dated after the riot that support fully what we… what Joe learned from Nick." Jessie blushed as she caught herself in what she had been about to say. But Jim was rather fast on the uptake.

"Jessie, were you about to say that you can talk with Nick, too?" His question and his eyes bored into her as he awaited the answer. However, Joe jumped right in.

"No, she didn't mean that. I tell her what Nick says, so it seems like she gets it from him, see, but it's only me who…"

"Joe," she said sternly. She turned to Jim and evenly returned his gaze. "The truth is that at first I couldn't relate to Nick directly at all, but somehow, later on I could see and hear him, just as Joe does. I'm thankful that I can talk with Nick, too." His suspicions confirmed, Jim decided to follow this lead as well.

"How would you describe Nick?" He prepared to wait her out, because when a silence presents itself, people tend to fill the void with talk. But in this case, Jessie was only too willing to discuss Nick with him.

"He's a young but ruggedly handsome man of about five feet, eight inches." She smiled at the thought. "Young, but at the same time over a hundred years old, of course." Jim chuckled at the irony. Jessie continued, more seriously now.

"He's not at all heavily muscled, but you can see he's strong. His arms are very sinewy-looking. In life I would suspect about 155 pounds or so. His slightly dirt-smudged face sports about a two or three day growth of whiskers. His hair appears to be dark brown. He has a prominent nose, and blue eyes that seem to reassure you it's okay to trust him. His hands appear to be large and powerful looking. He also has thick wrists." Joe looked at her quizzically, surprised that she noticed so much about Nick.

"Do I have to worry about Nick stealing your heart?" he asked half-jokingly. Jim smirked.

"… So I can understand why Carmella loved him so much," she continued, feigning a glare at Joe. Everybody then broke into laughter, including the library staff.

"Let's talk about that. Why do you suppose Nick could talk with you, but not with other people?" Joe explained about his experience when Nick's spirit had apparently moved through his body on his way back into the cave.

"One more thing, Jim," he concluded. "I think there's a reason beyond mere chance that his spirit passed through me, but we're still trying to work that out." He glanced meaningfully at Jessie and the library staff to hold off on the Angelo angle for the time being. "We'll fill you in, once we are one hundred percent certain."

Jim nodded and checked his watch. "I see it's getting late. I think I have enough material for not just an article, but the start of a mini-series. Especially if the other contacts you mentioned decide to share with me," he added hopefully. "I think if I can get my editor's permission we can publish the first installment on the front page of the local section, this coming Sunday."

"And if some other things we are researching come to fruition, we'll share them with you, too," Joe added. "But, Jim? Please don't include that Jessie can see and talk with Nick just yet, okay?"

"I'll check with you first," Jim responded. "But meanwhile, I have a deadline on another story I'm working on, so I better be on my way." After they watched him pull out of the parking lot, Joe and the others chatted for a few more minutes, strategizing what information would be shared, and when.

Nan spoke up suddenly. "Joe, I just remembered something. A while ago you asked me to research something else for you, and I may have an answer. Interested?" She grinned at him. "Well, maybe we can hold it for next time."

"I don't think so," he said with a hint of playful menace in his voice. "No, I don't think so. Now, let's hear it, Ms. Cross."

It has to do with "Shades of Death Road. The most likely story I can find is this: When the area was first settled and for quite some time afterward, the road was bounded by thick groves of trees, probably hemlocks. Traveling it could be a very dark and intimidating experience for early settlers, especially when going through a particular dip in the road, which was even darker. People related that it reminded them of going through 'the shades of death,' so they named it that."

"Hemlocks?" Joe answered, with a hint of disappointment in his voice. "Hemlocks? I was thinking more like murders and hangings and human sacrifices and all that."

"I doubt it. Of course, there are some old unconfirmed tales of deaths, including suicide, but they may have been made up because of the name of the road instead of vice-versa. Also, I noticed references in the Internet of a stand of trees called 'shades of death.' There is also a Shades of Death Road in New Jersey, for example, with its own set of legends, and a 'shades of death' hiking trail in a state park in northeastern Pennsylvania. So, we aren't exactly unique with our strange road name.

"Well, I like it anyway," responded Jessie. "And on that note," she said, turning to Joe, "we should let these nice people close up their library and go home.

"It's the public's library, not ours," Carol responded. "But we will close it up and go home."

"And next, we should cheek with an old friend named Andy," Joe remarked, getting back to the reason for their visit to the library. "And also call a very nice old lady named Carmella. It will be up to them, but they just may decide to chat with young Mr. Reporter, too."

CHAPTER FORTY-FOUR

This school board meeting is taking an ugly turn, Joe reflected in growing alarm as he watched the situation deteriorate before him. Brenda Jones had just finished her tirade with escalating support from the public and from the board.

"...so, why didn't you check this Bailey person out more thoroughly, Principal Landers?" the hawk-nosed board member continued, reveling in his glory. "Is that responsible administrative behavior?" The audience was eating it up now, and even the white-haired board member was visibly shifting her chair in the speaker's direction. Only the board chairperson and one other, lone member were still in Administration's camp, but even they showed signs of conflict.

Now, Granger was at it again, continuing where Jones had left off, demanding the jobs of the principal "and all staff members associated with planning the outing." Jessie sat, unbelieving, between Joe and Les. She clutched Joe's hand with her nails piercing his palm and was clearly on the verge of tears. Joe brushed aside the knife-like pain. Granger played to the crowd and the three television cameras. Sensing blood in the water, the guy with the video was murmuring encouragement to Granger. The chairperson reached for her gavel, but drew back her hand.

Doesn't anybody else see that this is scripted and choreographed by the troublemakers? Joe wondered. How it had turned so bad, so fast eluded him.

Suddenly a snippet of conversation that protruded through a lapse in the nearby buzz smacked into Joe like a ball bat. "...Nut that thinks he talks to ghosts," a man remarked aloud. A woman snickered in agreement, furtively glancing Joe's way.

"Thank you, Julie," the hawk-nosed guy repeated for the fourth or fifth time in the last five minutes. "You may take your seat." He had clearly taken control of the meeting and the chairperson was having less say as the meeting wore on. He turned to her. "I move that we go into executive session to discuss personnel matters." Shaken, the chairperson nodded. With the motion quickly seconded and approved, the security guards opened the doors so the audience could file out until the public portion of the meeting resumed.

"My God, the bastards are going to fire Principal Landers and Jessie!" Joe muttered under his breath. But Jessie's sharp hearing picked it up. She began to sob quietly as the crowd nearby stared at her in morbid fascination. An elderly woman reached out to console her. How much worse can this get? Joe wondered.

Then Joe uncontrollably screamed, "NO!" at the top of his voice as people nearby stared in alarm. Les reached out to calm him down.

"NO! NO! NO!" Sitting upright, staring straight ahead, he found that he had thrown his sheets clear off the bed. "NO!" he shouted once more before getting himself back under control and into reality. The crowd and the board had faded after the second or third "no." Joe wiped the sweat streaming into his eyes with his t-shirt.

I don't think I'll tell her about this dream, he decided. He quickly began his morning routine, forcing all vestiges of the nightmare from his consciousness. He still had Jessie's arrival to look forward to, and she was due in less than a half-hour.

***

"Nick," Joe began, as he and Jessie sat side-by-side in their accustomed places. "As you said, we just don't know how much longer you'll be with us. We hate to lose you, but we must be prepared for exactly that. We understand that this just isn't the right place for anybody to spend eternity." Jessie smiled encouragingly at him and squeezed his hand as he searched for the words.

"Thanks for pointing that out to us last time," she added. "Things are starting to move pretty fast out there. Les has already spoken to the coroner and the state police, and he contacted the United Mine Workers local union. It isn't general knowledge yet, but efforts to recover your… your," Jessie choked on the words. "Recovery will probably take place sometime next week."

Nick nodded sadly, wistful about the end of his time with these two remarkable people. "I hate to lose you, too, but the more I think about it the more I want to move on. I never mentioned this before, but did you notice a hostile attitude when we first met?"

"I did detect a kind of sullenness, Nick. Sort of an underlying anger or maybe a well-masked rage. But it didn't bother me much. And you seemed to get past it pretty well," Joe responded.

"To tell you the truth, I was getting pretty upset being down here. But then you came along and I had somebody to talk to – somebody who could tell me things about life out there. That helped. That helped a lot. In fact, I've been telling some of the other boys down here about you. They're feeling better now, too. It's like they can see a light at the mine portal, so to speak. They think you can help us. I'm sure you can."

Jessie answered quickly. "We will do our best, Nick. And you can tell them that. But these other boys... are they men who died after the riot?" she asked.

"They all died after the riot. They're all out there, or their bones are, anyway."

"How many are there?"

"I know of eight others for sure. There's Andy, you know about him. Tony was an Italian, John was colored, George was Slavic like me, Alex and Frank were Hungarian, Chuck was born in this country, and Pete was from Poland. But you know something?"

"No, Nick. Tell us." Joe's spirit fell upon this sudden, personalized verification that there were other bodies out there and other spirits that hadn't moved on. The names were what did it. These were *men*, he realized. Men with names. *People.*

"Not one guy cares at all about where he's from. They all just want to go on, to wherever they're going." Nick paused. "Like me."

They sat in silence for a while, but then Jessie suddenly brightened. "We do have another piece of news for you. Those louts who were here when we came the last time threw off our plans to tell you what has been happening. We overlooked one wonderful piece of information." She smiled at Joe, who had a sudden flash of understanding.

"Yeah, Nick, we do have something to tell you. Do you remember when we were here and you said that Angelo and Mike and Carmella were waiting for you… waiting for you to move on?" Nick smiled at the prospect and stared off toward the ceiling. Joe thought he stared beyond it.

"Wherever they are, they're waiting for me. I know it in my heart."

Jessie could hold her news no longer. "They are very much waiting for you. But first let us tell you what we saw when we visited Mike and Carmella's grave." Nick Jerked his head back down, concentrating on her with a sudden fervent stare in his eyes, hoping against hope that the news would be good.

"They prepared a third grave, right next to Carmella. Mike is on her right side, and…" Nick gasped audibly and looked as though he would collapse.

"…and they prepared a place for you on her left." Jessie broke down in tears.

"Nick," Joe picked up the story. "They prepared a headstone with your name on it and your dates of birth and death. They obviously thought it to be symbolic, because they surely knew that your body would never be found. But there's a grave there, all ready for you." Joe wiped away a tear, too.

"Are you saying that their final resting place will be my place, too? My body will rest next to Mike and Carmella?"

"Apparently so, Nick. Yes, I'm sure of it."

Nick's face took on a serene expression. "I could never have hoped for that much."

Jessie struggled internally, trying to develop a plan. She finally asked, "Nick, how can we know where the others are buried? We must help them, too. But you can't just walk around and show us, you know."

"I've been thinking about that," he pondered. "You know how I always can tell when you're standing outside the cave, and I can talk to you?" They nodded. "I think I could lead you around the ground outside, from below. For example, old John isn't buried very far from here. Do you want to try just one place now?"

Jessie's face positively lit up, excited and enthused. Joe thought that it must mirror his own expression. "Let's try!" they both exclaimed in unison.

"Alright, then. Outside the cave entrance you walk toward the west, back toward the tunnel and just follow my voice. You won't be able to follow me directly because of the terrain up there. You know. Gullies, rocks and thick brush in places, but I think I can get you there all the same. Ready?"

"We're more than ready, Nick!" Joe exclaimed. "I'd sprint out of this cave if I could." Without wasting another word in useless conversation, they quickly crawled out. They gave their eyes a moment to adjust to the bright sunlight of mid-afternoon, and then started walking west.

"Do you hear me? I mean feel my words?" Nick asked. "By the way, the burial places are lined up because we all traveled from west to east. Not in a straight line, of course, but still generally west to east."

"We can hear you, Nick. Just keep us moving the way you want," Joe responded.

"Now the important thing is that you have to keep talking, at least at the start. Sing if you have to. I have to be able to tell the exact place where you are." Excited, they couldn't think of any conversation, so Jessie began to sing: "Row, row, row the boat..." They could hear him chuckling.

"Now, walk along this ridge, until I tell you to turn. And keep on singing, or hum if you have to. I'm getting better at knowing where you are." After a few minutes, he told them: "Stop here. Now, start down the hill... Keep moving to your left. This is tricky," he continued, "but I think we can get better with practice." They stumbled along, intent on his direction, with only a few mis-steps.

"Ouch!" Joe complained, after he bonked his head on a low tree branch.

"Okay, careful now," Nick continued, undeterred by Joe's pain. "On the other side of this slope is a little gully. Walk along it toward a big tree stump and some boulders." They stumbled along the slippery slope, with Jessie pitching forward onto her hands and knees. "You're just about there. Now, just ahead of you, you should see a low pile of rocks. That's where they buried old John."

"We can find this place again," Joe remarked. "And when we do, I'll bring a topo map and my GPS locator. We can also mark the site with surveyors tape. And you were right, Nick. It did get a little easier. I think we can become good at this. With a day or two of walking, we should be able to locate and mark all the sites. Then experts can recover the remains later."

"I don't understand what you just said about all that stuff but it sounds like you have a plan," came the voice from under the soil.

Jessie dropped to her knees and lowered her head for a silent prayer over John's burial site. After a moment's hesitation, Joe did the same.

"Thanks," Nick said after a minute. "John and I appreciate the prayers."

Finally, the two stood and prepared to leave. "We'll come back to your cave in two or three days," Joe said. "And when we do, we can work on finding and marking the other sites. But we should be getting home. There's a school board meeting tonight. I hope we don't have a problem, but we should be there just in case."

"So long, Nick," Jessie offered. "See you soon."

The two started the trek back to the car, each engrossed in their own private thoughts.

CHAPTER FORTY-FIVE

"So, why do they have two school board meetings every month?" Joe asked as he stood in front of the bathroom sink, rinsing toothpaste from his mouth. Jessie, in the other room, was changing into clean clothing after showering away the sweat and grime from the hike. She had brought a change of clothing with her that morning, just in case the hike ran long.

"They have one meeting on the second Wednesday to discuss agenda issues. They reserve some discussion and voting for the second meeting, on the third Wednesday," she explained. "I think it's because they have so much to go over each month that they split discussion into two meetings rather than try to cram it all into one long monthly meeting. Also, if something has to be researched before a vote, the administration or the solicitor can do so between meetings.

"It also gives people like Granger, Jones, and the guy with the video cam a chance to reload between meetings," he pointed out. Jessie grunted her agreement, as she pulled a striped shirt over her head and smoothed it into place.

"Now, give me some more bathroom time so I can finish up," she commanded.

"Yes, ma'am!" Joe acquiesced, thinking as he did so that if she would only stick around, he would be happy to give her all the bathroom time she wanted.

They finished freshening up just in time to pick up Andy and head for the high school.

***

If anything, the crowd at school was even larger this time. They weren't really all that shocked, considering the ruckus at the last meeting and the subsequent newspaper article and Channel Eight coverage. "Some of these people are out-of-towners," Les whispered as he joined them. They watched as the custodians wheeled in dollies loaded with more chairs and then set the chairs up at the back of the cafetorium. "This room can hold close to 300 people for school plays and it's mostly filled."

"Principal Landers told me that while our jaunt in Cross Creek Park will not be an agenda item, two community members have requested time – again – to complain about appropriate staffing for outings," added Jessie. The stack of agendas had been depleted before their small group arrived. Rumor had it that the librarian and a crew of students were hurriedly making more copies.

"Don't those people ever give up?" Joe asked under his breath. Jessie's sharp hearing picked it up.

"I've seen them take an issue and run with it for months," she said. It can be pretty hard just to get regular business done sometimes. People ask questions out of the blue and make unexpected accusations. Administration has to answer the same questions repeatedly, do research into any new ones they raise, and make copies of numerous documents just for them," she whispered. "And staff spends a lot of time looking over their shoulders, concerned that somebody has their guns trained on them." Joe squeezed her hand. "By the way, I see that we have three television stations represented here tonight." Turning, Les and Joe saw the three cameramen in the back of the room. Channels Six and Nine had joined the party. Or, Joe wondered pessimistically, would it become a feeding frenzy?

"The meeting will come to order," intoned the president of the board. After the last of the shuffling had died down, she thanked all in attendance for their interest in school issues, and began the meeting. The agenda items were routine and quickly dispatched. The board seemed distracted and apparently wanted to get the meeting over with as soon as possible.

The time had finally come for public input, and the two registered speakers didn't disappoint. Mrs. Granger strode purposefully to the front and turned before her rapt audience. Smiling at the television crews and reporters, she paused for effect. She must do this a lot; she's very good at it, Joe thought. The crowd waited breathlessly.

"We are still not satisfied," she began, "with the inaction of this board and the school's administration. What has been done to make sure that this never happens again, that a man who continues even today to talk with ghosts, can never again volunteer at our school?"

She stopped and purposefully settled her eyes on Joe, causing much of the audience to look his way.

"I guess my secret's out," Joe muttered in a low whisper. "Now even the out-of-towners know where I am."

"Not much of a secret," Les observed.

"Everyone in town is talking about this man," she continued. Joe ruefully considered her prominent role in that gossip. "My demand is that you ban him as an unsuitable chaperone for our children. And that you discipline those who appointed him as a volunteer." A few people in the audience gasped.

The president cleared her throat, and with a determined set to her expression, responded. "The background checks on staff and volunteers are performed according to policy set by the state. Are you suggesting that we now investigate people's personal lives and town rumors?" Twittering rippled throughout the room.

"Well, if something is widely known about a volunteer, then I think it should be considered, too," the hawkish-nosed board member interrupted. "Please continue, Julie."

Julie, huh? Joe pondered. Yep. *He's* impartial alright.

"And we know something about this Bailey person. He thinks he talks to ghosts. Or spirits, or whatever. Therefore, he should be banned. It's as simple as that. Who knows what he'll be up to next? Probably chatting with demons." The audience gasped loudly, as of one voice.

A blue-haired board member sitting next to the president breathed a few words into her ear. She nodded and made up her mind. "If you and Mrs. Jones are willing to give up the remainder of your time, perhaps we should let Mr. Bailey speak again." Put on the spot, Mrs. Granger acquiesced, and Mrs. Jones had to go along. "Mr. Bailey? Would you care to speak?" Joe sighed and approached the microphone. A hundred quiet conversations built into a low roar. But before the president could gavel the room into submission, the noise dropped off into an expectant silence, as though somebody had shut off a valve.

"Madame President, board members and guests. I don't intend to rehash what I said at the last meeting. But I will tell you what we – what I have been up to lately, and I assure you that I have not been talking to demons. Furthermore, as I pointed out last week, I haven't been talking to ghosts, either. But I have communicated with the spirit of a miner named Nick Shebellko." This was nothing new, so except for a whispered word or two the audience sat mutely, hoping that he would reveal something even juicier this time.

"To bring you up to date, research has identified descendants of Nick's friends and of his fiancée, Carmella Antonini. I'm not prepared to reveal tonight who they are, but you will learn their names in due course. He glanced at Jim Christopher, who flashed a fleeting smile at him and then returned to his writing. "We have also confirmed a living descendant, right here in this audience, of one other miner killed in 1922. That miner was also buried in an unmarked grave in an unknown sylvan location.

"In regard to Nick, himself, perhaps I can fill you in on what we have planned. It will become public soon enough." The audience waited in anticipation. The television cameras continued to roll.

"Nick disclosed to us – I mean to me – where his remains may be found." Three hundred voices erupted in a raucous roar of questions and side conversations.

The board's solicitor whispered something to the president, who nodded with an exasperated look on her face. Visibly shaken, she gaveled the room into silence, and – clearly regretting putting Joe in the spotlight – she said in a croaking voice, "please continue, Mr. Bailey."

"Nick told me where his remains are located. We are assembling a team composed of state police, the county coroner, diggers from the United Mine Workers local union, and possibly a forensic anthropologist's team to actually remove his remains for proper burial." The room, bathed in the bright lights of the cameras, was spellbound. He continued: "I understand that a place has already been prepared for his re-interment."

As Joe allowed his words to sink in, he watched face after face move from incredulousness into confusion and then comprehension. Obviously, he thought as he stood there studying their expressions, he had put himself into a position with no way out. The media and the public would demand concrete proof of what he had said. "Please, Nick, you have to come through for me now," he whispered under his breath. He felt that he was heard.

Joe decided he might as well go all the way. "There is one

more thing." The room, hanging on every word, waited. "Nick has already revealed to us the location of one more burial site." The superintendent, who had been shuffling papers nervously, reflexively pushed them forward off the table, toward the main floor eight feet below. Joe and the others gazed hypnotically as various documents and reports fluttered downward. When the last sheet hit the floor, the room erupted into pandemonium. The president began to gavel the room back to order, but once again the effort wasn't really necessary. The audience quieted down of its own accord. Obviously, everybody wanted to hear Joe's next revelation.

"Nick told me there are eight other miners buried along a general west to east route from the State Line Tunnel toward Avella. He promised to locate every one for me. We hope to respectfully remove every one for proper interment later. The coroner will be in control, of course. And the forensic anthropology team will likely be involved. It's time these men had a proper burial. We will make every effort to identify each set of remains, independently of what Nick tells us. For example, the first set of remains that Nick directed us to was that of a man named John Brown, an African-American miner." The room sat in stunned silence.

"Whether I actually speak to a spirit will soon be proved or disproved," Joe went on. "But if my reputation is at stake here, I will gladly put my faith in my friend, Nicholas Shebellko."

The president of the board cleared her throat. "Mr. Bailey. You have referred several times to 'us' or 'we' in regard to getting information from this... this Nick. Are you saying that another person can also hear and see him?"

Joe hesitated, again prepared to fib to protect Jessie. But then she stood up in the middle of the audience and proceeded to walk determinedly toward Joe. She took the microphone and stated in a clear voice and with conviction: "My name is Jessica Randall. I can also see and communicate with Nick."

CHAPTER FORTY-SIX

"Well. Just another routine meeting of the Avella school board," Leo remarked dryly. "Nothing ever happens there." The others sitting around Andy's kitchen table laughed, the tension finally eased.

"I say this in all sincerity," Joe ruminated. "When we left for the meeting I only wanted to be there to defend Jessie's job and my own reputation. I never intended to spill our secrets to twelve counties on television. I hope I didn't make a fool of myself," he added, his voice pleading.

"You didn't make a fool of yourself in front of the cameras, Joe," Les assured him. "You sounded very reasonable, if beleaguered. But one thing's for sure. When we go looking for Nick, he damn well better be there." He paused as they considered the implications of what he had just said. "Jessie, you really put yourself on the line tonight when you admitted in front of everybody there plus three TV audiences that you can see and hear Nick, too. If Nick doesn't come through, your job could be at stake. Not to mention your reputation as an educator.

"He'll come through for us. I have faith in him," she said firmly. "He won't let us down. And even more importantly, we won't let him down. Him or those other men," she added.

"Some firefighters are taping the three news programs tonight, and then in the morning and over the next few days," Les said. We don't want to miss anything. But for now, why not turn on Channel Eight? It's nearly eleven p.m." Andy poured fresh cups of coffee as they waited.

"Here it is now," Leo reported, waving them over.

The announcer intoned:

"*Last week Action News Eight viewers were the first to learn about an astonishing controversy brewing in Avella, a sleepy former coal mining community nestled in the hills of Northwestern Washington County near the West Virginia border.*"

A map of the area appeared, showing Avella along Route 50.

"After being questioned at this evening's school board meeting, Mr. Joseph Bailey, a well-known real estate agent with Viewpointe Real Estate in Pittsburgh, confirmed that he has been communicating with the spirit of a Nicholas Shebellko. According to Mr. Bailey, Mr. Shebellko was shot and killed in 1922 during a coal mine riot. He states that the killing happened just over the state line at Cliftonville, West Virginia."

A graphic appeared on the screen, showing the State Line tunnel, Avella, Penowa, and Virginville, with the site of the former Cliftonville mine highlighted.

"We were able to interview Mr. Bailey and his friend, teacher Jessie Randall of the Avella Elementary Center. Here is the feed we recently received from our remote unit, now returning from Avella."

The next four minutes consisted of parts of Joe's interview with a female reporter in the hallway of the high school. He briefly explained about the riot and the upcoming efforts to reclaim Nick's body and the remains of the other miners. Jessie appeared briefly, telling about how she had also come to see and hear Nick, and fleshing out some details to Joe's summary. She omitted reference to jumping through Nick's spirit, because that would have sounded – well – just weird, she later said.

"...So who are these descendants, Mr. Bailey?" The on-camera reporter pressed.

"I can't reveal that information just now, but I assure you that at least one name will be very surprising indeed."

The in-studio ken-doll anchorman with the perfect hairstyle continued the news story, relating that the nearest prominent forensic anthropology department was located at Mercyhurst College in Erie. It had been archaeologists from the University of Pittsburgh and later Mercyhurst that excavated the world-renowned Meadowcroft archaeological site, also near Avella. The anchorman promised that as details developed, Channel Eight viewers would be kept informed during Action News and via breaking news reports. He also added that NBC's news division had been informed of this human-interest story of potential national interest.

Leo remarked: "I wonder. How many legitimate news stories got bumped or minimized today so they could hurry that report onto the news?"

"They always say that if you do something wrong, hope it comes to light on the same day as a big story breaks," Joe observed. "Not when they are scratching for news. It could be that Jessie and I are covering for several crooked politicians and petty criminals tonight. Their misdeeds never got any airtime." Jessie, sitting next to him on the sofa, squeezed his knee reassuringly.

"We are in this together, Mr. Bailey," she said firmly.

Once the TV clicked off the group started showing signs of fatigue, beginning with Andy. Jessie suggested that their best move now would be to get a decent night's sleep. The next week or two promised to be very busy indeed. Les and Leo drove to their homes and Andy hauled himself off to his bed. Joe and Jessie walked next door.

After settling down into the couch and sipping her soft drink, Jessie slid back a few inches, turned to Joe and stared directly into his eyes. "Joe," she began. "I've grown to care for you very much, but I'm not sure that I feel comfortable feeling this way about you. Do you understand what I'm saying?"

"I think so. I think you're afraid of getting hurt… again." He saw a haunted look flicker across her eyes. "Jessie, I would never intentionally hurt you. Right now you are the most precious thing in the world to me. I know that's strange for me to say, us only knowing each other these few weeks." He hesitated, his eyes revealing his own inner torment. "I never told you about Kathy, did I?" Jessie frowned and shook her head.

"Kathy and I shared a very trying time this past winter, while some bad people from her past were causing her trouble. I don't know if it was because of the danger or her vulnerability or actual love, but I put my heart and soul into that woman. But she couldn't handle all that was going on in her life, though, so she left me. Not once, but twice. I was still trying to get over her when I met you." Jessie's eyes and her doubts skewered him. He couldn't fault her for what she was undoubtedly thinking.

"Are you saying that ours is a rebound relationship?"

"No. Not at all," he answered her. "With you I think I may finally be experiencing genuine love. Do you see? The difference is that I was Kathy's anchor, her center of strength in a dangerous time.

We were drawn to each other and we 'circled the wagons,' we might say. And inside the circle we shared a kind of love." He paused and then continued. "But it may have grown more from need than anything else. Now I wonder if it was love at all, even though it broke my heart each time she left."

"So what are you saying, Mr. Bailey? I need to know. If she came back tomorrow, would your love be rekindled? Would you be torn between us?" Now her eyes took on an even more intense, searching look, exploring his core.

"I don't think so, Jessie. Now that I've come to know you I don't see how she could ever have a place in my heart again." He sat back for a moment, closing his eyes and absorbed for the first time in just how much he cared for this woman. Not just cared for her, but how he truly loved her. Opening his eyes again and fixing on hers, he searched the windows to her soul, hoping that she would not shut him out when he confessed his next words.

"I love you, Jessie. You're the only woman for me. If you will accept my love, I give it to you," he said simply.

Her eyes glowed, revealing the light in her heart. "I love you, too, Joe," she confessed, taking his hands in hers. "I love you." Her smile lit up the center of his being, where the private Joe Bailey lived. They shared a lingering kiss, before searching each other's eyes once more, their gazes locked, each with the other.

She looked at her watch and said sleepily, "I think I'm too tired to drive home this late at night. Would it be okay if I slept here? I'd be happy with the couch."

CHAPTER FORTY-SEVEN

After waking up early the next morning, Jessie drove home for a fresh change of clothing. She returned at about nine o'clock, carrying a Washington newspaper and the Pittsburgh morning edition. They went next door to Andy's, to drink coffee and to read.

"Jim did a nice job with his report," Jessie exclaimed, after skimming through it. "While he is objective, he doesn't use the underlying sneering tone that the Pittsburgh writer displays." She then observed, "of course, we gave him lots of information, including backup materials. His series will prove to be very interesting."

"Did I tell you I think Jim's a real nice feller?" Andy asked. "When we talked, he showed me a lot of respect, and he seemed very touched when I told him about my dad." Joe nodded, having picked up a strong underlying decency in Jim.

"It says here in the Pittsburgh paper that even though what we say has a basis in fact, we could have used those facts to make up our story. They say they're keeping an open mind. But I wonder just how open it is," Joe offered. "They don't actually dispute what we said, but they sure aren't jumping on board the possibilities, either." He scanned the next few paragraphs and added: "But he does acknowledge that I'm so far out on a limb that I will hang or be proven right. He says we need evidence – obviously, bodies."

They heard Les's truck abruptly pull to a halt in the gravel space. "It sounds like he's desperate for something hot to drink!" Joe laughed, but with some trepidation, realizing that something far more important than coffee might be driving his friend.

"I make good coffee, but somehow I doubt it's that," Andy remarked, reading Joe's thoughts. Les burst in the door.

"Coffee, please!" he requested as he sat at the table, disproving the both of them. But then he added: "I saw the early show and the Channel Six news this morning. You two are quite the celebrities, I must say. I'm impressed." Joe looked at him narrowly, expecting a punch line. "No, seriously. I think you got close to two minutes on ABC's morning show as a remote feed from Pittsburgh, plus a good four minutes on Channel Eight's morning news program. Both shows used footage from last night's meeting and the interviews you did in the hallway."

"So how did they treat the story? As a joke or as credible news?" Jessie looked for any sign that Les was holding back to spare their feelings.

"I can't say for sure. Right now the network seems to be treating it as a quirky local interest story, like a barbeque ribs cook-off in Duluth or something. The Pittsburgh television people are comparing it to the Meadowcroft rock shelter, where at first there seemed to be nothing more than a few arrowheads. They learned back then just how important that archaeological dig turned out to be, when evidence of the earliest human habitation in North America was found right in our own back yard. So, they're trying to show an open mind this time. Of course, it doesn't hurt that the area involved is right in the same vicinity as Meadowcroft."

After a few more sips he went on, "the anchorwoman made it pretty clear that the 'local people' – he inclined his head toward Jessie and Joe – have definitely put themselves out on a limb."

"There's that limb thing, again," Joe remarked morosely. "But I refuse to carry a hand saw out and I hope you left yours at home, too, Miss."

Continuing to leaf through the Washington paper, Jessie suddenly burst out, "Wait! The first article in Jim's series! They moved it up to today's edition." She began to read the feature story out loud:

Improbable friends

By James Christopher
Chronicle Staff Writer

This is the story of an area controversy, rooted in an event that occurred in 1922. It has become newsworthy during the past two meetings of the Avella Area School Board, when certain Avella area citizens accused a local school volunteer, Mr. Joseph Bailey, of "talking to ghosts." We will leave it up to our readers to evaluate what I have written, based on personal interviews with Mr. Bailey.

Bailey arrived in the small town of Avella a few short weeks ago, intending only to take a break from his real estate career with Viewpointe Real Estate in Pittsburgh and to renovate an inherited house. He also wanted to do some hiking along the area's wooded trails. But how could he have anticipated what the Avella area had in store for him? For example, one of his first new-found friends has been dead for over eight decades.

Very few residents are even aware that the town's history includes the "Cliftonville Mine riot." But Bailey learned about it soon enough.

The story began long ago, on July 16, 1922, when a group of desperate miners decided to take matters into their own hands. New owners had taken possession of the coal mine at Cliftonville, West Virginia, just over the state line in Brooke County. Cliftonville was situated next to the Wabash Railroad line near the western portal of the State Line tunnel.

At the time, most of the country was embroiled in coalfield strikes and production of coal had sunk to a historic low. To make matters worse, idled Avella area miners learned that union miners normally employed at the mine in Cliftonville had been evicted from company property. The displaced men and their families had then set up a tent camp between Cross Creek and the railroad tracks across from the mine. A delegation of miners from Cliftonville made the trek to Avella to ask for help.

What made the Avella miners' decision to intervene more compelling was news that the replacement – or "scab" miners in the vernacular – had been brought in by rail from Alabama. Most were ex-prisoners from the Alabama judicial system. People said they had been transported in boxcars, "just like animals."

Men from area mines met at Avella before walking in a large group down the railroad tracks toward the State Line tunnel. Some of the miners were armed. At another rally at Penowa, a mining village just before the tunnel, their numbers swelled to 400 or more. Under cover of darkness, they moved into the area around the Cliftonville mine. Some news stories reported that the miners' primary purpose was only to shut the mine down, rather than attack it.

Meanwhile a Wellsburg area farmer who had traveled through

Avella that same day had already alerted Ronald Davis, Brooke County's sheriff, of the miners' plans. Sheriff Davis established defensive positions at the mine, deploying over twenty armed deputies, mine guards and specially deputized citizens.

On the morning of July 17, at 5:15 a.m. the whistle from a departing train signaled the men to march on the mine. In little more than an hour, eight miners lay dead on company property while Sheriff Davis also lay dead from gunshot. The surviving miners beat a retreat back into Pennsylvania, in some cases assisting, dragging or carrying their wounded. Folklore has it that some of the more severely wounded attackers were buried en route after they expired from their wounds. According to Bailey, one such miner was named Nicholas ("Nick") Shebellko, age 22.

Bailey asserts that when he arrived in Avella he knew nothing of its past, except vaguely that it had once been a mining town. However, while hiking one day he discovered a shallow cave wherein he rested and ate his lunch. He suddenly felt an intense coldness there. The next night while asleep, he began to have vivid dreams of battle, coal mining and village life. Prominent in his dreams was a man named Nick, whom he dreamt was back at the cave. He decided to again hike to the cave, where he discovered that he could see and converse with Nick's spirit. The spirit told him about the Cliftonville riot and about his own life in Avella and the P and W coal mine patch from 1920-1922.

According to Bailey, Nick also told him of a close friend named Angelo Ballino and another good friend named Mike Zaretsky. He also reminisced about a young woman whom Nick called "the love of my life," Carmella Antonini. According to Bailey, Nick told him often of the fact that he and Carmella were planning to marry. Even today, says Bailey, Nick remains very concerned about whether his three friends went on to enjoy happiness. He is especially concerned about Angelo, who was involved in the riot and then helped to bury Nick during the homeward trek.

This story might never have come to light, except that Bailey recently accompanied a group of elementary school students on a local nature walk, along with Avella science teacher Jessie Randall and eight parent volunteers.

The daughters of Mrs. Brenda Jones of Jasper Lane and Mrs. Julie Granger of Brown Hollow Road, both of Avella, participated in that nature walk. Jones and Granger complained at the school board meeting that Bailey should not have accompanied their children because their daughters overheard him saying that he "talks to ghosts." However, the school board decided that the school district's administration and Miss Randall had followed procedures, and thus were not negligent in inviting Bailey on the field trip.

Bailey had easily passed the state-required background check prior to the outing. He is a former police officer from the Phoenix, Arizona, area. While a real estate agent, he made Pittsburgh news in January of this year when he helped Pittsburgh and Orlando, Florida, authorities break the Vestco money-laundering case.

As a follow-up to the first school board meeting, this reporter interviewed Bailey and subsequently talked with several other people who have information in support of his story. I am conducting additional interviews with other people associated with the case. Their stories will be told in future articles.

Editors note: *The details of the riot and the arrests and trials that followed have been cross-referenced with microfilm newspaper accounts of the day. In a future edition we will print a more comprehensive follow-up series of articles on the mine riot, the deaths and the criminal court trials that followed.*

Tomorrow: An Old Man's Father

"It looks like your story will be next, Andy," Jessie said as she carefully folded and placed the newspaper on the table. "Jim did a pretty nice job, hitting the highpoints for readers. He has an open mind, too. Something tells me that his series on Nick and his times will be very readable. I hope it wins some sort of award."

"Well, sports fans," Joe commented. "The roller coaster car has definitely left the platform and it's climbing the first hill. There's no stopping it now, so let's hold on tight for the ride. I hope it'll be as half as enjoyable as it will be exciting."

CHAPTER FORTY-EIGHT

The next morning Les, Joe, Jessie and Leo sat arrayed in their hiking gear at Andy's house, ready to dig into breakfast. "I've been thinking," Les remarked. "When we mark those burial sites today, we can't leave any permanent identification in place. I mean, how would it look if we had stakes and surveyor tape in place saying 'Burial Site #1'? Creeps like those you met the other day might try to dig them up, just for any personal possessions they could recover or to satisfy some weird, macabre obsession.

"I spoke with Dr. Briceland, the forensic anthropologist from Mercyhurst, about it. Your idea of using GPS readings marked on a topo map is a good one. But instead of physically marking each site, we'll photograph the immediate area thoroughly at each GPS-identified burial location and measure distances to certain nearby trees or boulders. That way, they'll be easy to find again, but impossible for the ghoulish or curious to identify." Les paused, wondering how to say the next thing on his mind. "Of course, in his opinion as well as the coroner's, there are no bodies."

"No bodies?" Jessie blurted. "What do you mean? Of course there are bodies!"

"Let's face it," he continued. "He says, and I can fully understand where he is coming from, that information from someone who claims to talk to a spirit is hardly proof of bodies lying scattered throughout the woods. He does agree, though, that if we excavate in the cave and find Nick's remains, they will investigate a second site. If that effort yields skeletal remains, he'll commit his entire team to a full-scale recovery effort."

"I just hope you can out find where my dad is located so I can get him buried next to my mom," Andy broke in. The others grew silent, realizing that they had been chatting clinically about nine sets of remains while Andy dwelled on the fate of his own father.

"We're sorry, Andy," Joe consoled the old man, who looked even older this morning. "We'll do our best. Nick tells us he's out there, and I'm confident he's telling the truth. We'll find him for you."

Andy turned away, in a sudden rush to go wash his hands in the bathroom.

Turning to the others, Leo spoke their implicit sentiment. "We can't let him down. If we accomplish nothing else, we have to come through for old Andy."

"One more thing," Les offered, to divert the focus from Andy when he walked back into the room. "Dr. Briceland agreed that if Nick's body were found in the back of that cave, free of rodents and insects and relatively dry, it could be in a desiccated or mummified condition. It could be intact." The five pondered the possibility that when they finally laid eyes on Nick, he could be recognizable as a man, still wearing his bloodied clothing and laid as Angelo had placed him so tenderly.

"Well, we better be on our way!" Joe said abruptly, to break the spell. "And, Andy? I have to swing by the supermarket for food and laundry detergent. Just let me know what all you need."

As Andy looked after them, they trooped out the door and headed for their vehicles. He slowly turned and started for his kitchen sink. He had dishes and mugs to wash. It stuck in his craw that he couldn't join them, nay even lead them. But at least in this way he could help. Andy also smiled with silent satisfaction, knowing that there was at least one way that he could still join them. They just didn't know it yet.

***

"Damn," Joe said under his breath. "There they are again." One truck and a car were the same, but three other vehicles were parked there as well. Les and Leo had already parked, and it was evident in their expressions as they alighted from Les's pickup that they, too were silently cursing.

"I think they brought reinforcements today, since the last time one man and a woman with a stick forced them to leave. That might have been a bit much for their manly pride," Joe explained. After a moment's study of the trailhead, he also noticed that at least one all-terrain vehicle had been pressed into use. "Lazy bums," he said aloud.

Again they started off at a fast pace, hiking up the trail. "Look at this stuff," Leo complained. "Wrappers and litter strewn along the trail." Soon they entered the meadow and approached the cave mouth. An ATV was parked outside and it was apparent that somebody on a dirt bike or ATV had been tearing up the sod nearby.

"It sounds like a party in there," Joe said aloud. No sooner had the words escaped his lips than he and Jessie heard Nick's complaint.

"Get them out of here, Joe. I want them gone now! Or if you can't I'm gonna figure out a way to throw rocks at them. Big rocks."

"Nick's really pissed," Joe explained. "I think he'd chew gravel if he had teeth."

Les and Leo glanced at each other. "You heard him say something?" Leo looked quizzically at him.

"We both did," Jessie chimed in. "He wants them out, and he wants them out right now." She took her stout walking stick in both hands and started for the cave in a very threatening manner. Les chuckled in admiration at her outraged display.

"Let me go in first," Joe suggested. "And then Jessie, like last time. You two brutes bring up the rear." He ducked down and crawled through the cave entrance.

"Well, look who's back!" exclaimed one of the young guys from the last episode. "Are you gonna throw us out?" He motioned to five other boys and men sitting against the walls, plus two girls. "Or are you gonna finally let us see the ghosts?"

Jessie had crawled in behind him. "Awwww. There's the lady with the big stick. Are we supposed to be *afraid*?" His friends snickered at his joke.

"It stinks in here with all that smoke... do I smell marijuana, too?" Jessie wrinkled her nose at the empty beer cans and their unsuccessful attempt to build a campfire. Just then the intruders noticed that Les and Leo were crawling in, too.

"It's getting crowded in here," Leo told the guys against the wall. "I think you should leave." Looking more mature and fit and carrying more muscle, the deadly-serious-looking firemen took away most of the intruders' bravado. After exchanging glances, the people in the cave began to file out. "And take your empties with you," Leo ordered. They silently began to stuff their empty beer cans and trash into the take-out plastic bags.

"Remember that we wrote down your license numbers and

photographed your vehicles. We also got a good look at you, so you should think twice before doing anything to our rides." The intruders sullenly left the cave, grumbling. The four heard the ATV outside start up and roar away.

"My big, strong men were here to protect me…" Jessie sighed.

"And we had our 'lady with the big stick' to protect us!" Les added.

"So, where are you?" She inquired, looking around expectantly. Nick came out from the rock wall, where Jessie and Joe immediately fixed their gaze. "These are two great friends, Nick. I think you and they would have gotten along. Les and Leo, that's Nick over there."

"We'll have to take your word for it," Les said sardonically.

"You really sounded upset, Nick," Jessie said in consolation. "Hopefully this won't happen again."

"The word Joe used was 'pissed' wasn't it? I think I like that word. It describes how I felt."

"He liked Joe's usage of the word 'pissed.' I don't think they used it to mean angry in his day," she explained to Les and Leo. "Well, Nick, are we ready to get started?"

"Just a minute," he replied. Jessie and Joe saw him approach the two firemen with a gleam in his eye and an outstretched hand. Jessie stifled a giggle. Nick touched both Les and Leo on the bicep with his fingertip, obviously trying not to go too deep through the skin.

"Hey!" They exclaimed in unison, jumping back, after he had touched them. Leo began to rub his arm, as did Les. "Was that him?"

"I think that was just in case you believed we were talking to the wall and not a real spirit. He did that to me, too, before I got the full treatment by jumping through him," Jessie laughed. I think his fingertip concentrates his coldness, somehow. Okay, Nick. Where do we go first?"

"We should go toward the tunnel and start back this way. It's over a mile to the first body. Then we'll work eastward back to here and another half mile or so toward Avella," he responded. After taking a sip from their water bottles, the troop crawled outside. Les and Leo caught on to the program pretty quickly. By the end of the day eight more burial sites, including John Brown's site, were catalogued and recorded in a logbook. They identified the miners by names as provided by Nick, digital photos of burial sites, measurements to landmarks and GPS readings. Jessie stopped to pray at each one, joined by the men.

"It's starting to get dark, so we better be on our way, Nick. We should be seeing you soon," Joe spoke, directing his words toward the ground. "By the way, things are happening pretty fast out there. I'll tell you about it the next time we come. My guess is that before too long we could be seeing your body, too."

The four friends carefully followed the trail back to the car as dusk turned into darkness. They finished the last stretch of their tiring trek under a cloudless, star-filled night sky. "It is beautiful, isn't it?" Jessie remarked. Nobody disagreed with her.

CHAPTER FORTY-NINE

The next morning the group reconvened at Andy's Diner. "I got a call from Jim," Joe reported. "He wants to buy us all dinner sometime because of the information and the leads we give him. He says that even the major newspapers and the networks are trying to play catch-up, but they have no chance of matching his work. He says he owes it all to us; that we're making him into a star.

"The Associated Press and Reuters have even inquired about picking up the series, sight unseen, because they just can't match his detail or timeliness. Once his stories reveal new sources and information it becomes old news for the others, who are running around scratching for crumbs. He's totally in his glory. His editor and publisher have given him carte blanche, as long as he runs everything by the editor first."

The others smiled at the thought. "He's a good kid and a good writer. I'm glad we could help him, but of course the credit really goes back to his fairness and objectivity and his initiative in calling me." Joe stopped shuffling through the paper and began to scan a page. "Oh, here's his article for today, the one about Andy and his dad." He began to read aloud.

An Old Man's Father

By James Christopher
Chronicle Staff Writer

Yesterday we introduced our readers to Mr. Joseph Bailey and the story of his friend, Nick Shebellko. According to Bailey, Nick had been mortally wounded during a coal mine riot in 1922 and was subsequently buried during the retreat. In this segment, we feature a surprising development.

After moving to Avella, Bailey met 96-year-old former miner Andrew Polack, of Gardner Drive, Avella. During a conversation with Bailey, Mr. Polack mentioned that his father, Andrew Polack,

Senior, had failed to return from the mine riot. According to him, other miners reported burying his father on the way back to Avella after he expired from wounds suffered in the battle. Here is the rest of his story...

...As Joe read Andy's story detailing the life of a twelve-year-old boy in a mining town whose father didn't come home, even the men were surreptitiously dabbing at their eyes. He concluded reading the article:

Mr. Polack, who insists that we call him Andy, maintains: "What Joe Bailey tells is true and factual. He just knows too many things that he has no right to know otherwise. I know in my heart that my dad will be found and laid to rest next to my mom. It was meant to be, and it had to happen in my lifetime. Joe is only the instrument that was needed to make things right. He's like the fuse in a charge of black powder that we needed to blast a section of coal loose so it could be dug."

As for the people who are trying to discredit Bailey, Andy maintains that: "Nobody can stop the right thing being done. They can try all they want, but it's like spitting in the wind. All you get is a face full of spit."

Everybody in the room chuckled at Andy's familiar simile. "You certainly have a way with words, old buddy," said Joe. "I see that next week's piece will be called 'A Place was set Aside.' I think we all know whose story is next." He set the paper on the table surface and rubbed his chin. "Good for you, Jim Christopher," he said. "Good for you. And we will take that free dinner.

"What puzzles me," Joe then wondered aloud, "is that despite all the initial skepticism people are somehow buying into my tale. What is it? Are we that convincing? Is the evidence that strong? There really *isn't* any evidence yet, is there? We don't have one tangible thing."

"Habeas corpus," Les interjected. "Or, as they say: *'Produce the body.'* The truth is that we haven't even found a body yet."

Jessie said thoughtfully, "I just think people want something to believe in – something beautiful and hopeful that shows there's something beyond their limited lives."

"I'm glad I have everybody taping the news programs," Les blurted out. "This story is beginning to explode all over the national news, and as I said, we haven't even found a body. When we dig for Nick, there could be up to three television trucks on hand with network feeds. They must really think this is a human interest story, because it's not exactly hard news."

"I worry about wackos trying to cash in," Leo observed. "All we need now are psychics and spiritualists traipsing all over the woods trying to earn a paycheck from some supermarket tabloid."

"I don't think we can do anything about all those woods, but we can try to protect the cave," Les offered. "The state police have already agreed to post the cave area and string police crime scene tape because there are reports of human remains inside, the result of an unlawful incident. And the company that owns the wooded land has agreed to post the entire area with "No Trespassing" signs and to cooperate with removal efforts.

"Meanwhile, the plan for the excavation is coming together pretty well. Next Wednesday, volunteer miners will brace the roof and dig out the fallen rubble that's concealing Nick's body. The coroner will be there, along with state police and our rescue truck, in case somebody gets hurt. Assuming his body is found, Coroner Walsh will call Dr. Briceland, who has agreed to receive it at Mercyhurst for examination in their laboratory.

"Again assuming that Nick's body is found," Les continued, "we'll schedule the next step. Dr. Briceland will bring his team to excavate what should be John Brown's burial site. If human bones are found there, they'll be taken back to the Mercyhurst lab, too. He says his crew is well trained, and they should be able to excavate and remove the remains within about an eight-hour time frame per site, one each day. He has people tasked as photographers, diggers, note-takers, screeners, and even 'go-fers.' I found his briefing very impressive."

Leo chimed in. "They should know pretty quickly if the bones found are human. Then back at the lab an examination of the remains should reveal any healed injuries and ethnic features that could help to identify a specific person. For example, Andy said that his dad had a broken right arm as a boy, and he suffered a broken collarbone in a mining accident. That should make it easy for them to identify him. Of course, scraps of clothing, shoes and metal objects would also provide clues."

"Doctor Briceland also told us that bodily injuries from the battle might be evident as unhealed damage. The injuries – mainly to bone – could reveal how each man died," Joe added. Looking up from his concentration, he saw the old man. "Sorry, Andy. We didn't mean to..."

The old man stopped him. "That's okay. I know my dad was shot and they had to bury him. I came to terms with that long ago. I just want it to be over, so I can see mom and dad together again." He stirred his coffee, fascinatedly watching the little whirlpool that formed there. Satisfied, he stopped. "Did you know that she never remarried? But, heck. I stayed a bachelor, too. After me, there are no branches on the Polack family tree. I'm the last one still alive. We'll close things up nice and tight when we bury dad."

"You never married?" Leo asked, grinning. "That explains how you lived so long, I suppose." The men glanced at Jessie for the anticipated glare. They weren't disappointed.

"You like to live dangerously, I see," Joe remarked. "Don't you remember 'the lady with the big stick'?"

Jessie released the big grin that had been forcing its way through her expression. "And I know how to use it, too!"

"By the way," Les interjected, in part to save Leo. "The coroner has already received inquiries from people claiming to be descendants of missing miners, including those descended from John Brown's family. Not counting Andy, of course."

Andy's mood brightened suddenly. "So, when do we do the day and night walk to Cliftonville?" The others looked at him in astonishment.

"But how can you walk that far?" Jessie asked concernedly. "We had a hard time doing it. Are you sure you would be up to it?"

Andy smiled as he revealed his secret. "I plan to ride in a car to Penowa, and then walk the tracks through the State Line tunnel. I'm sure I can do that. I've been walking more and more everyday while you youngsters were out on your hikes. These old legs will carry me okay."

Joe looked unconvinced. "If you insist on going, your ride should take you all the way to the railroad grade crossing, so you only have to walk the last few hundred yards to the tunnel. Remember, the tunnel itself is over 1500 feet long so your walk will be half a mile. But anyway, we can't make any promises just now." He touched Andy's hand. "We'll do what we can, old buddy.

"Anyway, gang, Saturday should be a go. The weather outlook looks good and I'm more than ready. It'll only be July the first and not the sixteenth like when they did it, but at least we'll walk during the same month as the miners."

Jessie clapped her hands excitedly. "Saturday! It should be perfect. We'll start in the afternoon, stop at the old Penowa ball field, and then around midnight we'll walk through to Cliftonville." She then decided to reveal what she had been mulling over. "You do realize that the tunnel is under the surface of the ground, don't you? We could meet an old friend as we walk through." The realization hit the men all at once.

"We might see Nick as we walk through the tunnel?" Joe exclaimed.

"It sure is possible," she responded.

"Give me some time and I can arrange to have a van waiting over by Virginville to give us a ride back," Les offered. "I just can't see us walking all the way back to town in the dark after a hard day and night of trudging on railroad ties."

"And listen to this," Joe interjected. "When I checked moon cycles on the Internet and in newspapers of the day, I learned that the marchers in 1922 walked under a full moon and cloudless skies. Looking ahead, I found that the full moon this month occurs on July the second. And as you know, this dry spell is supposed to extend through next week, so we should have a bright, clear night with plenty of light from the moon and stars. It should be perfect." He smiled happily. "And if Nick meets us, it'll be even better."

CHAPTER FIFTY

Saturday dawned as bright and cloudless as advertised. To brighten Joe's day even further, Jessie pulled into the parking space right on schedule. She practically ran to Joe's front door, where he met her with enveloping arms and a probing kiss. "Wow!" She breathlessly exclaimed. "Does that mean you missed me?" She clutched him and passionately kissed him back, before she pushed him inside.

After they finally separated, she studied his eyes and asked, "Well, are you ready for that little jaunt to Cliftonville?" Smiling, he stepped back and admired the enchanting green eyes; the ones that had so attracted him on the day they first bumped into each other. He would have traded the inconvenience of a few dropped snacks any day, he realized, to discover such a woman and friend as this one.

"I sure am. And I understand that a few of the other firefighters have decided to tag along. We might have a group walking this time. Les told me that while we were making plans for the exhumation, the word got around within the department." He finished packing his daypack, including an extra water bottle and, more importantly, his filter. "Ready to head next door?"

"You betcha!" she said, her eyes dancing happily. "Let's go! Oh, we should also check Andy's shoes to make sure they'll hold up. Even though it's only a thousand yards or so, it won't be easy walking."

Andy met them with the usual two mugs of steaming coffee. "I'm ready for today," he said with obvious pride. "I hope you kids don't tire out on me!" But then more seriously: "My old friend Jim Jenson's gonna give me a ride to Penowa to meet with you young folks, and then he'll tote me over to the grade crossing, where I'll wait for you kids to catch up. But he can't meet us by Virginville, because that'll be the middle of the night, and it'll be way past his bedtime." He stopped and his eyes took on a merry look. "Then I'll be your responsibility," he laughed. "Are you up to it?"

Joe chuckled at the old geezer. "No problem. With our paramedic and the emergency truck parked at Penowa, we should be able to take care of you okay."

Jessie interrupted, "no, Andy, somehow I doubt that you'll need any help. Anyway, we should be heading downtown now."

When Joe and Jessie arrived at the War Memorial area next to the train station, Joe's eyes met those of a totally bewildered Les Wilson. "Who are all these people?" Joe asked as they alighted from his Caddy. There were over a dozen cars parked nearby, and well over fifty men, women and children were standing around; some of them appeared to be stretching.

"I don't know," Les replied, shaking his head. "They've been telling us that they heard about our day-night hike in honor of the miners, and they said they wanted to walk, too. Look at all these people!" Joe noticed two more cars parking along the tracks with several people spilling out of each. Close behind came a van and a pickup truck loaded with boy scouts from the local troop, who promptly climbed from their vehicles in the characteristic mayhem of well-organized but exuberant youth.

As the scouts lined up behind patrol leaders, the scoutmaster hurried over to Joe's group. "We hope you don't mind, Mr. Bailey, but some of the other district troops have been asking us to let them know if we ever do anything to honor the miners. So we told them about this commemorative march. Here comes the Hickory troop now!"

"But this isn't a commemorative march!" Joe cried out in frustration. "This was my own little walk to celebrate the miners' courage and sacrifice." He finally shrugged. "Well, whatever you told them will be fine with us. Thanks for thinking of the miners."

"Joe." Jessie said quietly as she tugged at his shirt and then pointed to a new arrival. "It's Jim, and he has his hiking shoes on, too." Sure enough, their new journalism friend, Jim Christopher, had just parked a car emblazoned with the newspaper's logo and was walking toward them, looking surprisingly buff in his hiking garb. Just after Jim's car the ubiquitous Channel Eight news truck pulled in.

"That news crew must have some kind of Avella news radar installed," Les remarked. "Leo," he continued pragmatically. "We better get some traffic cones out and start diverting traffic down to the fire department lot. This place won't hold very many more cars. Some people are already double-parking."

"Yes, sir, chief, boss, sir," Leo responded, striking a sharp

English-army type salute, palm forward. He then waved over a few other firemen and they hurried off to the fire hall. The rest of the party turned their attention to the approaching camera crew and Jim Christopher.

"So you were going to keep this commemorative march secret, were you, Joe?" Jim asked, grinning, as the television camera man hoisted his unit to his shoulder. Jim thrust his tape recorder forward as the newswoman from Channel Eight did the same with her microphone. Joe noticed Leo and the boys coming back with traffic cones and a portable bullhorn with loudspeaker.

More vehicles were arriving and being diverted to the fire hall parking area and the municipal lot down the street. Another troop had just unloaded and the scouts were approaching, shrugging into their backpacks. The people nearest Joe began to quiet their excited chatter as he faced the news cameraman and the two reporters. Jim asked the first question just as people began to gather around.

"Mr. Bailey, what made you think of having this march to Cliftonville to commemorate the striking miners' march on the mine?" The crowd hushed as they closed in tight, straining to hear his reply.

"I never intended to have a commemorative march. I just wanted to walk the tracks alone. But then Miss Randall decided to go, too. And… well you know what happens when you try to tell a woman she can't do something," he said sheepishly. The crowd laughed. "And then a few of my fire department buddies decided that they'd like to tag along." He stared, bewilderedly, at the throng. "When we started to drive down here a few minutes ago, I thought that there would be ten or twelve people, tops."

He looked around in amazement. "How many people are here now? A hundred? Two hundred? Three?" A man standing nearby blurted out: "Word started to get around about your walk, Mr. Bailey, so we just decided that if we walked, too, it could celebrate the lives of all those men." Joe shook his head in wonder.

"Are you saying you didn't plan this big march, Mr. Bailey?" Jim asked.

"No, not at all," Joe responded again. "Frankly I have no idea who most of these people are. Look! Here comes another group of boy scouts. The scouts might be physically fit, but I don't know if most of these other people have any idea what they're getting into."

A woman stepped forward, knifing her way through the crowd. It took him a moment to recognize Julie Granger. "Mr. Bailey," she began tentatively. "Brenda and I have come to realize that we were wrong in the way we went after you at the school board meetings and how we didn't give you a chance. If you don't mind, we'd like to walk along on your commemorative march." Joe was taken aback by this simple declaration that had obviously cost her plenty in swallowed pride. "Carmella's story in the newspaper this morning sealed our decision for us," she added.

Joe shot Jim a comprehending look. "The paper printed Carmella's story? We have to get a copy.

"Of course, you're welcome to join us," he said, turning back to Mrs. Granger. And then louder: "You're all welcome to follow us as we honor those miners of so long ago. But first my good friend Les Wilson, the Avella fire chief, has some things to say. Les?"

Les stepped up over the low wall and stood on the elevated platform of the war memorial. As he watched the additional hikers filling the square, he held the bullhorn microphone to his lips. "Please understand that this is not an organized march. Rather, our small group intended it to be a private walk down the tracks, emulating what the miners did in 1922 when they walked to Penowa in the afternoon and then to Cliftonville during the midnight hours. I will brief you on what we have planned, and then I want you to seriously reconsider your participation, especially if you have health problems or any serious medical condition.

"I see that many of you have sturdy walking shoes and appropriate clothing. Most of you are also carrying water bottles and some have packs. But even so, you should reconsider whether you want to walk along with us. I'm aware of at least two people who plan to ride to Penowa and then walk through the last tunnel with us. If you wish, you can also ride to Penowa and meet us as we arrive, and then go home or follow us through the tunnel. But please understand that walking along railroad tracks can be very hard on your feet and legs."

The television camera alternated between Les and the ever-growing crowd. "The firemen will bring along every light we can muster for tunnel and night-time hiking, but if you have a flashlight you should carry it, too. We learned several days ago that the tunnels can be very dark inside. The State Line Tunnel will be wet, too, with water dripping from the ceiling onto the track bed where we will be walking. We arranged that the Jefferson Fire Department will have a rescue vehicle available at Penowa. We will also send our own rescue truck down there, just in case.

"We will be starting our walk at two o'clock. Please, each of you should think carefully about whether you want to attempt this walk. We will be traversing two tunnels and several railroad trestles over the creek before Penowa. The final tunnel will be the one that brings us out into the area of Cliftonville and Virginville. If you can do so, you should arrange for somebody to either pick you up at Virginville, or at the railroad crossing in Pennsylvania after we walk back through the Tunnel." With dismay, he saw several more people walk up after having parked their cars. "We're not sponsoring an official march here," Les added, "and while we can't prevent you from following along, neither can we be held responsible if you are injured." Seeing the scores of determined faces, he lowered the bullhorn and stepped down.

"Les," Jessie confided, "there have to be three hundred people here, maybe four. I hope some of them are here only to watch the excitement or to see their friends off." She looked up as a commotion occurred at the far end of the square. Somebody from the convenience store had delivered cases of bottled water that they began to distribute to grateful people.

Les checked his watch. "Two o'clock." He raised his bullhorn and explained that they would now be starting their walk to Penowa. Anybody who decided to follow along would do so at his or her own risk. Joe, Jessie, Les and Leo walked over to the tracks and started on their trek. Throngs of people followed along.

Looking back just before they passed under the overpass bridge, they noticed that several dozen people had remained behind, having thought better of attempting the grueling hike. But that meant there were still three hundred or more walking.

"What have we gotten ourselves into?" Joe wondered as he reached for Jessie's hand.

CHAPTER FIFTY-ONE

"The boys bringing up the rear tell me everyone's holding up okay," Les said after clipping his radio back to his belt. "A few are struggling, but it looks like they should make Penowa all right. The main complaint is about the uneven walking surface, but we knew all about that, right?" The others groaned in appreciation. The head of the line had just passed through the Craighead tunnel, and was approaching the Buxton. The full line of marchers had now spread out over more than a half mile, the slowest ones still trying to painstakingly step from cross tie to cross tie.

Having caught up to the front, Jim was asking questions about a wide variety of issues, including how this march had come to be. Joe ruefully observed that Jim was in really good shape, even better than him, able to ask questions non-stop while walking along at a steady pace. The leaders answered him patiently, albeit with a more halting breath. Jim mentioned that Carmella Cook had been a delightful interview, and his editor confided in him that the paper would likely submit the article to a newspaper award competition.

"The Buxton tunnel!" Leo suddenly blurted out, gesturing at the black hole in the green, leafy hillside. The local Boy Scouts had quickly closed the gap and were listening intently to the adult conversation. Joe had the impression that the scouts could have easily run on by them, but were holding back from taking the lead out of respect.

After traversing the tunnel, they found the place where they could cross to the old Penowa ball field. There, they saw the rescue vehicles and an ambulance waiting, along with the Channel Eight truck and a few dozen cars.

"Here's where the miners met for their last big meeting. They recruited more men from the local Waverly, Penobscot and Seldom Seen mines," Joe explained to Jim. He could hear the long-awaited word spreading back along the tracks from group to group: "Penowa!" The marchers understood that by far the worst of the walk was over, and they would now get to rest and quench their mounting thirst. Joe secretly hoped that some of the least hardy would quit here, satisfied with their participation in the remarkable event.

"Is that a school bus?" Jessie asked rhetorically as they approached the wide-open area that was once the ball field. The answer was apparent. A giant, yellow school bus waited welcomingly for anybody who wanted a ride back to town. One of the Jefferson firemen who had been walking close to the lead group explained that somebody had called the local school bus company and suggested that they have a bus or two available. Apparently the owner had decided to do so, at no cost.

"Looks like 'Jack's Tavern' broke out their supplies, too!" Leo said dryly, indicating a flurry of activity near a building. The innkeeper had brought cases of sport drinks and water bottles outside, and was distributing them freely. Grateful hikers rewarded him handsomely anyway, just for having the refreshing liquid there. A few people had already wandered inside the large, welcoming frame tavern, obviously in search of a nice, cold beer.

The Jefferson fire chief, Paul Bryan, sauntered over to Les and clapped him on his back. The Avella fire chief introduced him to Joe and the others. "I hear that all donations will be used toward a memorial if we decide to build one," he explained.

"A memorial?" Joe turned the thought over in his mind. "A memorial! How about that? A memorial! Thank the owner for the idea, Paul. Maybe we'll start thinking about designing one." Jim scribbled feverishly away in his note pad.

By now, the last of the marchers had come straggling in. The two fire chiefs walked to the center of the group, along with Joe and Jessie. "We have plenty to drink, so don't hold back on hydrating yourselves," Paul said, raising his voice above the thrum of conversation. "And welcome to Penowa. Now, we have at least two more things from Jefferson Township's history to be really proud of, the miners meeting place... and your march. To go along with the Meadowcroft Museum and archaeological dig, of course."

The group cheered in response. "For those who planned to be picked up here, your rides are parked over by the tavern. The bus will also make as many trips as necessary to get you back to Avella. You'll see that we have two rescue trucks and an ambulance here, for anybody who might want or need medical attention. Now, you should hear from the people behind today's march: my friend Les Wilson, the Avella chief, and Joe Bailey and Jessie Randall."

"Thanks for joining us in our little stroll down the tracks," Les began, eliciting a loud chorus of groans from tired marchers… tired, but apparently still in good spirits. He joined them in their laughter. Though they had sore legs and feet and more than a few blisters, he didn't think there were many quitters there. "It's now just after five-thirty. Our plan is to walk the tracks through the tunnel to the area of Cliftonville. We will start well after dark, between eleven p.m. and midnight." Somebody approached Paul and said something quietly. Paul leaned over to Les and relayed the information, as Joe took the microphone.

"My name is Joe Bailey," he began. "As most of you already know, this is the place where several hundred men stopped for a final rally and to gather local miners for the march into West Virginia. Just as they waited here for darkness and the midnight hour, we plan to do the same." He handed the mike back to Les, who clearly had some urgent news.

"I've just been informed that the Brooke County Sheriff has learned of our little unscheduled march…" Loud gasps rippled through the crowd as people realized the irony of the news. "But this time they'll be there to welcome us and to keep us from harm. They just ask that we be careful and not disrupt the little community of Virginville. It's okay with them if people have cars waiting to pick them up, but they would prefer buses.

"We can make the process simpler if some of the marchers can walk back through the tunnel to the grade crossing on this side. Then people can be picked up on both sides of the state line. This might be a good time to make those arrangements. Meanwhile," he said, rolling his shoulders slowly and extending his arm, "show me a nice, soft patch of grass where I can lie down!"

Joe saw the crowd separating as old Andy walked determinedly forward. Grasping the old man's hand, Joe asked for the microphone.

"Please let me introduce a very special man to you, and one of my best friends," he began, and the crowd renewed its attention. This is my neighbor, Andy Polack." A series of exclamations burst out as crowd members realized the identity of the 96-year-old man who had lost his father in 1922. "Andy has decided that while the entire march would be too much for him, he wanted to be here with you. He also intends to walk through the tunnel to Cliftonville." Scattered applause evolved into a resounding series of whistles, shouts and handclaps. Andy took the microphone.

"I just want to thank everybody here for walking the route that my dad and his buddies walked. It all turned out pretty bad for them, because so many were killed or wounded, and more went to prison." If a pin could have been heard falling into the grass, it would have been audible in the rapt silence.

"I know that I can make that walk through the tunnel, and in honor of my dad, I'm gonna do it. And after they get my dad out of the ground and we put him where he belongs next to my mom, I can die a happy man. But not just yet," he concluded, to everybody's relieved laughter.

***

Five hours later, Joe leaned over and gently kissed the sleeping woman. "Wake up, sleepy head," he quietly urged her. Others nearby stirred from their rest as Jessie opened her eyes. "It's eleven p.m.," he informed her. Joe had slept very little, instead watching a game of morra going on at the edge of the crowd. "Morra's a really cool game!" he told Jessie. "It's so far beyond paper-scissors-rock that it's beyond comparison. And it forces a person to know at least a small part of a foreign language. I tried it once using English numbers, but it lost most of its charm."

"Are we ready yet?" Jessie asked dreamily, ignoring his morra report, before reaching up and kissing him enthusiastically in return. Looking around, she saw card games breaking up and people pulling their hiking shoes back on, having aired out their sweaty socks and weary feet.

Les pointed out the television trucks from the Wheeling and Steubenville stations that had just pulled into the parking area in tandem. "Looks like we're getting even more coverage," he remarked. He walked over to meet with the reporters. Shortly the camera lights were on, and combined with Channel Eight's light, they illuminated the area brightly.

One reporter explained that somehow the unusual modern-day march on Cliftonville had become general knowledge and everybody wanted to learn more about it. The cameras rolled as Les explained the original intent of the small party of friends to enjoy a day-and-night hike. However, it had somehow ballooned into what they see here. Joe and Jessie answered questions about both the original march in 1922 and the walk today. Then, Les stepped forward with his bullhorn.

"We will now begin the final part of our walk. Andy Polack and a few other senior citizens will meet us at the crossing on this side of the tunnel. Again, if any of you want to follow us, it will be at your own risk. We did not organize your walk and neither could we prevent you from following us." He stepped away from the television cameras.

"Les," Jessie stopped him, standing on her toes to whisper into his ear. "We may stop in the tunnel because somebody might be waiting for us, so you should mention that there could be a delay in there." Les again picked up the microphone and alerted the marchers to the possible delay. "But to set your mind at ease about stopping in the tunnel, the railroad has informed us that the next train won't come through here until tomorrow morning about seven o'clock."

The Channel Eight reporter, apparently blessed with excellent hearing, asked: "Who is this 'somebody'?" She persisted: "It's not Nick Shebellko, is it?" The other reporters jostled to get close to Joe and Jessie. "Is it Nick?"

"All I can say is that the tunnel is in fact under the surface of the ground, so it could be possible. The tunnel is similar to Nick's cave in that way." He thought to himself, *I hope he does show up. I'd really like to introduce him to Andy Polack.* And then aloud: "We should get started."

CHAPTER FIFTY-TWO

They began to walk toward the tunnel, the throng following with renewed energy. If anything, more new faces had joined them in Penowa than had dropped out there. At the crossing, Andy and seven other older people had already climbed out of a Senior Citizens Center van. He explained that some were second-generation descendants of early 1900's coal miners.

The maw of the tunnel awaited them about two hundred yards or so down the tracks. As they approached it, Joe shined his light on the abutment with the legend "1904" painted on it. Others following did the same. As they entered the tunnel, Jessie drew closer to him.

"Remind the people back there that water will drip from the ceiling in here and there's no avoiding it," Les told Leo, who did as ordered. They walked through the water droplets, not minding at all the cooling effect in the warm and sticky air. As they approached mid-tunnel, complaints bounced off the walls from behind as people stumbled on the uneven track bed.

"Turn off your lights," Jessie suggested as the group came to a standstill. All along the line people stopped and turned off their lights. Soon the entire tunnel was enveloped in darkness, except for the dim light at the two portals. Bursts of nervous laughter could be heard as most people tried to be silent and appreciate how much like a coal mine the tunnel seemed.

"The men who marched that night had only a few miner lamps that cast very little light. Imagine how difficult it must have been for them to walk." Her words rippled through the entourage, with people murmuring agreement.

"I think I like our lights better," piped up a young boy scout who sported a bright, white LED light mounted on a band around his head that illuminated wherever his head pointed. Those near him laughed. "I do, too, son," Les answered. One by one, and then by the dozens like fireflies in a June night sky, the lights were turned back on again. After another hundred feet, Joe and Jessie both stopped suddenly, the people behind them colliding into each other like a long string of dominoes. "What happened?" somebody further back called out.

"We just saw a friend, is all," Jessie responded quietly. "Hello, Nick."

"It's Nick!" The information ricocheted back along the line. Jim wrote feverishly in the tablet balanced on his tape recorder, his flashlight wedged between his arm and shoulder. "Be sure to fill me in later on everything he said," he whispered.

Nick stood near the wall, looking as ruggedly handsome to Jessie as he had in his cave. "Who are all these people?" he asked. I only expected to meet a few of you, but it looks like you decided to bring the town of Avella." He paused. "Not that I mind, though. At least here they're not crowding into my cave."

"These people heard we were walking down here like you did back then," Joe responded. "And they wanted to come along." He paused, looking back over the long sea of heads. People squeezed along the tunnel walls to get closer. "They decided that a few of us walking wasn't good enough. They all wanted to join us in commemorating what you men did."

"They are doing it in honor of you and the others, Nick," Jessie explained. "There must be four hundred people behind us." Nick winced. Even after all the time that had passed, what the men did in 1922 still touched the hearts of so many people.

"Nick is really here?" Jim asked quietly. "I believe you, but it's too bad that we don't have any proof."

Nick grinned. "He wants proof, does he?"

Jessie and Joe grinned back. "You better get ready, Jim," Jessie quietly warned him. With that, Nick did his routine.

"Hey!" he shouted in alarm. His pen, notepad, flashlight and recorder went clattering onto the railroad crossties. "What was that?" He rubbed his upper arm as two boy scouts retrieved his still-shining and quite durable flashlight and reporting implements.

"You remember what I told you about Nick's touch?" Joe reminded him. "Well, you've just been treated to a demonstration!" he said, laughing. "By the way I think he's really starting to like that."

"Hey! Could Nick touch me, too?" exclaimed Johnny Black, who had been trying to stay near Joe and Jessie all day.

"No, Johnny. I don't think so," Jessie said compassionately.

The scoutmaster and the others nearby chuckled. "Otherwise people would line up and keep the poor ghost busy all night!"

Joe motioned Andy over. "Nick, this is Andy Polack, the man I told you about. Andy Polack's son. He was twelve years old when his dad went away. You didn't happen to bring Mr. Polack along, did you?"

Nick smiled. "So this is Andy's boy?" Tell him I'm proud to meet him." They passed on Nick's greeting. "Yes, Andy is here, and so are the others. They can see you, but you're limited in being able to see them. Tell him Andy is pleased to see his boy. He's proud of him, too."

"Andy," Jessie said gently. "Nick says your dad is here and he is proud of you." Andy snuffled loudly as tears ran down his weathered face. Most of the people standing nearby wept openly and as the word was relayed through the crowd line the din of weeping grew louder.

After a few moments, Andy struggled to force out, "tell him that while I was broken hearted that he never came back, I was always proud of what he done. But all I want now is to get him put next to mom." Nick informed them that Mr. Polack wanted that too, above everything else. Like the others, he just wanted to find his peace. Jessie passed the information on to Andy and the others standing nearby.

"I think you should get on with your walk now," Nick observed. "The people behind you are getting restless." Joe agreed, and they quietly began to walk toward the western portal, where they could just begin to make out the moonlight sifting through the opening.

The group talked in low murmurs as they walked along, as though passing through a cemetery. While the occasional stumble brought on an exclamation of surprise, and sometimes of pain, the people seemed to take it all in good spirits. As they passed the spring gushing from the tunnel wall, many stopped and drank thirstily.

Finally they reached the exit, aware that West Virginia and the former village of Cliftonville lay just a few hundred feet ahead. The first of the marchers emerged into a moonlight and starlight that, after the tunnel's darkness, shone brighter than they could have expected. Many turned off their flashlights. Joe and his group continued halfway to the railroad crossing, where they stopped to allow people to catch up.

After a few minutes the stragglers had emerged from the tunnel and moved as close to the leaders as they could, filling both the track bed and the paths alongside. As they waited, Joe noticed lights approaching around the bend in the tracks, from the direction of Virginville.

A state policeman walked up to him, along with a sheriff's deputy. "Are you the folks from Avella?" He shook Joe's hand and those of the others nearby. "We're proud to have you visit us tonight. We just want you to be safe until you can ride on home. There are school buses up ahead, waiting for you." He paused, and then continued. "Here comes Sheriff Blankenship now. We understand that some folks from up your way had a run-in with one of his predecessors a while go," he said wryly. The sheriff was a lean-looking man of about fifty years, without the paunchy belly of the archetypical motion-picture sheriffs. He grinned from under the thatch of red hair that protruded from under his uniform hat.

"We kind of wish that we had more notice, but according to the news you didn't plan a big event," Sheriff Blankenship began. "We've been following your story in the newspapers and on television. What do you want to do?"

"Thanks, sheriff, for the welcome. All we want to do is to walk along between Cliftonville and Virginville a short way," Joe said. "I had planned to fill them in on what we learned about the incident in 1922." The sheriff nodded and joined the group as it resumed walking toward the crossing. Joe hesitated when he saw a television crew approaching from the Virginville area. After they arrived and began to film, he started.

"We just crossed into West Virginia back there. The state line isn't marked now, but a photo I saw from the early 1900's featured a round sign on a post. Now, according to Nick, his group would have stopped about here and then slid down this embankment on the left, toward the banks of Cross Creek. Down there in that bottom they met some miners from the tent camp over there to the right, between the creek and the railroad tracks, who showed them where to ford the stream." The people, including a few locals from Virginville, packed closely around him, listening attentively as the television camera recorded the monologue.

"Meanwhile the rest of the miners, two hundred or more, had already moved into position on that ridge above the mine. The portal was over there, on the hillside," he said, pointing. "This area was the main camp, and what they called New Camp was over there..."

He continued telling his story as they walked slowly onward. Several state police and sheriff department cars were positioned with their lights flashing. A fire truck and two rescue trucks were also visible, just in case medical aid or rescue had to be performed. "When I saw how big this was getting, I had Leo call the Wellsburg and Follansbee fire chiefs to be ready, just in case," Les confided.

"Good heads-up decision," Joe replied. "I'd hate to see anybody get hurt without rescue equipment anywhere around."

Joe went on to relate the details of the battle as Nick had told it, and as he and Jessie had learned in the newspaper articles published in the days following the fight.

Meanwhile, more folks from Brooke County had approached the group and were also listening attentively. Nearly half an hour later Joe concluded: "...The sheriff's son found his body up there on that hillside on a rock outcropping, and the miners who could walk or be helped from the scene fled back into Pennsylvania, that way." He pointed through the woods to the east.

"Nick was aided by his good friend, Angelo Ballino, and several other miners who took turns helping and then carrying him. He finally died and they buried him along the way. He and eight other miners that we know of."

Joe then shocked the group with his next announcement. "We have already identified where Nick's and the other miners' remains are located." Les and Jessie glanced at him, also in surprise. They had clearly not expected him to reveal that information just yet. A stunned silence greeted this unexpected news.

He looked at Les. "Perhaps it's time that we broke this thing up so these kind folks from Brooke County can get on home, and we can get our people back to town. They must really be tired." Les nodded agreement and informed the crowd that it was time to go home; that school buses were waiting near Virginville and also back on the other side of the tunnel.

While still excited about their adventure and the lesson in local history, the participants were fast losing energy and were obviously ready to go home. Most walked over to the buses positioned near the railroad crossing before heading up over the hill and back toward Avella. Andy and the other senior citizens climbed into a waiting van. "See you back at the train station in Avella!" he shouted before the door closed. The five friends – Jim now included – waved and then turned back toward the tunnel; followed by the boy scouts and several score marchers who were obviously not quite ready to close out this part of their adventure.

As they traversed the tunnel again, Nick appeared next to Joe. "Do you mind if we walk along with you? We're really touched that so many people would remember us this way." Jim and the others knew without asking that Nick had reappeared. As they exited the eastern end of the tunnel, Nick and the invisible eight miners remained behind.

Glancing up, the party gratefully saw two buses awaiting them at the grade crossing.

"How can she be so darn peppy?" Joe asked, rhetorically, after returning the school bus driver's cheerful greeting and then plopping into a seat. Letting their heads slump against the seat backs, bus windows and each other, the spent marchers barely noticed the winding ride back to town. After twenty minutes or so, a very weary group stepped down from the buses next to the war memorial. It was already after three a.m.

"You're not driving home tonight," Joe told Jessie resolutely. "Twenty-five miles is just too far."

"No. I'm not," Jessie affirmed sleepily. "I'm staying at your house."

CHAPTER FIFTY-THREE

Our Affiliate in Pittsburgh sends us this report on a surprising march that started in the small Western Pennsylvania town of Avella yesterday.

The television image cut away from the New York studios of the morning program to a female reporter standing near a camera truck in the midst of a throng of people.

This is Amber Bridger of Channel Eight News reporting from the small Washington County village of Avella, where an incredible story is in progress. Over the past few days what began as a minor controversy at a school board meeting has evolved into a human-interest saga. As we previously reported, Mr. Joseph Bailey maintains that he regularly speaks with the spirit of a deceased miner. However, the story took an unexpected turn after hundreds of area residents decided to join Mr. Bailey on a difficult six mile walk down the railroad tracks to the site of a 1922 mine riot. I am reporting from the Avella War Memorial plaza and train station, before the beginning of that march...

The next few minutes included snippets of interviews with Joe, Jessie and several of the gathered throng, including one Boy Scout who excitedly said: "We just want to help Mr. Bailey by walking the same route as the miners did. That's all." He then added, "and this will be our first night hike."

After showing some footage taken later in the evening at Penowa with video of the State Line tunnel, the feed from Pittsburgh ended and the network went back to their normal morning programming.

"Cut over to Channel Six," Jessie yawned as she tried to waken herself with another cup of Andy's high-octane brew, made even stronger today due to everybody's flagging energy levels.

"It looks like three hours sleep just isn't enough for you or your tired, old educator's body," Joe cracked.

She looked at him contemplatively. "You don't look that much stronger, old fella." Inwardly he had to admit that his show of energetic machismo just wasn't fooling anybody, least of all her. Or even him.

"Channel Six news is on now," Andy interrupted. Joe considered his old friend, who seemed to be in better shape than he or Jessie that morning. But then he rationalized that Andy hadn't walked the whole distance. But, on the other hand, Andy hadn't gotten any more sleep than they had.

"What, Joe?" Jessie asked, having heard him muttering to himself.

"Oh, nothing. Shhh, look!"

... And now, another related story. We have been informed that the three-person gravesite, said to have been prepared in advance by Nick Shebellko's former fiancée Carmella and her husband Mike Zaretsky, has apparently been discovered. After reading news reports this week, Mrs. Mildred Brown of Meadowlands noticed the Zaretsky headstone as she arrived to tend her mother's gravesite in the Hillside Cemetery. We understand that as the word spread, there has been a veritable pilgrimage to the Zaretsky burial place.

"We now bring you a graveside report...

A female reporter spoke in low tones, as the camera first focused on the Zaretsky and Nicholas Shebellko headstones. The camera then panned the crowd of perhaps forty people standing respectfully nearby, talking in hushed tones. Suddenly, two little girls of about six or seven years walked forward and bent over, carefully adding small bouquets of flowers to those already accumulating in front of the headstones. Another sweep of the camera revealed that more than a dozen cars were parked along the roadway through the cemetery, with several more pulling to a stop behind them

We can't keep them out! I mean, how can we keep them out? Exclaimed a frazzled-looking man, apparently a cemetery custodian. *We have a funeral coming at eleven o'clock...* he muttered, walking away and shaking his head.

We have confirmed that the gravesite described by Mrs. Carmella Cook – but with no location given – has been discovered, the reporter continued.

That poor man, a woman standing nearby was heard to say. *I hope they find him and bury him here. He belongs here.*

After hesitating a moment, the reporter concluded: *And if this site is ever used to inter Mr. Nicholas Shebellko's remains, we plan to be here to report on the burial ceremony. Back to you, Kevin.*

The rest of the report rehashed the march with clips from the day and evening before, including part of an interview with Andy at Penowa.

And finally, the anchorman intoned. *Our research has confirmed that an estimated 400 men likely made the march in 1922 and then suffered through the battle. Early estimates are that over 400 people participated yesterday in the unplanned march, but under more peaceful circumstances.*

The news program then cut away to a report on an overnight shooting outside a bar in Pittsburgh.

"Now, ain't that something!" Andy exclaimed, just before noticing that both of his guests were sound asleep on the sofa. "Youngsters," he added, smiling paternally as he turned down the sound volume on the set. "And they missed my speech. Good thing I taped it!"

***

She was shaking Joe awake. "Sleepyhead! Time to wake up. We've slept for three more hours. I'd think your public is out there somewhere, wanting interviews and autographs." Joe roused himself groggily, wondering how she could be that chipper that fast. *Was* he getting old?

"Jessie, while I was sleeping I saw the men attacking the mine again. It made me think about the inconsistencies we noticed in the microfilmed news accounts of the day. Do you know what I mean?"

"Yes, I remember," she responded thoughtfully. "Especially in the first reports when the papers were hungriest for details. We noticed that there were lots of inconsistencies – perhaps dozens, including incomplete and conflicting information. I remember some of it. Let me see… we saw numbers of marchers from about 300 to an outrageous 1000. That was straightened out pretty quickly. There were probably 400 or so."

"And various reports showed that either the miners definitely started the shooting, or nobody knows for sure," he recalled. "For all anybody really knows, the defenders might have fired the first shot. Of course, the first accounts were by defenders who gave heroic accounts of actions by the lawmen, as you might expect. One report even had 100 or more miners from Ohio supposedly arriving by train, and then leaving before the fighting started. That didn't make any sense at all," he continued.

"We wondered about the timing, too," she said. "It seems logical that the meeting in Avella would have been held in daylight hours, despite reports that had it from eight p.m. to ten p.m. at night. That timing doesn't allow adequate time for a meeting and then a march to Penowa followed by a big outdoor rally with speeches. How could they still traverse the tunnel and approach the mine premises around midnight? It makes sense that the meeting in Avella must have been held during the day with an afternoon march to Penowa. A meeting there would have been held in the afternoon, logic would dictate. Especially since the Brooke County Sheriff was warned no later than eight p.m. One report has it that his forces were already marshaled by then.

"A glaring inconsistency was the names of the miners," she continued. "Some names changed practically every day – or at least the spellings did – making you wonder if the same miners were being renamed or if other men were being identified. That would probably be because of the foreign-sounding and strangely-spelled names of the immigrants, especially those from Eastern Europe. Not to mention that when interviewed, some of the immigrant miners could speak little or no English, and even that was heavily accented."

"What struck me as a major inconsistency was the guns and ammo issue," Joe recalled. "Some reports said that lots of guns and ammunition were shipped in and provided for the miners. But how does that square with the casualties?"

"You mean that so many miners were killed or wounded, but the defenders suffered only two casualties, including only one death?" she asked. Joe spread his arms as though befuddled. "Exactly. If most of the attackers carried guns against twenty-some defenders, then why only two casualties among the sheriff's forces? I'd think that many of the defenders would have been injured or killed, or would have fled in panic. In fact, the sheriff himself should have understood that… wait! Let me think." He paused and then continued. "I was going to say that the sheriff was killed after he left cover and went up the hill after a group of miners, right?"

"Correct…" she responded.

"Well, if even half of the miners were armed do you think he would have ever considered leaving cover? Who would be crazy enough to chase – they used the term 'try to outflank' – a large group of heavily armed men? No lawman I know, and I was one." He developed the thought for a while.

"I assume the sheriff was a professional lawman," he continued, "or at least a reasonable man. I just can't see him running off to his possible death against a heavily armed force. The odds would have been prohibitive against him and the small group of deputies who went with him. It would have been tantamount to suicide." Joe brightened as the thought jelled in his thinking processes. "The miners had some guns, but could not have been heavily armed. He wouldn't have chanced that encounter otherwise. He had to be too smart for that.

"I'd wager that they only had the guns and ammo that they could scrounge up, probably hunting rifles and shotguns, with maybe a few army revolvers thrown in. Most would have been unarmed. It couldn't be otherwise, or more defenders would have been killed," he said with finality. "Now, let's go and find today's newspapers."

CHAPTER FIFTY-FOUR

"Put it over there," Steve directed. The coal miner, who had identified himself only as Pat, followed the instructions as he continued to unload the ATV carrying the miners' equipment. Steve, the foreman, turned to Joe and his small group. "We just can't tell you how honored we are to be doing this excavating work for you. We really want Nick's body to be found in there, and we want to be the ones to find him." He stared toward the cave. "He's been in there too long."

"Yes, too long," Joe agreed. He admired the carefully organized digging equipment and roof supports, all placed near the cave's entrance. "Way too long."

Carl, the last miner to emerge after checking out the interior of the cave, agreed with the others. "This shouldn't be a problem. The roof fell in the one area. You say his friend pulled that section of the roof down using a branch?" Joe nodded. "The rest of it looks to be pretty solid and has held up 'til now. With careful excavating, we should be able to get through there okay. We just have to keep putting up the supports." He rubbed his chin whiskers and looked back toward the entrance. "No problem at all."

Joe gazed around, wondering at the remarkable day. Somebody had rewarded them handsomely for the efforts they were about to expend. The sun-splashed hillside was alive with scores of shades of green and other earth tones, interspersed randomly with the brilliant colors of wild blossoms. After recovering from the intrusion of humans and machines into their sequestered sylvan retreat, the wild birds had quickly resumed gorging on the nearby berries and were flitting about in full force. They had quickly realized that the bustling around of people, the clanks of metal tools and the thunks of wood supports being stacked were no reason to abandon their wild berry and insect buffet for flight into safe treetop perches. Their brunch was just too good to pass up and the humans wandering about were now at most an annoyance to be wary of.

Absently watching a groundhog pop its head out of a hole in the hillside before deciding against going out for a meal, Joe noticed that Steve was still going over details with the group. "I know you checked with the Bureau of Mines about getting a mine rescue team, but like they said we can handle it just fine. We got us a shallow cave. No poisonous gases – or you two probably never would have gotten out of there alive in the first place – and no other hazardous conditions. Just straightforward digging. We can handle it."

Joe surveyed the still-growing group between the meadow and the cave mouth. Paramedics, miners, state police, the coroner and his team, firefighters and Joe's usual entourage: Jessie, Les, Leo and Jim Christopher. Several television reporters and cameramen were standing further back in the meadow, kept away from the cave mouth per the coroner's edict.

Down below, Joe knew, were the television trucks, fire and rescue trucks, and numerous onlookers, including Andy, who had been given a place of honor in the headquarters tent. "They're calling for some rain later today," he said. "Shouldn't we get on with it?"

Coroner Walsh nodded his agreement. "Let's get started!" he directed. And, turning to Joe, he remarked: "You have a lot of personnel and resources tied up here today, Mr. Bailey. I hope for your sake that there is a space behind that rubble, and that there's a body in it. Otherwise, many of us will feel pretty stupid."

Joe recoiled, thinking of what somebody had said earlier that morning about 'Al Capone's vault.' Television reporter Geraldo Rivera had captured a large viewing audience some years back with the prospect of witnessing the discovery of hidden riches – or at least lost secrets – in a vault room that had supposedly belonged to the gangster Al Capone. But when the vault was finally opened, the result was nothing but abject disappointment. Of course, the Network's purpose had been fulfilled by the millions of viewers and advertising dollars. But there could be no positive outcome if Joe Bailey's vault were to come up empty as well. He would be humiliated and Jessie's reputation and career would doubtless be ruined.

Please let this not be another Capone's vault, and me a poor man's Geraldo, Joe silently pleaded as he cringed at the fleeting mental images. While Geraldo had long-term journalism credentials and a string of successes, Joe was only a real estate agent. He could even lose his real estate reputation and his career, he realized. He tore his attention away from those wretched images and forced his attention back to the six miners who had just stooped low and clambered into the recently enlarged opening, pulling their digging equipment in with them. Soon, those outside began to hear the sounds of rubble being dug and flung out of the way.

After nearly an hour, Carl came to the cave entrance. "It looks like this wall of rubble could be about five or more feet thick at the base, and maybe two-to-three feet on top. But we're making pretty good headway. There's not enough storage space along the cave walls, so we better start loading some of this stuff out."

Carl and another miner, a stolid, red barded man named Luther, began to bring rubble out by the five-gallon bucket loads, which they then dumped off to the side. "Make sure you don't disturb anything in there except plain rock and dirt!" Coroner Walsh directed. But the miners knew their jobs. Everything that came out consisted only of rubble. "And make sure you get roof supports up in there! I don't want to bring more than one body out of there," he said.

"I know, I know," a voice they recognized as Steve's floated out from within the cave's depths. "Wait!" Steve shouted. "I think we got through at the top of the fall." After another few minutes he could be heard muttering, "pass me that light." The group outside waited breathlessly. Joe knew that this was significant, because if a roof fall blocked an open space behind it, then his story about Nick's body was suddenly more plausible.

The television reporters and cameramen began edging forward. The policeman assigned to keep them back was apparently so intrigued that he didn't bother to stop them until they had gained fifteen more feet of ground toward the cave entrance. The scene outside the cave became deathly quiet after the initial excitement following Steve's announcement.

Jessie looked at Joe concernedly. He had been strangely subdued since their arrival at the scene. "Are you okay?" she asked him, looking carefully into his eyes. He shifted uncomfortably.

"I have a lot of things going on inside my head, Jessie," he answered tiredly. "My reputation – and now yours – rests on what is found behind that wall. And we are now fulfilling what fate has assigned to us. But that's not all of it," he concluded.

She nodded her understanding. "You aren't sure you want to see Nick's body, right Joe?"

"He's become such a friend that it could be hard for you," Les offered, looking at Joe sympathetically. Joe looked away.

"I think that about sums it up," he finally responded. "I mean, have you ever arrived at the scene of an accident in your rescue truck and then recognized the victim as somebody you knew well?"

Les nodded sadly. "Yes, I have. More than once. One time I came on a scene where one of my best buddies and his girlfriend were both… well, it was clear they wouldn't make it."

"I think that's how I'll feel," Joe said with resignation in his voice.

"Joe, we talked about this." Nick said from within the cave. Joe and Jessie both jerked into heightened alertness. "I told you that all they will find is my body. And it's not in that bad a shape, either. Just be strong, Joe."

Les looked at Joe and Jessie narrowly. "Did he just say something? He said something just now, didn't he?"

"Yes, he did," Jessie confirmed. "He assures us that they will find his body and that it's not in very bad condition, either." The others standing nearby, beyond surprise by now, just shrugged their shoulders and returned their gaze to the cave entrance as they saw more rubble being hauled outside. Jim jotted down some notations in his pad. The television reporters narrated excitedly. They also edged closer so the cameramen could frame them into the scene before the mine mouth, now only sixty feet away. The television crews had encroached another twenty feet.

The diggers dumped more rubble outside. "We need another jack over here," Steve demanded. They could hear wood and metal supporting members clattering as they were pushed into place. "I see something!" Steve shouted. "We have about a foot of clear space under the roof now and I can see something on the floor… Give me that halogen lamp!" After another few seconds of breathless anticipation: "It's a... it's a body! We got us a body!"

"That's me," Nick said, simply. Joe and Jessie clutched each other's hands as they started toward the sound of Steve's voice.

"He says it's him," Joe repeated. "Way to go, Nick." Under his breath he intoned: "Thanks, Nick. I should never have doubted you." And then aloud. "May I go inside? I have a hard hat."

Coroner Walsh spoke up. "Is it safe for Joe and me to come in? We'd like to have a look." He glanced toward the woman standing there glaring at him. "And Miss Randall, too?" Jessie's gaze softened, and she rewarded him with a dazzling smile as she pulled a hard hat on over her piled-up curls.

"Should be okay," responded the voice from inside. "There's enough room. But I'll have a couple of the guys step outside and stretch their legs, just to be sure." Carl and another, burly miner whose name Joe couldn't remember, clambered outside, stretching in the warmth of the sun.

The three entered the cave mouth, where only two of them saw a grinning Nick. "Hey, Nick," Joe smiled. He and Jessie were, as far as the others could tell, just talking to a section of the wall. But by now the others also knew better. "Over eighty years now," he continued. "And you're finally getting out."

"They're doing a good job taking that rubble out of the way," Nick remarked admiringly. "Tell them another miner thinks they're doing just fine. They'll have that wall down in no time."

"Nick says you're doing a good job, fellas," Joe explained. "He mined coal and he knows."

"Thank him for us, Joe," Steve remarked gratefully, wiping his brow.

"He heard you."

"The wall is partly down now and supports are in place. Want to have a look?" Coroner Walsh moved to the wall and peered over, using the light of Steve's helmet lamp, as Carl stepped back out of the way. "Bring the halogen lamp," Steve ordered.

"I think I see him. Come on over, Joe. Just be sure to keep your hard hat on."

"Interesting thing," Joe commented, still standing in the same place, "As a cop, I saw my share of dead bodies. But I'm not sure I want to see this one."

"I'm going. Come on over with me," Jessie said encouragingly. He sighed and took her hand. They went to the wall together. They found a nearly two foot space above the wall and gazed over, leaning forward with their chests against the rubble. Jessie squeezed his hand so intensely that it hurt. He leaned forward as far as he could.

"That's me," Nick said quietly from just behind their shoulders.

"We know, Nick," the lady said quietly. "You seem to have a layer of dust on you. We can't see your face because of that piece of cloth."

"You folks better let us get back to work," Carl finally interjected. "Do you mind clearing out for a while so we have a little room to dig?" Silently, they left the cave.

"It's him," Joe said after they emerged under the overcast sky and into the gazes of those waiting. "It's him." Jim placed his hand on Joe's arm, but said nothing. "We'll stay out here for the rest of the recovery." Joe averted his eyes from the gaze of the others and walked away.

After another two hours, Coroner Walsh began to give instructions to his photographer and the rest of his staff. "It's about time. We need another roll taken plus some digitals, all angles, from the cave entrance inward. And then photograph every action we take until we get him in the box. And be gentle with him. After all, he's over a hundred years old."

"They are showing proper respect," Nick said from inside.

"I knew they would," Jessie said.

"Huh? What?" Jim asked, and then: "Oh. Sorry."

"The wall is down now, so you can do your work," Steve said as he emerged from the cave. The other miners came out, too, tired but happy. They each sucked down an entire bottle of water and started on another.

Wordlessly, the coroner's team went inside, carrying their plain, wooden, handled box.

The bystanders anxiously waited for them to come out with their precious cargo. After another hour or so, their impatient vigil was rewarded. "I don't exactly know what will happen to me now," Nick remarked. "I can't say for sure, but I'm just about scared. I don't even know how long I'll be here before I have to go away." He then voiced what had haunted all three for the past few days. "Joe? Jessie? I better say goodbye, just in case. You were good friends. I hope Angelo,

Carmella and Mike and I can get together with you some day. But not too soon," he added.

Jessie clutched Joe in an embrace and together they wept in both relief and sorrow as the miners carefully carried Nick's box out. They delicately loaded the box on the back cargo compartment of an ATV for the slow, respectful journey down the newly enlarged trail. The television crews followed, filming all the way.

"Here they come!" exclaimed a state policeman when the entourage came into sight, with walkers preceding and following the ATV. The procession slowly exited the trail, led by the six miners; still carrying their digging implements. They stopped in two rows of three and held their picks and shovels overhead like crossed swords, paying due respect to a fallen brother as the ATV passed through their ranks. The local television trucks broadcast their signals to be relayed to network feeds. Hundreds of thousands across America would wipe away tears as they sat in front of televisions in their living rooms and in bars.

The box was carefully loaded into the coroner's van. "We'll now take Nick's remains to a cold storage room," he explained. "We'll take good care of him. And we'll soon make arrangements to get the others out, too."

CHAPTER FIFTY-FIVE

"I'm happy that we could finally meet, Mr. Bailey," offered Dr. Briceland as the two men shook hands. "And you, too, Miss Randall and Mr. Wilson. My team is beginning to set things up now. The staging area you suggested should work out just fine."

"I see you're setting up two tents along with your working shelter. Will somebody be staying here overnight?" Jessie asked as she surveyed the tight-looking encampment. Evidently, the forensic anthropologist's team had performed this sort of task numerous times before, but rarely under such scrutiny

"While most of us will be staying in a motel in Washington, four of the younger team members decided to remain on-site. Youth," he sighed. Looking up, he viewed an overcast sky, but with no hint of rain until at least the weekend. "Perfect weather," he commented. "How did you arrange it?"

"Spiritual help," Les joked. "By the way, most of the assets are in place or will arrive soon," he reported. "State police, fire and rescue services, constables and special security detail for crowd control and media management. I see that Coroner Walsh is ready for the press conference now." They walked over to the media area where television and print reporters were waiting.

"Good morning," Coroner Walsh began. "This morning we will begin the process of locating and removing the eight sets of remains that we have been told are still located in the project area. A team from Mercyhurst College, headed by Dr. Frederick Briceland, forensic anthropologist, will manage the process. Perhaps Dr. Briceland will explain his procedures."

Dr. Briceland stepped forward. "Our team is comprised mainly of highly-trained graduate students, each of whom has a specific task. We expect to manage one site per day, finishing in eight working days. Hopefully, with eight sets of remains," he added. "So, perhaps we should get started."

Les guided the team to a trail leading to the first identified burial site, that of John Brown, the black miner as identified by Nick.

As they approached it, he conferred with his GPS unit and compared the surrounding terrain with the 8.5x11 inch black-and-white photos. "See?" he said, pointing to the first site and comparing it to the photos. "Here we are now. The site is eleven feet from that outcropping and seven feet from that sycamore, right in there. You will notice that it's slightly mounded and has stones mixed in with the dirt. It also lines up with a small dry ravine." The team stood back and visually assessed the site. Two members carefully approached it and marked an area of two meters by two meters, with a centerline and a line crossing at the mid-point. The team photographer, who had been photographing from various angles, continued his work. One member began to make notes in a log as police started to fasten crime scene tape from tree to tree on the perimeter.

After the site was lined up, two people, apparently tasked to dig and sift, began their work in one quarter of the layout. Joe and the others walked off to the side to allow the team members to continue their painstaking duties. After a short while they heard: "We have a fragment here," and then: "and another one." Walking over to the tape now marking off the site, they saw a small bone being carefully brushed. It had apparently been found about 15 inches under the surface of the ground. "It could be a metatarsal, because there are more with it." The photographer snapped photos of it as the note-taker logged the entry. Dr. Briceland turned to Joe and his friends. "We may have a valid site. By the way, this will be very tedious and time-consuming work. Feel free to take a walk or go and rest down below at the headquarters tent."

"Yeah, Joe. Why not give these people room to work," Nick suggested.

"Nick says we should leave you alone for a while," Jessie related. Turning to the two men she said, "Let's take a walk over to Nick's cave and see what's left of it." She started off, giving them very little choice. Les grinned at Joe with his all-too familiar "if you stay involved with her you'll be in for it" look. Joe only sighed before following along in her wake.

***

The cave area was still marked off with crime scene tape, but it had been pushed down and stepped over in places. “Look at that,” Les remarked. “No sign of litter, but somebody has been here.” They walked on toward the enlarged cave entrance, which was still open but blocked by sawhorse barriers.

“Flowers,” Jessie gasped. “Somebody has been bringing flowers.” She was visibly moved. “It looks like the ghoulish creeps who were coming before have been replaced by more caring people.” Several flower shop arrangements plus bunches of wildflowers had been placed neatly in front of the cave entrance.

She delicately stepped over the tape, followed by Joe and then Les. They approached the cave mouth. “It looks like nobody’s gone in, but they’ve been peeking inside. And some left flowers just inside the entrance,” Les remarked. “Now how about that? They think old Nick is worth flowers!”

“There’s some in here, too,” Nick informed them. “And what does he mean by ‘old?’ I’m only twenty-two.”

Peering inside, they found several bunches of flowers and a teddy bear. “A teddy bear?” Jessie remarked. “Why would somebody leave…? Never mind. It must have been a child who came with her family and decided to leave it.” She leaned forward and picked it up. Noticing a note pinned to it, she began to read aloud. But then her voice caught:

“Dear Nick, This is because we are sorry that you were never able to marry Carmella and have kids. Janey and Carl (and mommy and daddy).”

Even Nick was speechless. After a few minutes, he said: “I think you should take that to Carmella’s daughter before it gets ruined by the weather.” They mutely agreed, and Jessie held it close to her breast.

“He says we should give it to Carmella, Les,” Jessie explained.

“I see that they have a lot of old John out now,” Nick continued, in an obvious attempt to break the bittersweet mood. “But if we dug coal the way they dig bodies out, all us miners together couldn’t have dug enough to run a steamship,” he joked.

“Nick,” Joe began, broaching a very touchy subject. “Your body is being examined right now in a lab, using all kinds of medical equipment. But you’re still here. I mean, we love to talk with you, but we can't help wondering when you will go or be taken away."

"I rightly don't know," he responded. "Maybe after the final miner is out or maybe after they finally plant me in the ground. I just don't know. Something's holding me here and I don't know what. But I don't mind, for now anyways." After again noticing the obvious fatigue in their voices, he continued, "one thing I do know is that you three are mighty tired. I think you should leave all this stuff to the experts for a while and get some rest."

Joe and Jessie glanced at each other and reached silent agreement. They were tired – exhausted, in fact. "Nick says we should get some rest. I think he's right," Joe explained to Les. Let's head on down the trail."

As they emerged from the trailhead, Jim and a Steubenville reporter, plus the Channel Eight on-site person, rushed over. "What's happening?" Jim asked anxiously, as they held their microphones and tape recorders forward.

"Right now, they are recovering what appear to be the remains of John Brown," Les began. "But you might be interested in this." He pointed at Jessie.

Carefully holding the stuffed animal out for inspection by the media and all those others nearby, Jessie paused, gathering her thoughts. Then she explained the circumstances of the little toy's recovery at the cave and read the note. "Nick says we should give it to Carmella before it's ruined. The cave isn't watertight, especially now that the opening was enlarged," she explained. Besides, we doubt that he'll be around very long to enjoy it." Her eyes began to cloud. As the two men quickly turned away they noticed the eyes of the others present beginning to brim with tears, even as they concealed their own.

"Let's get some sleep for a couple hours," Joe suggested. "We can come back later." He and Jessie walked to the Caddy, politely refusing more requests for information and interviews. Les remained behind to help with the logistics of the recovery.

Jessie snuggled tiredly against him as he drove home. Just before she dropped off to sleep next to him, she murmured: "Notice that I don't drive to my apartment much anymore?" Joe smiled. Of course he had noticed that.

At his house they lay together, napping throughout the middle part of the day.

***

When they finally returned, refreshed, to the recovery site they were just in time to see Dr. Briceland and Coroner Walsh wrapping up a press conference. Dr. Briceland opened the team's van, wherein a plain, functional-looking box had been carefully placed. It contained all that was left of John Brown's remains, including the residue of his clothing and personal items.

"Just to recap for you, Mr. Bailey, the remains seem consistent with those of a person who has been covered by soil for between 50 and 100 years. We noted bone damage and fragments that could have resulted from a gunshot wound to the radius and ulna bones of the left arm. There was also severe damage to two ribs, probably from gunshot."

Coroner Walsh interjected: "By the way, we neglected to mention this morning that preliminary data on your friend Nick Shebellko indicate a penetration wound through his shirt consistent with gunshot. It was heavily saturated with dried blood residue. The wound continued through his upper body just below the clavicle, or collarbone, with damage to his scapula, or shoulder blade. The wound would surely have been mortal without medical intervention. He likely bled to death," he concluded.

Quietly declining to grant interviews, Joe and Jessie drove back home to spend time with their dear neighbor. They had to help prepare him. His father's site would be next.

CHAPTER FIFTY-SIX

The next morning, Joe and Jessie were finally well rested and wide-awake. They didn't want to miss out on the excavation of Andrew Polack's burial place.

She gently suggested: "Let's go on over to Andy's as soon as we can, okay? He was pretty stressed while we were chatting last night, and he could still be having a hard time of it." Joe agreed immediately. After they brushed their teeth and donned their hiking garb, they headed next door. As expected, the lights were on, but nobody awaited them at the door with coffee mugs in hand. They followed the sounds of Sinatra's "It Was a Very Good Year."

"Andy, how are you doing this morning?" she quietly asked the man sitting at the kitchen table, staring straight ahead. "Are you okay?" He jerked his head around in sudden realization that he had visitors.

"Oh, hello," he finally said as he switched off the radio. "Yeah, I think I'll be okay. But you know they're going after my dad this morning, right?" He slowly got up and tottered toward the coffee pot.

"We know," Joe said. "And we'll stay by you until it's over."

"Thanks," he replied. "Today I could use a little support. I'm feeling my age today and I don't like that feeling."

They received the mugs of hot brew that he offered them and then sat and listened as he told stories of his dad and him when he was a boy. Upon Jessie's tender urging he also unloaded tale after tale about how hard life was without a dad in a coal-mining town.

"...And I worked every day I could on farms until I could start in the mine," he continued. "I worked for money and I worked for food for the table. I dropped out of school because mom needed my help to keep the bills paid. And as soon as I could I learned to mine coal. But that wasn't a good time, you know."

"What do you mean?" inquired Joe. Andy sighed and continued.

"They hooked me up with an old miner because I didn't have a dad to teach me. But he cheated me all the time. He put his check on a third of the cars I loaded. I decided to get out of there as soon as I could. My mom and family needed that money. It wasn't my fault that he was getting old and couldn't keep up. Mom needed all the money I could bring home." His countenance took on a very sad expression. "He cheated me and my family until I could get my own room to dig. Durn his soul."

After a few minutes more he turned to his friends and asked beseechingly: "Shouldn't we be leaving?" They headed toward Joe's by now very dusty and mud-spattered Caddy and set out for the staging area.

At the staging area the team had already departed for Andy, Senior's site, guided by Les, who returned as soon as he could. It was already 10:00 a.m.

Les posed a question to Andy. "Today's site is only a few hundred feet off the road. Would you like to see it?" While the suggestion shocked Joe and Jessie, Andy was elated.

"I'd like that just fine. Those men told us how they buried my dad and how respectful they were. I don't want to watch them dig his bones up, but I think I'd like to see where the men planted him."

Les waved his identification at the policeman guarding the trail, but it was hardly necessary. They walked slowly up the trail, assisting old Andy whenever necessary. "Don't want to spoil my old age with a broken hip!" he joked. Within fifteen minutes, they arrived at the site.

The forensic anthropologist looked up from his notes and then walked over. "This is Andy Polack, Dr. Briceland," Les explained. "This is his dad's site you are working today. Several of the team members suddenly looked up, as startled as Briceland, who took Andy's trembling hand and gently shook it.

"You have my sympathy, Mr. Polack. And you have our word that we will take good care of his… of him. Several of the team members crowded around to also shake Andy's hand, while others just bent back to their work, wiping their eyes with their sleeves from time to time.

After a few minutes, Andy finally broke the tension: "We should go back down the trail and let these good people get back to work."

Down below, he told more old-time stories, triggered by Jim

who had finally decided to ask about his glass eye. But the audience that started out at six quickly grew to over twenty, as others drifted over to this people-magnet of a nonagenarian. "You don't want to get me started telling stories," he cracked after the one about winning the final point that meant victory for his morra team. "And our team only had one Italian on it, too! I can bend your ear all day," he warned. But nobody wanted him to stop, especially because he – and also they – needed a way to reduce the stress of waiting.

When Andy began to run short on stories, Jim reached into his car for a copy of that day's Washington Chronicle. "We have some new stuff in here," he explained as he offered the paper to Joe, just before a speedy feminine hand intercepted it.

"Do you mind if I read it to you?" she asked, while browsing the front page. "There's the headline!" She held it up for everyone to see, and then read aloud:

Miners Death Story Confirmed?

The strange story that had Washington Countians chuckling only a few weeks ago may have been confirmed. Reports released by Washington County Coroner Richard Walsh confirms that a body recovered from a cave is that of a miner, as described previously by Joseph Bailey of Avella. According to Bailey, the nearly intact body found on Wednesday is that of Nicholas Shebellko, who was shot during the Cliftonville Mine riot of July 17, 1922.

Lending further credibility to his tale was the discovery yesterday of long-buried human remains found in the exact location identified in advance by Bailey as the burial place of Mr. John Brown. He says that Nick Shebellko's spirit gave him the locations of nine burial sites, including his own and Mr. Brown's.

Based on the two-for-two success to date, forensic anthropologist Dr. Frederick Briceland's team from Mercyhurst College plans to work each of the remaining sites at a pace of one per day. The Mercyhurst team will attempt recovery today of the remains of Mr. Andrew Polack. Mr. Polack's son, 96-year-old Andrew, Jr., still lives in Avella. He plans to remain near the recovery site until the remains are brought out..."

Jessie continued to read the story, moving on to page A-2. It went on to detail recovery efforts and the immense public interest generated by the story of the miners who died in 1922. After she finished, there was a prolonged silence among the two-dozen people standing nearby. "There's more," Jim finally said. "Try page B-1."

Turning to the front page of the second section, she quickly found Jim's by-line. "Here it is," she began.

Nine-For-Nine?

By James Christopher
Chronicle Staff Writer

On July 28, 2002, the rescue of nine Quecreek coal miners in Somerset County was heralded with the triumphant call going out: "Nine-for-Nine!" All of the nine miners trapped in a flooded mine on July 25 were successfully extricated under the glare of floodlights and in full view of well-wishers grouped in front of their television screens world-wide. Those nine miners returned to the welcoming arms of their families. They also entered a world that they could not have imagined two short weeks before, one of interviews and celebrity appearances on television talk shows.

In this anniversary month, on July 19, scientists are laboring in a humanitarian mission to bring closure to the anonymous burials that followed an ill-fated July, 1922 attempt to close a non-union mine. A letter to the Opinion-Editorial Page published yesterday has already generated a wave of references to this effort as "Nine-for-Nine;" that the remains of all nine miners buried anonymously will be found, brought out, identified, and given decent burials.

Coincidentally, if the one-a-day schedule is achieved, the date of removal of the final set of remains will be July 27, only one day removed from the anniversary date of the Quecreek Mine rescue...

When Jessie finally reached the final paragraph, Jim's smile broadened. "Bet you haven't heard about the "Nine-for-Nine" coincidence, have you? I know how busy you've been, and how tired.

But I understand that the slogan appears to be catching on, big-time."

"Nine-for-Nine…" Andy turned the words over and over. "I like it. They saved those nine men, but what they are doing now for these nine will mean a lot to some families. These men couldn't be saved, but this is the next best thing."

"I understand that the descendants of John Brown's brother have already inquired about receiving and properly burying his remains. When we make the other names public, we expect that others will come forward, too," recounted Jim. "And I understand that the Polar Star Club has asked about 'adopting' any miner who has no identifiable descendants."

"Hold on," Les interrupted. "It looks like they're coming down now." Jessie clutched Andy's hand, while Joe stepped to his other side. Sure enough, a small group could be seen walking back down the trail. It soon became apparent that they were carrying a wooden box.

"It's okay," Andy explained. "I've been getting myself ready for this." He walked over to the group led by Dr. Briceland, then put his hand on the box reverently. He continued: "I just want to thank everybody who helped get my dad back. When do you suppose I can have him…" He broke down disconsolately and placed his head on the box. "Daddy," he breathed.

After a few moments he choked out: "Guess I wasn't as prepared as I thought."

"It should only be a week or two before we can release him, Mr. Polack," consoled Dr. Briceland. "Will you be all right?" Andy nodded wearily.

After another few minutes, as the others remained gathered around him in genuine concern, Andy suddenly brightened. "I got my dad back!" he exclaimed. Shaking off the hands that had been supporting him, he headed over toward Joe's Caddy, with more spring in his step than he had shown for days.

CHAPTER FIFTY-SEVEN

Over the next several days, as each new set of remains was exhumed and removed to Mercyhurst for examination, the effort became less newsworthy. The final recovery of Mario Ferrari had only a brief mention as a news item, mainly because it was the last set and the project had been completed. The entire story still had some "legs," however, as attention shifted more to the burgeoning plans for burials. A proposal to erect a memorial and possibly have a public ceremony also took on renewed life.

"Joe," Jim asked, trying to dredge up even a scrap of fresh news fodder. "I really appreciate what you've done for me. My reports have gotten me plenty of notice, and some have been reprinted in Pittsburgh and national publications. Newsweek even wants me to collaborate on a comprehensive feature story. Heck, a few weeks ago I was paying my dues, covering municipal and school board meetings and writing the minor articles that more senior reporters didn't want to be bothered with. A junior writer has to prove himself from the bottom up.

"But I have to give my editor credit. He realized that my sources gave me valuable information, and rather than try to force a top reporter into the mix, he went with me. And thanks to you, I haven't let him down." He paused, looking a little troubled.

"But now it's becoming a case of 'what have you done for me lately?' He needs some fresh material to feed the public's voracious appetite. Can you help me out?"

Joe studied his young friend. Jim had been a straight arrow during this time, beginning when Joe's image was at its worst. His stories helped to portray Joe as a reasonable and stable man – an ordinary man who had found himself enmeshed in extraordinary circumstances. "Jim, there is one other thing…" he began. "Ben Jenkins, the genealogist at the public library, began a search into whatever happened to Angelo and Carmella. I just wanted to bring closure to Nick's concerns about how their lives played out. You already know about how Carmella's life went. In fact, her daughter is now a local celebrity. Although she prefers her privacy, I don't think the publicity is bothering her too much, now that Nick will be buried next to her mom and dad next week."

Jim nodded, thoughtfully recalling the series of reports since he first wrote Carmella's story and the tri-partite grave was discovered. He waited for Joe to go on.

"Well..." Joe continued. "Ben's search revealed that Angelo relocated to Detroit…" He enjoyed his young friend's widening eyes as he revealed what he had learned from Ben, and some additional fragments that had surfaced since that time – including spotty information that Joe's mom and dad had provided.

"… Anyway, they told me that they never knew much about my great-grandfather Angelo, because he was close-mouthed about his coal mining days in Pennsylvania. Apparently, the memories were too hurtful and he wanted to keep them private. You might say he was the polar opposite of Carmella and Mike, who held those days dear to their heart and talked about them often, building an oral history. My granddad Nicholas was more like his father, especially after he Americanized his name. He became very successful as a business executive, and I suppose his early death obviated him having a change of heart later." He stopped again, to re-group his thoughts.

"Dad tells me that grand-dad would say that his family was 'in mining back East.' Well, he *was* telling the truth I suppose." Joe smiled, wryly. "Dad and mom are in their mid-sixties now and don't feel up to making the trip back here for Nick's funeral, because the whole Nick, Carmella and Angelo thing is so new to them. But they say they've been following it on television and in the news magazines. "And they say they're proud of me, too, for sticking to my guns."

"And the hook, a very logical hook indeed once you consider it," inferred Jim, "is that Nick was attracted to you without even realizing it, because you are descended from Angelo? You share Angelo's bloodline, so your spirit somehow called out to Nick's?"

"I think that sums it up. Neither Nick nor I suspected it was anything more than chance. He just passed through my body and then invaded my dreams. We developed a connection. But now it seems to be far from coincidence. Over more than eight decades, there were lots of other people who entered that cave. He never touched any of them. I don't think it was an accident." Joe smiled, remembering another incident.

"And of course it was no accident with Jessie either. She did what any woman like her might have done. She saw an opportunity and took matters into her own hands. She flung her body through a space and then landed on the hard floor of the old mine.

"You know, I kinda miss her." Jessie was visiting her parents in New Castle for several days. He smiled again, wistfully. "She's headstrong – much more so than most women I've ever met – but she's really nice to be near. Know what I mean?" Jim knew exactly what he meant. He had enjoyed seeing how much spark Jessie had infused into Joe's bachelor existence. He also envied Joe a little.

"So what are you going to do with this?" Joe asked tentatively.

"I think I'll give Ben a call and ask him to put the fine touches on details about Angelo's genealogy. You should see what I do with it, either in Thursday's edition, or possibly on Sunday."

Before leaving, Jim added: "By the way, we have a staff writer looking into this drive for a memorial. A groundswell of sentiment is building. It would be in memory of all the men who died in the attack, to complement the United Mine Workers obelisk in the Patterson Mill Cemetery that only memorializes five specific men. But there's a larger issue here and I have to warn you that the editor and the publisher will not avoid it."

Joe's expression revealed his surprise. "What do you mean? Are you saying the paper might come out against it?"

Jim nodded. "The editor questions the appropriateness of honoring men who broke the law and in the process killed a lawman. Is there really any justification for that? He understands that many of the miners were killed and their proper burial is appropriate, but he wonders if memorializing criminals is beyond what is fitting. He agreed to accept an opinion piece from you or anybody else willing to write in favor of memorializing these men. If you can convince him, then he might put the power of his press behind the effort. But if not, he could even run an editorial against it."

"I could have something typed up by tomorrow, Jim.

"Great! Then we can run it in the Sunday Op-Ed page."

CHAPTER FIFTY-EIGHT

On Sunday morning Jessie arrived bright and early, Washington and Pittsburgh newspapers in hand. "When I picked up the papers at the convenience store, people were all smiles, Joe. I'm anxious to read whatever's in there." Joe concealed his glee that people now associated her with him automatically – in fact acknowledged that they were an "item." She smiled brightly and kissed him happily. "And I really did miss you. I'm glad to be back."

Joe kissed her back, enthusiastically. "I missed you, too, babe. But maybe we better head next door. Andy won't forgive us if we don't read the newspaper with him."

Once fortified by a mug of the old guy's strongest, Joe opened the paper to the Op-Ed page. "Here it is. Want to read it to us? I already know what I wrote." She took the paper, skimmed the first few lines, and began to read.

Why Not a Memorial?

by Joseph Bailey
Avella

As this newspaper has reported several times, grassroots interest has surfaced in favor of a memorial to commemorate either all the men who marched on the Cliftonville mine, or at least those who died during and after the battle. However, one compelling question has been posed: "Why erect a memorial to remember – even honor – the men who marched on July 16, 1922 and then participated in the battle on July 17?" It can't be ignored that those men broke the law. In fact, at least forty survivors of the fracas were sentenced to three to ten years' imprisonment in the West Virginia state penitentiary at Moundsville. While they were mostly convicted of conspiracy, the charges against them included murder of the county sheriff.

by Joseph P. Bogo

So, the question remains; why memorialize men who broke the law? In contemplating the question, and while trying to develop a reasoned answer, I went back to the reports of the day.

The entire country was embroiled in strikes in the 1920's, including the coalfields, railroads and steel mills. The coal companies had been routinely cutting pay per ton for miners who dug coal, as well as the wages of mine workers who were paid hourly. It became more and more difficult for these men to support their families, in the mining camps or back in the "old country." They were also burdened by the company store system that essentially indentured them, always keeping prices high and never quite letting them catch up to their company housing and store expenses.

Stories are still told about men who would work without pay, removing rock and soil to expose a coal seam. They would then load six, seven or even more mine cars in a day, just to be cheated on the coal they sent to the surface. In fact, unionization in the early 1920's was not merely for better pay and working conditions, but also to establish a "union check-weighman" to assure that the coal cars that the miners sent out of the mine were counted and weighed honestly.

During drives to unionize mines, the mining companies would sometimes fire the regular work force and evict the men and their families from company housing. The companies would bring in replacement miners, or "scabs," to take their jobs. In fact, some miners were driven to such desperation to feed their families that they themselves resorted to scab employment.

This was the setting: the company held all the cards. They had gained the upper hand by hiring mostly immigrant labor, concentrating on those who spoke little or no English and shared no common language. They essentially set up a "Tower of Babel," wherein the miners could not effectively organize against them. But after a time, the miners did begin efforts to organize.

The companies also hired the feared and hated "yellow dogs," or coal and iron police. This mounted force intimidated the miners and enforced the companies' edicts. The companies had the economic power and political influence to advance their interests.

Another factor was the dangerous working conditions in the mines. The threat of explosion and cave-in was constant; women watching their men set off to work in the morning knew they could become widows before the end of the day. The dreaded mine whistle would result in a flood of families racing to a portal, fearful that the injured and dead men being brought out were their own husbands or fathers. Also, "black lung," where coal dust suspended in mine air would clog the miner's lungs, was even more a reality back then than today. However, there was no compensation for injuries, deaths or disability.

Finally, I remind readers that the miners who had been evicted at Cliftonville reportedly asked the Avella area miners for their help. The men took on a caring mission, trying to right one of many wrongs. While some of the miners were armed, it appears that most were not. Some newspaper accounts reported that their goal was not to attack the mine, but instead to shut it down – to prevent the replacement miners from going to work, or to "bring them out" of the mine. An armed force was ready for their arrival. The fact that the outnumbered defenders suffered only one death and one injury attests to the un-preparedness of the marchers for a gun battle.

I also learned about society in the communities both in and outside the mining camps. The newspapers of the day revealed the disparity. As the miners and their families led lives of deprivation and quiet desperation, outside society was less troubled. I read of preparations for the county fair, hymn sings and social visits with out-of-town relatives. There were drives for foreign missions and newspaper advertisements for musical programs, movies and plays, and new cars. This was well before the Great Depression; so much of outside society enjoyed a genteelness that was at least comfortable if not prosperous. In fact, some in the society at large looked down on the "ignorant foreigners with the funny-sounding names."

I bring this up only to show how a bipolar society used the sweat, blood and even the lives of these men to feed their economic engine, while denying them a fair place in the community. It could be said that the "Roaring Twenties" roared away, leaving many behind.

The marchers may have broken laws while trying to shut down the mine at Cliftonville and aid those displaced mine families, but they also paid a heavy price in lives lost, injuries, jail time while awaiting trial and imprisonment after conviction. In fact, rather than abandon their fellow miners who died in the woods, they gave each one the best burial they could under the circumstances.

These men who marched merely wanted to improve their lives and the lives and futures of their families. They fought against incredible odds, moving against a well-defended mine and an even better funded establishment. In doing so, they laid a bloody foundation stone for building the wages and better working conditions of today's workers.

It's unfortunate that many of the men who died can never be recognized nor remembered. Several bodies were found burned in the tipple fire, bloated after days out in the July sun, or otherwise unidentified on mine property. At least nine others were buried in unmarked graves in the woods after the battle. Others were said to have been interred in "midnight burials" in the days following. Their precise numbers are unknown and unknowable.

Yes, in my opinion they deserve a memorial. And it's long overdue.

Jessie quietly placed the paper on the coffee table and then rested her hand on Joe's knee, as Andy averted his gaze. "I couldn't have said this as well," she said sincerely. "You became the voice of those departed men."

Joe broke the spell. "Let's see what Jim wrote."

"Here it is," she offered. "Page B-1."

She began to read.

Blood or Coincidence?

By James Christopher
Chronicle Staff Writer

A fundamental question has begged answering since the first mention of long-deceased miner Nick Shebellko. What is the relationship between Nick and Joseph Bailey of Avella, who first disclosed the existence of Nick's spirit? The story has been told repeatedly since the story of the Cliftonville Mine riot re-surfaced that Nick's spirit passed through Joe Bailey's body, resulting in a connection that enabled the two to communicate. Barring any evidence to the contrary we assumed that their bond was merely the result of a chance happening. However, it may be that is not necessarily the case.

Jim went on to report on the direct bloodline connection that had been discovered between Joe and Nick's closest friend in life, Italian immigrant Angelo Ballino.

...And so the question remains: When Joe Bailey decided to move to Pittsburgh from Phoenix and then inherited property that required him to live in the Avella area, was it merely coincidence? When he decided to renew his interest in hiking instead of continuing his accustomed daily runs, was that also coincidence? And finally, when a hike took him to a small cave and Nick's spirit passed through his body upon re-entering the cave, was that coincidence? Was it chance, or was it fate? We will leave the question to our readers to ponder.

"Well, the secret's out," old Andy commented. "For good or bad, the secret's out."

"I think it's for the good," Jessie said quietly.

But then she turned to Joe. "Maybe you and I should take a hike. It's been a week since we last visited the cave."

CHAPTER FIFTY-NINE

As they approached the cave, Nick called out impatiently: "What kept you?"

"Jessie's been away for a few days, Nick, and I've been involved in preparations for the funerals. I'm sorry that we've not visited much lately. But I brought something for you!"

Jessie looked at him suspiciously as he plunked himself down next to the wall, but then turned to Nick. "We don't want to miss out on your company, because we may lose you soon. Are you getting an idea how long it could be?" She eyed Joe, as he opened his daypack.

"I don't think it'll be long, now. I'm beginning to feel like I'm losing my attachment to this place." He also looked warily at Joe's efforts, as the cave finally fell into an expectant silence.

After pulling out a few other items, Joe revealed a small package wrapped in a sandwich bag, and then a pack of matches. "Oh, no," Jessie muttered. Out came the pack of stogies.

Nick broke into a big smile. "Thanks," he said.

"Well if you're going to have one, give me one too," she said. "I'm not leaving because the boys club wants to smoke."

"I have to warn you that I may have passed out the last time I did this. It might have been the smoke buildup in here reducing the oxygen. Two cigars could make it worse. And anyway, you don't smoke."

"I won't inhale. So hand one over, buster. I'll take my chances." He handed one over.

Before long, they were puffing away, and Nick seemed as heady as if he were smoking along with them. Poor Jessie suffered coughing fits several times before settling into a smooth routine. Nick appreciated her efforts to keep up and liked his connection with her feminine persona. They sat in companionable silence for a few minutes, before she spoke up.

"One thing I'll always be jealous of is that you took Joe on some kind of trip. More than once, too, and I missed out each time. But I better stop puffing before I get sick," she said, shakily. Stubbing out her partly finished cigar, she looked at him challengingly. Well?"

Nick sighed. "Close your eyes." As they closed their eyes, the last thing they saw was Nick, grinning through the thick smoke filling the space around them.

After a few minutes, as they verged on falling asleep, Joe commented weakly: "I think you just want my cigar."

***

"This is my friend, Angelo," Nick explained. After giving Nick a warm embrace, the big man reached out and shook Joe's and Jessie's hands. He had very large hands. They could tell that he was restraining his strength.

"So you're Joe and Jessie? I've been hoping to meet you." Jessie wondered that Angelo could see them, because Joe had told her that he was practically invisible in his other trips back.

"Let's take a walk," Angelo suggested. After the shock of meeting Nick's closest friend, not to mention Joe's own great-grandfather, they finally took in their surroundings. Jessie realized that they were standing on a dusty road, bordered by rows of drab two-room cottages. She gasped audibly, wondering exactly what had happened to bring her here. One look at Joe told her that he was beyond surprise, having made trips like this one before.

She returned her attention to Angelo, who stood nearly six feet tall, with a lean muscularity. It was clear, even in his rough and dusty clothing, that he was a ruggedly handsome man. His face featured a prominent nose, strong jaw and craggy eyebrows. His mustache seemed very heavy and unkempt, but that only added to his apparent masculinity. His blue eyes, she suddenly realized, were practically the image of Joe's eyes that she had memorized so well. But still, her gaze flicked back and forth, from Angelo's face to Joe's. Angelo examined the fleeting emotions visible in her expression; and the suspicion suddenly hit her that he could read her thoughts. He smiled and broke the little stare-down that had just begun to develop.

"By the way, I'm proud of you, Joe," he said, before turning his attention up the street. They began to walk. But unlike Joe's last time here, the streets were otherwise deserted. It felt like they were alone in town. "I have to show you something," Angelo explained.

This is surreal, Jessie pondered to herself. *But it's not quite how*

Joe told it. Where are all the people?

"Where are all the people?" she finally asked.

"Just watch," Angelo responded. Presently, several small children came spilling out of a shack, looking both excited and distressed. One of the older girls – who appeared to be about fifteen – ran to a neighboring house. An old woman quickly came out, tying a babushka – or colorful scarf – around her head, covering her hair. They hurried back to the cottage. Meanwhile, a little boy ran to a much larger house down the street. "The mine super's house," Nick explained. "I think he went to call for the doctor."

Shortly a black sedan drove up the rutted red-dog road trailing a billowing cloud of road dust and parked in front of the cottage. The doctor hurried past the children, carrying his black bag. Jessie began to twist her hands nervously. "What's happening?"

"Mrs. Babich has been in labor," Angelo responded. "I think her time has come. I hear that this one has been very hard on her, not easier. After six children it should be easier, but she is almost forty years now."

One little girl sobbed uncontrollably as her older sister held her close, comforting her. Two little boys began to fight, causing the old lady to come out the door and chastise them. "The children are all scared," Nick explained. "A new baby will be an excitement for them, but it will also make their lives harder. There will be less food for each."

"Why don't they stop having children?" Joe asked innocently.

"The women try many folk traditions to stop 'getting in a family way' – just about every one they hear of," Nick explained. "But the law doesn't let the doctors help them to stop having babies, and their religion forbids it."

"And I'm sure that the women have to give in when their husbands want sex," Jessie concluded.

"There are few pleasures when a man is in his house, except drinking and being in bed. And a man works hard," Angelo answered. How times have changed for the better, Jessie reflected.

Presently, the doctor left the house, stopping to give each child a piece of penny candy before driving away. The old woman invited the children inside. A boy came running out, shouting: "I have a baby brother!" He ran to a house down the street to spread the news.

"People love their little girls, but a boy is one to grow up and take care of a family." Nick explained. "He can work on a farm and then go into the mine when he is old enough. The father will be very proud." Jessie left her modern, enlightened views unspoken, recognizing that she was in a male-dominated place and time.

Angelo resumed walking down the road, scuffing his boots in the cinders and causing little clouds of dust to spring up. Clearly, he was dwelling on something that troubled him. Finally he stopped. "Men live and then they die." He stood quietly, until a procession began to come into view, rounding the bend in the road.

"A man should never die without marrying. Marrying makes him whole – a full member of the community. And a woman should marry too," Nick remarked. They could now make out a hearse traveling at a walking pace down the road.

"Who are those girls?" Jessie asked, confused. "And why are they the only ones walking?"

"The young man died before he could marry," Nick explained wearily, perhaps groping with the irony of his statement. "The six girls dressed like bridesmaids are ceremonial. It is like he has now married. They walk beside the funeral car from the house to the church, and then to the grave. The pallbearers and the others can ride, but the girls walk." He sadly pondered the scene. "It is tradition where I come from."

The girls were walking beside the hearse car, three to each side. With several other cars following, the procession slowly passed them by. It was as though the watchers weren't even there, or that the tragedy of the young man's death made all else inconsequential. They watched the procession move on down the road. Angelo looked at Nick sorrowfully, and then he was gone.

Joe and Jessie slowly came to in Nick's small cave, surrounded by the now-diminishing smoke from the stogies. They were alone; not even Nick sat there with them. She turned to Joe and remarked seriously, but with a light gleaming in her eyes: "I have to look into some things," she said as she began to rise. She squeezed his hand. "Bear with me on this."

CHAPTER SIXTY

The next morning, Joe received word from the local funeral director that all of the remains had been released by the coroner, including Nick's and Andy Polack, Senior's. Positive identification had been made on those two, as well as on three other sets of remains. The authorities had then officially identified all of the others according to the information that Nick had provided.

Old Andy went about the task of organizing his father's reburial with a renewed vigor. "I'm past crying, Joe," he said. "I didn't know how I would face this day, but it's the happiest day of my life. We can put my dad next to my mom on Saturday."

"Is it true that you want to keep the service and burial low-key?" Jessie asked.

"Yep, I just want a regular church service at Saint Michael's Catholic Church, and then a simple burial next to my mom. The cemetery folks say there's enough room there. I don't want lots of television trucks, but if reporters want to tag along, that's okay. Especially young Jim."

"I understand all the other sets of remains have been claimed," Joe interjected. "And funerals are being scheduled in Avella and as far away as Cleveland. They should all be held in the next two weeks. We'll be kept pretty busy for a while, visiting the funeral homes and attending services. Of course, there will be no traditional viewings because the other remains are skeletal," he added.

"How about Nick?" Andy asked. "He's already at the Avella funeral home, right?"

"He's there, alright. But a real viewing won't be possible, because his mummified body hasn't been properly embalmed. The casket will be closed when people stop by to pay their respects and when we have the church service and burial." He hesitated, and then added: "I saw the photos. All things considered, he looks pretty good. Nowhere near good enough for an open casket, but pretty good."

"I got the church scheduled for a week from Saturday," Jessie added. "And other things are falling into place. The cemetery will be ready for his interment next to Carmella and Mike. Thanks for letting me take care of the details, Joe.

"I hear planning for the memorial is coming along, too," Joe added. "The scout troop has designed a temporary memorial of landscape timbers and sandstone, to be placed near the train station. The historical society has already given permission for it to be built there. Les is on the committee that's planning to have a permanent memorial designed and built within two years. The contributions to the fund already total more than $5,000."

"Joe," Andy said unexpectedly. "I think I can die happy." After the two looked at him, startled, he winked and added: "But not just yet." Jessie gave him a spontaneous hug and kiss.

"I think you already used that one on us. But you sure better take your time leaving this world, mister!" she exclaimed.

"I'm lucky to have such good, young friends," he commented.

"We're even more lucky to have you, you old coot." Joe retorted.

***

"Well, Andy," Joe began as they finished their Saturday morning coffee. "Time to head on down to the funeral home." They knew that the last viewing of the casket would be held at nine o'clock a.m., followed by the church service at Saint Michael's, and then the interment at the cemetery near Independence.

As they drove to the funeral home, Joe and Jessie both noticed old Andy's atypical silence. Yes, atypical, but hardly unexpected. They let the old man dwell in his private thoughts.

"Look, Joe!" Jessie exclaimed as they approached the funeral home. "The municipal lot is full and the street is parked solid." Joe noted that as each car pulled out, another pulled into its place. More people were walking down the street from the fire department and train station lots. He eased his cleaned-and-polished Caddy into line behind the hearse, in the space reserved for him. "There are at least twenty cars already in line behind yours," she continued.

"It's about eight-thirty, he commented. I hope the crowd doesn't build much more."

"I had to press some of the guys into traffic control duty," Les explained as he opened the car doors for Jessie and the old man.

"Well?" Joe asked as he remained behind the wheel in his seat.

"Open your own door," Les smirked, as he took Jessie's arm and started toward the funeral home's private side entrance.

The visitation went off without a hitch, with several hundred friends, townspeople and visitors filing past the closed casket. The guest register had only one blank page left when they were ready to depart for the church.

As the last of the visitors filed out, Andy, Joe and Jessie stayed for a private few minutes with Andy's dad. "Andy," Joe commented as his hand rested lightly across the old man's shoulders. "I really do wish that I could have known your dad like I knew Nick, or at least seen him in the tunnel."

"I appreciate that. I reckon he would have liked to meet you, too. But at least we know he saw you." He stared silently at the head of the still-closed casket. "And he saw me." He finally broke down, sobbing like the 12-year-old boy in him who lost his daddy. Finally he wiped his eyes and put his kerchief away. "Them were happy tears," he explained. The others there knew the tears were a mixture of happy and despondent.

He nodded to the funeral director, who motioned the six United Mine Workers pallbearers into the room. Steve, the foreman who had worked on excavating Nick's remains, stepped forward. "Thanks for asking the union to provide pallbearers, Mr. Polack. Carl, Pat, Luther and the other boys were happy to help out. We had to beat other volunteers away with a stick. But we were the ones who dug Nick out, so we wanted to do this for Andy. It's an honor."

Finally the procession wended its way down the street and up the hill toward the Catholic Church, where a traditional funeral mass would be held. "Did you notice the second law-enforcement car in line?" Jessie asked. "It's the Brooke County Sheriff's Department."

The traditional funeral mass went off without a hitch, with the church barely able to hold all the attendees, including standing room. From the church, the procession then followed a winding route four miles to the cemetery for the interment. Andy maintained his composure throughout, alternately lost in prayer and triumphant that his dad was finally home. As the crowd sifted through the cemetery on the way to their cars, he explained: "I'll come back and cry some other time. But now, let's go to the fire hall and eat."

At the fire hall the mood was much happier, bolstered by liberal servings of rigatoni, fried chicken, vegetables, salad and cake. Andy's success at reuniting his mom and dad after eight decades dominated the conversation.

As they waited for the old guy to return with his second helping, Les offered: "I understand that the abandoned mine you found will be sealed permanently. There's just too much chance that somebody will be killed poking around in it."

"That's good," Joe responded, breathing a sigh of relief. "I think we could have been hurt in there, and we were pretty darn careful, not mention we had an expert miner to keep us from doing anything too stupid. By the way, I think all the arrangements are about ready for next Saturday."

"Just about all ready," Jessie answered as they finished their soft drinks. Les looked up. "What do you mean by that?"

"Oh, nothing much. I've just been pulling some details together, is all," she responded.

***

Later at Joe's home, Jessie turned to him from the kitchen sink where she was rinsing some glasses he had washed. "Joe, there's something we need to discuss." Her mood had been transformed over the last few minutes from cheerful to contemplative. It now sounded troubled.

"You better let me have it," he responded. "What's been bothering you?"

She wiped her wet hands and his with a dishtowel and led him to the couch. "I don't know how to say this, other than to say it," she began. "You know I finally achieved my principal's certification and have begun applying for an administrative position. While I love to teach, I always dreamed that I could do more by leading other teachers and caring for an entire school, not just one class."

He felt a sick feeling suddenly develop in his stomach. He didn't like the direction of this conversation, at all. "And?" he responded, feeling a weakness beginning to pervade him.

"I had put out some feelers in the early spring about openings that I thought were coming up. They were just some inquiries through a few contacts. I had planned to apply for openings as they occurred this summer. But since I met you and the Nick thing occurred, I never bothered. Also as our notoriety began to spread, I had the feeling that nobody would want me. Probably the most I could hope for was to keep my teaching job."

Joe reached out to her, taking her hand. "Go on," he said, resignedly.

"Well, I was right. For a while I was merely the woman teacher who was unwise enough to associate with a guy who talked to ghosts. And even worse, she began to talk to them, too. My administrative prospects had diminished to practically nothing. But then, something strange happened." She looked deeper into his eyes and forced a small smile. "We were vindicated by finding Nick and the others, and the publicity turned more and more favorable. Instead of a woman who claimed to talk to ghosts and probably didn't, some people saw me as a strong educator who could stay the course through difficult times to a successful conclusion."

"I can see where this is going, and I'm not sure I like it." Joe had unconsciously withdrawn his hand from hers. It now rested on his own lap.

"Anyway, several school districts have inquired about my availability for assistant principal positions, including an elite private school in Maryland. That one is intriguing. Joe, any one of them would pay $25,000 more than I am making here; possibly much more. But none of them are local." She paused, searching his eyes for whatever they could tell her. So far, there was no hint as to whether he approved of the idea at all. "I love you, Joe. And I don't know what to do," she said. "I don't know what to do."

"I want the best for you, Jessie. I love you, too. With all my heart." But his hand never moved, remaining retreated from hers.

"I worked hard all my professional life…" she paused, chuckling humorlessly at the fact that her entire professional life had only been eight years to date. Joe caught the irony, too. He reached out, took and then squeezed her hand. His hand then remained there, becoming one with hers.

"But I want any new opportunity to be because of my academic and professional merit, not just because I was part of a freak show. I want to become known as more than the woman who helped find Nick." She looked at him beseechingly, hoping for both validation and encouragement. As of yet, she had found little of either. She only saw confusion and his emotions in turmoil. She waited.

"Jessie, I see one bright spot. At least some schools are looking at you for a leadership job. You haven't been ruled out by all of them. I think if you accept the right position you'll surely prove your merit. Over time, I mean. No matter where you go, the Nick thing will follow you. Or, more likely, precede you. There will be no escaping it for at least the next few years." He brightened. "Actually, this could be a career boon. If Nick helps you to land that first job, then all you have to do is deal with the temporary Nick and Joe Bailey distractions while you prove yourself.

"And prove yourself, you will." A dark shadow crossed over his spirit, apparent to Jessie. "But Maryland?"

"Any local positions have either been filled, or I'm not being considered for them. Not everybody wants a qualified but inexperienced Ghostbusters applicant, you know."

They sat in silence for a few minutes, holding hands and sharing in their confused states. "What will you do?"

"Well, they do sell real estate in Maryland…" she ventured.

"That thought fleetingly passed through my mind just now," he revealed. "But I have a home in Collier, and I have to stay here in Avella for at least another ten months. Old Albert's house won't be fully mine until then, and neither will his bank account. It's not a whole lot, but I can't pass it up. Besides, I've not done much in real estate this summer, so I'll need the money." He hesitated. "I just couldn't turn my back on that inheritance."

"I would never ask you to, Joe. I love you too much."

"So, what will you do?"

"I just don't know," she replied sincerely. "If we had not met, I'd probably be packing my bags by now… assuming they formally offered me a job. But now, I just don't know." Again she looked into his eyes, probing for any emotion or signal – for or against – that may have been hidden there. But she found none, only bewilderment and impending heartbreak. "I just don't know."

Joe reflected for a minute and then smiled. "I know. Let's make chocolate chip cookies."

CHAPTER SIXTY-ONE

Over the next three days, Joe refrained from asking Jessie how she was leaning in her assistant principal quandary. It wasn't that he wanted to give her space to decide as much as he was hiding from his growing concern about losing her. He certainly didn't want to chance driving her away. Perhaps his escapism came down to "no news is good news."

Also, preparations for Nick's funeral were so time-consuming and detail-filled that little time was left for anything else. Interviews were given and arrangements were made. Restrictions on television truck placements were agreed upon. Work on old Albert's house had come to a standstill weeks ago.

Thursday finally came around, the day that Joe had decided to make one final trek. He just wanted to have a little private time with his friend. He doubted that he would have much time left with Nick – if any at all – after the funeral. That would be the most likely time for Nick to move on to his reward. Jessie had taken an overnight trip to Frederick, Maryland, so Joe hiked alone in a steady rain.

"Why do I bother with these ponchos?" he muttered as he slopped his way up the muddy trail. "I'm wetter inside the poncho than it is on the outside." He ruefully realized that he had made this complaint before. Finally, he rounded the bend into the meadow. The recent excavations and heavy traffic had turned up most of the sod, making for a very unpleasant, muddy walk. "Nick!" he cried out. "Here I come!

"…Nick, old buddy?" He stopped and listened, but received no answer.

Did I lose him already? He stopped outside the cave and then entered, stepping over the mostly wilted flower arrangements. Even in their poor condition, he didn't want to defile even one blossom under the heel of his hiking boots. "Nick?"

Joe sank to his place, leaning this time against piled rubble from the excavation instead of his accustomed smooth wall; disconsolate in the sickening realization that he may have missed his last chance to say farewell. "Nick! Hey, Nick!" he shouted, his voice reverberating off the cave's walls. "Come on, Nick! If you're hiding in the rock, it's not at all funny."

"I know, I know," he chastised himself, aloud. "If Nick were really around, there'd be no reason to shout. And he wouldn't play silly games." He leaned back against the cave wall, hoping to at least gather a little of the feeling of Nick. "Why did I neglect him by staying away? It's been way over a week." He groaned, and then sagged weakly to his side. He finally placed his daypack under his head. Within a few minutes, he had fallen sound asleep.

"Where am I?" Joe asked aloud, before realizing he was still in the cave. Looking around again, it dawned on him that there would be no response. No spiritual figure shared the cave with him. After another few minutes, he resignedly decided to leave.

As he reached the cave's entrance, he whirled around to look behind him. Still nobody. Breathing a final, despairing sigh, he began his trudging walk along the slippery trail, not bothering to put his poncho back on.

"I lost Nick, and now I'm losing her," he sighed. "I really did blow it, didn't I?" he chastised himself as he opened the car door. His muddy boots caused a mess on his floor mats that he knew would not be easily removed. "I don't give a damn about anything, anymore."

***

"Did you have a successful trip?" he asked Jessie after they had embraced and kissed passionately. She stepped back and probed his gaze with hers, and then studied his face.

"It went well. The trip to Frederick took less time than I thought it would. But I'm glad to be back. Sorry I had to leave when I did, but with the school year coming up, they wanted to interview me right away. It's a very nice private academy, with mostly female students and staff."

"Well?" he asked. Again, she studied him carefully.

"I liked the place, but they haven't yet decided whether to offer me the position. I think they're leaning my way." She stopped and hesitated before continuing. "It would be a tremendous opportunity for me, Joe. But on the other hand, perhaps I should delay that decision for a year or two, until the Nick thing dies down. Then I could be more certain that a school is hiring me for the right reason, because of my professionalism. Anyway, I haven't decided how to respond if they do offer me the position."

Joe changed the subject. "I better get going. I have to get my caddy detailed for the funeral tomorrow. If you come along, we can chat during the drive to Washington." Of course, Jessie beat him to the driver's door.

"...I really do love this fine, old car," she breathed happily, as she handled the controls. "Hey, look at all this dried mud!" While she drove, Joe explained about the missing Nick. "I didn't even sense his presence anywhere around, Jess. And he didn't play any of his tricks on me, either. I think he's just... gone."

"And I missed seeing him again, too," she cried. "I know that we said goodbye to him several times – just in case. But I still wanted to say a final goodbye, before he left. Damn, I really would have liked to give him a hug, but that could never have happened anyway." She sighed heavily. "Well, it will be a big day for us – for everybody – tomorrow. Are the final arrangements in order?"

"They're pretty much set. Except for the weather. Despite my best efforts at staving off the rain, it's supposed to pour down buckets."

CHAPTER SIXTY-TWO

Saturday had finally arrived, a day they had looked forward to for Nick's sake, but also a day they hated to see arrive. There was no doubt it would totally draw the curtain on their time with him and it would cement the loss of his very comfortable and accustomed companionship. As though that were still an issue, considering his early departure. Jessie's Camaro pulled into the parking space in front of Joe's house at seven o'clock a.m.

"The weather's beautiful, Joe!" she exclaimed, after receiving and reciprocating an enthusiastic kiss. "Butler and Beaver Counties got hit hard up north, but we only have sunny skies and a few delicate clouds!" She paused. "Could there have been a spiritual hand in that?"

"I don't care how it happened, I'm just glad it did. Nick deserves a break. A nice hillside cemetery on a clear day is just what the doctor ordered. Interesting thing, though. While I chatted with Carmella Cook on the phone, she guaranteed a clear day. 'No question about it,' Carmella told me. 'It will be beautiful weather, for mom and dad and Nick to be reunited.' Hmmmmm… wonder if she could pick out a lottery number for me?"

***

They weren't really surprised to see the crowded streets when they made the turn by the convenience store. Even with an hour to go before the final casket viewing at the funeral home, all available spaces in the lot and on the parking side of the street had been taken. "I don't understand," Joe remarked. "People are already leaving." He pulled into the space reserved for him behind the hearse and the pallbearers' limo. Glancing across the street, they saw the Channel Eight satellite truck.

"We had to let people come in early, just to file past the casket," the funeral director explained. People just wanted to do that and then go their way. Otherwise it would have been impossible here."

"Good move, Barry. There was no other choice. As it is, the street outside is as crowded as it is in here."

Joe turned and shook hands with Les, who had followed them inside. "Mrs. Cook has already paid her respects and is waiting in a quiet room with her family," Les reported. "She says she doesn't feel up to receiving people today, but she wants to see you." The small group entered the room and found Carmella, her daughter Carla and Carla's husband, and Jenny and Joey.

"I hope you don't mind that I decided to stay in here," Carmella apologized, as she brushed away another tear. "But I… I think you know," she finally concluded. "This is rather difficult for me. I am very happy, but also very… distraught, I must say."

"I understand fully, Carmella. I'm just glad that you could make it." She accepted hugs from each of them. "Well, we better go and pay our own respects to our friend."

"Do you feel his presence?" Les whispered as they stood before the casket, where the line had been interrupted for them. Joe and Jessie shook their heads sadly. They then took their seats as the procession past the casket resumed, each visitor taking a moment to kneel or bow his or her head. Occasionally some man who was obviously a retired miner would place a small memento on the casket, such as a mine car check, name tag or union badge.

"Pardon me, sir," a man said tentatively as he and a friend paused in front of their chairs. "I'm Joe, too. And this here is Phil. We came down from Quecreek. We're two of the men they rescued after the mine accident there. We just wanted to pay our respects." Joe stood again, for what seemed like the hundredth time, to greet them. "We see a couple of our rescuers here, too, but they said they didn't want to bother you."

Deeply touched, Joe and Jessie shook their hands, and Andy did the same while still seated. He had already warned that he "wasn't getting up one more time, unless the President of the USA shows up."

"Please, send them over. We'd be honored to meet them. We were so happy to watch your rescue on television. Our eyes were glued to the set, way into the night." Phil went off to get the rescuers, who came over to shake Joe's hand and those of the others in his party.

"Many of the people here this morning are miners or former miners from throughout the tri-state area," Joe explained. "They introduce themselves with pride or just sign the book, indicating the mine they work at or their UMW local union. We can also tell because many of them have taken to saluting Andy as they leave."

"Well, we think of you as rescuers, too," a man from Quecreek told them. "And we heard about how people down here have been saying 'nine-for-nine.' We like it."

"Look," Jessie quietly said as she touched Joe's arm. "Carmella and her family have come out to receive well-wishers. I'm glad." After the Cooks had taken hastily vacated seats, people immediately began stopping by to console them. "I think it will mean a lot to people that they could share a few words with her about how Nick's story has touched them."

The time for the regular viewing came and went as scores more people filed through the viewing area, some pausing in nearby rooms to reflect before moving on. Many who waited would be in the funeral procession of locals, miners and dignitaries who would follow the hearse to the Byzantine Rite Catholic church.

After the room had been cleared, and as the pallbearers waited in a nearby room, the small group paid their final respects to Nick, praying over his casket. With a nod to Barry, they departed and the six union miners returned.

"I'm glad you didn't accept the complimentary limo, Joe," Jessie said as they waited in his car for the pallbearers to emerge from the funeral home. "But I'm glad that Mrs. Cook and her family did accept one. They can ride in comfort."

"I like my car," he said. She touched his arm as the front door of the funeral home opened and the six men emerged and received the casket that had been rolled on a dolly to the door. A hush overcame the several hundred bystanders who had been waiting in the blocked-off main street. "I appreciate that the television people have agreed to be non-intrusive," he remarked. "There should be ample time for interviews afterward."

After the casket had been loaded, the fire truck started up its lights and slowly moved down the street, followed by a state police cruiser, the Washington County sheriff's car and the car from the Brooke County Sheriff's office. The procession followed the winding, uphill route past somber groups of bystanders and onlookers gathered on front porches. The head of the procession finally stopped in front of the unusually designed Byzantine Rite Catholic church as others parked in the lot out back and in a nearby freshly-mowed field.

"What a marvelous piece of architecture!" Jessie exclaimed. "It's... pagoda-like?" Joe understood exactly. The building with the sweeping, curved roof that hung so low over its sides had always intrigued him, and now he would finally enter the edifice.

As they entered and moved to the front of the polished wood interior Joe noticed several teenage girls dressed in simple white dresses. Already seated in the second row, their heads were bowed in prayer. He glanced quizzically at Jessie, who smiled back as they and the Cooks were seated up front. After all the seats had been filled by mourners with others lining the walls, the casket was carried in and placed on the dolly to be rolled to the front of the altar. The pallbearers were seated together in the first row and the funeral service began. Repeatedly during the service, Jessie's eyes wandered in rapturous wonder over the exotic beauty of the church and its colorful representations of saints.

***

"...The icons and other decorations were beautiful, Joe," Jessie breathed to him as they filed out. "Some of them looked like intricate mosaics! I didn't understand a lot of the service, but I couldn't help but appreciate the beauty of the setting. And the man who read from the scriptures and sang had a beautiful voice."

Finally the cars were loaded in preparation for the fifteen mile drive to the hillside place where Carmella and Mike Zaretsky rested, waiting for their beloved Nick. "I see another limo has moved into line," Joe remarked

"It's for the girls," Jessie confessed. A stunned Joe watched as the girls arranged themselves in two rows of three, on either side of the hearse, as the pallbearers slid the casket into its place.

"You remember the procession Angelo showed us, Joe," she said as they watched the pallbearers and the girls enter their limos. "...The one with the six young women. Well, I spoke with Nan Cross at the library. She told me that she recalled such a tradition. She said it actually went further than what we saw with Nick and Angelo, when the girls walked beside the hearse. She explained that if a girl or unmarried woman died, six young men would walk, dressed in their best clothes. She explained that the men could also be the pallbearers. But women or girls couldn't serve as pallbearers back then.

"I afterward talked with people from the church and a Slavic society about what I had in mind. They were immediately caught up in the idea. The girls were easy to recruit. They are all descendants of Avella area miners from Nick's day and are members of the Byzantine Rite Catholic Church. They said they felt honored to respect an old tradition."

"So," Joe added, still shaken by his realization of what Jessie had accomplished without his knowledge. "Our friend, who was denied his marriage in life, will be made complete in the afterlife according to tradition. And he will also be reunited with Carmella, Mike, Angelo and his other friends. The ultimate circle will finally be closed."

They sat quietly, lost in their own thoughts, as Les drove the caddy in the procession. At every intersection, police had other traffic stopped for nearly five minutes so that the long procession could continue unimpeded.

"I also mentioned it to Jim and to Amber, the Channel Eight reporter," she said, offhandedly. Joe shot her a sharp glance. "And to Les, too, so he could help. Sorry," she added. But she didn't appear to be particularly sorry after having surprised Joe. She pecked his cheek in feigned repentance. Joe noticed the back of Les's neck reddening slightly as he concentrated on following the car ahead. His face in the mirror, though, exhibited a huge grin.

"I don't see any television trucks," Andy commented from the front passenger's seat.

"The Channel Eight truck went on ahead to find a strategic place in the cemetery, not too far from the grave site but not close enough to be intrusive. I hear there may be another truck or two there, as well," Joe explained.

After more than a half-hour the long, reticulated procession slowed to a stop outside the welcoming arch of the cemetery. The doors of one limo opened, but only one. The six young women emerged and took their places on either side of the hearse. The procession resumed, but now at a walking pace, as the girls began to softly sing a hymn – one that Jessie recognized from the funeral service. Ahead of them, the television cameras rolled as the reporters quietly spoke into their microphones. The image of the six white-clad girls was broadcast into hundreds of thousands of homes across America.

We understand that the six bridesmaids are part of an old and nearly forgotten Eastern European tradition... Amber, the Channel Eight reporter, said into her microphone. *It has to do with the death of a young man or woman who has not yet married. We are told that in olden days, they would have accompanied the casket from the viewing at the house to the church and then the gravesite...*

She went on to relate the tradition as their researchers had determined it.

... And since Nick Shebellko was denied his marriage to his beloved Carmella by a merciless gunshot, the tradition was renewed...

She continued her report, relating Joe and Jessie's experience viewing such a procession, as the hearse neared Nick's final resting place. A very large canopy covered the gravesite under the brilliant mid-day sun.

Finally, the procession stopped. The pallbearers removed the casket from the hearse and carefully placed it on supports over the open grave, next to Mike and Carmella's final resting places. The people gathered around, packing in as closely as possible, before the priest began his brief service. Joe and Jessie remained standing, their hands clasped, while old Andy sat next to Carmella Cook on a folding chair.

Jessie turned to Joe with a small smile, and quietly whispered into his ear: "I think I've made my decision. We can talk it over later, okay?" Probing her eyes questioningly, he thought he saw her meaning.

"Joe!" she abruptly exclaimed aloud. "Look!" Glancing up, Joe quickly noticed an old friend, standing not far outside the group of mourners. "It's... It's Nick!" she whispered. A few people nearby, including Carmella Cook, looked in that direction but saw nothing.

As another form came into view, a visibly shaken Joe whispered, "and Angelo." They were beside themselves with joy.

They hadn't missed out on seeing their friend for the last time. The two stared together into a terrain devoid of all but tombstones, as others slowly caught on that something unusual was happening. The priest droned on, unaware, with his service.

Gaping in that direction, they saw other figures taking shape, including two whom they quickly recognized from Mrs. Cook's photos as Carmella and Mike. "Carmella is beautiful," Jessie whispered. Both she and Mike had joyful, shining expressions on their faces as they moved next to Nick. Joe clutched Jessie's hand as she squeezed his in return. She leaned forward and gently squeezed Carmella Cook's shoulder. "Your mother and father are here, Carmella, and they are very happy." Mrs. Cook sobbed quietly.

And then, as they stood awestruck and uncaring of what others might think, eight more figures slowly appeared, taking shape before their wondering eyes. One was a black man, and one bore a striking resemblance to the photo of Andy's dad. All appeared as young men in bright, clean miners' garb, and each smiled encouragingly at Joe and Jessie. None had the griminess that darkened Nick's appearance in the cave. All seemed to exude a luminescent glow that only enhanced their rugged features. Joe whispered to Andy, "your dad is here with the other men and he looks very proud." Andy just nodded his head.

"And so is your great-grandfather, Joe" Jessie whispered. Joe's heart leapt.

The gravesite grew still as it finally sank in to every person there that something magical was occurring. Joe and Jessie, unmindful as to the others at the graveside, beamed happily at their friend and his companions. Finally, Nick spoke.

"Thanks for all you did for us. You are good friends." He hesitated and continued: "We are happy now. We are complete." The other figures nodded toward Joe and Jessie and slowly dissipated in the shimmering light of mid-morning. Glancing up, Joe noticed the last, diaphanous cloud in the sky slipping away. Only the four friends remained standing together.

"Goodbye, Nick," Jessie said aloud, and then Joe responded unabashedly, "goodbye, old friend." Then Nick, Angelo, Carmella and Mike turned and walked together toward the hilltop, before vanishing from view under the brilliant sky.

Joe and Jessie slowly refocused on the service that had come to a standstill. The priest resumed where he'd left off and, finally, Nick's casket was lowered into the accepting space that had been waiting for him for lo these many years.

The end

An extra for the reader: Some newspaper clippings

In researching the Cliftonville battle and its aftermath, I noticed some newspaper snippets; most are unrelated to the battle. I thought you might like them:

56 MINERS LODGED IN OHIO COUNTY JAIL DO NOT REALIZE SERIOUSNESS OF THEIR POSITION

"...Prisoners worked all day yesterday in cleaning the third floor of the county jail which has heretofore been used to store stills and liquor confiscated in raids...

...Although many of the foreigners can speak but little English, this deficiency is wiped out by their singing ability. Contests are held nightly to determine the best soloist and quartet in the county jail..."

(The Wheeling (W.V.) Register July 20, 1922)

SHOOTS WIFE 5 TIMES; SHE DOESN'T COMPLAIN

New York, July 18 – Declaring that she "deserved to be shot," Mrs. Margaret Maher refused to lodge a complaint against her husband, George, who shot her five times... "He forbade me to go out with the other man," said Mrs. Maher... I did go. He caught me several times. I refuse to sign any paper against him."

(The Wheeling Register July 19, 1922)

SHOP WORKER GETS TAR AND FEATHERS

Lakeland, Fla., July 19 – R. J. Sanders, employed at the Atlantic Coast Line railroad shops here, was taken from an automobile in front of his home today by twelve men, given a coating of tar and feathers and warned not to return to work at the shops. Sanders said tonight he will comply with the warning.

(The Wheeling Register July 20, 1922)

CRACK SHOT MAKES THREAT TO CROOKS

Oakland, Md., July 22 – R. S. Jamison, captain of the famous Haymaker rifle team of 30 years ago, threatens to exercise his skill as a sharpshooter... "They are milking my cows on share by taking two-thirds and leaving me one-third. I shall try to give the surgeons of this community a job of picking a lot of No. 8 shot out of my friends' anatomies," he warned...

(The Wheeling Register July 23, 1922)

ROOSTER COMES HOME DRUNK; STILL FOUND

Cumberland, Md., July 18 – Henry Winthrop, South Cedar Street, complained to the police yesterday that a large red rooster came staggering home in the evenings and would fall over in a torpor, to revive in the morning. Then he would start out, and Winthrop, following him to where the Cedar Street sewer empties into the Chesapeake and Ohio canal, found him gorging on a menu of mash... and other chickens were partaking of the feast... city sewer workmen brought out yards of what Street Superintendent Adam Lebeck said was "assorted mash." The workmen said the clogged sewer had a stench from the fermenting mess that almost gave them a "second hand drunk." It is evident that persons in the neighborhood are pouring mash from their home stills down into the sewer, and the police were asked to break up the practice...

(The Wheeling Intelligencer July 20, 1922)

SIX BROTHERS ARRESTED AT CLIFTONVILLE

... It was learned that six of the miners arrested were brothers. They leave a widowed mother and a sister at home in Avella, Pa., without any visible means of support while they are confined to jail.

The prisoners gave their names as Victor, Jules, Louis, Murrel, Joe and Telio Martinelle...

(The Wheeling Register July 29, 1922)

Joseph Bogo was born in Washington, PA, and grew up in the small, formerly coalmining town of Avella. He served for five years in the U. S. Air Force, including a year in Vietnam. He graduated from West Liberty State College, West Virginia with a bachelor's degree in Psychology and Sociology. He served as an administrator in a state mental retardation institution and a state mental hospital in western Pennsylvania. He currently sells real estate in Washington County, PA.

He is active in the community, including publishing two community-oriented web sites and a local newsletter. He is a life-long writer, principally for enjoyment, although a few pieces have been published. He has already completed a second, unpublished novel. He has been married since 1971 to high school librarian Carolyn Bogo. They have two children, Jennifer and Joseph. Jennifer, currently the senior science editor at Popular Mechanics magazine, provided editing assistance for Holes in the Hills.

The United Mine Workers monument to five miners killed at Cliftonville

View from the State Line railroad tunnel, WV end. Site of Cliftonville to the left.

How many miners still lie under unmarked tombstones of rock and tree?

The tracks went into and straight through that dark, forbidding hole... and he knew he must do the same.